Congratulations to

Bennett Sims

Winner of the
2014 Bard Fiction Prize

⤳

Bennett Sims, author of *A Questionable Shape*,
joins previous winners
Nathan Englander, Emily Barton, Monique Truong,
Paul La Farge, Edie Meidav, Peter Orner,
Salvador Plascencia, Fiona Maazel, Samantha Hunt,
Karen Russell, Benjamin Hale, and Brian Conn.

⤳

The Bard Fiction Prize is awarded annually to a
promising emerging writer who is an American citizen
aged thirty-nine years or younger at the time
of application. In addition to a monetary award
of $30,000, the winner receives an appointment
as writer in residence at Bard College for one semester
without the expectation that he or she will teach
traditional courses. The recipient will give at least one
public lecture and meet informally with students.

For more information, please contact:

Bard Fiction Prize
Bard College
PO Box 5000
Annandale-on-Hudson, NY 12504-5000

COMING UP IN THE SPRING
Conjunctions:62
EXILE
Edited by Bradford Morrow

From the moment homes and homelands rose into being, exile ensued. While narratives of exile share themes of banishment, loss, and longing, they are at the same time as diverse as the human experience itself. Writers as different as Homer and Heinlein, Aeschylus and Camus have addressed this crucial subject.

In *The Satanic Verses*, Salman Rushdie conceives of exile as "a dream of glorious return. Exile is a vision of revolution. It is an endless paradox: looking forward by always looking back." Its permutations know no bounds. The political dissident deported, or jailed, under house arrest. The defected spy. The classic prince banished by his royal father from the city gates.  The communal exile of the diaspora. The private exile of the abused runaway. The immigrant caught in an endless limbo of displacement. The existential exile evoked by Primo Levi when he proposes that "the most immediate fruit of exile, of uprooting [is] the prevalence of the unreal over the real."

Conjunctions:62, Exile, explores the ramifications of expulsion and ostracism, of being proscribed, cast out. Contributors include Edie Meidav, Can Xue, Maxine Chernoff, H. G. Carrillo, Stephen O'Connor, Christie Hodgen, and others.

One-year subscriptions to *Conjunctions* are only $18 (two years for $32) for more than seven hundred pages per year of contemporary literature and art. Subscribe or renew online at conjunctions.com, or mail your check to *Conjunctions*, Bard College, Annandale-on-Hudson, NY 12504. For questions or to request an invoice, e-mail conjunctions@bard.edu or call (845) 758-7054.

CONJUNCTIONS

Bi-Annual Volumes of New Writing

Edited by
Bradford Morrow

Contributing Editors
John Ashbery
Martine Bellen
Mei-mei Berssenbrugge
Mary Caponegro
Brian Evenson
William H. Gass
Peter Gizzi
Robert Kelly
Ann Lauterbach
Norman Manea
Rick Moody
Howard Norman
Joan Retallack
Joanna Scott
David Shields
Peter Straub
John Edgar Wideman

published by Bard College

EDITOR: Bradford Morrow
MANAGING EDITOR: Micaela Morrissette
SENIOR EDITORS: Robert Antoni, Peter Constantine, Benjamin Hale,
 J. W. McCormack, Edie Meidav, Nicole Nyhan, Pat Sims
COPY EDITOR: Pat Sims
ASSOCIATE EDITOR: Jedediah Berry
PUBLICITY: Darren O'Sullivan, Mark R. Primoff
EDITORIAL ASSISTANTS: Tina Acevedo, Zappa Graham, Emma
 Horwitz, Joss Lake, Linnea Marik, Amy Pedulla, Asif Rizvi, Soli Shin,
 Maggie Vicknair

NATIONAL ENDOWMENT FOR THE ARTS
A great nation deserves great art.

CONJUNCTIONS is published in the Spring and Fall of each year by Bard College, Annandale-on-Hudson, NY 12504. This issue is made possible in part with the generous funding of the National Endowment for the Arts.

SUBSCRIPTIONS: Use our secure online ordering system at www.conjunctions.com, or send subscription orders to CONJUNCTIONS, Bard College, Annandale-on-Hudson, NY 12504. Single year (two volumes): $18.00 for individuals; $40.00 for institutions and non-US. Two years (four volumes): $32.00 for individuals; $80.00 for institutions and non-US. For information about subscriptions, back issues, and advertising, contact us at (845) 758-7054 or conjunctions@bard.edu. *Conjunctions* is listed and indexed in Humanities International Complete and included in EBSCO*host*.

Editorial communications should be sent to Bradford Morrow, *Conjunctions*, 21 East 10th Street, 3E, New York, NY 10003. Unsolicited manuscripts cannot be returned unless accompanied by a stamped, self-addressed envelope. Electronic and simultaneous submissions will not be considered. If you are submitting from outside the United States, contact conjunctions@bard.edu for instructions.

Cover design by Jerry Kelly, New York. Cover art by Sir Edwin Henry Landseer (1802–1873): *Isaac van Amburgh and His Animals*, 1839. Oil on canvas, 44.8 x 68.8 in. Royal Collection Trust / © Her Majesty Queen Elizabeth II 2013.

Available through D.A.P./Distributed Art Publishers, Inc., 155 Sixth Avenue, New York, NY 10013. Telephone: (212) 627-1999. Fax: (212) 627-9484.

Printers: Edwards Brothers Malloy

Typesetter: Bill White, Typeworks

ISSN 0278-2324

ISBN 978-0-941964-77-7

Manufactured in the United States of America.

TABLE OF CONTENTS

A MENAGERIE

Edited by Bradford Morrow and Benjamin Hale

EDITORS' NOTE

A CIRCUS LION GETS LOOSE in a small town in the Midwest. A rhinoceros languishes in his pen on the Boulevard du Temple as the French Revolution rages outside. B. F. Skinner's research pigeons are conscripted to guide WWII aircraft. An eyewitness offers a true account of hunting for okapi with the Mbuti people in Uganda. A medieval monk journeys to the Holy Land in search of a unicorn. From snow leopards to kraits, lemurs to lions, okapi to eels, pigeons to dogs, rhinos to wolves, giraffes to squirrels, gators to crocodiles, cats to cows, *A Menagerie* gathers writings about the vast world of our fellow beasts who occupy the earth, oceans, and sky.

Sharing a deep interest in animals and having both worked on books in which they play central roles, we decided to approach a number of very different authors with the simple proposal that they write about an animal of their choice. The choices—not only of subjects but of forms in which the works are composed—were more diverse than either of us expected, resulting in a literary bestiary of delightful range. Ben arranged an interview with the great animal scientist Temple Grandin, and Brad discovered his previously untranscribed conversation about animals with William Burroughs from many years ago, making this menagerie anthology all the more diversified.

We hope readers who have a like-minded love for animals will enjoy this collection of fictions, nonfictions, poems, documents, dialogues, observations, fantasies, speculations, dreams, and zoologies.

—Bradford Morrow & Benjamin Hale
November 2013
New York City

A Permanent Member of the Family
Russell Banks

I'M NOT SURE I WANT TO TELL this story on myself, not now, some thirty-five years after it happened. But it has more or less become a family legend and consequently has been much revised and, if I may say, since I'm not merely a witness to the crime but its presumed perpetrator, much distorted as well. It has been told around by people who are virtual strangers, people who heard it from one of my daughters, my son-in-law, or my granddaughter, all of whom enjoy telling it because it paints the old man, that's me, in a somewhat humiliating light, or maybe humbling light is a better way to put it. Apparently, humbling the old man still gives pleasure, even to people who don't know him personally. I half expect to see a version of the story appear, drained of all sadness and significance, in a situation comedy on TV written by some kid who was in a college writing workshop with my granddaughter.

My main impulse here is merely to set the record straight, get the story told truthfully once and for all, even if it does in a vague way reflect badly on me. Not on my character so much as on my inability to anticipate bad things and thus on my inability to protect my children when they were very young from those bad things. I'm also trying to reclaim the story, to take it back and make it mine again. If that sounds selfish of me, remember that for thirty-five years it has belonged to everyone else.

It was the winter following the summer I separated from Louise, the mother of my three younger daughters, the woman who for fourteen turbulent years had been my wife. It took place in a shabbily quaint village in southern New Hampshire where I was teaching literature at a small liberal arts college. The divorce had not yet kicked in, but the separation was complete, an irreversible fact of life, my life and Louise's and the lives of our three girls, Anthea, Caitlin, and Sasha, who were six, nine, and thirteen years old. A fourth daughter, Vickie, from my first marriage, was then eighteen and living with me, having run away from her mother and stepfather's home in North Carolina. She was enrolled as a freshman at the college where I taught and was temporarily housed in a studio I built for her above the garage. All of us were fissioned atoms spun off at least three different nuclear families, seeking new, recombinant nuclei.

I had left Louise in August and bought a small abandoned house with an attached garage a quarter of a mile away that felt and looked like the gatehouse to Louise's much larger, elaborately groomed Victorian manse on the hill just beyond. Following my departure, her social life, always more intense and open-ended than mine, continued unabated and even intensified, as if for years my presence had acted as a party killer. On weekends especially, cars rumbled back and forth along the unpaved lane between my cottage and her house at all hours of the day and night. Some of the cars I recognized as belonging to our formerly shared friends; some of them were new to me and bore out-of-state plates.

We were each financially independent of the other, she through a trust set up by her grandparents, I by virtue of my teaching position. There was, therefore, no alimony for our lawyers to fight for or against. Since our one jointly owned asset of consequence, that rather grandiose Victorian manse, had been purchased with her family's money, I signed my half of it over to her without argument. It had always seemed pretentiously bourgeois to me, a bit of an embarrassment, frankly, and I was glad to be rid of it.

Regarding the children, the plan was that my ex-wife, as I was already thinking of her, and I would practice "joint custody," a Solomonic solution to the rending of family fabric. At the time, the late 1970s, this was seen as a progressive, although mostly untried, way of doling out parental responsibilities in a divorce. Three and a half days a week the girls would reside with me and their half sister, Vickie, and three and a half days a week with their mother. They would alternate three nights at my house one week with four nights the next, so that for every fourteen nights they would have slept seven at the home of each parent. Half their clothing and personal possessions would be at my place, where I had carved two tiny, low-ceilinged bedrooms out of the attic, and half would be at their mother's, where each child had her own large, high-windowed bedroom and walk-in closet. It was an easy, safe stroll between the two houses, and on transitional days, the school bus could pick them up in the morning at one parent's house and drop them off that afternoon at the other. We agreed to handle the holidays and vacations on an ad hoc basis— postponing the problem, in other words.

That left only the cat, a large black Maine Coon cat named Scooter, and the family dog, a white part-poodle mutt we'd rescued from a pound twelve years earlier when I was in graduate school. A neutered female unaccountably named Sarge, she was an adult dog of indeterminate age when we got her but was now very old. She was arthritic, half blind, and partially deaf. And devoted to everyone in the family. We were her pack.

Louise and I agreed that Scooter and Sarge, unlike our daughters, could not adapt to joint custody and therefore would have to live full-time in one place or the other. I made a preemptive bid for Sarge, who was viewed as belonging not to either parent alone, but to the three girls, who were very protective of her, as if she were a mentally and physically challenged sibling. Despite her frailty, she was the perfect family dog: sweetly placid, utterly dependent, and demonstrably grateful for any form of human kindness.

Scooter, on the other hand, was a loner and often out all night prowling the neighborhood for sex. We had neglected to castrate him until he was nearly three, and evidently he still thought he was obliged to endure mortal combat with other male cats for the sexual favors of females, even though he was no longer capable of enjoying those favors. He had long been regarded by Louise and the girls and by himself as my cat, probably because I was an early riser and fed him when he showed up at the back door at dawn looking like a boxer who needed a good cutman. And though neither of us overtly acknowledged it, he and I were the only males in the family. He ended up at my gatehouse down the lane not because I particularly wanted him there, but more or less by default.

In keeping with the principle of dividing custodial responsibilities equally between ex-husband and ex-wife, since the ex-husband had been claimed by the cat, it was decided that the dog would stay at the home of the ex-wife. She insisted on it. There was no discussion or negotiation. I balked at first, but then backed off. Keeping Sarge at her house was an important point of pride for Louise, I saw, the one small tilt in her favor in an otherwise equitable division of property, personal possessions, and domestic responsibility. It was a small victory over me in a potentially much more destructive contest that we were both determined to avoid, and I didn't mind handing it to her. Choose your battles, I reminded myself. Also, claiming Sarge as her own and not mine was a not-so-subtle though probably unconscious way for Louise to claim our daughters as more hers than mine. I didn't mind giving that to her either, as long as I knew it was an illusion. It made me feel more magnanimous and wise than I really was.

Back then there were many differences between me and Louise as to reality and illusion, truth and falsity, and a frequent confusion of the causes of the breakdown of the marriage with the symptoms of an already broken marriage. But I'd rather not go into them here, because this story is not concerned with those differences and that confusion, which now these many years later have dwindled to irrelevance. Besides, both Louise and I have been happily remarried to new spouses for decades, and our children are practically middle-aged and have children of their own. One daughter is herself twice divorced. Like her dad.

At first the arrangement went as smoothly as Louise and I had hoped. The girls, bless their hearts, once the initial shock of the separation wore off, seemed to embrace the metronomic movement back and forth between their old familiar family home, now owned and operated solely by their mother, and the new, rough-hewn home operated by their father a few hundred yards down the lane. With a swing set and slide from Sears, I turned the backyard into a suburban playground. It was a mild autumn with a long Indian summer, I recall, and I pitched a surplus army tent among the maples by the brook and let the girls grill hot dogs and toast marshmallows and sleep out there in sleeping bags on warm nights when there was no school the next day. Back in June, when I knew I'd soon be parenting and housekeeping on my own, I had scheduled my fall term classes and conferences for early in the day so that I could be home waiting for the girls when they stepped down from the bus and came into the house. With Vickie living over the garage—although only sleeping there irregularly, as she now had a boyfriend at school who had his own apartment in town—my place that fall was like an after-school summer camp for girls.

The one unanticipated complication arose when Sarge, the beloved old family dog, trotted arthritically along behind the girls as best she could whenever they came from their mother's house to mine. This in itself was not a problem, except that, when the girls returned to their mother's at the end of their three or four scheduled nights with me, Sarge refused to follow. She stayed with me and Scooter. Her preference was clear, although her reasons were not. She even resisted being leashed and went limp like an antiwar demonstrator arrested for trespass and could not be made to stand and walk.

Within an hour of the girls' departure, Louise would telephone and insist that I drive the dog "home," as she put it. "Sarge lives with me," she said. "Me and the girls."

11

Custody of Sarge was a victory over Louise that I had not sought. I had never thought of her as "my" dog, but as the family dog, by which I meant belonging to the children. I tried explaining that it appeared to be Sarge's decision to stay with me and assured her that I had done nothing to coerce the dog into staying and nothing to hinder her in any way from following the girls up the lane when they left. Quite the opposite.

But Louise would have none of it. "Just bring the damn dog back. Now," she said and hung up. Her voice and her distinctive Virginia Tidewater accent echo in my ears these many years later.

I was driving a Ford station wagon then, and because of her arthritis poor old Sarge couldn't get into the back on her own, so I had to lift her up carefully and lay her in, and when I arrived at Louise's house, I had to open the tailgate and scoop the dog up in my arms and set her down on the driveway like an offering—a peace offering, I suppose, though it felt more like a propitiation.

This happened every week. Despite all Louise's efforts to keep Sarge a permanent resident of her house, the dog always managed to slip out, arriving at my door just behind the girls, or else she came down the lane, increasingly, on her own, even when the girls were in their mother's custody. So it wasn't Anthea, Caitlin, and Sasha that the dog was following, it was me. I began to see that in her canine mind I was her pack leader, and since I had moved to a new den, so had she. If she didn't follow me there, she'd be without a pack and a proper den.

There was nothing that Louise and I could do to show Sarge how wrong she was. She wasn't wrong, of course; she was a dog. After about a month, Louise gave up, although she never announced her capitulation. Simply, there came a time when my ex-wife no longer called me with orders to deliver our family dog to her doorstep.

Everyone—me, Sarge, the girls, I think even Louise—was relieved. We all knew on some level that a major battle, one with a likelihood of causing considerable collateral damage, had been narrowly avoided. Yet, despite my relief, I felt a buzzing, low-grade anxiety about having gained sole custody of Sarge. I wasn't aware of it then, but looking back now I see that Sarge, as long as she was neither exclusively mine nor Louise's, functioned in our newly disassembled family as the last remaining link to our preseparation, prelapsarian past, to a time of relative innocence, when all of us, but especially the girls, still believed in the permanence of our family unit, our pack.

If Sarge had only agreed to traipse up and down the lane behind the girls, if she had agreed to accept joint custody, then my having left my wife that summer and fall could have been seen by all of us as an eccentric, impulsive, possibly even temporary, sleeping arrangement, and for the girls it could have been a bit like going on a continuous series of neighborhood camping trips with Dad. I would not have felt quite so guilty, and Louise would not have been so hurt and angry. The whole abandonment issue would have been ameliorated somewhat. The children would not have been so traumatized, their lives, as they see them today, would not have been permanently disfigured, and neither Louise nor I might have gone looking so quickly for replacement spouses.

That's a lot of weight to put on a family dog, I know. We all lose our innocence soon enough; it's inescapable. Most of us aren't emotionally or intellectually ready for it until our thirties or even later, however. So when one loses it prematurely, in childhood and adolescence, through divorce or the sudden early death of a parent or, more usually, war, it can leave one fixated on that loss for a lifetime. Because it's premature, it feels unnatural, violent, and unnecessary, a permanent, gratuitous wounding, and it leaves one angry at the world, and to provide one's unfocused anger with a proper target, one looks for someone to blame.

No one blamed Sarge, of course, for rejecting joint custody and thereby breaking up our family. Not consciously, anyhow. In fact, back then, at the beginning of the breakup of the family, none of us knew how much we depended on Sarge to preserve our ignorance of the fragility, the very impermanence, of the family. None of us knew that she was helping us postpone our anger and need for blame— blame for the separation and divorce, for the destruction of the family unit, for our lost innocence.

Whenever the girls stepped down from the school bus for their three or four nights' stay at my house, they were clearly, profoundly comforted to see Sarge—her wide grin; her wet, black eyes glazed by cataracts; her floppy tail and slipshod, slanted, arthritic gait as she trailed them from the bus stop to the house. Wherever the girls settled in the yard or the house, as long as she didn't have to climb the narrow attic stairs to be with them, Sarge lay watchfully beside them, as if guarding them from a danger whose existence Louise and I had not yet acknowledged.

Vickie wasn't around all that much, but Sarge was not attached to her in the same intense way as to the three younger girls. Sarge pretty much ignored Vickie. From the dog's perspective, I think she was a

13

late-arriving, auxiliary member of the pack, which I hate to admit is how the three younger girls saw her too, despite my best efforts to integrate all four daughters into a single family unit. No one admitted this, of course, but even then, that early in the game, I saw that I was failing to build a recombinant nuclear family. Vickie was a free radical and, sadly, would remain one.

Mostly, when the children were at school or up at their mother's, Sarge slept through her days. Her only waking diversion, in the absence of the girls, was going for rides in my car, and I took her everywhere I went, even to my office at the college, where she slept under my desk while I met my classes. From dawn to dusk, when the weather turned wintry and snow was falling, if I was at home and my car parked in the driveway, Sarge's habit, so as not to miss an opportunity for a ride, was to crawl under the vehicle and sleep there until I came out. When I got into the car I'd start the engine and, if the girls were with me, count off the seconds aloud until, fifteen or twenty seconds into my count, Sarge appeared at the driver's side window. Then I'd step out, flip open the tailgate, and lift her into the back. If the girls weren't there I still counted, but silently. I never got as high as thirty before Sarge was waiting by the car door.

I don't remember now where we were headed, but this time all four daughters were in the car together, Vickie in the front passenger's seat, Anthea, Caitlin, and Sasha in back. I remember it as a daytime drive, even though, because of Vickie's classes and the younger girls' school hours, it was unusual for all four to be in the car at the same time during the day. Maybe it was a Saturday or Sunday; maybe we were going ice-skating at one of the local ponds. It was a bright, cloudless, cold afternoon, I remember that, and there was no snow on the ground just then, which suggests a deep freeze following the usual January thaw. We must have been five or six months into the separation and divorce, which would not be final until the following August.

Piling into the car, all four of the girls were in a silly mood, playing with the words of a popular Bee Gees' disco song, "More Than a Woman," singing in perfect mocking harmony and substituting lines like "bald-headed woman" for "more than a woman," and breaking each other up, even the youngest, Anthea, who would have just turned seven then. I can't say I was distracted. I was simply happy, happy to see my daughters goofing off together, and was grinning at the four of them as they sang, my gaze turning from one bright face to another, when I realized that I had counted all the way to sixty and

14

was still counting. That far into it, I didn't make the connection between the count and lifting Sarge into the back of the station wagon. I simply stopped counting, put the car in reverse, and started to back out of the driveway.

There was a thump and a bump. The girls stopped singing. No one said a word. I hit the brake, put the car in park, and shut off the motor. I placed my forehead against the steering-wheel rim.

All four daughters began to wail. It was a primeval, keening, utterly female wail. Their voices rose in pitch and volume and became almost operatic, as if for years they had been waiting for this moment to arrive, when they could at last give voice together to a lifetime's accumulated pain and suffering. A terrible, almost unthinkable thing had happened. Their father had murdered the beloved animal. Their father had slain a permanent member of the family. We all knew it the second we heard the thump and felt the bump. But the girls knew something more. Instinctively, they understood the linkage between this moment, with Sarge dead beneath the wheels of my car, and my decision the previous summer to leave my wife. My reasons for that decision, my particular forms of pain and suffering, my years of humiliation and sense of having been too compromised in too many ways ever to respect myself again unless I left my wife, none of that mattered to my daughters, even to Vickie, who, as much as the other three, needed the original primal family unit with two loving parents in residence together, needed it to remain intact and to continue into her adult life, holding and sustaining her and her sisters, nurturing them, and more than anything else, protecting them from bad things.

When the wailing finally subsided and came to a gradual end, and I had apologized so sincerely and often that the girls had begun to comfort me instead of letting me comfort them, telling me that Sarge must have died before I hit her with the car or she would have come out from under it in plenty of time, we left the car and wrapped Sarge's body in an old blanket. I carried her body and the girls carried several of her favorite toys and her food dish to the far corner of the backyard and laid her and her favorite things down beneath a leafless old maple tree. I told the girls that they could always come to this tree and stand over Sarge's grave and remember her love for them and their love for her.

While I went to the garage for a shovel and pick, the girls stood over Sarge's body as if to protect it from desecration. When I returned, Vickie said, "The ground's frozen, you know, Dad."

"That's why I brought the pick," I said, but the truth is I had

15

forgotten that the ground was hard as pavement, and she knew it. They all knew it. I was practically weeping by now, confused and frightened by the tidal welter of emotions rising in my chest and taking me completely over. As the girls calmed and seemed to grow increasingly focused on the task at hand, burying Sarge, I spun out of control. I threw the shovel down beneath the maple tree and started slamming the pick against the ground, whacking the sere, rock-hard sod with fury. The blade clanged in the cold morning air and bounced off the ground, and the girls, frightened by my wild, gasping swings, backed away from me, as if watching their father avenge a crime they had not witnessed, delivering a punishment that exceeded the crime to a terrible degree.

I only glimpsed this and was further maddened by it and turned my back to them so I couldn't see their fear and disapproval, and I slammed the steel against the ground with increasing force, again and again, until finally I was out of breath and the nerves of my hands were vibrating painfully from the blows. I stopped attacking the ground at last, and as my head cleared, I remembered the girls and slowly turned to say something to them, something that would somehow gather them in and dilute their grief-stricken fears. I didn't know what to say, but something would come to me; it always did.

But the girls were gone. I looked across the yard, past the rusting swing set toward the house, and saw the four of them disappear one by one between the house and the garage, Vickie in the lead, then Sasha holding Anthea's hand, and Caitlin. A few seconds later, they reappeared on the far side of the house, walking up the lane toward the home of my ex-wife. Now Vickie was holding Anthea's hand in one of hers and Caitlin's in the other, and Sasha, the eldest of my ex-wife's three daughters, was in the lead.

That's more or less the whole story, except to mention that when the girls were finally out of sight, Scooter, my black cat, strolled from the bushes alongside the brook that marked the edge of the yard, where he had probably been hunting voles and ground-feeding chickadees. He made his way across the yard to where I stood, passed by me, and sat next to Sarge's stiffening body. The blanket around her body had been blown back by the breeze. The cold wind riffled her dense white fur. Her sightless eyes were dry and opaque, and her gray tongue lolled from her open mouth as if stopped in the middle of a yawn. She looked like game, a wild animal killed for her coat or her flesh, and not a permanent member of the family.

I carried the body of the dog to the veterinarian, where she was cremated, and brought the ashes in a ceramic jar back to my house and placed the jar on the fireplace mantel, thinking that in the spring, when the ground thawed, the girls and I would bury the ashes down by the maple tree by the brook. But that never happened. The girls did not want to talk about Sarge. They did not spend as much time at my house anymore as they had before Sarge died. Vickie moved in with her boyfriend in town. By spring the other girls were staying overnight at my house every other weekend, and by summer, when they went off to summer camp in the White Mountains, not at all, and I saw them that summer only when I drove up to Camp Abenaki on Parents' Weekend. I emptied the jar with Sarge's ashes into the brook alone one afternoon in May. The following year I was offered a tenure-track position at a major university in New Jersey, and given my age and stage of career, I felt obliged to accept it. I sold my little house down the lane from my ex-wife's home. From then on the girls visited me and their old cat, Scooter, when they could, which was once a month for a weekend during the school year and for the week before summer camp began.

Handling the Beast
Sarah Minor

8000 BCE, THE BLACK PÉRIGORD of southwestern France: A cave system is forming. At the end of the last ice age, water seeps into fissures in the high cliffs along the Vézère River. What begins as the slow drip of melting glacier soon becomes a subterranean river that carefully slices 250 meters of branching passages within the limestone bluff, opening what will later be known as La Grotte de Lascaux. The extensive cave paintings preserved within show that early *Homo sapiens* crept inside by widening the entrance to this grotto during the Upper Paleolithic period, and used the protected walls of its interior not for shelter but as canvas upon which to create the first known art.

————

(Of the four hundred figures depicted at Lascaux, only one is anthropomorphic. One semihuman figure with a birdlike head rests, angular, perhaps fallen, before an eviscerated bull with innards dangling from its open belly. Human figures are rare in cave art from this period. When they exist, their bodies are disguised with wild appendages, roughly rendered as compared to their nonhuman counterparts. The legacy those first conscious beings left to speak for them is not one of written texts, complex shelters, or machines, but representations of the wildness outside of them. At the moment they hopped the crevice spanning the animal and human brains, they began to imagine, to create art, to grapple with the beasts they had been. Some prehistorians theorize that the Lascaux paintings reflect how, in the first moment humans developed the gray matter, the wherewithal to make art, they also recognized that it made them different, and thus drew the other creatures repetitively as their first expressions of mankind's loneliness, a consideration of separation, of the animal still inside of them, a nostalgia for wilder days.)

————

1869 CE, the French Caribbean: Aesop's fables are being translated into Creole. Through volumes like *Fables créoles dédiées aux dames de l'île Bourbon* (Creole fables for island women), colonists in the Seychelles are impressing French culture upon native island peoples via literature. Most of the stories these books hold are *beast fables* or *beast epics*, short texts that contain speaking animals and their sly scrutinies of human behavior. Beast fables were passed in oral tradition long before Aesop's recording of them. These fables are especially evident in the bestiaries of medieval Europe, illustrated volumes describing various real and mythical animals that served as symbols in the visual language of Christian art of the period. Bestiaries exist as a kind of collection of beast epics related to religious teachings, a cataloging of animals and the ways humans can learn by their example.

———

(It wasn't that our species was without the physical capabilities for art making before the Upper Paleolithic; one of the main benefits of bipedalism was its freeing the hands for activities other than forward motion. The Neanderthal could plod upright, bowlegged, could raise a high flame, craft hand tools—but she did not bury her dead, did not, as far as we know, leave any record of representational art. With a sharp blooming in her species' cranial capacity came the advent of a "creative explosion" that marks the birth of *Homo sapiens*, the first artists, and their newly vast imaginations. *Homo sapien* pressed five toes into the Dordogne River sand, a burier of grave goods, a self-adorner, a grinder of manganese pigment created for art alone.)

———

157 CE, Bergama, Turkey: Galen of Pergamon eviscerates an ape before the High Priest of Asia. He then fully mends the damage to the primate's body, winning himself the post of physician to the priest's gladiators, human men hired to battle the formidable beasts brought to Bergama from the untamed corners of the continent. Both men and beasts were kept in cells off the stone corridors below the floor of massive arenas where Galen sometimes worked. Ever the student, Galen referred to the wounds of his patients as "windows into the body."

Following his post as physician, Galen would become one of the most prominent researchers of antiquity. He performed countless animal dissections in his research, primarily of the tissues of the Barbary ape. Galen produced the first detailed drawings of the inner musculature of an ape's hand, which contains all of the structures present in humans, differing only in the tapering of the ape's slender wrist and fingertips, and in the proportional development of muscles rendering the ape's thumb only partially opposable. These drawings served as a model for the crude surgical processes of many ages that followed.

––––––

(When one studies the cave art at Lascaux, it becomes clear that the natural formation of the wall was considered as a primary influence of a figure's placement upon it. Often an existing rock shelf became the ground on which a painted herd ran; a sharp cleft gave dimension to the tucked neck of an equine. We can imagine the earliest human artists planning their work the way their successors would in millennia to come, by skimming palms along the inner rock faces, tracing grooves with fingertips in search of spines, a sinuous flank. When the first artists grazed these pigments to stone, it was not their own likenesses, but those of the creatures around them that they drew. These animal figures were layered, stacked in lines or packs suggesting procession or stampede. They were dusted with patterns, empty to suggest whiteness, heavy bellied, bent. None were captured in stillness. These first attempts at representation proved detailed enough that humans living thirty-five thousand years later could identify and catalogue 605 of the 900 depicted species, and counting.)

––––––

1994 CE, outside Montignac, France: I step across a threshold of limestone into the slick chill of French subterrane. My damp palm is wrapped in my mother's long fingers. A hard pool of sunlight at the entrance quickly fades as we descend farther into the rock face and my mother ducks her forehead down toward mine. I let her lead me forward blindly and tilt my head back to gaze beyond the brim of my sun hat where flat figures are streaming slowly overhead. *Fais attention*, she warns, practicing our French. Our flashlights skip across the sharp ceilings in a flickering that recalls torch light, that stretches and plucks at those painted skins until I am sure they are tugging across the rock in the darkness, somewhere swimming beneath. I remember wondering how the images had been placed there and why we didn't just take them back out into the light with us. I remember guessing that we had shuffled miles into the dark, that the black passages opening in the swoop of yellow beams were endlessly descending into the earth.

———

(The musculature of a hand cannot be dissected without a hand. Nor can its tunnels and crevices be detailed and recorded without the precise crafting and then wielding of a pen. Thirty-five thousand years before Galen of Pergamon pressed fingerprint to fingerprint, split the skin of gladiator or ape, Paleolithic artists and dissectors of southern France commanded the same manual precision in their own renderings, in their excavations of anatomy. We know this because they left finger bones behind. Today, we can guess at the contours of flesh that once encased the marrow of the first artists through the study of similar existing species. The recorded curve of the earliest human musculature presents itself to us only in handprints stenciled on the walls of Lascaux. To create these distinctly human marks, early artists blew crushed pigment directly from their mouths onto the bare stone between their five spread fingers—perhaps a kind of signature, a symbol of their existing this way, or at all.)

———

2007 CE, Iowa City, USA: My mother is chewing her cuticles. They are shining, raw down to the first knuckle, deeply stripped around nails she leaves beautiful, intact. She normally chews while reading her medieval history, historical fictions, but with me away at college her erratic nerves are singing at a higher frequency. In leaving, I seem to have taken with me part of the order she imposed upon her days. She refuses medication, is frantic, forgetful. *Fais attention*, I warn into the phone. I lie in my lofted bed, feeling deeply guilty for leaving her behind—that's how I think of this. I lie and imagine I possess a specific kind of psychic power to ease our anxieties—those that, like my mother's, slept inside me until adulthood. I imagine that I can conjure freeze-frame images of the people I love, in whatever motion they are making at that exact moment. Something like an instant X-ray or simplified stick figure upon an empty background. With this ability, I might check to see if they assumed positions of comfort or attitudes that required my attention. Were fully intact, or otherwise. Maybe this seemed a less invasive kind of checking in than calling my mother or sister for the fourth time that day. Maybe it felt more plausible than bird's-eye viewing them satellite style, like the universe was more likely to grant me *this* specific skill. If it did, I could squeeze my eyes shut in the dark to see if my mother was curled C-wise in her bed, or with skull cradled in palms. If my sister's feet were tapping a dance floor or angled along the slope of a highway bank, in dire need. What worried me was the forms I could not imagine, the positions that pained them most, those I never knew. Lying there, I picture their stick figures in succession, asleep in beds, reading in armchairs, laughing in TV glow, and I slowly find sleep.

―――――

(Some theories concerning the intent behind the paintings at Lascaux suggest that the animal figures there are acts of "sympathetic magic," early humans' attempts to influence reality through representation, the way modern practitioners of voodoo still do today. This theory suggests that the Paleolithic hunter made her first kill on the walls of Lascaux to prompt the kill incarnate to present itself on the hunt. Others have suggested that, as at similar sites, the symbols placed upon the body of the drawn animal detail effective wound placement—the first art recorded and instructed in successful killing techniques. These theories suggest that each drawing marks an expression of early human desire, that together the figures display a chorus of individual hopeful voices, of unique signatures moving in a pack.)

―――――

1940 CE, outside Montignac, France: September. A village myth: A small dog named Robot wanders away near the Vézère River. He leads the four teenage boys in search of him to the mouth of a cave where perhaps no human foot has padded for tens of thousands of years.

"We have learnt nothing!" exclaimed an exasperated Pablo Picasso upon his visit to La Grotte de Lascaux the year of its discovery. This encounter with early human art would have been especially unnerving for the famous postimpressionist who favored bulls both in his early paintings as a child and in his best-known works as an adult.

The rendering of figures at Lascaux was also uncannily similar to the thick black outlining favored by Picasso and his contemporaries who were nicknamed *les fauves*, the wild beasts.

The bulls that Picasso noted were actually the aurochs, an extinct species of massive oxen among the most dominant species at Lascaux. The site's Great Black Bull panel, depicting a seventeen-foot aurochs, is the largest animal painting ever discovered in cave art. Long after its first known rendering, the aurochs served as an important game animal and attained mythic significance for numerous human cultures. Like domestic cattle, the aurochs carried a cross-shaped bone in its heart, believed to be a sign of its magical powers.

―――――

(The figures at Lascaux present a unique puzzle for modern visitors and historians. They are singular but overlapping. Differing species are placed in procession alongside one another. Some decorated panels contain only one very small or large figure; others hold many. Because two entrances once existed, it is difficult to discern in which order the paintings are intended to progress. Though fossil records of the Périgord show that the animals depicted there lived in the cave's vicinity, by no means are all species accounted for upon its walls. Initially, finding no clear patterns in their rendering, historians entertained the theory that the paintings at Lascaux were doodles, were created as art for art's sake.)

―――――

1900 CE, the cave of Mas-d'Azil, the southern French Pyrenees: In the deep corners of a cave through which a highway will someday run, French explorers discover the skull of a young girl with her teeth removed, with circular reindeer vertebrae set within her empty eye sockets. They find a reindeer horn carved with three detailed horse heads. The first carving depicts an intact equine head, its flared nostrils clearly delineated; the second shows a head stripped of most tissue, its skull deeply shadowed; the third head has been lightly skinned, so that the contours of the surface muscles can be detailed. These carvings reveal that the earliest human artists were curious about the inner parts of creatures, about how life resulted in the combination of physical structures, and was absent in their separation.

———

(The cave paintings at Lascaux are read as a kind of bestiary by pre-historians who understand each species as a symbol or allegory—like hieroglyphics, like an alphabet, like pixels. Each animal there is linked associatively to form our most ancient recorded narrative spanning the entire cave system.)

———

1491 CE Florence, Italy: A teenage Michelangelo describes his carving process as one of bringing existing figures out from within slabs of raw marble. The moody young Italian was among the first artists to conduct dissections of cadavers to better understand anatomy, was practiced at seeing its inner forms. Michelangelo first considered a section of stone, imagining the statue encased within it, and then began to delicately excavate the curves he saw beneath its roughened surface, revealing a crooked knee joint, a draped hand, a lifted heel.

———

(The aurochs, after stags and equines, are the species most numerous in Lascaux imagery. Absent from the paintings are reindeer, which prehistorians believe to be the primary food source of the Lascaux artists. It seems, to these researchers, that the creatures the upper Paleolithic artists chose to represent were those formidable in size or capabilities, those they feared or interacted with closely but did not consume, the beasts they respected, those they thought a match for their newly conscious minds.)

———

2009 CE, outside Minneapolis, USA: I sit tucked into an obscure corner of level 3½ at Rolvaag Library studying art history. My hands rest, clawlike in LED light, as the seventeen-thousand-year-old cave paintings from Lascaux float across my screen to eerie, echoing notes via the official French website. The caves were first closed to visitors in 2008, during attempts to battle a black fungus that began to crawl across the walls after the introduction of AC units, high-powered lights, twelve hundred daily breathers and their bacteria. This year, they were closed permanently, indefinitely. The entrance was locked, and a replica of two halls was buried two hundred meters away. Cross-legged, I am studying the earliest example of human art in the only way a human can these days—via replication. The official website is fitted with an interactive virtual tour that winds the visitor's gaze through tunnels rendered in pixels. From my vantage point, I can consider the paintings the way I might with my nose inches from the curved walls they rest upon. Under a camera's spotlight, evidence of alterations and edits are visible in the faded aging of a stag's amber pigment. Long extinct felines lurk in low profile in the small, darkest corners of the painted world, the way they did in life. A bull bends its shoulder into the sharpened edge of a crevice as if it had grown just there. Scattered among these creatures and upon their flanks rest slender hook and arrow symbols, laced patterns, stacks of orbs. Missing entirely are any representations of the surrounding cliffs or river, any fore- or background landscapes, renderings of any kind of vegetation. The theories behind the paintings are numerous, farfetched, contradictory, impossible to enumerate. Few prehistorians can agree on basic interpretations, and I feel no inclination to choose among theirs.

———

(Two existing photographs taken a decade apart capture Pablo Picasso wearing a bull-head mask. One was taken for the cover of *LIFE* magazine and the other by Edward Quinn. In each photograph, Picasso is bare chested and gesturing with his arms. Some have speculated that the mask is a reference to Picasso's Spanish heritage and the country's association with bullfights, while others suggest that the hybrid portrait references the presence of the bull as a symbol throughout his work.)

———

2012 CE, Tucson, USA: On-screen, a small black girl stands inches from a massive bovine whose wide nostrils stare back into her eyes. Earlier in the film *Beasts of the Southern Wild*, children living in the mythical Bathtub, a piece of land below sea level mirroring coastal Louisiana, are warned by their Creole teacher of the coming of the terrible aurochs. This teacher, who bears an aurochs tattoo upon her thigh, describes to the children a boar-like beast that consumes humans and will soon be freed from the melting icecaps in which it was imprisoned during the ice age. In one scene, the protagonist, Hushpuppy, climbs inside a cardboard box as her home burns down and records her life on its inner walls. She wonders, "How're people going to look back on my civilization?" Later, Hushpuppy's father instructs her in survival techniques by encouraging her to crack a crab shell without the use of a knife, to lure a catfish with her tiny wiggling fingers, to pluck it from the water just as it clasps hard above her knuckle.

———

(In *Beasts*, the aurochs is painted as an apocalyptic beast, a predator accompanying disaster that serves as a symbol for a number of narrative themes. Among them: evolution, extinction, human fear, and the human grappling with the order of the cosmos. This twentieth-century film echoes themes that earlier prehistorians recognized in connecting biological behavior to cosmic pattern at Lascaux. In these theories, the real aurochs processing in lines among other painted species symbolized the progression of seasons and, alongside other beasts, represented the rhythm and circular, regenerative cycles of nature and time.

Early humans were perhaps the first beings to contemplate natural systems, parts of the cosmos they could not comprehend. Art served as these creatures' first method of ordering the world, of articulating their newly complex human fears and desires. They drew what they were decidedly not—the beasts they had been. They pointed at the line between and toed back across it. They engaged in just what their minds were built for—in making meaning from component parts.)

Some Early Exxxperiments in Behavioral Science: A Bird's-Eye View

James Morrow

AT LONG LAST THE PRAYERS of this humble rock dove have been answered. Electric typewriters have come on the scene, which means I can employ my hunting-and-pecking skills to tell the whole story of my brave lab mates, Burrhus Frederic Skinner, and our collaborative effort to cripple the German Navy during the Second World War.

Rest assured that I intend to give B. F. Skinner, dean of behaviorists, all the credit he deserves, though you won't find herein much enthusiasm for his argument that the mind of any given pigeon—myself, for exxxample—is merely an epiphenomenon of its body. (I apologize for the above typo; the xxx key on this machine is sticky.) By the time my tale has ended, I hope to have convinced you that every member of my species enjoys an inner life and aspires to the condition called dignity.

I needn't remind you that over the centuries your earthbound race has sustained three major blows to its self-esteem. First Nicolaus Copernicus dislodged you from the center of the universe, then Charles Darwin demolished your myth of special creation, and soon thereafter Sigmund Freud dashed your hopes of ever knowing yourselves in full. Now circumstances compel me to heap a fourth humiliation upon your head. It concerns the natural ability of pigeons to communicate telepathically with humans. To be perfectly frank, every time we read your thoughts, we become bored to tears. Evidently my species has little to learn from an animal that cannot travel at thirty-eight miles per hour under its own power, navigate by a planet's magnetic field, or spread its wings and fly. I don't mean to give offense. That's simply the way it is.

Call me Reuben. Hatched on April 17, 1938, I came of age in Professor Skinner's laboratory, back when he was teaching college students and exxxperimenting with allegedly lower animals at the University of Minnesota. At first my generation was happy to let Skinner believe that a rock dove is essentially a black boxxx with feathers. As long as he kept the rewards coming—the popcorn, the coconut flakes, the

Chexxx cereal—we gave him ostensible sovereignty over our psyches, allowing him to train us to play ping-pong, knock over tiny bowling pins with marbles, and engage in other inane activities. But then Hitler invaded Poland, and kibble became the least of our concerns.

You would be hard-pressed to find a more patriotic vertebrate than the pigeon. Our military exxxploits are the stuff of legend. We have not always fought on the morally superior side, but we invariably perform our duties with distinction and élan. I think especially of a female Great War veteran named Cher Ami (not Chère Amie, for her gender became known only after her death). On October 3, 1918, during the battle of the Argonne, this fearless bird soared across German lines bearing a dispatch from a lost battalion: WE ARE ALONG THE ROAD PARALLEL TO 276.4. OUR OWN ARTILLERY IS DROPPING A BARRAGE DIRECTLY ON US. FOR HEAVEN'S SAKE STOP IT. Cher Ami arrived at Division Headquarters shot through the breast, blind in one eye, and covered in blood, the leg holding her message capsule dangling by a tendon. Army medics immediately went to work on Cher Ami, saving her life and fitting her with a wooden leg. Her heroic flight delivered 194 American soldiers from annihilation by friendly fire, a feat for which she received the Croixxx de Guerre and, when she left France for her home in New Jersey, a personal send-off from General Pershing.

Not long after the Nazis went on the march, a consensus emerged within the community of Skinner's winged exxxperimental subjects. We would devise a scheme for thwarting the Third Reich and then, breaking our vow of silence, solicit the great psychologist's aid in implementing it. This plan, we agreed, should go far beyond the usual employment of pigeons as an organic telegraph system. Our *beau geste*, when it came, must be unprecedented and classy.

Months passed. No strategy suggested itself. The Japanese attacked Pearl Harbor, bringing America into the war: a catastrophic event, though one that would surely reinforce Skinner's patriotism and hence his sympathy for our cause. We passed the early days of 1942 letting Skinner believe he was conditioning us to peck out tunes on a xxxylophone, but our minds remained fixxxed on Hitler and the abominable things he was doing to the doves of central Europe.

The breakthrough occurred one chilly Minneapolis morning when a pallid young entrepreneur named Victor Peabody appeared in the lab seeking Skinner's opinion of his nascent scheme, Project Canine. Peabody hoped to dazzle the research department of the state's largest industry, Minnesota Mining and Manufacturing, with his design for an antisubmarine weapon: depth charges strapped to dogs conditioned to follow faint acoustic signals emanating from the hulls of U-boats. Was the renowned author of *The Behavior of Organisms* willing to endorse this idea? Skinner said it sounded feasible, and he would write to the 3M people, urging them to give Peabody a hearing.

My lab mates and I later learned that Project Canine never got off the ground, largely because the president of 3M had a tender spot in his heart for dogs. But a spark had gone to flame in our collective avian imagination. The longer we mulled over the essentials of Peabody's brainstorm—lightweight missile, sentient navigation system, suicide mission—the more convinced we became that Hitler might be checkmated through an astute deployment of self-sacrificing pigeons.

For a full month we researched Der Führer's arsenal. By persuading the US Navy that its most coveted enemy targets were vulnerable to bird-controlled bombs, we reasoned, Skinner would acquire the necessary funding in a trice. Eventually we set our sights on the German fleet. Although the formidable *Bismarck* was now at the bottom of the North Atlantic, her sister battleship *Tirpitz* still roamed the seas, preying on Allied shipping, and the heavy cruisers *Gneisenau* and *Scharnhorst* also remained at large.

On the morning of his forty-first birthday, after ascertaining that he was the only human in the lab, we entered into telepathic communication with Professor Skinner. He behaved exxxactly as one would exxxpect of such an organism, stammering incoherently and dropping a tray of white mice. The container hit the floor, and the startled creatures scurried toward a familiar habitat, a rodent-scale maze in the far corner. Skinner flopped into his favorite lounge chair, stared at the ceiling, and moaned. Prematurely bald around the temples, he was a slender and agile man, with a gracefulness not normally found outside the *Columbidae* family. I genuinely liked him, and not just because he occasionally rewarded us with euphoria-inducing cannabis seeds.

"Am I losing my mind?" he asked the skylight.

"Tut-tut, Doc, you know that the mind is nothing but a scientifically uninteresting phantom of the central nervous system," my little brother, Sasha, reminded him acerbically.

"Give us a moment of your undivided attention," pleaded my comely cousin Hannah.

As the clan's official ambassador, I apprised the psychologist of our resolve to help secure an Allied victory. Somehow Professor Skinner must convince the US Navy to underwrite the development of pigeon-guided missiles intended to blow Kriegsmarine vessels out of the water. If our dream failed to become a reality, we'd never be able to look ourselves in the mirror again.

"I can't believe I'm communing with pigeons," Skinner averred.

"There are more things in heaven and earth than are dreamt of in your psychology," I retorted.

"I appreciate your antifascist sentiments, Mr. Pigeon—"

"Reuben."

"Reuben, but you see before you an exxxtraordinarily busy man. I'm teaching three classes this semester, supervising a major rat exxxperiment, and trying to be a good husband and father."

"*Gneisenau* is out there, causing untold misery," my cousin Thomas proclaimed. "Also *Scharnhorst* and *Tirpitz*." He pivoted toward me. "There's a gang of mites in my bib."

Promptly I removed the parasites from Thomas's throat feathers, *peck, peck, peck, peck, peck.*

"Thus far the good guys in this war have failed to devise a single servomechanism capable of delivering a payload to its target," noted my scrappy sister, Elvira. "The US Navy aims its torpedoes and hopes for the best. The RAF drops its bombs and prays for a lucky strike."

"If the War Department needed the services of an exxxperimental psychologist, I'd be the first to answer the call," Skinner asserted. Tugging on the ends of his bow tie, he rose defiantly from the lounge chair. "But I don't take orders from birds—even birds who've somehow conditioned themselves to engage in telepathic verbal behavior."

"Let me put it this way, Doc," I declared. "You have many splendid achievements behind you and an even greater career ahead of you. Reward the right people, outwit your antagonists through negative reinforcement, and before long you'll be running the psych department at Harvard. Ah, but that happy outcome depends on your feathered friends keeping mum about their subjective selves."

"You have enemies, Doc," my cousin Aaron reminded the boss, "and I don't mean the Nazis—I mean the cognitive psychologists. I'll wager Jean Piaget would be tickled to learn that pigeons worry about phenomenology. I think he'd *love* to enter into a postwar correspondence with B. F. Skinner's exxxperimental subjects."

"You're indulging in exxxtortion!" protested Skinner. "Conscious and deliberate exxxtortion!"

"Didn't you read your own book?" I asked. "We have no free will in the matter. We're acting this way because similarly unscrupulous behavior on our parts was rewarded in the past."

"Please think it over—or whatever you do that the rest of the world calls thinking," suggested Thomas.

"I'll think it over," said Skinner, sighing as he sank back into the chair.

"Happy birthday, Doc," I said.

So the great psychologist thought it over, and he came to the right conclusion. He would acquiesce to our blackmail, secure his future at Harvard, and perhaps, *en passant*, destroy the armored heart of the Kriegsmarine.

After consulting with the engineering department at the University of Minnesota, Skinner concluded that our proposal should turn on the Navy's latest scheme for an air-to-surface missile: an unmanned, unpowered, wing-steered plywood glider called the MK-7. In January of 1942 only three prototype MK-7s exxxisted, but the weapon would go into mass production the instant some genius devised a radio-activated or radar-dependent guidance system and installed it in the spacious forward chamber. Owing to this outsized nose cone, the creators of the MK-7 had nicknamed it the Pelican, in homage to the limerick by ornithologist Dixxxon Lanier Merritt.

> *A wonderful bird is the pelican,*
> *His bill will hold more than his belly can,*
> *He can take in his beak,*
> *Enough food for a week,*
> *But I'm damned if I see how the hell he can.*

Skinner proposed to attach a camera obscura lens to the tip of the nose cone, secure an eight-inch translucent disc along the focal plane, and tether a trained pigeon vertically behind the viewscreen, its harness wired to translate its head and neck movements into course corrections. He called this hypothetical rig an "organicon," short for "organic control," and it promised to make MK-7s the most accurate missiles in the world, each exxxplosive-laden glider pursuing a precise flight path as the pilot tapped his beak against a live projected image of a battleship, submarine pen, munitions factory, or other such stimulus.

As a first step in selling the military on Project Organicon, Skinner requested—and received—an audience with the Navy's Civilian Scientist Liaison Committee in Cambridge, Massachusetts. Little brother Sasha and I went along, secured in a wire-mesh carrier beneath a passenger seat in the DC-3. The trip was not unpleasant. The stewardess, who thought we were adorable, gave us some crushed almonds and a thimble of Chianti. Then Skinner pulled a blanket over our carrier, and Sasha and I went to sleep.

The meeting transpired in a cramped and drafty office on Brattle Street, Commander Roger Quillin presiding, flanked by two MIT professors named John Philipoff and Fred Wapple. While the humans smoked their Pall Malls and Chesterfields, Sasha and I roamed the room, consuming crumbs from a recently spilled boxxx of Cracker Jacks. I exxxperienced a fleeting impulse to poop on the brass base of the floor lamp but managed to subdue the urge.

Not surprisingly, the notion of piloting missiles via sacrificial live animals occasioned within the committee an epidemic of rolled eyes and skeptical frowns. Undaunted, Skinner unfurled a poster of the German chancellor on the carpet. He told the committee that through "carefully calculated schedules of reinforcement" he'd conditioned Sasha and me "to perform dentistry on dictators." I admired his chutzpah—for in fact we'd received no such training: The boss had simply briefed us an hour before the DC-3 took off.

Sasha and I played our parts with aplomb, systematically exxxtracting Hitler's visible teeth with our beaks. As a coup de grâce, we removed the eyes. Quillin, Philipoff, and Wapple grunted approvingly, prompting Skinner to claim that in less than a month he could condition a squad of pigeons to peck repeatedly at cutout silhouettes of *Gneisenau, Scharnhorst,* and *Tirpitz.* Place such a specialized bird in a Pelican nose cone, outfit the organism with a head-and-neck rig designed to convert its gyrations into directional-control signals, convey the glider via transport plane to within range of a German battleship, present the avian pilot with a camera obscura image of the stimulus, and—voilà!—the bomb would fly straight to its target, exxxploding on impact.

By now the committee was electrified, especially Professor Philipoff, who noted that, since the proposed servomechanism employed only "the visible segment of the spectrum," it would be "resistant to jamming," as opposed to a system dependent on radio signals or radar waves. Quillin straightaway offered Skinner a $25,000 grant to inaugurate Project Organicon, then got on the phone and arranged for 3M to place its research facilities at our disposal. Before the meeting ended, the commander promised to ship an MK-7 aircraft to Skinner posthaste, along with two additional nose cones—though he added a severe caveat: Pigeon-steered missiles would enter America's arsenal if and only if the prototype passed muster with Admiral Scott Plantinga, head of the Navy's Office of Special Devices.

Back in Minneapolis, my siblings, cousins, and I endured several weeks of intense tedium while Skinner and a quartet of 3M engineering prodigies set about adapting the glider to the brave new world of *Columbidae* navigation. The whiz kids soon realized that a Pelican nose cone could accommodate three separate bird cockpits, each equipped with its own lens and viewscreen. If one pilot lost track of the stimulus, his copilots would keep the glider on course. Brilliant.

A month into the project, Skinner and his colleagues started worrying that the proposed head-and-neck rig would prove unreliable under combat conditions. Because the noise and vibrations from flak might cause a pilot to jerk about and disable the gyroscopes—a possibility my lab mates and I couldn't discount—the whiz kids decided to incorporate the viewscreen itself into the pneumatic-steering mechanism. They installed a valve on each translucent disc at twelve o'clock, three o'clock, sixxx o'clock, and nine o'clock. If the missile drifted laterally from the target, the pilots' corresponding pecks would trigger the appropriate valve, east or west, delivering corrective jets of air to the wing flaps via rubber tubes and causing the glider to bank. If the missile drifted medially, then the north or south valve would come into play, moving the ailerons to make the Pelican climb or dive.

After two additional months of fiddling, futzing, tinkering, and tweaking, Skinner felt ready to let Admiral Plantinga render a verdict on Project Organicon. Determined to give the most dramatic demonstration possible, the psychologist and his team outfitted the hull of a nose cone with a ball-bearing collar bolted to the interior of a horizontal, open-ended wooden barrel, then connected the steering tubes to a manifold forged to simulate the effects of aileron movements. Every time the avian pilots adjusted their pecking behavior in response to target displacement, the outside observer would behold the suspended capsule bank, climb, or dive. To understand exxxactly how an attack on a German battleship might play out, Plantinga and his staff needed merely imagine that the nose cone was attached to a Pelican glider and its lethal payload.

Satisfied that his bearing-and-barrel contraption would spellbind the Navy brass, Skinner crated it up and sent it COD to the Office of Special Devices. On the evening before our scheduled departure, the psychologist gathered together his three best birds and led us to his

3M office for a briefing. He served us cannabis seeds and addressed us in a somber tone.

"Whatever happens tomorrow, you will make no mental contact with any Navy personnel," he declared.

"You can count on us, Doc," I replied. "I'll pretend my skull's as empty as one of your damn ping-pong balls."

"Zero telepathy," Skinner persisted.

"None whatsoever," Sasha promised.

Skinner said, "Plantinga and his staff will arrive at tomorrow's meeting with a cognitive understanding—"

"Hey, the boss said 'cognitive,'" I noted in a sardonic tone.

"What's this 'cognitive'?" Thomas asked Sasha with mock bewilderment.

"An illusory domain invented by softheaded nonbehaviorists," Sasha exxxplained, pooping on the stand of a hat rack.

"Shut up," Skinner responded. "Plantinga and his staff will arrive with a cognitive understanding that the Pelican is steered by birds. But once they see the capsule hone in on the *Tirpitz* cutout, they'll forget what's going on in the cockpits."

"There's a couple of mites in my auriculars," Thomas told Sasha, who set about ridding his cousin's ear feathers of the parasites, *peck, peck, peck, peck, peck.*

"Sounds like you're planning to keep us out of sight till the last possible minute," Sasha hypothesized, facing Skinner.

"Exxxactly," said the boss. "By the time they decide to see what's happening behind the scenes, they'll be totally sold on organicon navigation. They won't care if they find hamsters under the hood— or rabbits or bumblebees or rubber bands or yo-yos."

"Most ingenious, Doc," I observed.

"You're one bright cookie," Thomas proclaimed.

"Somebody's been reinforcing your more intelligent traits," suggested Sasha.

"You birds drive me crazy," seethed Skinner.

On the morning of December 16, 1942, the psychologist, Sasha, Thomas, and I flew from Minneapolis Airport to Washington National along with a backup team comprising Hannah, Elvira, and Aaron. The journey proved entirely wretched. No almonds, no Chianti, and, because our carrier lay adjacent to the cacophonous starboard engine, sleep proved impossible, even after Skinner draped a blanket over the carrier.

The instant our DC-3 skated to a halt on the icy runway, Skinner frantically collected his luggage—suitcase, carrier, valise holding the *Tirpitz* cutout—and hailed a taxxxi. He told the driver to get him across town as quickly as possible. Against the odds, we arrived at 1401 Pennsylvania Avenue a full hour ahead of schedule. The Pelican nose cone lay in the far corner of the conference room, afloat inside the open-ended barrel. After hiding the backup team in a broom closet, Skinner set the capsule on the polished oak table and secured Sasha, Thomas, and me in our respective cockpits. He closed all three hatches. Lifting one leg, I puffed up my feathers and took a nap.

Within the hour I awoke. Although the nose cone muffled their voices, I could hear the Navy brass greeting Professor Skinner, who proceeded to exxxplain the basics of the system: operantly conditioned avian pilots, redundant pecking screens, pneumatic course-correction valves. To pass the time, Sasha, Thomas, and I chatted telepathically.

"Nervous?" asked Thomas.

"I feel like I'm walking on eggs," Sasha replied.

Alas, the tension was getting to me as well. I sensed feathers loosening around my throat and along my left wing.

"I hear the Army Air Corps plans to attach incendiary bombs to thousands of bats and release them over Japanese cities," said Sasha. "The bats will roost in the eaves and attics. Built-in timers will ignite the bombs, causing firestorms."

"Clever idea, but I wish the poor mammals could consciously volunteer," I said. "Otherwise it's murder."

"Agreed," said Thomas.

"I believe that bat-human rapport, like bat-pigeon rapport, will always be a distant dream," said Sasha.

"Have you ever wondered what it's like to be a bat?" asked Thomas.

"I've tried, but I can't wrap my mind around echolocation," Sasha replied.

"Professor Skinner, I suggest we get on with the show," said some Navy big shot—probably the admiral.

"For purposes of this demonstration, you should imagine that a Douglas C-47 Skytrain is towing our Pelican glider to within striking distance of *Tirpitz*," said Skinner. "Admiral, perhaps you'd like to play the transport plane's pilot."

"With pleasure," said Plantinga. "Commander Culkin, you'll be my navigator. Maintain present course!"

"Maintain present course," echoed Culkin.

"Lieutenant Kresky, you're the bombardier," said Plantinga.

"Aye aye, sir," said Kresky.

"Bad news, guys," said Sasha. "The tension's getting to my gizzard. I think I'm about to poop."

"Oh, please," said Thomas.

"I'm not in great shape either," I confessed. "I've lost some hackles and a few secondary remiges."

"Same here," said Thomas.

"Visual contact!" cried Plantinga.

Suddenly the cutout of *Tirpitz* appeared on my viewscreen, her four pairs of 38-cm guns protruding from their turrets like arms exxxtended in *Sieg heils*.

"You see that?" I asked my fellow pilots.

"Target acquired!" yelled Sasha, who'd apparently mastered his intestinal distress.

"Lieutenant Kresky, drop glider on the naught!" ordered Plantinga.

"Aye aye, sir," said Kresky.

Plantinga shouted, "Ten . . . nine . . . eight . . . seven . . . sixxx . . . five . . . four . . . !"

"The early bird gets the Kraut!" I told my colleagues, resting my beak against the viewscreen.

"We're with you, Reuben!" Sasha and Thomas replied in unison.

"Three . . . two . . . one . . . release!"

"Missile flying!" screamed Kresky.

"Bomb under organic control!" cried Skinner.

Transcending our anxxxiety, Sasha, Thomas, and I thrust our beaks back and forth, pecking till hell wouldn't have it again, *tap, tap, tap, tap, tap*. After twenty seconds somebody tried making our task more difficult, jerking the battleship cutout first to the left, then to the right, then up, then down. I cleaved to my target, hammering with the steely determination of Poe's raven, *tap, tap, tap, tap, tap*. The valves whistled madly, releasing measured bursts of pressurized air, *tap, tap, tap, tap, tap*. I could feel the nose cone banking, diving, and climbing as we faithfully tracked *Tirpitz*.

"Amazing!" cried Culkin.

"This is better than radar!" shouted Kresky.

Plantinga yelled, "Lieutenant Bissonette, move target closer!"

"Aye aye, sir!"

Bissonette did as instructed, simulating the Pelican's progress toward *Tirpitz*. Our mission became ridiculously easy, *tap, tap, tap, tap, tap*. Even a starling could hit a *Schlachtschiffe* at this range, *tap, tap, tap, tap, tap*.

Now somebody got the bright idea of covering my camera obscura lens with his palm, making my viewscreen go black.

"Fellas, I gotta drop out!" I informed my colleagues, lifting my beak from the strike zone. "I lost the target!"

"Lost mine too!" moaned Thomas.

"Sasha, it's up to you," I exhorted my little brother.

"I'm on the job!" shouted Sasha.

"Professor Skinner, I salute you," said Culkin. "Two servomechanisms knocked out, but the missile remains on course."

The mischief maker abruptly restored my *Tirpitz* projection.

"Stimulus reacquired!" I yelled, *tap, tap, tap, tap, tap.*

"Stimulus reacquired!" echoed Thomas.

"Now let's have a look at these hotshot pilots of yours," said Plantinga.

"Not yet," pleaded Skinner. "The missile hasn't detonated. I haven't said, 'Ka-boom.'"

Ignoring the psychologist's protest, Plantinga opened the hatch of my cockpit. Ambient light flooded my viewscreen, washing out the projected image, and I found myself pecking at a maddeningly vague battleship, *tap, tap, tap, tap, tap.*

"A pretty raggedy-ass bird you got there, Professor," said Plantinga. "I'll bet he's shed a dozen hackles."

"Ka-boom!" shouted Skinner.

"This one's even mangier," said Culkin, evidently commenting on Thomas's condition.

"Ka-boom! Ka-boom!"

"This last one's in the worst shape of all," said Kresky. "He's pooped all over the place."

And then it happened, the most undesirable development imaginable. Our presumed patrons stopped taking us seriously. Merriment gathered in the decorated breasts of Admiral Plantinga, Commander Culkin, Lieutenant Kresky, and Lieutenant Bissonette, and they all burst out laughing.

"P-p-p-pigeons!" cackled Culkin with unrestrained glee.

"P-p-p-pigeons!" echoed Kresky.

"Of *course* they're pigeons!" countered Skinner. "That's what you paid for!"

"A scruffy bunch of p-p-p-pooping p-p-p-pigeons!" snickered Bissonette.

"They delivered the bomb to the target!" wailed Skinner. "They sank *Tirpitz*!"

"They crapped in their cockpits!" cried Culkin, guffawing.

"Radar guidance might not work, but it doesn't get the runs!" said Plantinga, howling hysterically.

And from that moment on, it was clear to all of us—to Sasha and Thomas and me and even to the great psychologist—that Project Organicon was history.

Speaking from my perspective as an old, tired, postwar pigeon, I would predict that behaviorism does not have a bright future. To be sure, cannily forged stimulus-response bonds and sagacious schedules of reinforcement, positive and negative, will always boast great utility—ask any guide-dog trainer, porpoise handler, lion tamer, dressage artist, or elementary schoolteacher giving out gold stars—and yet I suspect that psychology will become a real science only by keying itself to biochemistry and neurology. OK, I suppose the field could go in the opposite direction, scorning materialism and embracing teleology, but Aristotle already tried that and scientifically it got him nowhere.

I am skeptical of behaviorism now, and my lab mates and I were skeptical of it when, ten years ago, the US Navy slammed the door on the Pelican initiative. And yet we stayed true to our word. The instant we reiterated our promise to keep our qualia to ourselves, convening no press conferences on the topic of *Columbidae* consciousness, Professor Skinner wept tears of gratitude. I continue to honor that commitment—indeed, I recently arranged for this memoir to remain under wraps until the second decade of the new millennium, by which time I'll be dead and Skinner also will have gone to his, as it were, reward.

Amazingly, the saga of Project Organicon has a third act. Like a phoenixxx rising from the ashes, the notion of biologically controlled bombs did not die on that dreadful afternoon in the Office of Special Devices. Instead it transmuted into a British plan to exxxploit behaviorism in the struggle against totalitarianism.

During the early weeks of 1943, however, none of us had any inkling of Project Columbine. Inspired by the exxxample of Cher Ami, my lab mates and I allowed ourselves to be drafted into the Allied Signal Corps. For nineteen months I delivered messages and dropped poop all over the European Theater without any disabling misadventures. But then, on October 17, 1944, while I was carrying a dispatch from General Truscott to Général de Lattre de Tassigny following

Operation Dragoon, a German bullet tore through my rump, and I lost my right leg plus half my left-wing feathers to a second enemy volley. The message reached de Lattre's headquarters, but I almost died on the operating table.

Realizing that I faced a long recuperation, de Lattre's personal physician transferred me to a clinic in Nîmes. The *vétérinaires* whittled a wooden leg for *le Reuben courageuxxx*, just like Cher Ami's, and spliced in replacement plumage to stabilize me until my feathers grew out again. Eventually I began to feel better. True, my soldiering days were over, but I figured I'd already made my contribution to the war effort. A bird could do worse than sitting out the rest of this global conflagration drinking Chablis in a therapeutic loft.

On the first day in November my little brother appeared at my side. He brought me a crouton and a newspaper article about my last mission. *Le Figaro* called me *"le héros volant de l'Opération Dragoon."*

"Any news from the family?" I asked.

"It could be much worse," Sasha replied, exxxtracting a mite from my nape. "Elvira's still with Patton's Third Army. She fractured a wing at Arracourt, but I'm told it healed just fine. Aaron lost most of his bill in the same battle. I heard he's adjusting well to the prosthetic."

"Somebody up there likes pigeons."

"Here's the really big news," said Sasha. "Looks like I'll be piloting a glider against the Nazis after all!"

Elaborating, he exxxplained that, two days after the Normandy landing, Skinner's bête noire Admiral Plantinga got to swapping stories with a British naval officer named Eric Strawson. Plantinga told Commander Strawson about his encounter two years earlier with a crackpot Minnesota psychologist obsessed with putting pigeons in gliders. But Strawson decided that a bird-steered bomb was a capital idea, and he lost no time talking it up with Winston Churchill's scientific adviser. Lord Cherwell immediately grasped the shrewdness of the system and inaugurated Project Columbine, whereby His Majesty's military would build a score of single-pilot gliders, each equipped with a camera obscura lens, a viewscreen, and a dove-size cockpit.

"Last month Cherwell's people asked our favorite psychologist to round up his twenty best pilots," said Sasha. "Skinner tracked me down in Luxxxembourg and gave me the task of drafting the other nineteen."

"I'm not well enough to guide a missile," I said, sipping Chablis.

"Good heavens, Reuben, I came to *visit* you, not *recruit* you."

Sasha proceeded to reveal that in four days he and the other volunteers would join Skinner aboard the British carrier *Indefatigable*, part of a convoy cruising Norwegian waters under orders to hunt down and sink German battleships. Evidently the boss wanted to be on the scene when all his hard work on organicon navigation finally paid off.

"This is my chance to redeem myself for pooping during the Plantinga demonstration," said Sasha.

"Plantinga would've closed us down whether you'd pooped or not," I said. "The man has no imagination. So what's your primary target? *Gneisenau*?"

"*Gneisenau* is out of action, torn to pieces in a bombing raid. *Scharnhorst* capsized last year during the Battle of the North Cape. Get this, Reuben. Four days from now a squadron of transport planes will tow me and the other pilots to within striking range of our old nemesis, *Tirpitz*."

"*Tirpitz*. Golly."

"Strange are the ways of fate."

"Promise me you'll be careful," I said, a ridiculous thing to tell somebody embarking on a suicide mission.

"Sure, I'll be careful. You bet."

"I'll miss you, Sasha," I said, encircling him with my good wing. "I'll think about you every day for the rest of my life."

"I love you, Reuben."

And with that avowal, my stouthearted little brother bobbed his head, cooed vigorously, and flew away.

I spent another week convalescing in Nîmes, after which the *vétérinaires* gave me a clean bill of health and discharged me. Before long I decided to go feral and settle in *le gaie Paris*. Now that the Germans were on the run, *la vie française* held a special allure for me.

At first I thought I would imitate my fellow ferals, dining on hibernating bugs during winter and, come spring, consuming baguette crumbs tossed by visitors to le parc des Buttes Chaumont. But soon I began to miss my old life as an exxxperimental subject, so I took to hanging around the main plaza at the Sorbonne. I was netted in less than a week, then brought to the laboratory of a grizzled scientist named Jean-Marc Delrue, a recent convert to behaviorism, too old for the fight against Hitler. Despite wartime austerity, the rewards were splendid: croissant flakes, brioche chunks, macaron bits. I spent many gratifying hours letting Delrue believe he was conditioning me to assemble children's jigsaw puzzles.

It was in the domain of *le professeur* that I met and courted my one true love, *une jolie colombe* named Marie. We bonded for life— I believe she was attracted to my status as an *héros de guerre*—and planned to start raising squabs after Der Führer abandoned his fantasies of a Thousand-Year Reich. Delrue must have sensed there was something going on between us. No sooner had he resolved to create a pigeon orchestra than he began teaching Marie and me to play duets on his great-grandfather's harpsichord.

Early in May of 1945, two exxxtraordinary events occurred: General Alfred Jodl, having arrived at Allied headquarters in Reims, signed unconditional surrender documents for all German forces—and Professor B. F. Skinner came to the Sorbonne to give a lecture called "Engineering Human Happiness." Shortly before he was to appear in the Amphithéâtre Richelieu, I importuned the great psychologist as he paced anxxxiously around backstage. He recognized me instantly. I bowed to him thrice. He reciprocated. Our telepathic conversation was brief but pointed.

I asked, "Can you tell me anything about—?"

"He's dead," Skinner informed me.

"I assumed as much." A nugget of grief coalesced in my crop. "Tell me more."

"The first missile to attack *Tirpitz* destroyed the aft turrets. The second strike turned the bow to scrap metal. And then came Sasha, piloting his glider straight for the main ammunition magazine."

"I can see him pecking his heart out," I mused.

"The exxxplosion tore an immense hole in the hull," Skinner reported. "The ship capsized and sank in a matter of minutes, and so the other strikes were called off. Thanks to his skill and courage, Sasha saved—"

"Seventeen pigeons and God knows how many British sailors."

"Quite so."

"You trained him well," I averred in a mildly sarcastic tone.

Skinner graciously disregarded my rudeness. "Sasha and the other fallen birds received Dickin Medals, the only ones awarded posthumously so far. The Victoria Cross for animals—have you heard of it?—very handsome, silk ribbon, bronze disc. The obverse reads 'For Gallantry' and, below that, 'We Also Serve.'"

"*Bonsoir, mesdames et messieurs!*" came the amplified voice of *le professeur*, who then introduced the evening's celebrated guest. I translated Delrue's remarks for Skinner.

"I wish I could've died in Sasha's place," I added.

"Do you mean that?" asked the psychologist.

"No," I replied. "I hope your speech goes well."

"My interpreter, a young man from Boston, is very competent. Allow me to offer my deepest condolences."

"War is hell," I observed.

"Je vous présente Professeur B. F. Skinner!" declared Delrue.

The psychologist offered me a soft smile and strode toward the stage. "Good-bye, Reuben," he called over his shoulder.

"Au revoir, Doc."

I didn't stay around for Skinner's lecture on "Engineering Human Happiness." The commodity in question, I feel, is not something one can engineer, and neither is avian happiness. And even if such a technology were possible, I would worry about the side effects.

So I left the auditorium and took to the air, headed for the lab and the lovely dove who awaited me there. Despite my war wounds I could still fly, albeit clumsily. Fluttering over the main plaza, I composed an epitaph for the recipients of the first posthumously awarded Dickin Medals.

> *A wonderful bird is the pigeon,*
> *Whose mind holds much more than a smidgeon,*
> *He can soar from the sod,*
> *To the left eye of God,*
> *And he does it without a religion.*

Adieu, noble Sasha. Farewell, little brother. Good-bye, *mon cher ami.* You were a mysterious and irreducible creature. But then again, aren't we all?

Here Be Monsters
Sallie Tisdale

DAN, THE YOUNG DIVEMASTER, set us up with weights and tanks for the required checkout dive, running through the park rules as he worked. The checkout dive was one of the rules. Taking coral or spearfishing outside permitted areas was against the rules; feeding fish was most definitely against the rules.

"Some idiot started feeding the moray eels hot dogs," he said, swinging a tank to me. I pretended not to stumble when I caught it. "Some *idiot*." He was half my age and naked except for a pair of ratty swim shorts. "They're myopic, the eels," he added. "They can't tell the difference between your finger and an octopus tentacle and a hot dog. A woman had half her finger bitten off last year." He paused. "Don't be *stuuupppid*."

I learned to dive in chill, dim Puget Sound, and promptly gave up on cold water. I had never dived in warm water or been to a sub-tropical island, except for Hawaii, where I went snorkeling for the first time and was seized with the need to go below, to stay *down* there. And Bonaire was a fever dream of a desert island, a tilting tabletop barely out of the sea. In the north, the narrow interior is scrub and cactus and tikitiki trees pointing to the southwest with the eternal wind. The arid land is filled with birds, wild donkeys, goats, and iguanas six feet long. The small towns in the center are sun scorched and still; the people are mostly African by descent, with Arawak and Spanish and Dutch and Portuguese mixed in. The south is salt flats, towering white cones lining the road beside giant loaders and pink evaporation ponds; twinkling crystalline drifts of salt powder float across the highway like low fog. A row of tiny slave huts is protected as a memorial, the size of dog houses and hot as saunas. A large flock of pink flamingos lives in the south. They step daintily through the shallows on silly delicate legs, turning their big heads completely upside down to feed on tiny shrimp. The birds chatter constantly, *cho-go-go, go-go*, the sound mixing with the wind, *cho-go-go, go-go, cho-go*, like gossip or the mild chronic complaints of old aunts. Sometimes they fly to Venezuela, fifty miles

43

away—the flock rising at twilight all at once like a vapor flashing flame in the last light.

Sand and scraped sky above the waves; below, an immense work of eons. The naturalist William Beebe said of the coral reef, "No opium dream can compare." The reef looks like the rumpled ruins of a great city, slumped boulders and bushes and pillars and branches cascading down and down, an architecture that is truly stone—the skeletons of tiny animals piled one atop another. I was a novice diver and a complete tyro on the reef. After a few days of barely coherent dives, I began to learn names: tilefish, wrasse, moon jelly, lugworm, overgrowing mat tunicate, southern sennet, whitespotted toadfish, honeycomb cowfish, porgy, the tiny scrawled filefish hiding in a gorgonian like a shivering leaf. I learned the names of things, but that is not the same as knowing the things one can name.

On the second day, I saw my first eel. Dan pointed to a rough rock near an overhang and I paddled over in stupefied and clumsy strokes. The big head, the jaws working—a green moray, all muscle and velvet.

Family Muraenidae in the order Anguilliformes. Hundreds of species of moray eels all created on the fifth day, if Genesis is to be believed. They are brown, green, ivory, gray, yellow, orange, black, and neon blue, and all these in combination: speckled, spotted, polka-dotted, striped, tessellated, piebald, brindle. A couple of the species are two-toned like saddle shoes. Morays live in every tropical and temperate sea, mostly in shallow water. They make dens in caves and crevices and holes in rocks; some live in hollowed-out burrows in the sand, mixing mucus and grains of sand into cement. They live alone, wolves sharing out the territory. The redface eel in the Atlantic and Indian Oceans is eight inches long at maturity; the slender giant moray in the Indian and the Pacific can reach twelve feet. A study in Hawaii found that up to 46 percent of the carnivorous biomass on the reef was moray.

They are fish but don't look like fish; they have no pectoral fins, no fishiness. Instead the dorsal fin runs the entire length of the body, fimbriated and smooth from the aerodynamic head shaped like a jet cockpit to the tapering tail. Morays are covered in mucus. The green moray is really blue. Or is it brown? Or gray? Or a funereal black? I'm not sure; sources vary. The mucus is green, or perhaps yellow; the mucus is poisonous. Or not; sources vary. These are no long-distance swimmers; they are immensely strong but slothful, like high-school boys on a Sunday afternoon. Morays are mostly nocturnal, shy, and spend much of the time curled in their dens, often with just their heads peeping out. Morays don't see well, but they have a great sense of smell, and mostly wait for prey to wander by—lobster, octopus, fish of all kinds. Divers and snorkelers are most likely to see only the wavering head, the long sinuous body curled out of sight in a den. (Often, if you look carefully, you can see that snaky body wound round and round the rocks and coral like loose rope.) Most morays stay in exactly the same place for years—the same part of the reef, the same den. Divers recognize specific eels, and tend to name the big ones.

Sources always vary in this world. Morays are dangerous, I read in a fish guide. They are aggressive, ugly, fearful beasts. Such adjectives recur again and again, in science as well as stories. My beloved Britannica says "they can be quite vicious," an oddly subjective entry in that careful publication. My well-worn Peterson Field Guide warns, "Before sticking your hand into a crevice, look into it carefully. A dreaded moray eel may be hiding there."

The mouth—that's what scares people. The big, wide mouth and all those pointy teeth, gaping at you. Morays have small gills; breathing requires them to open and close their mouths continuously to force water through. They look contemplative, like a man working off the novocaine. Fish have a second set of teeth in pharyngeal jaws in the throat, to clench onto captured prey and pull it quickly down into the gut. Pharyngeal jaws seem odd, but they are common. Human embryos have extra jaws that fade into the skull early in development. The moray, however, is unique. They catch prey with the long, needle-sharp front teeth and then the pharyngeal jaws shoot out of the throat like a questing blind skull and bite again. The front jaws let go and the pharyngeal jaws retract, and the prey ratchets down, gone in a second or two.

There are many videos on the Internet purporting to show moray attacks. Like *dreaded* or *vicious*, like *ugly*, the word *attack* is one colored by imagination. In many of the videos, divers are making faces and showing off, darting out of reach with a scared giggle, egging each other on. One of the most well-known shows a moray biting a diver's thumb off with a crisp pop. (If a moray bites your finger, the pharyngeal jaws won't let go—do we think they would reconsider if they could? Do we imagine an eel listening—*Let go, you shouldn't eat that?*) If the eel gets a finger, it simply bites the finger off. If the eel gets hold of something bigger—an arm, a thigh—well, there's not much to be done. The diver gets out of the water with the eel attached until someone can smash its head in and cut the jaws off. In the case of the thumb—in every case I've heard of in twenty years of diving—the divers were petting eels or teasing eels or trying to coax the eel out of its den to take pictures. These are big ones, eels with names, the reliable local celebrities that tourists want to see. They are conditioned to come out of their dens to be fed. Conditioned, but not domesticated. Mostly, the divers were feeding the eels hot dogs, which look, even to my human eyes, a lot like fingers.

One can let go of a surprising number of concerns underwater, drifting slowly down into the blue like a pebble in honey. After the first startled moment, the inside-out reorienting of the world that comes with sinking underwater, I'm at ease; at times, I'm so relaxed I can almost nap. Since that first dive off Bonaire, I've seen many morays: spotted and goldentail morays, dwarf and zebra morays, and once a chestnut moray, a trick to find. Off Glover's Atoll in Belize, I drifted down a huge boulder to a little sandy plain like a courtyard, falling without hurry through water clear as air. When I reached the sand I looked casually to the right and saw a green moray several feet long resting under a ledge with his eye on me: *Gymnothorax funebris*. Green morays can reach eight feet in length and weigh up to sixty-five pounds. *Gymnos* is thorax, and *akos* means the naked breast. The word *funebris* means funereal, for the dark color, perhaps. Or for the fear.

Later that day, in a cavern, my dive partner, Carol, kept gesturing vaguely at me, and when I shrugged at her—*I don't understand, what are you trying to tell me?*—she grinned and shook her head. Back on the boat, I asked her what she'd meant. "A moray," she said. "Right behind you in his den, the whole time."

In Roatán, off the coast of Honduras, the sand is smooth as white silk, and the foam flows along at the edge with a snake's hiss. The little village of West End is scattered with wanderers from around the world, many sporting cherry-red sunburns. I dove one afternoon with Sergio, a six-foot-tall Spaniard twenty years younger than me. Such pairings are the stuff of diving. We took a little skiff out to the reef wall at the end of the lagoon. Everyone on the island was in siesta, it seemed; there was no one in sight, no current, just the two of us buzzing on glassine water under a hazy sky. We hooked to a mooring and slid in, to drift slowly along the coral wall with barely a kick. The tumbled stone wall was interlaced with the lilac vases and greenish lettuce leaves of sponges, the twisted pipe cleaners of wire coral, and the wavering Christmas ribbons of soft corals called knobby candelabrum and dead man's fingers. Two huge crabs shuffled back and forth like gunfighters at high noon. A small, tight band of black margate formed a square wall to one side, turning in unison as we passed.

I was floating in the kind of sensuous abandon that drives time out of one's mind altogether, hearing only my own exhalation, when something slipped into my peripheral vision. I turned to see a great green moray right beside me, glorious and iridescent. He matched my speed, watching me with a thoughtful eye. Sergio was ahead, hovering, absorbed by some small creature. His tan, lean body hung horizontally beside the wall. The moray, with what seemed a meaningful glance in my direction, slid sideways toward Sergio and parked just above him, inches behind his head, like a semi heading smoothly into a truck stop. Morays smell through two small tubes like snorkels jutting out from the snout; the eel seemed to be inhaling the scent of Sergio's shampoo. Its huge, undulant body was as long as the man.

I slowly sidled over, trying to get in front of Sergio, wanting to catch his attention in a quiet way. I could feel myself grimacing a little. Finally he looked up and I gestured, *Come here*, with just my fingertips—nothing dramatic or abrupt. He must have noticed my darting eyes, because he turned around and then leaped away. He stopped beside me and there we hung; we watched the eel and he watched us and this just went on and for a long while. The eel was an elephantine leaf, a scarf, a nymph, a dragon. A sea monster, a dream. I longed to touch it.

Morays are hermaphrodites, sometimes transmutating male to female, sometimes fully both genders at once—screwing willy-nilly with whatever moray or Spaniard comes along. They court when the water is warm (who doesn't?) and they really gawp then—breathing hard, wrapping around and around each other's long, slippery bodies like tangling fringe, like braids, like DNA. Eggs and sperm are released together, and the eels return to their anchorite dens. When the eggs hatch, endless uncountable larvae called leptocephali dissipate, a million shreds of wide ribbon—tiny fish heads on long, flat bodies. The larvae float for nearly a year. (The ocean is always a bath of barely visible infants; one swims in a snow of newborns.) The survivors of that perilous year absorb their pectoral fins and grow into elvers, which is what juvenile eels are really called, and in time each finds an empty spot and makes a den and lives for decades. They have few enemies: a couple of the biggest fishes. Bigger morays. You.

The Roman aristocracy loved morays; they farmed them as live-stock and kept them as pets in elaborate ponds. Now and then a master fed his less obedient slaves to the eels, presumably in pieces; human blood was thought to fatten a moray nicely. Delicious or not, it's always a bad idea to eat an alpha predator. A bit like unprotected sex—when you eat the top of the food chain, you eat every link. A wee dinoflagellate (*Gambierdiscus toxicus*, a microalga that feeds on dead coral) produces a neurotoxin called ciguatoxin, becoming more concentrated in each successive species. It's possible to get ciguatera from herbivorous fish, and little guys like snapper, but the alpha predators bank it like gold. The toxin is a nasty one—almost everyone who eats a fish with ciguatoxin will get sick. Victims vomit and suffer diarrhea; their lips and fingers go numb; cold sensations switch with hot; they feel profound weakness and pain in the teeth and pain on urinating and arrhythmias and respiratory failure. The symptoms last for months and you can pass the toxin to others through sexual activity and pregnancy. King Henry I of England may have died of ciguatera; he collapsed after gorging on eels. At one Filipino banquet featuring a large yellow margin moray, fifty-seven people got sick; ten went into comas; two died.

Weeks of wind and rain lashing the sea kept us land bound on Cat Island. Carol made hats out of sticks and wrack. I restlessly walked the same path several times a day. One morning I found a perfect set of frog legs lying on the path. They had been nipped off at the waist. An hour later, they were boiling with brown ants. By afternoon, the ants had dug a hole beside the path, and tugged the legs halfway in; they were bowed, as though swimming into the earth. By morning, there was only skeleton; long, slender toe bones pointed to the angry sky.

The world is a strange place, for all of us—strange to me, strange to frogs, to ants, to eels. Strangely full of all those others, who are utterly unlike us, who look and act insensibly. If they are thoughtful, these are thoughts that have nothing to do with me; if the glance is meaningful, there is no way for me to know the meaning. But we do insist that we know what it is, that it is familiar in some crucial way.

Everyone wants the familiar. (Yes, people often say the opposite, that they crave the new and long for adventure and novelty. They really don't. What we call adventure is the process of meeting the new and turning it into the known as fast as possible. We want to name the unnamed and touch the untouched so that they are no longer unnamed and untouched. No longer strange. Then we can go tell people all about what we've found.) Perhaps it is always most difficult with the sea, to which so many are drawn as though by a piper, and where none of us belong. No shared fundament in the sea; coral and sponge and fish are a wonder to me, but there is nothing of me there.

Ah, we long for commonality. The idea that an animal is simply out of reach, forever opaque, is not to be tolerated. The unknown makes sociopaths of us all, turning animals into objects to meet our needs, affirm us, *befriend* us. So one imparts motive, emotion, even morals to an animal. And one sees what one expects to see. Perhaps a vicious sea monster. Perhaps a puppy who takes a biscuit from your hand. In both cases, one will be wrong.

Since that first trip to Bonaire, I've seen a lot of fish feeding. The point is a good photograph, an exciting moment—a good tip at the end of the dive. Hot dogs are used because they don't fall apart; frozen peas sink nicely in the sunny water. Cheez Whiz is quite popular—people find it amusing to squirt a can of Cheez Whiz under water and stir a school of damselfish into frenzy. As a species, we are easily amused. Besides the nice tip, fish feeding gives us control. It bounds the boundless. We've *interacted*, we've *made a connection*. Whether the damselfish or stingray or moray eel feels the same way is not at issue here (though people are remarkably quick to ascribe motives like pleasure or play or, God knows, *affection* to the behavior of a carnivore chasing a sausage). The last thing we want to admit is that they may be indifferent to us. We tiny fragile mammals, stunned by the danger of the world; we press our fear against the vast, improbable gestalt of the sea.

I like to dive at night; the reef is wide awake, softened and kinetic with a million little bodies. Slipping into black water is always a little spooky, a reminder: my legs dangling out of sight above the primeval deep. At night I carry only a little light and cover a smaller territory, so I can focus on one thing at a time. The stalk eye of a conch slowly turns as it hauls its great shell across the sand. Coral polyps dance like hands hauling in a net. Carol's fairy light bobs in the distance. A red snapping shrimp rises up to a boxer's stance when my light passes by. A basket star unfurls itself into a burnt-orange tumbleweed. And at the edge of my little circle of light, a moray slides across the ivory sand and is gone into the dark.

On one night dive, with a group too big for me, too much the herd, the divemaster led us to a moray's den, the young green eel's head caught in a dozen headlamps like a startled deer. It turned from side to side, trying to watch all of us at once. A German man with a big video camera kept darting in, trying to get a good close-up of the eel's face; finally, he took the camera and started bashing the eel on the head. I felt myself retract far deeper than the eel could go, retreat all the way out of the human species. *Bite him*, I thought. *What are you waiting for?* He had fingers to spare. But I also knew it would likely be the death of the eel. Finally the divemaster pulled the man away, and we ascended to a rocking sea. The sky was close and thick with stars; there was sheet lightning all across the horizon, silent, huge. In that moment I wanted never to speak to a person again.

Some time later, I was back on Roatán. Carol and I dove through a splendid set of winding, narrow coral canyons separated by rivers of sand. The day was bright and wide beams of sunlight shone down on the reef. We flew through the wonderland, this solid chunk of long time. We finned slowly up one canyon, around, and down the next, back and forth, watching the abundant schools of blue tang and sergeant majors like flocks of butterflies. I stopped to watch a glorious queen triggerfish hovering shyly in the distance. Then I turned around and saw a huge green moray hanging there, a single poised muscle a few feet away.

We hung eye to eye. He was more than five feet long, a dusky, piney green that seemed to shimmer in the light. For a half hour the eel stayed near us: flowing straight along the reef an inch off the coral, matching every curve; sliding over low ridges like, well, water; slipping sideways in and out of thin breaks and reappearing around a turn as though waiting. I felt blessed—not by some imagined connection, not by recognition or a meeting of minds, but by the strange that will remain forever strange and by its strangeness tell me who I am. We found ourselves fifty feet down at the base of a straight ridge, Carol and me and the big green eel, and then it spun around and swam straight up the coral mountain toward the bright sky and was gone.

Night Walks
Cole Swensen

1.15.13

Ambling around the neighborhood this evening—it really can't
even be called walking—it's too pointless, I'm reminded of the
French verb *errer* or *to err*—i.e., to go nowhere, or rather, to
wander, to go anywhere. It's the opposite of getting lost:
Everywhere you end up is exactly what you want. My neighbor
from the fifth floor passes on his bicycle, waves, and as he passes,
I see, tucked in on his little shelf under the seat, the white rat with
whom he lives, who looks back at me. He never goes anywhere
without him.

5.17.13

In a relatively quiet street that swells out at a certain point into a
small square overlooking the river, a man on a cell phone is out
walking his dog, milling aimlessly around the square as he talks, as
does a woman, also on a cell phone, also walking her dog, and, of
course, the two people don't notice each other, but the two dogs do,
and by straining gently but insistently on their leashes, keep trying
to arrange a closer exchange, which the two people, of course,
completely ignore, though finally the man gets tired of the
constant strain on his arm and, jerking the leash, stalks off,
heading east, leaving the distinct impression that his phone call
is not going as well as planned.

5.29.13

It's a world unmarred by color tonight, unjarred. Which is a matter
of the light, no doubt, perhaps its angle—perhaps its angle is
unusually sharp, what there is of it, as it's almost dark, what there

is comes in low and flat, and the shadows are black and the sky
that odd white that you only get right before nightfall.

Night falls. And all the dogs, too, tonight are black or white, with
everything else different—size, fur, ears—but then I notice, so
too are the cars, though occasionally one is black *and* white, but
only rarely.

6.21.13

Walking down a long, quiet street in the dark, thinking that this is
the shortest night of the year. For a while my footsteps are the only
sound I hear until I hear something up ahead, and the noise grows
louder, and soon is clearly a party in full swing, clearly coming
from a building down the block a bit, and as I pass the building,
I notice that every window of every apartment in it is dark.

I turn the corner and notice two people, somewhat similar in
appearance, yet with identical dogs—schnauzers—pass each other
without a glance and continue walking in opposite directions.

6.25.13

We have a cat. "We" is used here in the broadest sense, and in
this case, one that signifies a body constituted by affection, and,
in this case, for a particular cat—one with black and gray stripes in
that odd but very common way in which the gray actually has a
slightly green cast. The cat slithers through the café, particularly
the sidewalk part of it, a few times a night, always clearly heading
somewhere else, does not look to the left or right, but leaves in its
wake this "we" who affectionately watch it pass.

7.5.13

Seagulls crying in the dark over the park or the not-so-dark, their
cries sharp and always sounding so far away, though in fact they're
circling aimlessly albeit gracefully right overhead as I pass by the
darkening park on the second day of summer weather, thus the

streets are busier at 11:00 p.m. than they've been all day long, and no one is going anywhere.

7.13.13

The eve of a major holiday, so everything is very busy, very loud, with people absolutely everywhere, some of them literally dancing in the streets—it's really quite nice. I turn into a particularly busy street, no cars—there's no room for them—but down which a young couple is trying to negotiate a stroller in which sits a very miserable little girl, maybe four, crying her eyes out and clutching a cat. A very patient cat, which she brushes across her face to dry her tears, then goes on crying, while the cat continues to stare straight ahead.

7.19.13

In the course of my nightly walk, I stop, as I often do, at a certain sidewalk café, often to write down the thoughts and impressions of the walk of the evening—or of the night, depending on how late it's gotten. And out of the corner of my eye, I see a cat scooting by, or perhaps I should say that I have the *sense* of a cat's fleeting form against the face of the granite curb at the edge of the street just off to the side. It's an unusually high curb—it amounts to a screen about a foot high. And this happens several times—several cats, all black and all zipping west at a good clip, which, after a while, I think, seems a little odd—when I happen to look up at just the right moment to see that, in fact, it's nothing more than the shadow cast by bicyclists hit by a streetlight not strong enough to strike the building beyond, but turning the curb (much closer) into a *lanterne magique*. People walk by too, but because they're moving much more slowly, their shadows can't turn them into animals.

7.25.13

Cooler this evening, particularly crossing the bridges, where the wind picks up and is making a mess of the surface of the water.

Cole Swensen

People walking, lots tonight, and almost in rhythm, as if it were a way of collectively resisting the wind. I stop and look over the parapet, down onto the quay, where five pigeons seem to be marching in step in a single, evenly paced line. I know this is only the projection of a human attachment to order onto random avian behavior, but still, it's a remarkably straight line and remarkably evenly paced.

Fables

Bennett Sims

1.

THE BOY BEGS HIS MOTHER to buy him a balloon. As they leave the grocery store and cross the parking lot, he holds the balloon by a string in his hand. It is round and red, and it bobs a few feet above him. Suddenly his mother looks down and orders him not to release the balloon. Her voice is stern. She says that if he loses it, she will not buy him another. The boy tightens his grip on the string. He had no intention of releasing the balloon. But the mother's prohibition disquiets him, for it seems to be addressed at a specific desire. Her voice implies that she has seen inside him: that deep down—in a place hidden from himself, yet visible to her—he really does want to release the balloon. Otherwise, why bother to forbid it? The boy feels stung by her censure. He grows sullen at the injustice. It isn't fair. He didn't do anything. They approach the car in the parking lot. The day is bright and all the car roofs glint. His fingers fidget, his palm throbs. Before, the balloon had been just a thing that he wanted to hold. Now, he cannot stop thinking about letting it go. He wants to release the string, to spite her. But he knows that this would only prove her right. By forbidding a thought he hadn't had, she has put that thought into his head; now, if he acts on the thought, it will be as good as admitting that he already had it. He glowers up at the balloon. Why had he begged her to buy it in the first place? What had he ever planned on doing with it, if not releasing it? Maybe she was right. For there is now nothing in the world that he more desires—has always desired—than to be rid of this balloon. The boy knows that it is the prohibition that has put this idea into his head, and yet, he can't remember a time before he had it. It is as if the prohibition has implanted not just the desire, but an entire prehistory of the desire. The second the thought crossed his mind, it had always already been in his mind. The moment his mother spoke to him, he became the boy she was speaking to: the kind of boy who releases balloons, who needs to be told not to. Yes, he imagines that he can remember now: how even in the grocery store—before he had so much as laid eyes

55

on the balloon—even then he was secretly planning to release it. The boy releases the balloon. He watches it rise swiftly and diminish, snaking upward, its redness growing smaller and smaller against the blue sky. His chest hollows out with guilt. He should never have released the balloon. Hearing him whimper, his mother turns to see what has happened. She tells him sharply that she told him not to release the balloon. He begs her to go back into the grocery store and buy him another, but she shakes her head. They are at the car, and she is already digging through her purse for the keys. While she unlocks the door, he takes one last look above him, raking that vast expanse for some fleck of red.

2.

One day at recess, alone behind the jungle gym, the boy spots a crow perched on a low pine branch. He is used to seeing entire flocks in this tree. At dusk dozens will gather together on its branches, visible from across the playground as a cloud of black specks. They dot the treetop then, like ticks in a green flank. Even at that distance he can hear them cawing, a dark, sharp sound that they seem to draw from deep within the tree itself, their black bodies growing engorged on it. After school each afternoon, waiting for his mother in the parking lot, the boy will watch them, listening. Today, however, there is only the one crow, and although its beak hangs open, it does not caw. It is perfectly silent. It just sits there, cocking its head and blinking its beady eye in profile. The boy keeps expecting the crow to caw, to let the tree speak through it, in a voice infinitely older than it is. But its beak gapes and no sound comes out. If the boy listens carefully, he can distinguish the rustle of a breeze, some wind in the needles. And then it is possible to imagine that this hissing is emanating from the bird's beak, in steady, crackling waves, like static from a broken radio. That is the closest it comes to cawing. Maybe, if he startled it, he could get it to caw, the boy thinks. He kneels at the base of the tree, palming a pinecone from the ground. It is pear shaped, and imbricated with brown scales, like a grenade of shingles. Rising, he readies the cone at his shoulder, the way a shot-putter would. The crow keeps cocking its head back and forth on its branch, oblivious. Its beak never narrows. The jaw's twin points remain poised at a precise and unchanging angle, as though biting down on something that the boy can't see: an invisible twig, or tuft of grass. Materials for its nest. The boy waits for the crow to blink, then lobs the pinecone. It misses by a foot, crashing through the foliage and landing behind the tree some-where. The crow is unfazed. It retracts its head on its neck slightly, but it doesn't caw, and it is careful neither to open nor close its beak. It really is as if there is something in its mouth, something that it is determined not to drop. But its mouth is empty, and so the boy imagines that it is this very emptiness that it is bringing back to its nest: that it is building a nest of absences, gaps. The way it jealously hoards this absence between its mandibles, like a marble. Its beak must be broken, the boy decides, broken open. Or else, no: The bird is simply stubborn. It could caw if it wanted to. It is resisting only to spite him. He gathers four more pinecones. The longer the crow doesn't caw, the louder its silence becomes. The gap in its beak magnifies the still-ness around them, until the boy can no longer hear any of the other playground sounds: teachers' whistles; the far-off squawks of his classmates on the soccer field. The boy feels alone with the crow, alone inside this quiet. He hugs the four pinecones against his stomach. He is determined to make the crow caw once before recess is over. He imagines that he is the teacher, the crow his pupil, and he remembers all the ways in which his own teacher calls on him in class: how the boy is made to speak, pronounce new vocabulary terms, say *present* when his name is said. Before recess is over, the boy will make the crow say *present*. He will pelt it with pinecones until it caws, until it constitutes itself in a caw, until the moment when—dropping that absence from its beak—the crow will finally announce its presence, say present, present its presence in the present sharpness of its caw. The crow looks up at the sky for a moment. Seizing the opportunity, the boy hurls another of his pinecones, this time missing its torso by a matter of inches. The crow spreads its wings and begins to bate on the branch. For a moment, it almost seems as if it is going to fly away. The boy grips a third pinecone tightly, until its spines bite into his flesh. Soon, he knows, the recess bell will ring. He squints at the crow, focusing its black body in the center of his vision. But just as he is about to throw the pinecone, the bird tucks its neck into its chest, looking down at him. It blinks its black eyes rapidly, agitatedly. Finally it closes its beak. And when at last it caws—rupturing the quiet around them, with a loud, sharp-syllabled *awe*—it is as startling as the first sound in creation.

3.

The boy walks his bike up a hill. In the middle of his street he sees a dead chipmunk, crushed evenly by the tires of a car. It has been flattened into a purse of fur. Around it, a red aura of gore. It makes a brown streak in the center of the lane, straight as a divider line. Ahead of him on the sidewalk he sees a live one. Only a yard away, a second chipmunk stands tensed on all fours, eyeing the boy and his bike. When it wrinkles its nose in rapid sniffs, the boy can tell that it is smelling the carcass stench, wafting in faint off the tarmac behind him. It must seem, to the chipmunk, as if the boy is its brother's murderer. He does not know how to correct this misunderstanding, or reassure the rodent that he means it no harm. He stands silent, trying to stifle any movement that might terrify it. It flees in terror anyway. In an abrupt about-face it dashes up the sidewalk, hugging the hill's concrete revetment; when it reaches a ground-level drain-pipe—barely bigger than its body—it squeezes inside. The boy walks his bike up to the drainpipe. He moves slowly, so as not to startle. But his wheel spokes make a sinister sound as he approaches: Each bony click seems to close in on the animal, skeleton sound of Death's scythe tapping. When the boy reaches the drainpipe he bends to peer inside. Huddled into a ball, the chipmunk is shaking violently, its walnut-colored chest convulsing. It glares out at the boy, trapped. The rear of the pipe is backed up with gunk: mud, pine needles, dead leaves. The sight of the boy there, darkening the aperture of the drainpipe, must be a source of unbearable dread for the creature. He starts to back away, but it is too late. Inexplicably, recklessly, the chipmunk rushes forward. It reaches the edge of the pipe and leaps free, landing on the sidewalk at the boy's feet. There it freezes, locking its eyes on his shoes, as if awaiting the killing blow. The boy is careful to stand behind the bike's front tire. He gives the chipmunk a barrier, a zone of safety. He reassures it, by his very posture, that he means it no harm. The chipmunk cowers, catching its breath. The wheel casts a barred shadow over its body, a cage of shade in which the chipmunk trembles, frozen amid the many spokes. Indeed, the way that the tire's shadow encloses the rodent, it looks like a phantom hamster wheel. Like the kind of toy Death would keep its pets in—all the mortals who are Death's pets. Maybe that is why the chipmunk dares not move, the boy thinks: because it already understands the nature of this wheel. To flee from Death is just to jog in place. Spinning inside one's dying. The boy takes the bike by the seat and rolls it back. As the front wheel withdraws, the shadow slides off its prisoner. Now the chipmunk is free to flee. But it hunkers to the ground, eyeing the boy's feet with coiled purpose. A second passes in which it does not so much as flinch, and the boy understands exactly what is about to happen: Feeling cornered, the chipmunk will charge him. In a brown blur it will scurry up his shoe and latch onto his pants leg, the way a squirrel mounts a tree trunk. As it claws at his pants for purchase, tearing through the cotton, the boy will be able to feel its bark-sharpened nails get a scansorial grip into his shin-bone. The sear of skin tearing; the beading of blood. He cannot help imagining all this. He will kick out his leg—as if it were aflame, he imagines—but the chipmunk will hold fast to him, out of rabidness perhaps. Then the boy will have no choice. Above all, he knows, he will have to keep the creature from biting him. After trying so hard not to frighten it, he will be forced to kill it. With his free foot he will have to scrape it from his pants leg, onto the sidewalk, and stomp the life out of it, flattening it as dispassionately as that car had flattened the rodent in the road. In this way, he will become everything the animal mistook him for: its murderer, its personal death. The boy stares down at the chipmunk, which has begun to vibrate like a rev-ving engine. Because it was wrong about the boy, it will prove to be right about the boy. Because it has mistaken the boy for a murderer, it will make the boy murder it. And so perhaps, the boy reflects, the chipmunk wasn't wrong after all: Maybe it could see clearly what the boy could not. That he had a role to play in its fate. The boy stomps his foot lightly on the sidewalk. Still the chipmunk does not run. It is ready now. It must have been waiting for this moment its entire life. Seeing the boy today, it recognized him instantaneously: He was the human who had been set aside for it, the boy it had been assigned from the beginning. *He* was the place it was fated to die. Now, at long last, it has an appointment to keep.

4.

On his walk home from school the boy pauses at the edge of his neighbors' yard. It is wide and well manicured and unfenced, and today their dog is out in it. A standard chocolate poodle—as tall as the boy's chest when standing—it is couchant now, in the middle of the lawn. It has not yet noticed the boy from where it lies. It pants happily in the midday heat, its long tongue lolling from its jaw. Some curls are combed into a bouffant on its forehead, where they seem to seethe, massed and wrinkled like an exposed brown brain. The dog's owners—the boy's neighbors—are nowhere to be seen. Far out of earshot, deep within their white two-story house. If the dog were to suddenly bark loudly and attack the boy—if the boy were to shout for help—they would not be able to hear. At least twice a week the boy passes the poodle in the yard like this. The sight of it always paralyzes him with fear. He will stop walking for a moment, then sidle slowly down the sidewalk, careful not to draw the dog's attention. What is to keep it from mauling him? The owners are never outside with it. Evidently they trust the poodle. It is allowed to roam unsupervised in the yard, which is not technically—but only appears to be—unfenced. In reality, the boy's mother has explained to him, it employs a so-called invisible fence: a virtual boundary of radio waves tracing the perimeter of the lawn. GPS coordinates are broadcast to the dog's shock collar, which is programmed to administer mild jolts of admonitory electricity whenever the poodle trespasses the property line. There is nothing—she reassured him—to be afraid of. After a few hours of behavioral training, the dog would have learned to obey the dictates of its collar. It would have internalized the limits of its prison. And so even if it noticed the boy one day—even if it bounded barking toward him—it would know to stop short at the pavement. As his mother was explaining this, the boy nodded to show he understood. But deep down he still does not trust the invisible fence. He wonders, for instance, how it is supposed to keep other animals *out* of the yard. All it would take is for a rabid bat, or raccoon, or chipmunk to crawl across the boundary line and bite and infect the dog. Then when the boy was walking home one day, he would see the poodle foaming at the mouth in the yard, with nothing but a symbolic cage of X/Y coordinates separating it from him. And what was to keep the dog—mindless with rage—from simply disregarding the fence, in that case? Assuming it could remember the fence at all. For the rabies might very well have wiped its memory clean, erasing its behavioral training. Then the dog would be incapable of recognizing symbolic cages, only real ones, and it would not think twice before bounding across the yard at the boy. He stares at the poodle. It is facing the house, panting. He does not know its name. Sometimes he imagines being attacked by the dog, and in these fantasies— which he indulges in involuntarily, standing motionless with fear on the sidewalk—he assigns it the name Gerald. He imagines the neighbors running across the lawn, calling, *Gerald, Gerald, get off him,* even as the poodle pins him to the pavement and snaps its jaws. This is always the most horrifying moment, for the boy, in the fantasy. How the dog can ignore its own name. How it can conduct this beast's balancing act, suspended between two minds: the mind that answers to Gerald and the mind that murders meat. For once it starts tearing into the boy's throat, it is not Gerald any longer: It has already regressed, passed backward through some baptism. Not only nameless now, but unnameable. That is what terrifies the boy. The name cannot enclose the dog forever. It is just a kind of kennel you can keep it in. The boy pictures all the flimsy walls of this poodle's name: the collar's silver tag, engraved *Gerald*; the blue plastic food bowl, marked *Gerald*; the sound of its owners' voices, shouting *Gerald*. Each of them is just another invisible fence, which the dog can choose to trespass at will. The poodle turns to him now, cocking its head sideways. At any moment, the boy knows, the animal could transform from a friendly house pet into a ferocious guardian: a Cerberus at the gates of the hell that it will make this boy's life, if he makes even one move toward its masters. From his place on the sidewalk, the boy reaches out his arm. He extends it over the lawn, as over a candle's flame. Unfolding his hand, he holds it palm down inside the dog's territory. The poodle rises, stretching its hind legs and shaking the tiredness from its coat. It begins to cross the yard. Every few steps it stops, eyeing the boy. *It* is afraid of *him*, he realizes. The dog must recognize the threat that the boy poses. That he could snap. Attack it. That he is wild, unpredictable, unconstrained. From the poodle's point of view, the only thing holding the boy back is a kind of invisible fence, or else system of invisible fences. The name his mother gave him. The school uniform he wears. The fact that he walks with his back straight, and hair combed, and that he knows better than to murder his neighbors' pets. This is all that protects the poodle from him now, the poodle must be thinking. He imagines himself enraged like the dog, rabid like the dog; he imagines himself punching the animal, in blind mindlessness. Yes, it is possible. He can see himself that way, one day: suspended over a void where no name reaches. The dog approaches the edge of the grass. It stops a foot back, looking up at the boy's hand. Suspicious, it sniffs. It curls back its lip slightly, revealing a white incisor. The boy's hand is cold with sweat. It is exactly as he always imagined. He wants to call the dog's name, in soothing tones—*There, Gerald. There, Gerald.*—but he remembers that *Gerald* is not its real name. And so, not knowing what to call it, the boy says nothing. He stands there on the pavement. The dog stands on the grass.

61

5.

Behind his house one afternoon the boy finds a chunk of ice. It is lying on the sidewalk, fist sized and flecked with dirt. Someone must have dropped it there from a five-pound bag or a cooler. Now it lies exposed to the summer. It is the clear kind, blue-gray all the way through, except at its core, where a brilliant whiteness has condensed: sunlight, locked inside. Tiny hairlines of trapped light radiate outward, veining the ice's interior from corner to corner, touching the edges and returning to center. The radiance seems to ricochet around in there, bouncing off the walls of its container. Even as the boy is considering this, the ice jerks toward him. The chunk shifts a centimeter across the pavement, then stops abruptly, as if thinking better of it. The boy can hardly stifle his surprise. He knows that there is some kind of glacial principle at work: that as the chunk melts, it lubricates its own passage, and is displaced across the pavement in a basal slide. But still, the way it had moved. Exactly like a living thing. Bending down, he can see the darkened trail behind the ice, where it has wet the pebbled concrete. While the boy is studying this, the chunk scrapes forward again, another centimeter. The light at its center glints, melting it from within. Where is it headed? The boy's shadow stops an inch or two away, and it almost seems as if the ice is trying to crawl inside. As if, stuck beneath the sun, it is seeking shelter in his shade. Dragging itself into his shadow. And it's strange too, the boy thinks, how what melts it helps it move. That is the paradox the ice has been presented with: this light at its core, the light that is killing it, is what enables it to escape. It has to glide along a film of its own dying. The faster that it moves, the more of itself that it melts, and so it is alive with its own limit, animated by this horizon inscribed in its being. There is a lesson to be learned in this, the boy thinks. He watches the chunk, waiting for it to judder forward again. The ball of light sits calmly at its center, like a pilot in the cockpit. It will steer the chunk forward by destroying it. Death is what's driving the ice. It collaborates with the ice's other side, the side that wants to survive, and together these twin engines propel the chunk to safety. As the boy watches, a line of water melts off one edge, trickling down the sidewalk in an exploratory rivulet. Paving the way for the glacier. The boy was right: It is headed directly for him. He watches the tendril inch into the shadow of his head, worming blindly forward. It punches deeper and deeper into the darkness. This is the track that the death-driven ice will travel, the boy understands. Gradually the glacier will slide into his head. One-way into the shade. One-way into the shadow that his skull casts. There has to be some kind of lesson in this.

Where Have All the Animals Gone?
Dale Peterson

IN THE SPRING OF 1900, approximately one hundred ten years before the three of us—Karl, Dan, and I—are sitting in Uganda's airport transit lounge at Entebbe moaning about the state of the world, the British governor of the Ugandan Protectorate, Harry Johnston, was sitting in his house at Entebbe and listening to some Mbuti Pygmies from the Ituri Forest. They could have been moaning about the state of the world too, although I imagine they were more concerned about their own personal condition, since they had recently been kidnapped by a German entrepreneur who planned to exhibit them in Paris at the World's Fair. Once the entrepreneur traveled with his human cargo into the Ugandan Protectorate, headed for the coast and a boat, however, Governor Johnston put an end to all that nonsense. He freed the Pygmies and sent the evildoer back to Germany.

Governor Johnston encouraged the Pygmies to recuperate in Entebbe that spring as he made the preparations for their difficult journey back to the Congo. But the governor was an amateur cryptozoologist—interested in mythical or mysterious or undiscovered species—and since Europeans had yet to explore most of Africa's forested middle, he began quizzing his guests about their home in the Ituri. What did they hunt? What kinds of unusual animals did they know about?

The conversation between the Pygmies and the governor could have included a little spoken language and a lot of pantomime. But the governor also had a good idea of what to ask about, since he was familiar with an account published in 1890 by the Welsh-American journalist and explorer Henry Morton Stanley about a strange animal of the Ituri. Stanley had never seen this animal, but he had spoken to some Mbuti who described the elusive "Atti," a kind of forest-dwelling donkey, Stanley thought, whom the Pygmies captured with pit traps. They weren't actual donkeys, of course. They were some other kind of quadruped, adapted to live in the dark and leafy world of the rain forest. "What they can find to eat is a wonder," Stanley wrote. "They eat leaves."

Based on Stanley's brief account, Governor Johnston held up before his guests the picture of a donkey, and they confirmed that, yes, they were familiar with an animal like that. When Johnston pulled out a zebra skin, the Pygmies again confirmed a resemblance. They called this animal an "o'api," Johnston would later write. The word soon became Anglicized to *okapi*.

Johnston knew enough to be excited. Such an animal, never heard of by a European before Stanley's brief mention, never seen by a zoologist anywhere, never written about in any of the world's zoological literature, could amount to a great discovery for some enterprising person like him. He therefore organized a full expedition out to the eastern Congo and placed himself at the head of it.

By July of 1900, the expedition had made it as far as the Belgian outpost of Fort Mbeni, on the edge of the great Ituri. The Pygmies left at that point, returning to their village, while Lieutenant Meura, the commander of Fort Mbeni, declared that he too believed there was a donkey-like creature in the forest, although perhaps more horse than donkey. In any case, Meura provided Johnston with trackers and some extra supplies, enough for a several-day journey right into the hot heart of that oppressive place.

At least Johnston thought it was oppressive. Johnston's negative impressions may have been intensified by the malaria. He was soon stupefied enough that when his trackers showed him what they claimed to be o'api or okapi tracks, Johnston refused to follow— thinking, apparently, that he was about to be tricked by devious natives. Donkeys and horses, the governor knew very well, did not have cloven hooves. The tracks being pointed out to him were of a cloven-hoofed animal. Couldn't be an okapi.

He was wrong, of course, but by then everyone in the expedition was too wracked by malaria to think about it. They returned to Fort Mbeni, and from there back to Entebbe. Too bad for Harry Johnston.

Luckily, Lieutenant Meura was a generous sort who rummaged about and found two small pieces of okapi skin that had been sewn into a pair of bandoliers. He presented those to Johnston as a parting gift, and he promised to send more okapi pieces as soon as he could. Meura then died of blackwater fever, whatever that is, but his faithful second-in-command eventually sent to Johnston a full shipment of okapi pieces, including a complete skin and a couple of skulls along with, it seems, a jawbone. Cloven hooves also in the package, according to an accompanying note, disappeared in transit.

Still, there was enough specimen material to justify Governor Johnston's mailing it to an expert at the British Museum in London, who, after a quick examination, announced in 1903 the discovery of an entirely new mammal, a new genus and species, actually, which was named *Okapi johnstoni*. In that way, Harry Johnston acquired his own mote of immortality. But the important part of this story— and the main reason Karl (photographer of giraffes), Dan (ivory guy, along for the ride), and I (writer of a book about giraffes) are now strapped into a missionary plane and being bumped along in our passage above the green and misty sea of the Ituri Forest—is that the expert at the British Museum also announced that okapis are the only living relatives of giraffes.

How can that be? you ask yourself. When you first look at an okapi you don't see anything like a giraffe. You see a strange and ghostly beast, shy, with a bony face and a body that reminds you of a horse with a beautiful chestnut-brown coat that, in a filtered forest light, glows and turns dark chocolate with orange highlights. A horse with, when you examine him or her more fully, horizontal zebra stripes wrapping the forelegs and, at the rear, a wavery burst of zebra emerging from the rump, fanning out and spreading forward in a feathering of wavery horizontal stripes. The stripes look like strips of sunlight reflecting off a fan of rain-wet leaf layers. Ghostly? Especially the face, which is bony with black circling around the eyes and nose, with a dusting of white or gray cast gently over the rest of the face. It's a gray mask, making this animal look like a horse dressed up for Halloween and wearing a horse-skull mask topped absurdly by a pair of moth-eaten donkey ears. Donkey? Horse? But then you look down at the cloven hooves.

I forgot to mention the tongue, which is bluey-black and long enough to wrap halfway around the animal's snout—in fact, a lot like a giraffe's tongue, which is one unlikely clue to the okapi's obscure ancestry. It's true that okapis don't have long necks, but neither did the direct ancestors of giraffes until only a few million years ago, so the fossils say. It was, in any case, a generally hidden anatomy that convinced the expert in the British Museum back at the start of the twentieth century that he was looking at pieces of a giraffe relative: particularly a specialized set of lower canines that are notched in the middle and flattened into a couple of spoon-shaped lobes on either side of that notch. It's an odd feature but useful for both giraffes and okapis as a specialized tool for stripping leaves off branches and twigs.

Then there are the okapi horns, which, like a giraffe's horns, are actually what some experts call *ossicones,* meaning they began life as pieces of cartilage that eventually turn into bone. Okapi horns are a lot smaller than the horns of giraffes, though, and they're pointy at the ends. Also, only okapi males have horns, unlike giraffes, while the females are just left out . . . even though, again unlike giraffes, *la femme est plus grosse.*

The French I'll let you figure out. It's being spoken right now by a handsome and vigorous man named Jean-Prince M'Bayaa at the Okapi Breeding and Research Station, which is where Karl, Dan, and I now happen to be, having just, with the help of the missionaries, magically dropped out of the sky and landed in the middle of the Ituri Forest. We're actually inside a 13,700-square-kilometer patch of the Ituri called the Okapi Faunal Reserve, not far from the village of Epulu and right next to the rushing, roaring, cool-watered Epulu River.

Here at the Okapi Breeding and Research Station near Epulu, thirteen okapis are living inside fenced pens, but the pens are very large, with plenty of giant trees and other vegetation inside, so it's possible to look through the chain-link fence and at least imagine you're looking at wild animals in the forest, rather than ones who have just been suckered into pit traps and put in prison. Anyway, it's a nice prison. The okapis don't seem frustrated or unhappy, and they appear to have plenty to eat and, possibly, enough to keep them mentally occupied if mental occupation is what they desire.

Jean-Prince has just brought out a green-painted wooden wheelbarrow full of bundled leaves and personalized in white lettering with the name Tatu, and now he opens a gate to the pen for a female named Tatu. He enters the pen and starts tying the leaf bundles onto an outstretched rope. It looks like he's putting green laundry on a clothesline, which seems a silly way to feed wild animals, but it probably reproduces the okapis' usual feeding posture in the wild. Tatu seems satisfied with the deal.

In the wild, Jean-Prince tells us, okapis eat the leaves of a hundred fifty species (or maybe it's fifty species, and I misheard the French), while here at the station they're fed leaves from about forty-five different species. The Pygmies—Mbuti Pygmies—go into the forest every day, harvest the leaves from those species, and bring them into the station.

67

*

Three days later, Karl and I, followed by our minder, follow a couple of the Mbuti workers on their morning route into the forest to harvest leaves. The minder, a young, quiet, and rather sweet-looking African named Michel Moyakeso, wears green military-style fatigues and carries an old rifle. He works for the Institut Congolais pour la Conservation de la Nature (or ICCN), which officially runs the reserve from a headquarters based next to the Okapi Station. For some reason, someone at the ICCN has assigned Michel to follow us with his gun whenever we leave the station grounds.

The two workers, Bernard Mtongani and Abeli Doki, are both wearing black rubber boots, standard issue for the project, and carrying machetes. Bernard is older, with a ski-jump nose in a small face beneath a big wool watch cap. When he talks, his face lights up with the pleasure of communication. He's the talker. Abeli, not so much. Abeli is dressed nicely in an Okapi Center T-shirt and fancy jeans with zippered back pockets and the name Obama embroidered in bright yellow letters going down the front of his right leg.

In the wild, Bernard tells us (his unfamiliar words translated into French by Michel), okapis eat leaves from over a hundred species, while his and Abeli's daily job is to collect the leaves from thirty to thirty-five different kinds.

We follow these two as they wander through the forest, locating the various species of plants, and then—maybe it requires shinnying up a pole-like tree or scrambling into a difficult, thickety branch somewhere over our heads—harvesting the leaves and packing them into little bundles tied with vine. Later on, Bernard and Abeli assemble the bundles into fuller packets, and at the end of the morning's harvest, which has taken altogether about three hours, the fuller packets are bound into big, clumsy bunches that are then skillfully balanced on their heads and toted off to the Okapi Station.

Once our rented car, complete with driver, shows up from Kisangani, Karl and I, with Dan now coming along (and, of course, our minder, Michel), visit the Mbuti village of Lembongo.

The driver takes us for a short while down the main mud road from Epulu and the Okapi Station and then off the road through a series of twisty ruts until we can go no farther. He stays with the car. On foot, the four of us walk until we reach the edge of the village, where we are greeted by a few sickly looking people, some with hair yellowed from malnutrition, and an old woman, her bare breasts flat and hanging like banana leaves, who sits before a blackened boiling pot resting on three or four logs hotly welded into a small fire.

The full village includes some beehive huts made of palm fronds and several cube-shaped, mud-and-stick huts: maybe four or five dozen dwellings altogether, casually spread out around three or four dusty, flattened centers, along with a few subdued, smoky fires, and one central pavilion made of poles and thatch. We sit down in the shade of the pavilion, and soon half the villagers have turned out for the occasion. We shake many people's hands, the men dressed in rags, some of the women wrapped in colorful cloth. Someone brings out a yellow-enameled bowl containing a treat of fresh, dripping honey straight from the hive, and the bowl is placed on the ground near where we're sitting. Several eagerly orbiting bees have already started drowning in the honey, and there's a reason why: It's delicious.

The village "chief," in Karl's assessment—but do Mbuti have "chiefs"? maybe he's just the oldest bloke around—comes out of his hut to sit down and chat with the visitors. He's wearing pants printed with a portrait of Jean-Pierre Bemba, the rebel commander from a few years back who was given a vice presidency as his reward for quitting the war. The old man's wife stays back inside the doorway of the hut, watching us quietly from the shadows.

His name is Myanamenge, he says, and he has a small, rounded face and a quiet reserve. He speaks in a language that Michel translates into French and then, since I'm missing a lot of the French, is occasionally turned into an explanatory bone of English tossed my way by Karl. Myanamenge says he doesn't know how old he is. His life has always been hard. He doesn't eat elephant meat. Sometimes hunting is good, sometimes not—and here Karl inserts his own opinion: "He's not going to say that in the old days there was a lot more game."

Meanwhile, as we're slurping the honey and exchanging words with Myanamenge, a hunting party from the village shows up and seems to confirm Karl's assessment about the game. We see only a small part of this returning parade, starting with a giant net rolled up like a household rug and looped around someone's head and shoulders, followed by a solemn-faced hunter with a thin goatee who is carrying a spear and knife. The hunter slips into his hut and then slips out again to greet us and show us the blue duiker he's just killed: about the size of a Chihuahua, with gray fur, tiny feet, no head. The hunter holds up the duiker. Karl takes a picture. The hunter, dressed in cutoff shorts, a dirty gray polo shirt, and a faded red baseball cap, now slips back into his hut and brings out the duiker's head, tongue lolling out, which he holds up. Karl photographs that.

Karl now photographs me standing next to the red-capped hunter, whom he calls "the chief's son," and the miraculous image at the back of his camera provides an interesting contrast between tall and short in one way and soft and hard in another. Then, after a good deal more random socializing and chitchat, we leave—having arranged to join the village on another hunt for another day.

And so, early one morning, we return to Lembongo as the hunters are fixing and straightening out their nets. The nets are fed and looped around the heads and shoulders of five sturdy men. A partner does the feeding and looping in the style of someone looping a hose or rope, pulling arm lengths of rolled netting, tossing it skillfully over the head and about the shoulders of the carrier, forming at last a large, thick doughnut of netting that settles onto the head and hangs about the face and drops back across the shoulders and down the back to the buttocks. From the front, the net carriers are half hidden by the nets, their faces solemnly peering out, the nets brown and piled high enough to make the carriers look like forest trolls with impossibly spectacular hairdos.

We all leave the village led by the red-capped chief's son: a party of (not counting Karl, Dan, Michel, and me) about a dozen men (net carriers and hunters gripping iron-tipped spears), a dozen women (including one or two adolescent girls and a mother carrying a baby), and four small brown-and-white hunting dogs. Both men and women are small and, at least some of them, rather delicate looking. The women have cut their hair short or fixed it into cornrows and snaky plaits. The men have given themselves more severe cuts, although, as if to make up for that severity, many have left a scattering of delicate growth on chin and lip. The women are wrapped in colorful print cloths, some of them with wicker baskets strapped to their backs, and the men are dressed in T-shirts and shorts. The men are all flip-flopped. Some of the women are barefoot, others flip-flopped. And one of the women carries the fire: glowing embers inside a log small enough that she can carry it in one hand.

After a long walk through the village gardens and other areas that look recently slashed and burned, at last we get into the tall forest. After another hour or so of walking, we come to a small, cavern-like clearing at the base of a giant tree. An old man stacks small pieces of wood below some outreaching branches of the giant tree and borrows the transported embers. With a leaf, he fans the embers into a flame—which he then stifles with green leaves, creating at last a steady column of rising white smoke.

Most everyone is sitting down now, and there's a good deal of relaxed conversation, some laughing, the women always grouped together tightly and focused on their own society, the men more spread out, several people smoking rolled-up cigarettes and luxuriating in this lovely moment before the hunt.

Now people are getting up and, one by one, bathing themselves in the smoke, walking over, and reaching with their hands into the writhing immaterial substance, splashing it back like water into their faces and hair. Next the net carriers step one by one into the smoke, thus smoking out the nets for some reason or other, maybe the practical one of neutralizing organic smells in order to confuse the game.

And then, quickly now, all are up and laying out the nets. A net carrier moves sprightly along a game trail, unlooping his long, long net, drawing out a netted line that stretches away along the trail until he's reached the end of his piece, whereupon another net carrier takes up the task. He begins unlooping his long net, drawing it out into a continuance of the netted line—and then another. The women, meanwhile, follow this unreeling act, expertly joining the nets together at the ends, while spreading them out at the sides and raising them up: deftly attaching one lengthwise side to bits of vegetation on the forest floor, raising up the other side and attaching it to any standing vegetation—bush, vine, small tree—at a height of maybe three feet. The net, which was a rolled line reeled off by the men and stretching along the forest floor for a mile or so, has now become a netted fence, and because the fence is woven from oily brown twine or liana fibers, and vibrating softly in resonance with the secret filtering of air and the quivering greens and browns of the forest, it turns invisible—as do, suddenly, the Pygmies.

Karl, Dan, Michel, and I are left standing in a sleepy daze near the invisible net somewhere around its midpoint, I believe, and everyone else has vanished. Dan smokes a cigarette, and as he does I can picture as in a dream that long net drawn out into a great crescent in the forest, with the Pygmies quietly slipping through the forest and over to the open face at the far side; and now I can hear, in the distance but gradually moving closer, a series of strange, dreamlike, high-pitched whoops and barks that sound like the faint cries of birds and dogs, which, after a while, sound like whistles and flutes, which, after another while, sound like women's voices. As this ethereal chorus approaches and gathers, closer, closer, I understand that the Mbuti must be chasing or driving or calling out for the game. They could be saying to the animals: *Where are you hiding, our sweet little friends? Where have you gone, our dear little ones?* And the animals, at first alert and drawn in by the mysterious whoops and barks but now anxious or afraid, might be saying to one another: *This is not good. We should run.* Some might say: *Let's go this way!* Others will say: *No, this way!* Another says: *Quick. Down this hole.* Yet another says: *No, not that hole! That one leads into the other world!* And so the animals are altogether scared and confused but generally headed, one can imagine, toward our part of the net at the closed bottom or pocket of the crescent. After a time, however, the disembodied chorus fades and dies out, and the four of us are left listening to silence, which isn't silence, of course, but more the in-and-out breathing of a sleeping forest, the eternal susurrus of insects, the turning clockwork of burps and chirps from small birds and hidden frogs. Silence for all practical purposes, though, and it is in this whispering silence that the Mbuti at last materialize and unhang and roll up the nets as deftly as they had earlier rolled out and hung them up.

With the nets rolled up once more and looped over the net carriers, we continue walking and walking until we come to another place that someone—Who knows how these decisions are made?—determines is right, and the nets are again laid down rapidly by the men, raised and fixed in place by the women, with the four of us again left standing near the bottom of the crescent. Again we hear the high-pitched whoops and barks in the distance and coming closer, and again at last the Pygmies silently materialize from inside the forest—but again, this second time, no animals: no nervous, leaping monkeys, no ragged, zigzagging duikers, nothing. Nada.

A third time as well the hunters spread out their great nets, fix them in place, whoop and bark, singing thus to push and drive the game into the pocket of the crescent—but the calls die out, and the Pygmies appear while the animals do not. This hunt has become a tedious vegetarian's exercise, and so the question one is provoked to ask is this: *Where have all the animals gone?*

*

Dawn.

I'm lying beneath the mosquito netting in my bed in my bedroom in our cottage beside the Epulu River at the Okapi Station. I open my eyes to look up through a cloud of netting overhead to consider the bullet holes in the ceiling. Still half asleep. Being awakened by an alarm clock, which is the temperature bird, a repetitive little fellow who hangs around outside the window and every morning wakes me up at the same time with the same monotonous query: *Temperature. What's the temperature? Temperature. Temperature. Temperature. What's the temperature?*

It's warm now and going to be hot soon.

I open my eyes again and once more size up the bullet holes in the ceiling, which seem now like a dangerous form of punctuation, like a stream of ellipses screwing the syntax of the synapse in the middle of a dream, like . . . and . . . and . . . that make one pause to wonder: Where have all the animals gone? They've gone, I think, into a black hole made by the soldiers and thugs who shot the bullets that made the bullet holes. Or maybe they've gone into a deep hole dug in the ground by the meat merchants and the ivory traders and timber thieves, the butchers, bankers, bosses, and bumblers. Or maybe they've just dropped into the giant hole being screwed into the earth by the mighty march of modern progress.

Temperature. Temperature. What's the temperature?

It's our last day at Epulu, and now, as I scribble these words into my little notebook, I hear a series of clinks, clanks, and clunks in the kitchen, a discordant concert conducted carelessly by Samuel, our cook, as he rummages about. He's early this morning, maybe because he's eagerly anticipating final payment for services rendered.

The Epulu River rushes past the Okapi Station and our little cottage in the station, creating a surfy roar day and night, nature's white-noise machine that I find mostly comforting, since it masks much of the rumbling of the trucks moving past the Okapi Breeding Station and the headquarters of the ICCN on Route Nacional 4 (RN4). That's the main clay track connecting east with west, in the process slashing open an orange gash right through the Ituri Forest and the Okapi Wildlife Reserve. A brief pause in the rumbling, as a truck stops momentarily at the security barrier in front of the ICCN barracks. Then the driver revs the engine, shifting gears, getting under way—although still carefully, one hopes, across the wood planks bolted onto the steel girders of the new bridge over the rushing Epulu River—headed, as he would be, west, on the way to places like

Nia Nia and beyond, as far perhaps as the big city of Kisangani. . . .

Or maybe the driver is pointed in the other direction, in which case he has already crossed the bridge before stopping at the barrier. It's still a momentary pause at the barrier (no inspections here) before he revs the engine, shifts the gears, and heads east to places like Mambasa and Irumu and on, perhaps, to Bunia and out to Uganda and beyond.

I sometimes think of Africa as the middle of the world. It is, in any case, a nucleus of evolution and a center of life, and the Congo—the great warm, wet, all-embracing Congo—is the forested center of the center. In 1989, the Democratic Republic of the Congo held more elephants than any other nation in the world, with an estimated population of 112,000 individuals. Surveys published in 2007, less than two decades later, concluded that only between 10,000 and 20,000 elephants were left. If those figures are reliable, one can conclude that somewhere between 80 and 90 percent of the elephants alive in the heart of Africa were, during the last couple of decades, wiped out, erased, extinguished, killed, or just shot full of holes and cut up into a hundred thousand pieces.

Such is the elephant holocaust: the sad, sad circus of Pleistocene refugees all lined up and marching trunk to tail in the grim program of extermination. What drives this bloody parade is the Great I-Want, the mysterious matrix of human desire, the unaccountable human passion for the peculiar luster and texture of the elongated front teeth of elephants.

Elephants have those teeth.

People want the teeth.

Too bad for the elephants.

Until recent times, ivory was sold openly and legally in the Congo, carved in dozens of workshops located in the urban centers of Kinshasa, Kisangani, and elsewhere. A ban in 1989 pushed Congo's ivory trade underground, while the war, beginning in 1996, brought it back into the open with a vengeance. Thugs temporarily employed as soldiers looted the forests for meat and ivory, and they looted all the settlements along the road, including the village of Epulu and the offices and barracks of the ICCN and the various buildings and guest cottages of the Okapi Breeding Station.

Aside from the dozen or so okapis cared for at the Okapi Station, Rosmarie and Karl Ruf (the Swiss couple who ran the place) also took in chimpanzee babies who had been orphaned by hunters, keeping the growing apes on two islands in the middle of the river. The thugs employed as soldiers killed and ate all those chimps but somehow were persuaded—who knows how? a promise, a deal, an appeal?—to leave the okapis alone.

Meanwhile, thousands of amateur miners had been moving into the Ituri Forest, scratching holes into the earth in search of gold, diamonds, coltan (critical for the manufacture of electronic gadgets), and cassiterite (for tin), while other extraction entrepreneurs moved in to mine the trees, the meat, and again the ivory. Mining ivory was easy enough. No shovels required. Mining ivory required little more than pointing an AK-47 in a certain direction and pulling the trigger, then hacking away an elephant's front teeth and getting those teeth out to market. But what market, where, how?

The dirt highway, the RN4, could help. On the RN4, elephants' teeth could be taken either west to Kisangani and from there on to the north or west. Or one could take the ivory on the RN4 east to Bunia and from there out of the country and on, ultimately, to China, where a rising middle-class has become the big market for big teeth these days.

The end of the war came after all the deals were finalized in Kinshasa, whereupon the various rebel chiefs signed papers, were given rewards, and the national army and police drove out the last of the thugs employed as soldiers. With the end of the war, a number of outside organizations—the World Bank, for example—moved in to make things better. The RN4, that link between east and west, the red-clay cut through the Ituri Forest and the Okapi Reserve inside the Ituri, had gotten bad. It was rutted, washed out in places, muddy, seriously unreliable. The World Bank financed the improvement work, hiring Chinese crews to do it right and even to build a beautiful new steel bridge across the Epulu River right in front of the Okapi Station and the ICCN headquarters.

That's the World Bank. That's development. That's progress. After the World Bank refurbishment, traffic on the RN4 went from a small trickle to a major rush: hundreds of trucks a month rumbling along the road. But the question the World Bank officers, teetering in their ergonomically engineered chairs inside their high-rise offices at the very tippy tops of cities in the First World, may not have addressed fully enough is this: What might be inside those trucks?

*

75

A good X-ray machine would help, since official barriers on the road are run by soldiers and police among whom many are not altogether averse to closing their eyes. As a result, the RN4 has become a major conduit for illegal timber, bushmeat, and ivory. A few weeks after the bridge at Epulu was finished, a giant double truck carrying twice the legal load, all of it illegally harvested timber bound for markets in Kenya, tested the tensile strength of the bridge girders and found it wanting. A two hundred–meter span of the bridge buckled and dropped into the river, along with the truck and its driver and the wood. Of course, the World Bank was quick to refinance the building of that bridge by a Chinese crew. The trucks soon returned.

Along with the illegal timber goes illegal bushmeat. There is legal bushmeat too, but in truth all animals of all kinds, including elephants and okapis, are chopped up and sent piece by piece on this road in both directions and sold as meat at the various village and town and city markets outside the Okapi Reserve.

Ivory moves in both directions on the RN4, and occasionally a truck is popped open to show us more particularly what it looks like. By "popped open," I'm referring to cases like the truck bound for Kisangani recently that crashed into another vehicle, whereupon 116 tusks stored in jerricans flew off the back. The ICCN rangers who monitor the barrier at Epulu are unusual in that they do not take bribes, so I have been told, but they have an additional motivation not to look closely into the trucks. A lot of the criminal traffic in ivory moving past their checkpoint is run at the direction of the general commanding the Thirteenth Brigade of the Congolese army, based not very far away in the town of Mambasa.

The general is a Big Man, as are most of the people at the free enterprise heart of the ivory mafia. These are the *commanditaires*: men of money and power who will organize the hunting expeditions at the start and take care of the ivory sales at the end. The *commanditaires* are military officers, government officials, well-established businessmen, and they hire the hunters and provide them with all the necessities: food and marijuana, guns and ammo. Guns are usually military AK-47s, owned by the Congolese military, but sometimes twelve-gauge shotguns with the lead shot melted down and reconfigured to make elephant-stopper slugs. An expedition might include a couple of hunters going out for a couple of days or perhaps a dozen or more hunters headed into the woods for a few weeks. The principal goal is ivory, which is the shiny prize that motivates the *commanditaire*, but the hunters may be rewarded with meat for themselves and their families or to sell or give away. Meat will come from antelopes, apes, buffalo, bushpigs, monkeys, okapis . . . any unlucky animal will do, including, of course, elephants.

Sold in the city markets at Kisangani, elephant meat goes for around $5 to $6 per kilogram. By comparison, antelope fetches between $3.60 and $4.80 per kilo, while monkey goes for $3.22 to $3.50 per kilo. Yes, elephant meat is more expensive than other meats, and apparently more desired, especially the succulent steak from trunk or feet. The skin of an ear makes a good drum head, while the hairs of the tail can be sold to make bracelets that are said to protect a person from lightning. The dung is used as a medicine to treat malarial convulsions among small children. But all that—dung, ears, feet, trunk, basketfuls of other body parts—is for the hunters and the traders and transporters to think about. The meat and by-products: That's their take. The *commanditaire* is just hoping to sell his cleaner and more portable ivory for his own nice profit. Right now, as I listen to the temperature bird outside my window and to the clinking, clanking, and clunking of Samuel in the kitchen working on breakfast, raw ivory sells for around $160 for a pair of five-kilogram tusks, $580 for two ten-kilogram tusks, and $1,680 for a pair of fifteen-kilogram tusks.

Temperature. Temperature. What's the temperature? Temperature.

Those price figures are based on the report Dan is just now working on, so they must be up to date. Before the trip, Dan had hired a couple of professional ivory spies—make that professional researchers—named Richard and André, two vigorous-looking young Africans, cool and self-confident, dressed well and wearing shades, who day before yesterday rode their motorcycle all the way up from Kisangani for 460 kilometers, in order to conduct their own interviews.

Dan gave them some money as a down payment, lent them a video camera, and sent them on their investigative journey up and down the RN4, west to Mambasa and east back to Kisangani, to meet and interview elephant hunters, transporters, marketers, and, if possible, a few middlemen or *commanditaires*. Richard and André have good connections in the area. They will do their job, while today—this morning, just as soon as we finish our breakfast and pay Samuel, the cook, for his services—Karl, Dan, and I will hit the RN4 on our own little mission that will include stopping in markets and making ourselves as inconspicuous as three daft blancs in the middle of the DR Congo can be, while checking various kinds of meats and their prices. . . .

*

But first, as I say, we must pay the cook, Samuel, who, as a worker contracted through the ICCN, has his own official prices that are carefully summarized on an official bill that he now—now that the breakfast dishes are cleared and left to soak in the sink—hands us.

We do the math and assemble the money: a small fistful of clean, crisp American fives, tens, and a couple of twenties. Samuel looks tentatively grateful, but he wants to make sure the money is good. He counts the bills once, twice, thrice, turning them all in the same direction, and then carefully, one by one, he goes through them once more to examine the dates. One five-dollar bill has a bad date. Luckily, though, Dan has a five that's better. Having satisfied himself about the dates, Samuel presses them up, one by one, against the glass at the window, using sunlight to check for any imperfections.

Ah! One of the tens has a crease that looks like it could be the beginning of a slow tear. He hands that back. Karl fishes around in his wallet to find a replacement.

But now, as Samuel examines the bills even more closely, he finds three of the bills—two fives and a ten—have actual holes in them. Pinpricks. He shows us, shaking his head with sincere concern. They won't do.

Dan, dripping with sly sarcasm, comments quietly: "This is unbelievable. I can't fucking believe it. Somebody has put pinpricks into our money!"

But patiently we go back to our wallets, and with a good deal of back and forthing, leafing through bills, considering the dates and holding them up to the window for new examinations, we finally come up with sufficient replacement money, making Samuel at last satisfied. Then we jam our bags into the car and hit the road.

Good-bye, Samuel.

Good-bye, Michel.

Good-bye, Jean-Prince.

Good-bye, Bernard, Abeli, and Myanamenge.*

---

*Two years later, an armed gang of poachers and illegal miners stormed the ranger station and the Okapi Breeding Center, looted and burned the physical structures, and killed six people. I can only hope these generous individuals were not among the victims. The criminal raiders also killed all the okapis.

Unnatural Habitats
Susan Daitch

GIRAFFA CAMELOPARDALIS

A STUFFED GIRAFFE, mottled and less than a tenth the height of the full-grown actual animal, began life in a factory in Jiangsu Province, China, traveled in a container ship across the Pacific to the port of Oakland, California, was shipped in boxes with other animals to the Bronx Zoo gift shop, bought for a child, discarded when outgrown, picked out of the trash, and then tied to the grille of a truck like a ship's figurehead, and in this position it crisscrossed the United States, Canada, and Mexico.

In 1826, the Ottoman viceroy of Egypt arranged to have a giraffe from the Sudan and her handlers follow the slave route, along with traders of so-called black gold up the Blue Nile, to travel all the way from Sennar to Khartoum to Alexandria. She had two keepers: Atir, Sudanese, and Hassan, an Egyptian. They knew nothing of cities of snow and ice, but the ultimate goal of the adventure, as they understood it, was to present King Charles X of France with Zarafa, named from the Arabic *zerafa*. The gift was intended as part of a grander, more secret scheme to keep the French from siding with the Greeks in their war against the Turks, to drive a wedge, to keep European from siding with European, a heavy burden to place on the sloping shoulders of an animal.

So unusual was the concept of capture and display that even the nature of what a cage might be for wildcats and large creatures had yet to be completely and reliably figured out. While Zarafa was waiting in the port of Alexandria, there were reports of hyenas and lions in disintegrating pens, and parrots from Yemen clustering in palm trees, none indigenous to the city and all occupying space somewhere between containment and the streets. Zarafa remained docile in her enclosure; the streets were full of recognizable hazards, the sea was deadly, there was no place to go. Fed milk from Egyptian cows who also had to be transported, she was loaded onto a Sardinian brig-antine, *I Due Fratelli*, set to sail from Alexandria to Marseille.

It was an uneventful crossing. The ship's first port of call was Messina, sentry for Europe, Africa, and the Levant, and the sight of a giraffe's head poking up through a hole in the deck lined with straw to prevent chafing was like a third mast, rotating, blinking, periscopal. As the port's towers and waterfront came into view, Messina was the first northern city her keepers, Hassan and Atir, had ever seen, and it appeared like a white arm curled into the sea welcoming in, but also keeping out. Though it was docked, no one could leave the ship. Because of the plague, a scourge of the fifteenth century, the city was still on its guard against contagion, any contagion, even if it might be a kind they had no name for. If anyone on board the ship wanted to buy so much as an orange or a handful of olives, their money, whether Egyptian piastres or Turkish *kuruş*, had to be disinfected by dropping coins into pots of vinegar before they could be touched by the local Messinesi.

Their next stop, Marseille, also had strict rules of quarantine. When the passengers were cleared to leave the ship, they had to move to the lazaretto. Fishermen stopped sorting their catch, stevedores rested their crates, children ran to the roads that led away from the docks. They stared at Atir's facial scars, parallel crescents etched above his eyebrows, and he stared back at them.

Within the fortress both men began to get a sense of how different life would be in France. One sat on chairs around a table, not on the floor, did not share food, did not eat with fingers but rather with forks and knives. Everyone had their own plate, bowl, glass. It was considered rude to use anyone else's. When they were finally allowed to leave the fortress, the sound of the giraffe's hooves on cobbled streets drew crowds.

Witnesses wrote about the giraffe as if she had human attributes, like shyness and flirtatiousness. She seemed to feel some affinity and affection for horses, though they were frightened of her. The giraffe, like all animals, had never seen herself and didn't know how to recog-nize her reflection. Her sense of herself, based on a small number of clues, was built on the appearance, sounds, and smells of other ani-mals, so to herself she was not a giraffe, since she'd had no memo-rable experience of interacting with others like her, and didn't know what a giraffe might be. If Zarafa had stayed in the wild, she would have recognized fellow giraffes, and identified predators and the dan-gers they posed, but from the moment she left Khartoum, Zarafa would never have seen another creature like herself, and as a stranger to involuntary speciation, would identify a horse as kin.

The five-hundred-mile walk from Marseille to Paris took three months and ended at her new home at the royal zoo. Le Jardin des Plantes had a violent and bloody history. During the French Revolution, Étienne Saint-Hilaire, a scientist who accompanied the giraffe on her journey to Paris, had written about the unhappy past of Le Jardin, a scene of massive slaughter, comparing it to entertainments staged at the Circus Maximus in ancient Rome.

> After the 10th of August 1792, when mobs attacked the Tuileries palaces, the menagerie of the late guillotined King at Versailles was pillaged: a beautiful dromedary, several small quadrupeds, and a great number of birds were either eaten or delivered up to the flayer. Only five animals, among them an Indian rhinoceros and a lion, escaped the massacre. But they had the misfortune to belong to the King and so were considered souvenirs of tyranny. They were deemed useless, had to be fed, and dangerous to the city. Their death was decided, and the Minister of Finances offered their skeletons to Le Jardin des Plantes.

Perhaps ghosts led to Hassan's flight. Once in France, he grew increasingly depressed, etiolated, and confused. If he strained to hear a muezzin call from across the sea, all he heard to mark the hours was church bells, an altogether new sound for him. Patterned shadows on walls from screens that separated men from women didn't exist in the land of goose liver and tall hats. Women wore dresses shaped like bells and took up too much space, their legs inside somewhere, hidden clappers, the top halves of their bodies almost naked. They could go anywhere alone or in odd groups, say or do, it seemed to him, almost anything they wanted to. The French language surrounded him like a shallow lake. He strained to find something to stand on, yet still keep his nose above the surface. In the name Simone, common and heard often, he heard the Arabic word *simoon*, a desert windstorm, and pulled his scarf tighter. When despair became overwhelming, he returned to Egypt.

Atir did not, as far as has been recorded, suffer from homesickness, regret, or longing. He moved into La Rotonde, a hexagonal brick structure that was to house both himself and Zarafa. During the day he groomed Zarafa with a comb attached to a long pole, and the expression "Do it or comb a giraffe" entered the language. It was

81

used when someone was reluctant to do a task, a retort issued to a footdragger. To reach his quarters, Atir needed to climb two ladders, but once in his perch he was eye level with the giraffe. It was a thrilling view, and with this promise, Atir became known as a seducer. Women flocked to his aerial roost in Le Jardin des Plantes.

When Zarafa went on public view that summer, she had sixty thousand visitors, but, as popular as she was, and as well intentioned as the king might have been in allowing the people to see his pet, in political satire the giraffe became a symbol not of the king's largesse, but of his censorship of the press.

There was competition in the realm of exotica. Passing through the city were a pair of serpentologists who exhibited never-before-seen clutches of reptiles from Africa and the New World; a beached whale was reported at Ostend; and perhaps the most spectacular of spectacles, six Osage Indians were brought from Missouri. How much freedom of movement was afforded the Osage is not known. They might have been given French or American jackets, shirts, shoes, and trousers and shepherded up the steps to Notre Dame or Sacré-Coeur, or down into the catacombs. They might have visited Atir and Zarafa as well, and been allowed to touch her fur, perhaps the first wild creature they'd had contact with since leaving the Ozarks.

Saint-Hilaire was interested in symbiosis, a relationship between two species that can be mutually beneficial to both or be beneficial mainly to the parasite, not the host. Sharks and pilot fish, he knew, had a symbiotic relationship. The pilot fish swim alongside the sharks and consume parasites who would otherwise infect or disable the sharks, and in return, are protected from possible predators because there the pilot fish are, swimming happily along, in close proximity to the sharks' jaws. Predator nations and prey can shift into symbiotic gear, at least temporarily. The gift of the giraffe, however, didn't allay the sultan's anxieties. The French entered the war on the side of the Greeks.

THE AQUARIUM

I've long found the edges of the city, those liminal spaces, the ends of what you could call a city, worth exploring, and the New York Aquarium occupies one of those margins. It's right next to Coney Island, as far south as you could go in the city before the hurricane, at least without getting your feet wet. The next landmass due south is the Turks and Caicos Islands, thirteen hundred miles away. The aquarium reminds me of the kind of optimistic modernism found in much of the architecture of the 1964 World's Fair, built just a few years later. Behind the aquarium lie projects. The Atlantic Ocean laps the shore a few yards from its front gate. So there you are at those gates, one foot in nature, the other in culture's version of nature, a sort of parking lot for some pieces of nature.

The gate is almost a whisper compared to the brass band that is its neighbor to the west, but the aquarium hides a spectacle of twelve thousand hostages, and, at the same time, is a panorama of preservation. It's a highly collapsed microcosm, a UN of sea life complete with tanks and simulated environments that reduce the seemingly infinite oceans to a few cubic meters of water.

In the early days of the aquarium, when it was located at Castle Clinton, the fish were collected in a more haphazard way. According to the WPA guide to the aquarium, "Wireless operators on ocean freighters obligingly carry to far-off corners of the world castoff clothes, whiskey, and other goods given them by the aquarium, and barter them for rare fish to add to the aquarium's collection." But now, it's against the law to swap a bottle of Lagavulin for a dolphin. As with zoo acquisitions of animals, the creatures here were bred in captivity or rescued.

As I walked around, I wondered, How are the animals selected? Why hammerheads, for example, and not giant squids? What's the system? Some animals were rescued or endangered; others came with certain iconography. Seals and penguins were chosen rather than the ordinary dinner-plate herring or mackerel. The two long-tusked Pacific walruses were flown from the Bering Strait to Brooklyn; wounded condors from the Andes occupied a perch on a 787 to JFK, to be transferred to a small craft destined for the Berkshire Bird Sanctuary, where they could safely roost on discarded construction-site spools; eleven elephants were flown from Swaziland to a zoo in Tampa, Florida. (Though they were heavily sedated, a keeper had to be assigned to stay with them in the plane. Elephant urine is corrosive to metal.) They landed in the confinement of artificial rocks, moats, and undisguised fences, but these man-made, constrained environments will save their lives.

One of the most animated exhibits, the one that draws by far the most visitors, is the shark tank, but a disturbing sign near its cavernous entrance tells you that sharks are more like people than fish. They reproduce through internal fertilization. Sharks mature in their teens, though many humans, it could be argued, don't grow up until much later, if ever. Most sharks bear young only every few years. Sharks produce fewer pups, or as the sign says, "babies," drawing an alarming image, and they are born alive. Neither we nor the sharks are kosher to eat. Sharks have no scales and are the *treyf* or pigs of the ocean, along with shellfish, catfish, and other bottom dwellers. We see them much as we see pigs, as creatures of unbridled appetites and ferocity, and yet with potentially homologous personality traits. As the sign says, we're not such strange bedfellows, the sharks and us.

It's feeding time, and dead fish are dropped into the water, but for some reason the sharks aren't interested. As they circle close to the edges of the tank, as animals tend to do in confinement, they swim right up to the glass, and a couple of big ones shit right in front of a group of children. The kids, noses and hands pressed against the glass, go nuts. They're dying with laughter. Sharks have been cast as ferocious hunters. This is not supposed to be part of their act.

It's hard to look at them with a marine biologist's eye and see a statistically harmless-to-man endangered species. The sharks in the tank have tiny eyes, rows of teeth going every which way, and look completely true to the mechanized fish automatons of *Jaws* or *Mega Shark Versus Giant Octopus*. We fear nature outsized and out of control, and this is what the independent and bigger-than-us eating-machine sharks seem to represent. One of the most horrific moments in Thor Heyerdahl's *Kon-Tiki*, perhaps one of the most frightening moments in all oceanic narratives, is when the crew is hundreds of nautical miles from Peru, and one of the nine giant balsa logs that make up the raft has taken on so much water it no longer floats. It drags the edge of the raft down. Heyerdahl takes out a knife, slices off a piece of balsa, and drops it into the Pacific, where it quickly disappears. The crew has no choice but to cut the saturated log loose, and it sinks to the bottom of the Nazca Ridge. Is this what will happen to the remaining eight? The sharks seem to sense this is a distinct possibility. They circle the raft.

The tank also contains stingrays, members of the shark family, and it's difficult to watch them without thinking of Leni Riefenstahl riding stingrays when she was in her seventies. The rays ripple and flop around at the bottom of the tank. If interested in still pursuing such recreation even at 110, Riefenstahl would take the F train to Coney Island, get in the tank, and swim around. These docile specimens would be as easy to ride as bits of sample carpeting, but then she'd be pretty old, so that might be all she could handle. Following the dip in the shark pool, she might go next door for a ride on the Cyclone, camera in hand. She would avoid the freak shows, the Sideshows by the Seashore; apart from the strong man, freaks are emphatically not her subject. She might wander over to the Human Slingshot in the Scream Zone, or, if it's New Year's Day, join the members of the Polar Bear Club in their annual icy swim. But if the Polar Bears are old and Russian, as is sometimes the case, she will not photograph them.

When I emerged from the shark tank, it was raining, so I ran across the plaza to the hall of Alien Stingers. The seascapes and aquatic environments no longer contain statues of Neptune, mermaids, sunken ships, treasure chests, rusty anchors, or painted backdrops that reflect the world of *Twenty Thousand Leagues under the Sea*, a locus of marine fantasy. Now tanks and environments are signs of the geographic origin of their inhabitants.

In an alcove near the jellyfish wing we are told, "Coral reefs are like underground cities." They provide an environment that balances food, shelter, and protection from predators, and in doing so creates automatic controls over population explosions. The closest thing I've seen to an underwater city, one that even resembles the aquarium's reef cities, appeared in *Amphibian Man*, a Soviet science-fiction movie made in 1962. Amphibian Man, part human, part shark, escapes his father's underwater lair to explore a small coastal town. Though it was shot in the Crimea, standing in for Argentina, *Amphibian Man* represents a kind of transenvironmental *The Russians Are Coming*. Amphibian Man's father, a utopian scientist, plans to build a classless utopian underwater society, but his son has his reservations. Once on land he meets a levelheaded socialist, a newspaperman who doubts that human nature, fundamentally greedy and sharklike, will be any different underwater.

There's something fragile about the Saarinen-like shell of the aquarium. The buildings that make up the park—the Aquatheater, the Sea Cliff exhibit, the Bathysphere, and the Shark Tank—could easily be fractured by an earthquake, a tornado. Man-made catastrophes, a missile, a drone, though unlikely, would reduce the plaster and glass to dust in no time. But because the aquarium, like many aquariums, is close to the ocean, Coney Island is in the blaring red zone, or Zone A, so far out in Zone A, it should be coded in some pre-alphabet symbol. Before the hurricane hit, the urbanized fish, rays, jellies, and marine mammals must have waited for a possibly liberating storm, when all the urban fish would just keep swimming,

swimming, and happily join the Gulf Stream waiting for them out beyond Montauk.

There are many precedents for animals escaping during natural or man-made disasters. In June, flooding at a Duluth zoo led to seal and polar-bear escapes. Cobras with Houdini-like powers have liberated themselves from the Bronx Zoo, crocodiles went missing from the New Orleans Aquarium during Katrina. During the Second World War, the Berlin Zoo and adjoining aquarium, the site of the Nazis' last stand against the Soviets, was bombed. Most of the animals, numbering over three thousand, were killed in the attack, though ninety-one animals—leopards, panthers, jaguars, and apes among them—escaped, crossing the Spree, if they were able to, and headed into the Tiergarten. Animals in the Baghdad Zoo in the recent war fared no better. During the 2003 American bombing, four lions escaped and roamed the city until put down by marines.

So not all aquarium dwellers would find freedom in the crashing waves. The representatives from the Arctic, those from the tropics, those accustomed to a lifetime of four daily feedings might think, as glass breaks and water meets water, What, me hunt? Forget it. They wouldn't last long. The walrus, for example, known as the "loudest voice in the Arctic," a thought that hints at what total silence must be like, would be in big trouble. The aquarium's explanatory text describes how the walrus uses "muscular whisker pads" to blow mud from shellfish on the ocean floor and then feast. But walruses would have to swim two thousand miles to get to their native habitat, Greenland, Ellesmere Island, Baffin Bay. And then the Arctic sea ice is melting at an alarming rate; the fish all have lead and mercury poisoning. So escape has its drawbacks. The walrus area is totally enclosed by glass and netting that extends maybe fifteen feet high and overhead, hinting that the three-thousand-plus-pound walruses, the Père Ubus of the animal kingdom, have the potential to become airborne. The hurricane hits. Water rises, and the walruses gnaw through the netting, and they're off. But they've spent their entire lives in a man-made environment listening to the constant five-minute cycle of screams from the Cyclone at the top of its track, at the top, then down, alternating less screaming in the troughs and dips, but interspersed is the barking of sea lions and seals. The two walruses might, as they swim toward Nova Scotia, feel nostalgic for the rounds of seal barking/Cyclone screams/seal barking/Cyclone screams.

After the hurricane, the Cyclone became silent anyway. The roller coaster and the Wonder Wheel were weighted down by tons of sand and garbage. The owners said very simply that this is what water does to wood: warp and bow. Metal rusts and corrodes. Barnacles take root, and the closed aquarium faces an amusement ghost town. This seemingly protected underwater city was no more invulnerable than the zoos of New Orleans, Berlin, or Baghdad. Maybe there are no true preserves possible, no zone that keeps out vandals, flood-waters, bombs, or real estate developers, and such a concept is a fantasy with an expiration date.

The developers' bulldozers were poised on the edge of Stillwell and Mermaid, waiting for the end of gas rationing. This is a break they couldn't even have prayed for, it's such a gift. Their plans and computer-generated models were delayed and kept at bay because this is, or was, a city landmark. At one point, it looked like the wrecking ball was going to be allowed to finish what the hurricane initiated, but then Coney rides were revived, and the aquarium is being restored. It will eventually again be a kind of aquatic environment where Amphibian Man can put up his flipperized feet, get his silver-sequined suit dry-cleaned at Oceana Cleaners or Professional Magic on Brighton Beach Avenue, where they speak Russian and might recognize him from their childhoods. He, like those of us who love these marginal parts of the city, will feel right at home.

DÜRER'S RHINOCEROS

The identity of the person who found the rhinoceros washed ashore in Liguria in the winter of 1516 is not known. What he or she thought the hulking creature might be, where it had come from—none of this has been recorded. We do know that, like Zarafa, when very young, it had successfully traveled from its home in Goa, southern India, to Lisbon as a gift to the king of Portugal. When it was fully grown, the king, familiar with bullfights, proposed a contest to pit the rhino in a fight against an elephant.* At the sight of the horned creature, the

---

*Watching *Game of Thrones*, my son and I observe brutality to animals signals a character is thoroughly evil and probably beyond salvation, whatever his past, whatever his reasons. When Cersei Lannister orders the execution of an innocent wolf or Ser Gregor Clegane summarily beheads his horse, that's it for them. As characters, they're done for the next thousands of pages or hours of viewing. With the fall of the sword there will be no redemption for them. They are the kings of Portugal, the executioners of Le Jardin des Plantes.

elephant had other ideas, bolting and crashing through the arena, requiring many people to recapture it beyond the broken gates. Since it was considered unable or unwilling to perform, the king planned to send the rhinoceros to the pope as a gift. Would it have wandered around St. Peter's, toppling statues, terrifying supplicants, cooling off in the Tiber? Whatever plans were made to accommodate the rhino in its new home, they were never realized. The ship carrying the animal sank in the Mediterranean. Despite the confusion and horror of those who found the carcass on a beach, it was gutted, stuffed, and sent on to the Vatican anyway.

Albrecht Dürer never saw the rhinoceros himself, but he did see a drawing of it that had been posted to Germany by a Portuguese artist, and from this sketch he made his own rendition in a woodblock print. In Dürer's version, the animal's body armor was closer to that of a triceratops than a rhino, but it was considered an accurate representation, often copied and disseminated widely, until actual rhinos were brought to Europe over two hundred years later.

Dürer lived in a land of no photographic images and very few printing presses. Even up to Kipling and Verne's time, a percentage of nineteenth-century readers of *Twenty Thousand Leagues under the Sea* or *The Jungle Book* might never have seen even illustrations of elephants, tigers, and monkeys and could only imagine what a narwhale might look like. As a citizen of the opposite kingdom, that of an infinite number of images, I'm fascinated by clips of an actual giant deepwater squid as it brushes by a submersible tasked with filming the Pacific floor or a mongoose beheading a boa constrictor in a courtyard. I confess I watch these clips from time to time, from cats driving Pontiacs to the possibly gruesome and extreme, but what's fascinating about stories that introduce the wild into manmade environments: pythons on the subway, a leopard in a Bronx apartment, a boxing kangaroo escaped from its thuggish keepers, elephants walking through the Holland Tunnel at 3:00 a.m.? It would be a fairy tale to believe some of these scenarios end well for the animals, but there is another way to look at these stories: as portents of animals saying, We're not extinct yet, and someday this will all be ours again.

Impersonal Affairs
Henri Michaux

—Translated from French by Gillian Conoley

TRANSLATOR'S NOTE

Henri Michaux (1899–1984), known for his forays into human per-ception, published over thirty books of poems, narratives, essays, travelogues, journals, and drawings. Throughout the almost sixty years of his creative life, he explored the darker, shadowy realms of human consciousness while concurrently searching for an ade-quate tool or medium of communication—language, drawing, paint—up to the difficulty of his task. Within his work one can trace the struggle for, and his disappointment in not finding, a universal language through gesture, mark, sign, and the word.

Michaux gave himself over to adopted or induced conscious-nesses that would wrest him from his own: travel, mescaline, imagined worlds full of creatures or beasts, Western and Eastern spirituality. This goal is relentlessly explored from his first book to his last, including the early My Properties *(1929), the half-imaginary travel journals of* A Barbarian in Asia *(1933), the invented lands and mythical animals of* Elsewhere *(1948), and the multiple tex-tual columns and dislocated drawings of* Miserable Miracle *(1956), written during Michaux's eleven-year experiment with mescaline. A teetotaler until he was fifty-seven, Michaux had a neurologist friend who encouraged him to try the drug. Michaux was drawn to mescaline precisely for its capacity to enhance a division in consciousness he was already encountering in his art, an experi-ence in which one part of the mind remained excruciatingly un-illusioned and lucid during vision, fantasy, or hallucination.*

Watchtowers on Targets *(Vigies sur Cibles), the book from which this excerpt is taken, was written in 1959, two years after* L'Infini Turbulent, *and three years after* Miserable Miracle. *Considered one of Michaux's mescaline texts,* Watchtowers on Targets *is un-usual in his oeuvre, in that characters, beasts, and animals appear unannounced, and without the narrative link we usually see in Michaux.*

Waking up, he felt a small belly in the palm of his hand. Whose belly? He didn't want to disturb it. Reflect first. While reflecting, he fell asleep again. When he woke up, no more belly. No more anyone.

There, as a prime example, one of the many disadvantages of reflection.

*

Around the violated shelter, there was hurried activity. Everyone wanted to attend the apoplexy of the swan.

*

How sad it would be, filled with rage, with phlegm, with weakness, to suffocate, a twisted body, in the bottom of a gourd.

*

In the white of the cry, the crime betrayed itself, threw itself, terrible in the consciousness of all those living in the neighborhood. It was necessary to open the shutters, the eyes and the languishing rest of the almost finished day. The criminal himself, pierced by the cry, stops and does not make a move. The red liquid with the minute stammering, called "blood," elsewhere *blut*, or *blood*, and even proudly *sangre*, the blade of the knife, the marks and the fingerprints will soon testify against he who now flees, but in whom, motionless, a vertical cathedral erected in one moment, the unexpected cry dwells and does not fade.

*

Coming from the forest, the flying larvae appear in spring. Large, larger than the largest birds, and in great numbers, they darken the sky, they darken the countryside and the villages, nestling together in the hollow of the small valleys, and wanting to nestle even more.

The counting of the monsters occurs once a year or every ninth moon. Fate is called to decide. Many perish, but enough survive so that the Haw monsters can monstrously gather again.

*

The fly is so well organized that it has been able to frequent man diligently for thousands of years, without being kicked out, or put to work. It has done all of this without interfering and without looking around stupidly like a cat pretending to be tamed. Going as far as to settle itself on the rim of one's eyes and drawing out from the admirably salted tears the exact chloride missing from its diet. With the same ease it frequents the comforts of the biggest mammals' eyes, no doubt dreaming of more perfect eyes yet, like saucers, sunken in rather than bulging out.

Here is the creature that every man should have studied in the slave era, instead of eagles, lions, horses, or . . . marshals who will never teach him what is most important: "How to live together without serving?"

*

"Me too, said Varisi, I would need sovereignty to cross countries and places, or at least to significantly settle there. But I do not have the bearing and height of the tree, I do not have the royalty and concentration of the tiger, I do not have the mass and the majesty of the mountain.
"What was the reason for this triple lack in my organism, I ask myself."

*

Telepathy from one star to another. It's on another planet that Christ would have been crucified! Ah! Ah! This would perhaps account for that which seemed so false, so true, so false . . .

*

By the hair of the soul, he held it while she waved herself in vain attempts of resistance, while she struggled in vain movements, in vain returns, in vain unlacings, slipping despite it all, slipping almost entirely suspended, with no support above the pit of shared desire.

*

There is in me, Raha said, a worm-like movement. I would utter stupidities in wanting to situate it better and not touch it more. Many other movements, it's still in me, holding me far from the action, far from the attention expected of me, and from which I could never become sober. Idiots who insist on inviting me. They do not know. Raha must be underground. How would he want to dig? . . . I have my borders near the center. I have to be quick, very quick, to ensure my confidence. One minute later and I'm abroad. But I know, I know in advance and guide myself according to its geography. Know its geography, Raha said . . .

*

"The mirror of the soul," said Agrigibi, "sometimes sends me back as a dog, sometimes a crab, sometimes an ant, sometimes a spider, sometimes a weasel caught in a trap, sometimes a young hedgehog with soft prickles, sometimes a wounded mosquito with its wings torn off, in short my willingness is mocked, defeated like a creased note in a prostitute's stocking."

The jagged being, who then will speak in its name?

How many times does Agrigibi not meet tornadic beings! Strange? Hardly. It's with a continual thunder of triumph that the healthy advance everywhere, brother of the lion and the steamroller. With force he throws, through his skin, through his eyes, a carousel of forks, to force, to pierce, to break weak points established tenuously themselves, which cannot bend the mechanism of the gust of wind that feels human and that is only spin, that whirlwind, that crushing, that persecution, that explosion, that ceaseless threat of explosion.

How to resist?

How to advance against the wall of trumpets?

*

So then, like a decoy greyhound, like a mad greyhound that begins to run inside itself, to run, to run in itself tirelessly, Agrigibi, helpless, animated by futile vibrations, "rushes backward," getting lost with dizziness in the unending hallways of his being.

*

Here the hours of the Mna rule.

At the nth hour, the orders are centaurs, half thoughts, half on foot. How? Its impulses are between revolt and dream.

The complication arose with reveille. While the bugles sound, which is my camp? What is my territory? Behind me (or to the side) I begin my pursuit, object of excitement and delirium.

With such ardor I wait for the windows to burst open.

Desires and turgescence listen to the octaves climbing. The large migration of small boats has begun, however. An even larger one is being prepared. A very, very large one, in fact.

*

He who loves will be like the river. Is this, really, what he wanted? Is that right, tomorrow that drives him, tomorrow a building on the ground, tomorrow dazed, tomorrow like a crushed tomato?

*

The phases of the view are these: First, there are four gray zones where columns of a darker gray are formed and intertwined: It's the morning of the eye, which may not coincide at all with the morning of the solar day, and can even happen at night.

Depending on the situation, there is a pleasing view, becoming more delightful little by little, or simply a small tickle can occur and will not be noticed.

Henri Michaux

Following next through flexible passages is a light that grows until the noon of the eye, after which there is a progressive darkening until the night of the eye.

The night of the eye doesn't come every day. Some are set to have it just once a year at best. Others, although rare, have never known it at all. But if it ever comes to them, there will be an exhibition that lasts for months, and, they, clearly obliged, will come, previously hidden and drawn away, like the crippled and degraded.

Such is the eye that doesn't follow life, such is the life that doesn't follow the eye.

—1959

Leviathan

Wil Weitzel

None is so fierce that he dares to stir him up.

—Job 41

THE HOUSE WAS SMALL and got you used to bird life. There were mynahs most of all, common mynahs, roosting in mating pairs in the winter and in large flocks in the springs and summers on the beach. They had bright yellow beaks with banded white tails showing smartly from behind when they were on the wing. In addition, the *honu*, or Hawaiian green turtle, would draw itself out of the sea and gradually turn the color of lava that had cooled and sat for years beneath the sun. A brown color once black that became, in the brightness of noon, hard to see at all.

Whole lives had been lived like this, for all Cal knew. The aromatic calm formed an unwavering picture in his mind, and since he'd been a child on family visits to the island, roaming the inlets of lava on the beach, he had understood the ocean in only one way, as something slow and warm with enduring comforts. Occasionally it occurred to Cal that in winter, while he was on the mainland, there were storms. But he pushed this knowledge away.

Now he crept quietly off the lanai, or grand Hawaiian porch, onto the beach. The sand, even at this late hour, was hot and the heat seeped into the pads of his feet and made him hasten toward the water. He stood perched on the lava looking not at the ocean but toward the house, toward Harold, who was round at the belly and lay back asleep, his head lolling with the startled fury of the beard gushing massive and wild, until it was the thing most conspicuous from the tide line.

Harold was new to the sea, comparatively, though they'd been coming to the house Cal had inherited from his mother, a rich San Diego dowager of the 1960s, for twenty years together now. The sea still seemed to mesmerize Harold, who hailed from Ohio and belonged to lakes and ponds. Warm summer ponds you could approach via long wooden jetties and, as Harold told it, you could splash into, with gaping strides through the air, in your youth. Cal had the impression when Harold spoke of these things that it was still possible to be young, that it was a place rather than a time, and one, moreover, you could still travel toward if you sought ardently the desires that had lived there.

In any case, Harold had never swum in the water in Hawaii. He'd dipped his toes, sure; he'd responded to coaxing by laying his considerable bulk in the tide pools, yes; he'd been nibbled by tiny, carnivorous glass shrimp, nearly translucent, and by juvenile raccoon butterfly fish. But he had never swum out with Cal to the drop-off where occasionally you glimpsed large pelagics, a spotted eagle ray flying with her calf, a pod of spinner dolphins swallowing long circles of rest, or, very rarely, a white-tip reef shark cruising the bottom structures, seeking then finding a ledge of coral under which to pause and drowse.

Nonetheless, Harold was clearly intrigued by large predators and sea mammals. Dolphins intrigued him. It was rare that dolphins visited the bay in their languorous sweeps of the shoreline but occasionally Cal would hear Harold exclaim. Then his lover would point vigorously, eyes squinting with the brush line of his brows buckling. "Spinners," he'd mutter a second time, collecting himself, in a voice that was calm and flat, belying his excitement.

"In that case, why don't we take the kayak?" Cal would watch Harold carefully in such moments, wondering if he was tempted, knowing him to be unwilling to don a mask and sink his broad body into the ocean.

"Oh, they'll be long gone," Harold would say quickly. Or "No need to disturb their rest."

Even so, Harold had clearly become a student of spinners, of the way they hunted at night and rested and bonded in their long circles during the days. They were smaller than bottlenose dolphins, more athletic, and Harold would watch them spin out of the sea, then crash back down with resounding slaps of what seemed to Cal like pure joy.

"Status and power," Harold would correct him. "They're either hunting or making displays." Then Harold would drone on in a dry monotone about impressing mates, territorial war, and bachelor factions shaking the structures of dolphin authority. He was really quite knowledgeable, Cal thought, for a man who never ventured into the water. Cal himself knew only what it was to swim beside a pod of spinners thirty feet down, to look them in the large eye that was deeply far from the end of the nose, to see the bright-white gleam beneath the gray of their flesh, and to feel them slow and patient beside him, as though awaiting the long, curving strokes of his fins. The dolphins, with calves gliding silently beneath mothers' bellies, with the thickness of their bodies slimming to thread whitely into broad tails, were the muscles of the sea, their gazes entering you through water and growing inside your lungs until you were forced to turn up for air.

Cal turned at last from Harold toward the water and scanned the bay. It was choppy with a seaward breeze that pushed at the incoming tide and made humps like the backs of things. This whole expanse, the ocean, would not make sense without the lanai and the stand of coconut palms he and his mother had planted and that now tilted and rattled in the wind. Nor would the placid bay live at all for him without the old man snoring in his chair. How could that be? Harold who never went into the sea. If it were up to Cal, after all, one would hardly get out of the ocean—

"Shark," yelled Harold from behind him.

"What?" Cal turned to face the lanai and Harold was standing, staggering, then descending unsteadily onto the beach.

"Shark," he yelled again, this time pointing with his whole giant hand as though it were a ventral fin, the thumb tucked in, palm downturned and level with the ground.

"Where?"

"There. Past the surge zone. Coming back in. That's a big one now. Huge one."

Cal turned and stared.

"Never seen one like that," and Harold was still hoarse and bellowing. Burbling on. Coming up sweaty and grabbing him by the shoulders, roughing him in his excitement so that Cal, who was lithe and tall, nearly fell down.

"See it," said Cal, straightening himself. "That does look large."

The dorsal indeed stretched surprisingly high off the surface, was wide at the base, and swiveled slightly, aggressively, in a way that Cal had never seen.

"Big sucker," whispered Harold, clearly fascinated. Now they could make out a shape beneath the water, again, surprisingly large, of a scale Cal had only seen in a young whale, in humpback calves he'd dived with off the northern coast of the island near Hawi.

"Jesus Christ," blurted Harold excitedly. And at last the shark was close enough to the shore that they could see, squinting out across

97

the lava breaks, that the dorsal was mottled, even banded at its base with jagged swaths of shadow crossing the blade. "Christ, that's a tiger."

Cal twisted free of Harold and ran to the side of the house. He grabbed the light hawser of the kayak and started hauling, running with it as best he could down the beach to the break and finally dipping the bow into the first crust of the waves.

"Get in here, Harold," he hollered, expecting Harold to begin shuffling backward as he invariably did when challenged, to start shifting his bulky shoulders in retreat, tracing a line with his heels up the beach toward the lanai.

But Harold stood transfixed and Cal, turning quickly, could see the outline of the shark clearly now, the sun cutting across it from the west, the big snub nose small in comparison with the bulk behind it and the scythe of its tail tall and proud and immense, sweeping far behind the head as if a sailfish were trailing the body and propelling it at a distance.

"Get in here, Harold," Cal yelled again, and Harold, to Cal's amazement, began to sidestep, still staring at the shark, which had turned to the south and seemed to be moving back along the surge line in their direction. Harold, for whatever reason, perhaps because the shark had taken him from his dreams and just at that moment he remained poised between worlds, or perhaps because he'd suddenly awakened to his bravery and found himself at last to be redoubtable, a crowing beast, or, most likely, because he was utterly beside himself—Cal didn't care what it was—now shuffled not backward toward the lanai but sideways. Then, as Cal steadied the kayak in the channel between lava floes, Harold stumbled in, nearly upsetting it. He even grabbed the paddle from the floor, as though it were a sword, still straining his eyes out toward the sea.

Cal had never seen a tiger shark in the wild and supposed, to the extent he supposed at all, that Harold, who seemed fascinated with anything large, found the prospect of witnessing the animal up close too tempting to resist. It was certainly true that tigers rarely, almost never, approached such shallow coral embankments during the daylight hours. Occasionally there were sightings by open-water swimmers along the shoreline south toward Kona and the odd attack on surfers, particularly when swells amped up and runoff from rains clouded coastal waters. But it remained an anomaly, something wild and mysterious, and Cal, for his part, did not hesitate to run for the kayak at the prospect of peering down at such power.

There was one other thing. Cal, who had dived with many sharks, had never been in the water with a tiger. They had a kind of mythical presence. When they did approach the shore, it was usually at dusk and they had been known to surf, literally to surf, to use their wide bulks to navigate wave troughs and fish along the break line when the sun had exited but still cast its gloaming rays. In other places, not Hawaii, Cal had sat on the beach and watched this happen. What had struck him then was not the danger of wading into the shallows but the need of such animals, the urgency that size brought to bear. There were stories of tigers slit open to reveal plow blades and tree branches and parts of cars.

Now he climbed in behind Harold to the seat at the stern and pushed off with his own paddle. They moved, incredibly, out toward the shark, as though they were one, as though the two of them had often, just before sunset, set off together in precisely this way, toward things you couldn't exactly envision from land but that, having lived them together in a kind of complicity and synchrony, they'd known for years and thrust into their knowledge of each other.

"That's it," purred Cal from behind, watching Harold work his paddle carefully, avoiding the outcroppings of jagged, coffee-colored lava. Then, "Now, good work," as they came to the surge zone, elongated and rough with breaks arriving in three irregular rows across the floe banks. Here, to his amazement, Cal watched Harold dig in, bending his broad back toward the water and hauling powerfully with his arms, the big bulk of him at work, the head lifted up as though seeking something, then the shoulders dipping back down to pull.

They were in a rhythm. It was maddening, thought Cal, to the extent that he was of a mind to think anything. Indeed, just at that moment he scarcely inhabited such a mind. He had almost no thinking in him at all except for a yearning for deep water, for the place he'd never brought Harold before where even from a kayak you could see depths, detect things displaced beneath other things, find animals passing beneath you and then, when you dove, gliding even above you, over you, between you and the air.

The shark was gone, so far as Cal could tell. Harold had stopped working his paddle and was sitting upright. The sun was blinding in the west and streaking through the surface of the sea into what was now a gorgeous blue, fine and clear at depth, marking out the place just ahead where the drop-off lay and beyond which other things, God knows what things, were alive and real, shooting into light you could scarcely see.

Out there, Cal knew, they would be beyond the tumult of the break line and the turbid, brown water of the shallows, past even the green of the lava holes and, because it was already July, outside the coral bloom that began along the structures at the surface and persisted until the reef gave off, where the substrate of the ocean floor bent down into the gloom.

Cal had dived out there on many occasions, equalizing three times and passing down toward the curve in the coral floor where it arched to a sandy bottom below sixty feet in places and descended across outcroppings from there. From those outcroppings he would turn, his lungs pulled tight while the sun at that depth fell through curved shafts into a set of slung hammocks against the sand. Then he'd sail upward, thrusting with his ankles locked together. Finally, as he rose above fifty feet, the air would begin to boom inside him.

But that had not happened for a while. It had been some time since he'd been down there like that. Perhaps years. In fact, Cal could not recall when he'd last felt alive in a way he'd once taken for granted, testing his body, feeling it wrapped around his mind like cords of energy he could alternately tense and release, tap into. Harold too seemed tired, had been tired, Cal suspected, for perhaps fifteen years. He had been terribly affectionate when they'd first met. Too affectionate, if anything. Making it difficult to sleep. Indeed Harold had been a wonderful lover, a great brute, a hurly-burly. And even now there were spurts of love, periods of grand warmth. But those too, if one thought it over, drew roots from an epoch of earthiness and treachery and reconfirmed belonging that had long passed. So at times it seemed to Cal as if they haunted separate spheres, as if for years he'd been walking slowly into the sea and the tide line was the breaking point where Harold left off and he began.

There was this, though—the impossibility of anything else was what you reached, what you earned. To Cal it seemed hardly conceivable that either of them at this late stage could ever renew or reset. Or be jolted. That too, he'd decided, was a kind of love, deep and trenching. And like the tide, it made grooves in you.

Now Cal could see Harold stiffen, the looseness in his limbs suddenly disappearing. Harold still held onto his paddle but it was in one hand rather than across his thighs and the blade dragged into the water, slicing the surface insignificantly. He was shifted awkwardly in his seat, craning his neck.

"Gone," said Harold bemusedly, and Cal turned the kayak so they could see behind them, in the direction of the shore.

"I suppose so," he agreed, not wishing to disturb the fact that they had alit here silently as though atop a wide sky, that they'd settled in the water as if on spreading boughs that were invisible and belonged to nothing.

"Christ," blurted Harold suddenly, but Cal was not sure why.

Now they both stared outward and to the west, squinting, and were motionless. The wind was already coming down, eddying elsewhere, stirring beyond the bay somewhere in the offing before it would stiffen again just as they lay back to sleep in the small bed beside tall, screened windows that faced the sea.

Cal dipped his paddle and shoved them forward, farther from shore, watching Harold, who was still swiveling, scanning the surface, and looking downward into water at last clear and deep.

When the shark came, it was from behind and beneath them, rising and sweeping under the kayak from the back. Its bulk was perhaps a yard under their feet at its closest, the dorsal fin alone filling much of that space. It was just to the starboard, coming below their right hands and passing massively, for a long time, the snout abrupt, then the black, intelligent eye, gills vulnerable and white on their ruffling insides, and the skin mottled by huge, broken swatches of dun. The upper lobe of the tail was what moved, long and smooth like a sail.

Cal could not see the look on Harold's face. He had not thought of Harold in the moment it took for the shark to pass. He himself was elated, as though a soft electric current had swept through him, had coursed through his insides, and he wanted to touch Harold, to make sure he too had felt this thing, this immensity.

"Fifteen, maybe sixteen feet," he shouted to Harold. But Harold was already falling. Having twisted around in his seat, his hands to his right along the thin rim of the kayak shell that lacked the deep gunwale of a dinghy, Harold had jerked himself forward to see the broad swath of the tail glide beneath him. Now, for an instant, he was curved sideways, grappling to regain his balance, hips hulked dangerously out away from his shoulders and left hand shooting to grab his seat. It was too late. Harold's bulk took him right, nearly overturning the kayak. Harold himself plunged into the sea, his shoulder in first then his jowls and head then the heavy rest of him, all of it disappearing for a moment before the pale back of the neck showed and he was bobbing at the surface, hallooing and monstrous, pouncing for the kayak as though there were something below him to leap from, tossing out his arms and letting them flop into the hollow below his seat before he was sinking back down again, returning to the ocean with his great throat sputtering and eyes in the waves.

Cal could see a moment of horror in Harold's face that held all moments. This, after all, was why you swam in the sea—the thought flashed in Cal's mind—so there was an element of readiness about you. As Harold had no experience of sharks, his legs, Cal imagined, would feel like bloodied meat, seeping even before their butchery, and Harold must sense them now hung languidly down for slaughter.

"Harold—reach out and take your paddle," yelled Cal. Unlike other pairs who'd invented bedroom names or other flip endearments, he and Harold through a kind of tacit formality and his own inveterate shyness had never taken such license. Now Cal leaned forward but could not quite reach Harold's paddle bumping on the surface of the blue ocean away from them.

"Swim out and grab your paddle, Harold." But it was like talking to a fool. Harold was clamoring madly, stabbing for a hold of his seat in the kayak with both hands and pulling the rim violently to the starboard.

Cal leaned left to balance him and began to crawl toward the bow in an attempt to gain a purchase on Harold's broad shoulders and heave him back aboard. But before he'd gone far he realized he would not have the strength to lift a man as big as Harold, and Harold, he knew, would soon spend himself in his panic and turn listless and deadweighted. For now, the kayak wobbled dangerously as Harold flailed and vainly sought a handhold, an oarlock, at last a gunwale that was not there.

"Stop splashing," shouted Cal. "It will attract the shark."

And Harold ceased, already exhausted, his eyes bright and strange, contaminated with fright in a way that Cal had not witnessed in anyone, that did not fit with what he'd known. Initially he'd thought to drag Harold beside the boat, to paddle him into the safety of the reef structures. But now he changed course.

"I'm going to flip it," he hollered. And Cal grabbed hold of the right rim of the kayak and shifted his weight to the left, letting himself splash down into the ocean on the far side of Harold and pulling the kayak with him until it was inverted. He guessed that the shark would be near, that there had been too much commotion for it not to circle and return, so he dove down several feet beneath the tide wash and gazed out, scanning into the water, his vision maskless and bleary, before he lifted his head to surface.

"Now we'll get on together," Cal said more quietly, "at the same time," trying to reach Harold with his eyes, Harold whom he could not see, as the broad yellow plastic of the kayak, built for tourists and novices, rounded out above the level of his vision. He weighted the back end and, to his surprise, there was Harold on the far side at the front, coughing and pulling himself up onto the inverted bow until the two of them were lying awkwardly in a line, facing the western horizon and the deep sea, their legs straddling the plastic and splayed out, chests full on the kayak bottom, and the whole enterprise sunk a foot, or a foot and a half, below the rocking surface of the waves.

Cal saw that Harold had a paddle wedged beneath his armpit. Cal had lost his own paddle, not thinking to grab it before he'd turned the kayak, and he cursed himself now for this omission. But Harold must have found it. Somehow, it must have floated to him. In any case, Harold had a grip on the paddle now, had shifted it into his right hand, and, to Cal looking across Harold's back toward the crown of his head, his partner seemed suddenly armed, as though he were preparing for something, girding for battle.

"If it comes to it, go for the butt of the snout and the eyes," Cal whispered. "If you can manage it, jab at the face, strike him above the mouth."

But Harold looked to be concentrating on the water just in front of him, fixated on something that Cal, from his vantage, couldn't quite make out.

"Stay close to the boat whatever happens," Cal went on. "We make a larger shape together."

Perhaps thirty seconds or another minute slipped by like this, with them lying on their chests, grasping the overturned kayak as though they were riding a wobbling missile through the air, their bodies largely submerged, the water covering their backs, and their heads moving on a swivel, eyes on both men scanning, feet and even knees hung more deeply in the sea on one side of the kayak or the other, then pulled up hastily, then dropped down again for balance.

"Stay quiet with your legs if he comes. Lift them out and shift them away from him."

But Harold gave no indication, had given no indication, that he

103

could hear Cal speaking from behind him in the stillness. He remained fixated on the water in front of the kayak, as though spinner dolphins were circling in the brilliant blue beneath them. Cal remembered that spinners and tigers were famously ill disposed to one another, that they were enemies. He thought perhaps in the winter they would laugh about all of this, the two of them holding one another on the beach like they had done regularly in those first years after his inheritance, basking in their good fortune. Harold, who was always more voluble in company, whom Cal would watch shyly and admire, would tell the neighbors the outrageous story of their humping a kayak and Cal would search out pieces of olivine in the sand and pile them on Harold's stomach while it rumbled and shook as he came to the part about dolphins. Perhaps, he thought, there were spinners beneath them now.

As the shark rose, its dorsal slit the surface evenly, sixty feet in front of them, without the conspicuous swivel that would suggest aggression. He was moving on them directly, however, in a line. Cal could see the large scythe of the tail working well behind the dorsal and breaking the surface at intervals on either side of the body. The sun was in their eyes as the shark came in and what they could glimpse was limited by the glare. Though Cal could not make out the head just yet, he knew where it was in the water.

"Coming," he whispered to Harold. "Stay steady."

The shark left its course and built a slow circle, perhaps fifteen feet in its radius, and now Cal, as the shark made its first pass to his port side, could clearly see the eye, which was round and jet black and seemed to stare at him directly. It was a magnificent eye, old and patient. Then it was behind him and though the shark finished its circle and completed one more, Cal did not see the eye again but was caught instead by the ravaged field of the skin, by opalescent scars ripped above the mouth and tattering the left ventral fin, by the breadth of the fish in its middle where it was wide as his Toyota, and by the tiger swatches, faded and worn and making the sides pass on and on, shapeless, great decorated walls that narrowed only after a long time to the tail.

When Cal watched the shark veer after its two circles and start to swing its tail wide, he barked, "No," but by then it was already in on Harold with its body arched upward and the head lifted nearly out of the water and Harold was falling backward and off to the left, the whole bow of the kayak momentarily jerked down from great weight and Cal himself raised up, grasping for the plastic as he came off into

104

the sea then clumsily stroking for the stern and hauling himself back on before finally, reinstalled and safe, searching wildly for Harold, who had disappeared.

Reports of attacks in Hawaiian waters that had circulated over the years in which Cal had followed them tended to highlight the same things. There was generally surf involved, one way or another, and victims tended not to be diving but stretched upon the surface or occasionally wading to the shoulders. Spear fishermen reported encounters but mostly with smaller sharks like blues and oceanic white tips, which could be dangerous but rarely attacked divers. The tiger, on the other hand, was famously unpredictable. It was the foremost attack species in the Hawaiian archipelago. Most of the time it would circle and depart but if there was activity or fear it could remain, become aggressive. The key was to stay calm, not to turn your back, and so long as your eyes were in the water, drop both legs together to show your length. In any case, Cal had purposefully skimmed over the rare articles pronouncing incidents on the grounds that he, in the event of a sighting, would be in a kayak or well beneath the surface and Harold, in all likelihood, would be watching from the safety of the shore.

Now a kind of fuzz occupied segments of Cal's vision, toward the peripheries, and a loud stillness sat in his ears as if the ocean had been amplified to the point where he ceased to hear it. He saw the shark surface to his right, perhaps thirty feet off. Seconds elapsed that he initially failed to register but that then filtered back as a vague gap in time. Harold, who somehow had been swept far left of Cal and slightly to his rear, emerged, surfacing loudly, still grasping the paddle and sputtering. In another moment he was performing the crawl, majestically and, for all that Cal could discern, steadily and calmly with the paddle crashing on the surface at the stroke of his right arm.

Yet inexplicably he was swimming outward, toward the depths, in the direction of the blue ocean. Cal hoisted himself forward to the center of the overturned kayak and called out to Harold in order to offer him direction. But, again, it was as though one or both of them could no longer hear, or as if the force of events had not only clogged Harold's ears but in so doing made off with his mind.

"Harold," Cal yelled, "over here." But it was for naught. To his horror, Cal watched as the shark swam toward the kayak and submerged, sinking its bulk only just under, so he could nearly reach down and touch those irregular bands and follow the shadowy markings with his thumb. It continued beneath him, still submerged, toward Harold, who, bizarrely, horribly, was swimming out to sea in a beautiful, noisy crawl, pointed toward Maui and the deepening trench, moving like a great, slow van of milkshakes and sugar cones that was ringing all its bells.

"Harold," Cal yelled again. "Shark!"

Now, as though this last word stirred something, awakened him, Harold lifted his head and peered in the direction of the voice, then sharply shifted course, his rough beard suddenly visible in the waves, his eyes heavily lidded at first, then wide open. He began swimming toward the tiger shark, and toward Cal, wielding the paddle out before him in awkward half strokes like a ridiculous spear. Then, without slowing his kick, which was shooting fountains behind him, Harold began jousting with his weapon, raising it absurdly and slapping the sea in front of him, spearing the space between him and the shark. If anything, it looked to Cal, lying motionless on the kayak, as though Harold was picking up speed and at last he was bellowing, making a noise that was unidentifiable but deep and final.

As the two of them converged, Cal could see the tall dorsal fin of the tiger shark that had been swerving on the surface rise mightily into the air and Harold begin to sink, as though he were cowering before a blow.

"No," yelled Cal once again, slapping his own arm impotently against the ocean and nearly losing his balance.

But just before contact, Harold reappeared. Having lowered himself, he raised his whole chest out of the water, or nearly, and, once reared, brought the paddle, blade first, down like a javelin with what looked to Cal like tremendous force. There was a jerk and Harold was brought sharply into the air while the tiger flashed its tail and rolled seaward, turning abruptly, the dorsal sinking off and away.

Cal, meanwhile, watched in amazement as Harold, after vanishing again for what felt like ten seconds or more, surfaced twenty feet off, again farther to the left and closer to the safety of the lava floes. After briefly wiping his eyes, he resumed his slow, recreational crawl, his giant fountain kick, this time shoreward, the handle of the paddle still in his hand, the blade and much of the shaft now broken off and missing. Every so often, Harold would pause as he proceeded toward the lava and turn, dipping his head beneath the surface as if to gaze into the depths behind him, then lifting his eyes to scan the horizon. In these moments, he would raise the jagged shaft of the paddle and wield it threateningly and, having waited for an instant, turn back to the grand strokes of his crawl.

Finally, Harold stood in the shallows and was yelling out to him, "Stay where you are. Don't move. I'm coming with the dinghy." In another few minutes, there was Harold, having dragged the dinghy down to the shore from behind the house, the mynah birds quarreling over him in the jacaranda or swooping onto the sand to swagger like field generals at his feet. Then he was rowing swiftly through the lava breaks. A few minutes more and Cal found himself being helped onto the dinghy, Harold's strong arms pulling him up over the gunwale and placing him gently onto the dry seat.

"Thank you, Harold," said Cal, gathering himself and watching as Harold turned back to the oars, taking his sweet time now, his arms from that angle appearing particularly round and wide, pulling the two of them in to safety with long, powerful, leisurely strokes.

When they reached the shore, Harold beached the dinghy and they stood together, quiet, the two of them staring for a short time out toward the sea and shifting their bare feet on the lava. Cal could just see the rocking hull of the kayak, largely submerged, humped like the yellow rind of a melon.

"Tiger's a brutal fish," he sputtered at last, shaking his head. "He'll kill you in an instant." And he felt his whole body quivering, as though a wildness had corded his limbs until then, and only now, in a single moment, swung them back to his frame. Cal realized for the first time he could recall that he'd been fighting to hold himself upright. He decided, moreover, if he did not monitor his breaths and broaden his stance he would need to lean on Harold, or at least take him by the shoulder. Finally, so as not to fall over, he squatted down.

There was another long pause while the sun began to falter. The remaining light was slung low and sharp. A breeze had come up.

"Now everything has a belly," said Harold softly, his voice even and serious. He placed his big paws on his own belly, which was beautiful, grand and drum-like, and began to chuckle so softly that Cal could scarcely hear him. Then Cal also began to laugh, glancing up at his lover, staring at him with a curious intensity, a kind of fascination, each of them coming to the other's eyes, and for a moment they were laughing together before Harold was moving up the beach, looking every so often back at the ocean then swinging his grand neck forward toward the spreading shade of the house.

"Harold," Cal called after him, but the sound got stuck in his throat. And he watched as that hulking form, still wet and scraped badly along one side of its ribs, the bright line of abrasion curving back almost to the spine, climbed surely, effortlessly, up onto the lanai as if it had only just stepped out from the froth of the waves, barnacled and metamorphosed.

"Harold, wait."

Yet again he was voiceless, silent. Soon Cal was stumbling into the sand. Trying to keep up. Struggling to move closer to the house and farther onto land. Exhausted, he hung there out on the beach attempting to master himself but, as the pure soot of darkness rolled in from the sea, dropped first to his haunches and then to his knees.

An Interview with Temple Grandin

Conducted by Benjamin Hale

DR. TEMPLE GRANDIN IS ONE of the world's most accomplished and well-known adults with autism. After earning a PhD in animal science at the University of Illinois, she went on to revolutionize practices for the humane handling of livestock in slaughterhouses. In North America, almost half of all livestock cattle are handled in a center-track-restrainer system that she designed for meat plants. She is the author of ten books, including the classic autism memoir *Thinking in Pictures* (adapted by HBO films as *Temple Grandin* in 2010), *Emergence, Animals in Translation, Animals Make Us Human*, and, most recently, *The Autistic Brain: Thinking across the Spectrum*. She is a prominent proponent both of animal-welfare issues and of the rights of people with autism and Asperger's syndrome. She lives in Colorado, where she teaches animal science at Colorado State University.

I had the great fortune of speaking at length with Temple Grandin by phone on a recent weekend, when we talked about horses, cattle, pigs, pigeons, agribusiness, dairy farming, corn ethanol production, dog breeding, domesticated foxes, rhinos, tigers, roosters, whooping cranes, bear cubs, and political polarization in Washington. There is something very familiar and refreshing to me about the way Temple Grandin speaks. Her conversation is colloquial, folksy, and no-nonsense—totally bare of sophistry. She is a matter-of-factly brilliant woman who would never, ever try to "sound smart." In Grandin's frank, direct way of communicating, her curiosity, her insistence on sticking to concrete particulars, her respect for pragmatic, hands-on problem solving, and her mistrust of abstraction, I recognized that refreshing worldview of someone for whom the quantifiable, observable reality of things is always the bottom line. I heard my own mechanical-engineer uncle's voice echoing in my head at her rather ornery complaints about the disappearance of practical-skills classes such as woodworking and metalworking from high-school curricula. What I admire most in her blunt attitude is her old-fashioned respect for those people who see the world for what it is and work with their hands—for, no matter what puffs of thought-smoke in the realm of art, politics, and philosophy may indirectly stir others into action, it is always such people who will be the ones to put one stone on top of another, to physically move the matter that results in real change in the world.

BENJAMIN HALE: What are the main things that people tend not to understand about the way animals think? What do you wish more people understood about animal minds that they don't?

TEMPLE GRANDIN: I think they need to realize that an animal is a sensory-based thinker. Animals don't think in words, so they've got to store memories in images and sounds and smells. In fact, I just found an interesting paper on the Internet today that says even insects can categorize different shapes, like star-shaped flowers versus more round kind of flowers. And they can then pick out something from that same category that looks different. You've got to get away from verbal language. That's the first thing that people have to do—totally get away from words. And think: What does it look like? What does it sound like? What does it smell like? What's it feel like? It's a very detailed, sensory-based world. Some research has shown that pigeons can be taught to differentiate Picassos from Monets, just by the style of the artwork. In my book *Animals in Translation*, I talk about a horse that was scared to death of black cowboy hats, but he was fine with white cowboy hats.

HALE: I remember that.

GRANDIN: The memory was sight specific. A white cowboy hat has never done anything bad to him, but a man in a black cowboy hat has done some really bad things to him. Animals tend to associate something that they're seeing or hearing with a memory. If they're looking at something, or seeing something while something bad happens, that's what they'll associate the bad thing with. So they see a person in a black hat again and they get spooked. I know a dog that's terrified of men wearing baseball hats. Any baseball cap. Take the baseball cap off, then it's fine. It's a sensory-based world.

HALE: Do you think that it's just humans' tendency to think verbally that prevents them from getting into the minds of nonhuman animals?

GRANDIN: Well, I'm not going to say that every verbal thinker can't get into the mind of an animal. But what I've observed over the years is some of the best people I've seen with animals—oh, they might be dyslexic. They've got some learning problems. There's a lot of people on the autism spectrum that really get along with animals. People who have a tendency to be less verbal in their thinking often tend to get along with animals a lot better.

HALE: I'd also like to talk about the difference between animal rights and animal welfare. You're a meat eater. I also eat meat, but I've always felt a little bad about it. Have you ever encountered an argument for ethical vegetarianism that made sense to you?

GRANDIN: Oh yes, I have. First of all, I can't function on a vegetarian diet. I've actually tried several times. I cannot function on it. And my mother's exactly the same way. When she goes to a hotel, she asks them to make sausage for breakfast. No bagels for breakfast—that doesn't work for her, and it doesn't work for me. I feel very strongly that animals that are raised for food we've got to give a decent life. That's really, really important. We've got to give them a life worth living. That's the terminology that the farm animal council in Europe uses. And another thing I've always thought about is, most cattle would have never existed if we hadn't, you know, put the bull and the cow together. We bred cows for food. Another thing is, you look at the layout of this country—about 40 percent of the US is range land. You cannot grow crops on it. The only way you can grow food on it is with animals. Grazing animals—cattle, sheep, goat, bison—grazing, herbivore-type of animals. And if you use them right, you can naturally sequester carbon. If you raise them badly, you can really threaten the environment. We've got some real problems right now with mining water for ethanol plants—making corn ethanol, and I don't think that's a very good idea.

HALE: What do you think the average consumer can do, who cares about animal welfare but who also eats meat?

GRANDIN: Know where your food comes from. And you get into the whole argument about big versus small. I have a video called *A Video Tour of a Beef Plant with Temple Grandin*, where I show how a large plant works when it's working right. I have a similar one called *A Pork Plant Video Tour with Temple Grandin*. And we just show it. And when things are working right, the animals walk up the ramp, and their behavior is the same as walking into the veterinary chute. I'm not going to say it's stress free, because the veterinary chute also has stress, but the stress levels—and they've measured in both places—is about the same. Now when things go wrong and things are not managed well, you can have a real mess really superquickly.

HALE: And so you would say that, for an average consumer, the main thing is just to be aware of where your meat comes from?

GRANDIN: Yep. In fact, what I'm seeing now in the slaughter plants are problems like lameness. Animals can be lame and have painful walking for different reasons. It can be genetics, or they push the animals too hard to go really fast. Or it could be they're lame because you fed them too much grain. It could be a lot of different things that make animals lame. Like dairy cows that are just being pushed, pushed, pushed, to give more and more milk, to the point where their body condition gets really low, and they get into what I call biological-system overload. Those are some of the biggest problems now. Problems that are going to have to be fixed on the farm. I've seen pigs with arthritis, and they squeal when they lie down because they're in pain. That's absolutely not acceptable. And then you've got housing issues, like sow-gestation stalls. That needs to go. In fact, I just got off the phone with a good friend of mine who consults for the pig industry, and she's helping them make the conversion from sow-gestation stalls over to loose housing, and she was telling me how much she wants to get them converted—[the pigs] actually like it, how nice and quiet the sounds are.

HALE: Do you think the best way to go about improving conditions for farm animals is through better policy and legislation?

GRANDIN: One of my big concerns in legislation, and I don't care what you're legislating, is what I call *abstractification*. We're dealing with a Congress now and a Senate that are so far removed from *reality*. I read the other day that forty-two senators, in their whole entire career, had never had a job outside of politics. I think that's a very sad thing. I think that's one of the things that's causing all this radical partisanship in the government, is everything becomes an abstraction. Nothing gets done until something *real* happens. Like the sequester was going to furlough the air-traffic controllers, and make [lawmakers'] flights get canceled—and then they instantly did something about it. Because now something *affected* them. And I think one of the big problems we have in government, and a big problem we have with our activists, is that they've gotten too far away from what is actually happening in the field. I think this is true for many issues. Animal issues, environmental issues, lots of different issues.

HALE: Do you think that this problem of abstractification is getting worse over time?

GRANDIN: Yes, I think it's getting worse. For instance, schools are taking out all the hands-on classes. Kids don't know how to sew, they don't know how to cook, they don't know how to do wood-working or steelworking or automobile shop. All those classes have been taken out. And those classes teach a kind of practical problem solving. And so issues turn into abstractions. And then it just turns into pure ideology, rather than, how do we solve problems?

HALE: Is this a big problem in animal science?

GRANDIN: It's a problem in many different fields. I'm not going to single out animal issues—it's also a big problem in environmental issues. People who work in the field, they may be right or left on an issue, but they tend to have more moderate views than people who just live in offices. And the other problem we've got now is that the Internet magnifies the voices of ultraradicals on both sides of the issue, both right and left. And that's not a good thing. That's not going to solve problems.

HALE: Do you think that the Internet abstractifies our thinking in other ways too?

GRANDIN: Well, you can't blame the Internet for all the problems. I think the thing that's doing the worst abstractification, I think it's very bad, is that somebody gets a college degree in political science, goes right into working with legislators and lobbying groups in Washington, DC, and then becomes a congressman, and they've never worked outside the Beltway. They've never done what I'd call a real job.

HALE: Do you think that people have less daily contact with animals than they used to?

GRANDIN: Yes. I witnessed a really disturbing thing—I did my book *Animals Make Us Human*, and I did a big book signing, where I was going to be at a big Costco store for eight hours. And I decided to just walk up to people and just show them the book, you know. I wasn't going to wait for people to come up to the book table, I was just going to walk up to them. So I walked up to all the retired couples and all the young families and I just said, My name's Temple Grandin, and I have a book about animal behavior. Do you have pets? And I was shocked to find out that in south Denver, about 20 to 25 percent of young families with children had no pet of any kind. No gerbil, no parakeet, nothing. Those kids are growing up totally away from animals.

HALE: So you think it's a good thing to grow up with pets?

GRANDIN: Yes, I do think it's a good thing. There's a wonderful book called *Last Child in the Woods*, and it talks about how kids don't play outside anymore. I think about growing up in the fifties—oh, we'd go out and collect leaves, and we built things, and we floated boats in the brook, and we were out in the natural world.

HALE: Here's a question I was thinking about just the other day. Just a few weeks ago, the black rhino became extinct in the wild. Whenever I read about something like the black rhino going extinct, or the fate of the orangutan, which is just barely holding on, it profoundly depresses me.

GRANDIN: It's bad. It's really bad.

HALE: And I've always thought of the conservation of endangered animals to be an inherent good, an end in itself. And then the other day I was talking to a friend about the whooping crane, and she was talking about how the people who have been trying to rehabilitate the whooping crane go to great lengths, dressing up in costumes and things like that, in order to revitalize this animal—and she said, To what end do we save these animals? Is it for the animals, or is it somehow for us?

GRANDIN: I think to let beautiful animals just disappear is a terrible thing. Especially animals like whooping cranes. And there's a lot of controversy about a lot of things, like the whale, and problems with elephants in captivity and things like that. I was reading a super-interesting book that I got a galley proof of, it's a book about a guy who raised bear cubs. And he'd take them out for walks in the woods, and then he'd be able to turn them loose in the wild, and they would function in the wild. In fact, they'd function both in the wild world and in our world. In other words, animals are very compartmentalized in their thinking: In this situation, I do these behaviors, and when I'm in this other situation, I do these other behaviors. And these bears would be functioning out in the wild, and he'd go out there and see them, and change the batteries in their radio collars. And he understood how bears communicate—he would watch their ears and know when they were starting to get angry, and things like that. I think it's a shame to lose all the wild animals. I want to conserve them.

HALE: In the case of the black rhino—

GRANDIN: Has that species actually gone totally extinct?

HALE: I believe the black rhino has officially been declared to be extinct.

GRANDIN: They have to make sure whether the black rhino is truly a separate species from the other rhinos. You've got things like different kinds of rhinos. I don't know much about the black rhino, but I know something about genetics. In fact, my book *Genetics and the Behavior of Domestic Animals* we just updated, and I talk about how genetics can affect behavior, and there's some discussion in science as to exactly what a species is. Now, I think everybody would agree that a tiger, an orange-and-black tiger, is definitely its own species. But then you get into, say, twenty-five different kinds of sparrows—are those really each a unique species? You see, evolutionary pressures work on animals. I read an interesting paper about—oh, I don't remember what kind of bird it was, but you know, birds get hit by cars. And the birds that manage to not get hit by cars ended up having shorter wings, for faster takeoff. And so in places where there tended to be a lot of roads around, the birds that went out on the roads ended up with shorter wings and faster takeoff. That's evolution. Is that shorter-wing-and-faster-takeoff bird a different species from a bird that lives away from cars that's got longer wings? These are animals that will interbreed with fertile offspring. One of the definitions of a species is: has to have fertile offspring. Where if you breed a horse and donkey, the mule is not fertile—you can't breed mules.

HALE: Is that your definition of a species?

GRANDIN: That's most people's definition of a species: two individuals that can make fertile offspring. I mean, it's possible to breed bison mixed with cattle and stuff like that, but most of those hybrids are sterile, they don't have fertile offspring.

115

HALE: In a lot of your work I've read about this really fascinating thing, and you were just talking about it a moment ago, about the relationship between genetics and behavior. For instance, I remember reading in one of your books about an experiment in Russia to domesticate a wild fox—

GRANDIN: That's in the genetics book—that's the Belyaev experiments. Years ago, they wanted to breed a fox that wouldn't bite your hand off, to raise for fur coats. And so they just selected for the foxes that licked your hand instead of wanting to rip it off, and they ended up with this black-and-white border collie fox-dog. In the updated version of my genetics book, there's a new chapter, written not by Belyaev but by some people who worked in the same lab, on the continuation of those fox experiments. And basically, you've got foxes that look like dogs and act like dogs.

HALE: Reading about that experiment, and also reading what you wrote about the hyperaggressive roosters that had accidentally been bred to be aggressive when they were breeding for physical traits—

GRANDIN: Yes, they weren't trying to breed hyperaggressive roosters. These things are side effects of selecting for other traits. Also, this has been somewhat corrected now. But twenty years ago, when they bred pigs to be really, really lean, they accidentally bred a pig that was really mean, and it was real aggressive, and it fought a lot. And nobody was deliberately breeding aggressive pigs. But the thing is, traits are linked in ways that can sometimes be surprising. The pigs turned out to be lean and mean. Now they've been selecting away from that, and a lot has been corrected.

HALE: The idea that behavioral and physical traits can be connected in surprising ways can have uncomfortable implications.

GRANDIN: I always say overselecting for a single trait will wreck your animal. And I don't care what the trait is. I was in the airport the other day, and I saw a dog that looked like a cross between a Pomeranian and an Australian Blue Heeler—you know how those miniature breeds often have those hydrocephalic, really rounded foreheads? And the lady told me it was a miniature Australian shepherd. But it wasn't. It wasn't! And now you've got a bulldog where the nose is smashed in, it can't breathe, it can't walk, it can't have babies naturally. And if you look at a picture of a bulldog from 1938—go on the Internet and type in "Bulldog's Dilemma"—you'll find the 1938

116

version, and he's actually got a snout, he actually can function.

HALE: Do you think it's unethical to breed dogs for physical traits?

GRANDIN: I think it's unethical when it gets to the point where it causes welfare problems. When they have difficulty walking, they have difficulty birthing, they have difficulty breathing. Those are big welfare problems. That is unethical. I think an animal needs to be sound. And that animal, the bulldog, is not physically sound. How do you get in a mess like that? You get in a mess like that because it happens *slowly*. So young people now coming in to the bulldog breed say, Well, that's just the breed. Yeah, but I'm old enough to remember when it didn't walk that way. It's interesting to go to a college or a high school where the bulldog is their mascot, and look at their old sports pictures, and the bulldog's not this monstrosity that you've got now. It is unethical. I think it's very unethical to breed animals that have got behavior problems, that have lameness problems, or they've got problems with giving birth, problems with breathing, heart-failure problems. I have a real problem with what I call biological-system overload. Now the dairy cows are starting to get some big problems. This is all developed genetically. They just push them so hard with genetics that you're having problems with the body condition. She's putting everything she's got into milk, there's nothing left for the dairy cow. So she's getting really skinny, really lame, and they're having a really difficult time getting her to rebreed.

HALE: You've written that in animal science, it's always the debunkers who are on the attack—you've said that you couldn't remember a single big academic fight where someone got fired or lost their funding for doing a study where the animal turned out to be *dumber* than people thought. Why do you think this bias exists? Do you think it's especially particular to academic science?

GRANDIN: I don't want to single out academics, but there's a tendency for people to get single-minded on a single thing. I'm an associative thinker. A lot of people are much more linear in how they think. You see, I tend to associate a lot of different things, and I'm concerned about overselecting for single traits. You see it with monocultures in crops too. We've had trouble with wheatgrass, and we're having trouble with a disease in bananas. I think one of the things that's difficult for a lot of people to understand is, what would be the optimal solution over time? What is the optimal milk production? You see right now, you push that dairy cow too hard, she'll only last

117

you for two years. It takes you three years to grow the heifer and make her into a dairy cow, and then you only milk her for two years. That's not great economics. If you cut back production just a little bit, she'll last you for three or four years. That would actually make more sense. But people just get single-minded on one thing. People are always looking for the one single magic thing. They don't tend to look at the whole system. And that applies to lots of things, not just farms.

HALE: You've worked with ranching and animal science for more than thirty years—how have they changed over the last three decades?

GRANDIN: People are thinking a lot more about ethical issues they never used to think about. When I first started, people just beat cattle up, and the treatment of animals was terrible. But what kept me going was there were some ranchers who really did a good job. I can think of Bill and Penny Porter, with their ranch in Arizona. It was people like that that kept me going. There were good people raising cattle. About 80 percent of them were bad, but there were some that were good. So that was sort of like the sun behind the clouds. And that was real important to me.

HALE: And that's what's changed?

GRANDIN: Well, one of the things that really pushes the big changes is when a major company like McDonald's insists on changes. I worked on implementing the McDonald's animal-welfare program, and then the other big companies like Wendy's and Burger King started implementing animal-welfare programs too.

HALE: I'm really interested in the categories that humans tend to put animals into. There are companion animals, like dogs and cats and horses, which we consider taboo to eat, and then there are other animals we think of as food animals, like cows and pigs. Do you have any ideas about how these categories of thinking develop?

GRANDIN: A veterinary student asked me one time, why do we have to give anesthetic to castrate a dog but not a bull, when they both feel pain? Dogs are an animal that we bred in a real special way to be hypersocial. We've bred them to be hypersocial and loyal, and there are lots of emotional traits in dogs that make them good companions. Cats have a lot more of the wild in them. And then food animals, we've tended to domesticate large, social animals simply because they're easier to manage.

HALE: So you think that pigs and cows have become food animals because they're easier to corral and things like that?

GRANDIN: And also they're herbivores, which makes them easier to feed. When agriculture first started, cows were just out on the pasture, they just grazed. There was a lot of grass around, so we didn't have to feed them.

HALE: Where do you see the future of industrial meat production going?

GRANDIN: We're running out of water, for one thing. And the only reason grain was fed to animals originally was because it was cheap. That's the only reason. We had surpluses. Now we're running out of water. Right now we're mining water to feed ethanol plants and then export ethanol. That doesn't make any sense at all. We have no net energy gain on ethanol. I am *not* a fan of ethanol. We've got to figure out *practical ways* to solve problems. And I recommend that anyone who wants to solve problems get out in the field and figure out what's *actually going on*. Get out of the office. Get out of the Beltway. You stay in Washington, DC, too long, you're going to turn into one of those pods—like that movie *Invasion of the Body Snatchers*? You know that old movie?

HALE: Yes, I know that movie!

GRANDIN: That's what people in Washington, DC, do—they turn into pods. Everything becomes ideology and power. They forget what the issue actually really is. And the thing is, when you really get involved, the right thing to do is always something messy in the middle. That's true for anything, I don't care what it is.

Two Poems
Andrew Mossin

ECLIPSE

Wave gull call

striped black fluent wave down an arm

Set back from the shore in blue water

a body in long strides walking in wrinkled shadows

      walking into the water there is a system

of working one's way out

wave by wave the common whiteness of grave

stones drenched in sunlight.

*

Coercive bridge and crease of elbow.   Shroud liniment applied to its surface.

Gulf bones dragged into human lots.   Back slotted spongy knots of coral.

Aroused one wakes on bone-mottled gray cloth.

And the wind that knots itself.   One gray-green scarf coiled around the hand.

Plastic tarps spread on shell-soaked ground.   Necklace bone shields borne out
[in a stream.

A grove of shells held against copper the color of sky at sunset.

The opacity of smoke.

*

(*prayer bell*)

Shoal surface shine.   To go down to it paler in light to see the pale waters
[removed.

Low gull cry spilled downstream.   Wind-yipped gulls in formation above.

Caught sight at dawn of barrier boom.   Stray slotted bloom of ash in palm.

Another broken from the first uncapped.   Bodiless mercy.   A line pulled in
[two directions.

Stained sea mottled black then blue.   *Line flowing into line a flower of*
[*hands almost.*

Stood under the surface itself a scenic cloud.   Musical almost. Weightless
[beam of water.

Our hunger for the ordinary.   Let's see the very thing and nothing else.

Night after night no night but forms of waiting.   One grows attached to
[the images.

A plume rising through half-light.   Well wide open.

Bell buoys rising underwater.   A crown of waves encircling soft black lines.

Plume night sail blue acquiescent at sea. Tar balls floating on ochrous flinty
[surface of foam.

Mute stars sited dusk inside its channel. Spume sea-white foam palm
[plankton side first.

Black wooded sea surface bucolic coral faded brown *and bees of paradise*

floating in ash.

*

A line in oil or sand is still a line.

To break the form of it to sing again.

Carrying some weight inside the song that opens and abandons one to what

cannot last.

White crystal under the tongue. Bleached hand folded black wing.

*

No child can wander inside its foamy circle.

Shed shards of its gull shape. Loose forms dragged bone. A pit where the
[hands were.

A child in the form of a bird landing beside it. Body's bell diving for salt.
[Bone stalks of

black sand on white.

Color disappears from the world when you least expect it.

Gulf tide looping climactic shifts.   Follow the cycle it comes around washed
[back to

shell-beaded shore.

Shapely brown combed shell carriers on shore gone on all fours.

An old man standing in the middle to find what is the middle of blackness.

Seeing anything gone seeing it go where it goes underneath it goes. . . .

Carried back again piles of white plastic bags arranged in rows of white.

Nude hands weighted without shovels.   Who is near when no one is near.

Edge to edge hooked smooth surfaces hooked together.

One colony below the surface one above shining aerial view of their forms
[silvery black lines

congregating at dusk.

*

No panic in the moon light it comes to nothing.

Surface of one then another like a hand

passed through black jelly.

Dipped below what one has lost or not known was there.

In place of it a shapeless moon eye. Beam and edge of beam

"the final mountain the last glowing tower."

*

Andrew Mossin

Sea bones passed through hands of the living. The blades of oars passed over
[and over

orange over black.

Bodies in a line of bodies
lined up to watch the sun rise fall silent.

Spectacle is what it says
it is. A sea garden dissolved within a beacon of forms.

The seal broken off.

*

Oyster shell in hand of a boy.

Hand the shells back to him they come back gray and black on white.

Small knotted pearls of flesh. Cupped hand of gray meat.

Not in his eyes he says it's over not in his eyes but his hands.

Pale boy's hands bearing no trace of black.

Gray husk meatless play of light on his hands.

*

(*prayer well*)

Refuge inside of it a column rises through black-tiered jewel of ocean.

Eyes shut or open opening into blue-green layers of sight.

The sun travels weightless over white sand refuge to what it leaves.

124

Without borders a slim space of light passing through the layers underneath.

Captive well capped light. A plume brown then black rising blue then brown.

No trace of their bodies when the rig is lifted like a tower into view.

What is redemption the cloud line of it rising then parting like prayer folds.

Stage by stage the serene story of living things below.

Green infused with brown blacking out the line
                                    between death and life.

                    *

To share the day blue then gray in passing.

Soft civil bird bent low to ground finding sky and sun bleached.

This shine in place of white passed over mottled summer.

A zone of blue then orange opening out to sea lanes blackening far as the eye
                                    [can see.

Sun when it sets black in the gray sky. Vigil in which characters speak

Against what they are seeing one speaks against half-pale reds in ocean sky

Gone black-sashed sky and sun bolted black to a black knot of oil.

Birds blackened foam-like waiting.

                    *

Bell buoys in motion beneath a cut-out moon.

Toothless black sky white sand coast hills no hills around the center of a

                    surface black tin scraping a plastic ledge.

Shivering heavy rains come down silver then white on black. Scarred lines
                                                  [of it.

Silver then black white surfaces blown open by white black hands.

Forged lanes of shiny black jettisoned to make memory a route of passing a
                                                  [phase

of unknowing. Bleached bones in a field of yellow sand winced leveraged
                                                  [back.

Laid end to end when the bags fill with them and are brought out put in
                                                  [a line.

As wind shears scatter salt grooves blackened newly tiered layers of black
                                                  [salt.

One's history caught entangled marsh grasses

matted with death.

                                          *

Marsh flowers stemmed slick.

Mute blaze field of wet flora

pressed into black. Sheathed

rib ends coarsened matted against hand-held silt.

Flown off wind

pelican beak wing forming one black ring.

Black pelican flight bright-edged wheel of stemmed flora

                                            cut ice coral blaze.

                              *

In the visible sea locate the invisible sea imprisoned there.

Notes disappear written out dissolve blue gray as metal in hand softens.

Coral rose darkened funneling out blue then black squall sudden plume of
                                            [gulls scattered.

Ledged sediment black conic silt uprising plume of salt whiteness as it burns
                                            [out.

Echoes coloring the lines meeting boom barriers faint sound of their color.

A vessel

sinks from view reappears colorless splotch in rear of scene.   Gull homes
                                            [black window.

Orphic column of orange light burning at sea

                              brown plumes forested glow.

                              *

Flown low bright steps of oil in a line of orange.

Refuge attached to each broken trace networks of foam

broken open like cloistered blooms bright silver.

Andrew Mossin

Rock surfaces submerged black green weighted down

waves crested rising against bolted shore.

*

Blue yellow sky and sun.

Bolted half piles of green white plastic.

Each lasting trace of black coating a surface of white green.

Buoy shell stern. Sun

clapped folds of crab shrimp sea turtle.

Netted pulled soft webbed shell.

Nubbed trace black silver needle beamed boat light.

Scarred bird-like no bird.

A scream softened settles downwind. Black

surface pluming beneath each edge of landscape

"swarming

with the changes that occur

living as and where we live."

Andrew Mossin

ANIMA MUNDI

And this is what the serpent told me. The one in my dreams.
She appears on the site of an ancient Greek temple. The temple is in ruins,
but the power of the place is palpable, running in electric currents through
my body. Olive trees with their gentle presence cover the hillside. She slithers
away through the warm grass and a deep voice cries out, "Why have you
abandoned me!"

But the meaning of her cry wasn't clear at first

I couldn't read the red bird inside a tree of fire

its meaning wasn't clear when the fire rose

inside a crown of red.

What came back years later?

The story of the snake reddening in wet grass

A boy inside the tale breathing its fire

Once again the tale told to others the tale

repeated until it becomes what it must

hold—

> Like a bashful virgin being lavished with compliments, it tried
> to conceal its pride in its beauty, and, having made certain of
> captivating its lover, the snake coyly twisted round and gently,
> gracefully, glided away until swallowed up by a crack in the
> wall. . . . I rose from my place, overwhelmed by the feeling that
> I was on the brink of a new world, a new destiny, or rather, if
> you wish, on the threshold of a new love.

*

Andrew Mossin

Do you remember waking I don't remember waking

by the sea in the serpent's house I don't remember the name of She

who led me there woke me by the sea in a serpent's tale

black like ash flakes in my mouth I tasted her metallic flesh

I don't remember waking by the sea near the serpent my Beloved

I was told nothing near the sea my beginnings

were like reddened wood in the fire where the spirits watched

for me one by one they came to watch my beginnings

in the forked place where the wood ran bloodless through our palms

I was led there in the infinite ash in the pale sky skin like a snake's

pale surface my palms cut bloodied on their hard surfaces

their twisted forms elongating in the dark

(*heard her say*)

I gathered by water I was alone the days it took

black days to see her form by means of two tiny fangs like pearls

and a golden tongue like a twig of arak wood

it smiled at me and fastened its eyes on mine

in one fleeting commanding glance.

The thought of killing left me the thought of

meeting her tongue like a twig of arak wood

I felt a current a radiation from its eyes

ordering me to stay where I was.

I became the serpent's bride

    I saw her in the realm of reptiles

    I tasted her flesh in the form of the djinns

    I coupled my form to hers I was brought

    beneath the red ash winged like a cut piece of flesh

    I was made to lie down until she fled at morning

    There was not whispering in the trees

A house near my vision the days going past one

by one I didn't count them I sat near the woodpile

and tasted fern and ash white palms struck

what the flames were what my body was

made visible against the light

    Whenever a snake appears, you must think of a
primordial feeling of fear. It is hidden and therefore
dangerous. As animal it symbolizes something

unconscious; it is the instinctive movement or tendency;
it shows the way to the hidden treasure, or it guards the
treasure.

*

What is forbidden?

Red wing dust birth what is forbidden

the snake's forbiddenness inside

the red hand revealing itself to

sight potent night a stain reddening

working its way into consciousness

the hawk's piercing eye from above

as the snake is a form of beginning

blended with red wings & clay

*

Lost everywhere without you I am black
teeth black on a ring of cypress I am holy
flesh of the goat pierced by fire I am the name
it carries stained red black meat on a red
flooded pyre.

*

(*after* Rumi)

And my branch of olive is bottomless

my ship steered under gray falconless skies my skin flecked

with ash one is returning one is forever not returning

And the root is a reed blossoming chain

Blood flows between the florets my mouth and gums bleed

to play its bony structure to hear itself in half measures

as if grieving as if in prayer to the goddess torn

limb from limb its heart eaten in the shade of cypress

> And the origin of its secret was lament
>
> And its reed a white palm of bone
>
> And the reed's sound an amulet of fire
>
> lifted to the Heavens
>
> telling of the road that runs with blood
>
> telling the tales of Majnun's passionate loves

The lover is a veil that roams without beginning or end

And their children were squandered edge to edge

Escaping its music the children

pled for their lives and did not return.

*

When I was a boy, thoughts born out of fear struck me in the
face and told me I was a coward. That was because I was still
bad at being afraid. Since then, however, I have learned to be
afraid with real fear, fear that increases only when the force
that engenders it increases. We have no idea of this force,
except in our fear. For it is utterly inconceivable, so totally
opposed to us, that our brain disintegrates at the point where
we strain ourselves to think it.

Nothing is when light is nothing

upon the flesh of the seeker nothing can

alter wood formations built on sea's inlet

And our skin is squeezed from within by black

coils of its being we are what it coils around

black speech in the mouth of a parrot

Let it endure us we are liable to say

Let it coil around our waist & begin the crossing

Let it settle around our torso's blade of black coral

And seduce our mother from her depths

And hasten our father to his death

*

Let me die near your coiled being let me know
fear of your metal black form of death my living wish
Being afraid does not mean feeling my body shake or
my heart beat . . . I want to experience the world as something
to shun as black ghost of kin.

*

But the woman and man were blind

in his dream they were blind walking into

daylight turning to one then the other

blind voices crying out to one then the other

And god was outside their solitude apart from where they lay

And the man arose and knew in the distance

their house with columns and saw her move from its interior

Blind as she was blind to see herself moving from within

A bright stone the color of water moving beneath them

And the serpent moved through their days & nights

And he saw what it was came before there were two of them

A door opening on the right onto a garden and the figure of

Odysseus reflected back through waves of light

"Do you know where you are?"

"I am a stranger here and everything is strange to me."

Andrew Mossin

"Do you know where you are?"

"I am a stranger to you and to all who come after."

*

As if bird & snake were messengers

One calling to the other in terror at dawn when the skies opened

And light poured forth upon them

Earth and light from above when the Heavens opened

And they saw themselves out of place

Orphans in each world

"My soul, my sister, from above. . . ."

*

See what has left us what begins anew
as if in a dream of paradise we can never know.

NOTE. Eleonóra Babejová's "She Will Wind Herself around You" (*Jung Journal: Culture & Psyche* 5: 3) and C. G. Jung's *The Red Book: Liber Novus* were the sources for many of the references and quotations in this poem.

Wolf Interval
Gwyneth Merner

INTRODUCTION

HOW DOES THE READER ENTER a story? Through the mouth of the author, over her tongue and teeth, against her ridged palate. I believe it is the duty of the book artist to create a new mouth, a space to house the word. In our craft, there is no book more suitable to render the mouth than the Wolf Interval, a structure I designed in 1988 with the critical aid of C. R. Bailey.

For this project, you will need to tear down a 25-inch-by-38-inch sheet of paper into sixteen folios, 6¼ inch by 9½ inch, grain long. I recommend Hern, seventy pound, text weight, though if you plan to letterpress the content of your book, you may prefer a paper stock of heavier weight and equal quality. You will also require a bone folder (do not settle for synthetic), a palette knife, PVA glue, book board, paste paper, book cloth, waxed thread, and a curved needle.

INTENTIONS

The clear difference between craft and art is intention. It is fundamental that your books should demonstrate both the solid execution of craft and abundant forethought. To expose my intentions, exactly as you will leave the Coptic-sewn binding of your sample book open to scrutiny, I would like to invite you into a personal history, into the throat of a story. In our cross-scrutiny, we will see fine, tight loops or untidy knots, a waxed trap.

In 1987, when I was still an apprentice printmaker at Magpie Press in Montague, Massachusetts, I decided to bike to Sunderland to see an exhibit on mobile dwellings at a small, informal gallery in a private home. It was entitled "The Wolf Interval: New Impressions of Nomadism." At the time, I had planned to purchase a vehicle that would serve as my home: something small, something that could be moved from plot to plot, and, foremost, affordable on my wages from a part-time job waiting tables at a vegetarian restaurant. As with any new project, I suffered from a kind of monomania—certainly a good trait for a book artist, but foolish when applied to other areas of my life. I suspected that the gallery visit would provide a break from the tiresome comparison of vehicle size, towing weight, engine horsepower, and added features like kitchens, bathrooms, and lofted bedding.

The gallery was in back of a white farmhouse on Route 47. It was close to the Connecticut River, which smelled of rust in early spring. The gallery owner, a sallow man with gray stubble and drooping lower eyelids, welcomed me and drew me through his living room (a sleeping orange cat on a couch, a hi-fi, and a wall of LPs), his small, impeccable kitchen (the scent of fried eggs) to a black-curtained doorway.

Behind the curtain, the narrow room felt like an aquarium after closing hours—cool, lapping blue light and the calm indifference of drifting invertebrates. The mobile dwellings, each no bigger than a shoe box, had been executed in painstaking miniature inside of odd, polygonal vitrines. The metal models flashed like sardines and sardine cans, the light fluctuating as though there was a short in the wiring.

Each of the six vitrines had a small descriptive label in navy card stock adhered to the front pane of glass. The labels were numbered, and so—enjoying order and deliberateness—I followed the recommended sequence.

I leaned over the diorama of a campground forested with pines and plane trees. In the middle of a foam block made to mimic concrete, I saw a pole topped with the plastic head of a camel supporting two swings. The VW van, tinted in a shade of burnt sienna, was parked in a rectangle of combed sand at the edge of a round of artificial grass—an ideal camping spot. Its white pop-top was propped at an acute angle. In front of the van's sliding side door were two lounge chairs upholstered in a minute floral print to match the paint. On a coffee table covered in yellow vinyl was an array of resin-sculpted foods: a baked chicken with a greased sheen, two green apples, two half-full cups of coffee, a bottle of white wine, and a plate of cheese slices with cut tomato.

1. *Julio Cortázar and Carol Dunlop's Volkswagen Kombi Van, 1982. Driven between Paris and Marseilles without leaving the autoroute in order to explore each rest area*

for multiple days and generate the expedition journal
"Autonauts of the Cosmoroute."

A dark green GMC truck with a white camper over its bed had been arranged in chalky, red powder, made to mimic dirt, and placed next to a pipe-organ cactus and a molded-plastic standard French poodle, sitting politely. The back of the camper had been sliced away to reveal the kitchenette with umber-colored appliances and a Formica fold-up table. On top of the table, roughly the size of a matchbook, was a black typewriter. I thought of the space of the book, the space of the author, the space of the informal home—I must have smiled.

2. *John Steinbeck's Rocinante, 1960. Steinbeck traveled in this camper truck, named after Don Quixote's horse, while gathering material for "Travels With Charley." Camper manufactured by the Wolverine Camper Company of Glaswin, MI.*

The next mobile home was parked perpendicularly across seven parking spaces at the edge of a lot. It was surrounded by rows of boxy toy sedans in black, red, and blue. The vehicle itself was long, chrome, and shaped like a loaf of bread. On the door was a red logo, "Spartanette," showing the featureless profile of a man in a winged hat. A line of ten light posts—eight pairs with the bulbs out, and the remaining twelve guttering—led to the two-dimensional facade of the Nugget Hotel. There were lights embedded in the wax-paper windows of the hotel and inside the Spartanette as well—everyone was preparing for bed.

3. *Spartanette, 1951. Manufactured by Spartan Aircraft Company in Tulsa, OK. Managing Owner: J. Paul Getty.*

Under a mock highway overpass was a trailer resembling an up-turned canned ham. Artificial weeds sprouted in cracks carved into the foam concrete. A light flickered inside the trailer's single window. It was a wretched place, even in miniature. Back then, my career still so precarious, I could imagine myself inside the trailer, listening to the sounds of moving cars overhead.

4. *Boles Aero, 1948. Manufactured in Burbank, CA.*

The second-to-last miniature resembled a tall, elongated hearse. Or, more accurately, a railway car on tires. It rotated on a round glass mirror within a dark frame inlaid with triangles of knotted wood. On both sides of the vehicle, I saw three white-curtained windows in the middle and two small portholes, one at each flank.

5. *Raymond Roussel's Maison Roulante, 1925. Manufactured by George Régis, coach maker, 14, Rue Sainte-Isaure, Paris 18ᵉ, at the cost of one million francs, measuring close to thirty feet long. Roussel had at his disposal a bedroom with a double bed, a studio, a bathroom, and a dormitory for two servants and a driver. The interiors were designed by Lacoste.*

The final diorama was at odds with the others; it lacked four wheels and a steel body. A she-wolf, carved in wood and painted delicately down to its blue irises, brown and gray fur, and the pink of its distended nipples, disgorged the upper torso of a girl through its sharp, yellow teeth. The girl appeared to be crawling out of the wolf—her hands were flexed and her chin was up, but her hair enveloped her face. The wolf's tail curled under its body and between its legs.

6. *Wolf Interval, 1922. An antiquated and largely ignored female form of touring. Last seen Wolf Interval: 1964, in captivity.*

As book artists, you may find that the books of your childhood have left an indelible mark on your craft, from the dimensions of your page to the color contrast between your paste paper and book cloth. In front of the wolf figurine, I recalled a long-lost book, bright blue with piano keys on the cover, a kindergarten songbook. Our class had a favorite song. It was one of those tunes that children sing—like "Ring Around the Rosie"—that attempt to obscure horror with a major key and distracting gestures. How did it go? *The she-wolf, the she-wolf, da da dum, da da da.* I still have not been able to track down the words. But I do remember a mistake: I used to sing *wishy-wolf, wishy-wolf.*

The song portrayed the dangers of traveling inside a wolf, of a daughter choosing to become the passenger of a Wolf Interval. The father shoots his daughter's wolf by accident, trying to protect his flock of sheep. The girl suffocates while the wolf around her dies.

140

The father discovers his intact daughter within an extra organ inside the wolf. He remembers her penchant for wandering and pledges that he will never kill again. In penitence, he becomes a star that protects travelers from misunderstandings.

I asked the gallery owner about the curator, who he was, if he had a business card. He handed me a small, perfectly square booklet with a dove-gray cover. The title had been letterpressed—the ink impression perfect—and was the same as the exhibit. The authors were listed as Lotte N. Pfeiffer and C. R. Bailey. I asked if the authors had made any attempt to explain the history of the Wolf Interval. A paper band prevented me from opening the booklet and scanning the text.

The gallery owner shook his head but agreed to let me remove the band. I was careful not to tear it or damage the fore edge. The title page bore a variant inscription: *Lotte N. Pfeiffer and the Wolf Interval: A Biography, by C. R. Bailey.* The printer had also neglected to provide a publication date or the name of the press. It was a single sheet, folded booklet (See Chapter 3, "Variations on the Accordion Binding"), the folds alternating between the spine edge and the head. A handmade book requires a quiet attention, and so I quickly paid the gallery owner what remained of a recent withdrawal from my bank account ($30, a dear sum), and returned to my apartment.

A RETURN TO CRAFT

Let us recall the importance of the grain. As you undoubtedly know by now (your sample books, your first attempts, may already have warped), the grain of the paper, book board, and book cloth must follow the direction of the spine. A book is a quick-tempered animal—you do not stroke a dog or a cat against the grain of its fur, do you? A sheet of paper folded into eighths and cut with a T-shape pattern will undoubtedly have two folds against the grain. This design flourish comes at the cost of preserving the booklet. But what wondrous spaces this form creates! What a joy to peek into a secret crease created by a fold at the head of the page!

As I read *Lotte N. Pfeiffer and the Wolf Interval: A Biography*, I was pleased by how it made me hunt for the content, how between pages of text I had to tent the pages with my thumbs to open into the hidden illustrations. The first illustration within a head fold was an etching reproducing the Wolf Interval sculpture from the exhibit. On the verso page was the following caption:

"How do I read this book?"
"Carefully, as though you are about to enter the mouth of the wolf."

* * *

Lotte N. Pfeiffer and the Wolf Interval: A Biography
by C. R. Bailey

ACKNOWLEDGMENTS

Before her death in 1975, Lotte N. Pfeiffer made it clear to me that she valued her privacy; it was in fact her inherently private nature that allowed her to retreat into the wolf on that summer day in 1914 near the Siskiyou Pass. In tracing Ms. Pfeiffer to her residence, in my efforts to record the reminiscences of the last Wolf Interval, I have stalked her in the manner that the biologically typical form of *canis lupus* stalks its prey. Ms. Pfeiffer, an altogether decent woman, responded to my incursions with the utmost grace.

Now that this volume is complete, I feel it is necessary to extend my gratitude to the Pfeiffer family. Without their comments and corrections, this work would have been a lesser animal.

INTRODUCTION

Lotte, in her white boatneck sweater and thick glasses, was not the imposing woman I imagined she would be. We sat in wicker chairs on the deck of her A-frame lodge and drank iced mint tea, enriched with ample helpings of sugar. As we set our interview calendar for the next two weeks, she called on me to research the etymological roots of the word "dwell" to understand the invisible history of the Wolf Interval.

Perplexed, I went to the modest library in the town of L. and consulted the dictionary. After several afternoons in conversation with Lotte, we agreed that this information would be better addressed in the addendum to this booklet. At her insistence, I have followed her exacting instructions for the physical format of each page. Lotte also

requested that I include a note that reading in sequence is not fundamental—"One is allowed to start at the end."

THE INTERVAL ORGAN

Lotte N. Pfeiffer was born in St. Louis in 1904. Her father, Leonard
Pfeiffer, died of tuberculosis two years later and Lotte and her mother,
Adeline, were left in the care of a distant cousin, Gustavus Pfeiffer,
an entrepreneur of a growing pharmaceutical company that specialized in effervescent lozenges, gum tablets, and mouthwash.

The specific details of Lotte's infancy and early childhood are valuable but nonetheless better off withheld, as they have no clear bearing on her departure from her mother's home in 1911. Between 1907
and 1908 Adeline had a decisive break with Gustavus and she took
her daughter west to Oregon by rail coach. They settled in the log-
ging town of R., close to the Siskiyou Pass, where Adeline became
the local schoolteacher. For a time, they lived in a cold, one-room
cabin close to the mill while their Sears and Roebuck Model 115 home
was constructed on River Street in R.

One day, while netting butterflies in a cluster of horsetail and wild
ginger, Lotte was troubled by an unusual smell.

> It was like rendered fat and almond extract. I saw white
> sparks in my vision and my palms went numb. Finally, I saw
> the she-wolf's eyes and her gray body move behind the thin,
> red branches and the silver leaves of the manzanita bushes.
> We watched each other for a long time and I became aware of
> the smell of her breath, its sweetness and acridity.
> She moved closer to me, not standing her full height but
> crouched low to earth with her ears flat against her skull. I
> removed my pinafore, my long-shirt, my wool stockings, and
> my lace-up boots and approached her. We came to an under-
> standing. She opened her mouth and though at first it seemed
> unlikely that I would fit, I put my chin and elbows on her
> velvety tongue and moved toward the spot where the ridges
> on the roof of her mouth ended. Once I had pushed half of my
> body into the wolf, I had to push with my heels on the backs
> of her yellowed canines to start the involuntary spasms in
> her throat.

The typical wolf esophagus leads to the stomach. In the Wolf
Interval, an interval organ bypasses the stomach. Like the stomach
it can expand to a great capacity but it is designed to adjust to the

contours of a small girl. What does it feel like to enter the interval organ? Accounts from the last three centuries have compared the squeezing to that of a boa constrictor. In the most recent modern accounts, the sensation has been described as a blood-pressure cuff tightening over the entirety of the body.

Lotte, in a compression stupor, contemplated death and the poor decisions that had led her to the she-wolf's mouth. She recalled her mother's repeated warning about playing in the woods: "Only the homely girl calls out to a homely wolf." But within the interval organ, the pressure eased. Let us remember that within the womb the child does not float in unbounded fluid. The fetus is pressed firmly from all angles. It was similar for Lotte within the wolf; she was blanketed in warm muscle, yet she could feel huffs of cool air within the dark cavity. Through the muscle she felt the wolf's quick pulse, and at intervals, it aligned with her own.

EDUCATION

> It was dark, but it was also vibrant. I had my eyes open the whole time and I might as well have been blind, but there were colors. Not colors that could be associated with the seeing spectrum but colors that could be felt in the throat—a kind of tickling. I could not conceive of a source or a purpose for this constant swallowing until I understood that it was how the Wolf Interval transmitted the outside space to me. At first these spaces were more like gestures, or cues. Then, slowly, the coloration fluctuated in transparency and opaqueness; it braided and thickened in the tubes and hollows of my skull. Now, even after all this time, it is difficult for me to look at you without feeling your shape somewhere between my jaw and my stomach. A side effect, I suppose.

Having just grasped reading and writing after months at the slate with her mother guiding the chalk in her hand, Lotte was used to fatigue and incomprehension. However, inside the discolored darkness of the interval organ, her wakefulness fostered a pristine form of awareness. Moreover, her imperative to observe nourished her; the colors made her strong and healthy. Even while the wolf slept, the dark red of hares in the brush trickled along the smooth contours of her inner cheeks. If the Wolf Interval awoke and caught the hare in its jaws, then she would be nourished by that as well—the wolf's pleasure in feeding would always be a thick, white lump close to her tonsils.

Many biologists have developed theories about the nature of the symbiosis occurring between the passenger and the Wolf Interval, but few facts have been authenticated since the presumed extinction of the subspecies. We can now be assured that Lotte's vigilance even during the animal's sleep cycle aided the wolf in catching prey.

It has been exceedingly difficult to dislodge the image of the "wild child" or the "child raised by wolves" from the collective imagination surrounding the Wolf Interval. Canonical imagery of the Wolf Interval always displays the external signs of motherhood—heavy teats and bowed ribs—these signs are not trivial. Lotte, unlike Remus and Romulus, never suckled at her vehicle. Instead, the teats discharged a fluid that resembled milk, which Lotte called "spill."

> Spill would not nourish any animal. It was my waste product. The interval organ kept me clean and warm and well fed. It purified my body. The speculation regarding the motherhood of the Wolf Interval is strange; my vehicle was barren and I assume they all were.

In traditional illustrations, the Wolf Interval is often depicted lying on her side, curled around the milk-fattened lost child. Rarely did passengers willingly egress the interval organ; they preferred the tranquillity of that unspoiled interior. To adjust to the growth spurts of a young girl's adolescence, the Wolf Interval occasionally required one to four days of emptiness. Not only did this vacancy allow the interval organ tissue to regain some of its elasticity, but it also fortified the animal's immune system.

> Whenever my Wolf Interval urged me out of her body, she made such wretched sounds—almost a woman's pule. In the cold air, my feet and palms were too tender, so I shuffled on my knees (they were hardened from the position of the interval organ against the wolf's ribs). In the snows I stayed crouched between the Wolf Interval's front legs. In the summers I covered my skin in mud and long grasses, but my vehicle licked me clean again. If I smelled a settlement nearby, I would sneak to the clotheslines at night and steal bloomers or a silken chemise. Silk was the only fabric I didn't find abhorrent. These I would roll into a ball and toss onto the back of my Wolf Interval's tongue so that she would swallow them. But she fought me. She spit the clothes up, and rent them in her jaws. She refused to allow any other foreign objects into her body.

It is here, with the dirty child stationed outside the Wolf Interval, that we begin to understand why so many of these shy creatures, masked in false maternity, were hunted and captured in the early decades of the twentieth century. The authors of the Interval Passenger Reeducation Act (IPRA) of 1922 expressed their opinions on the encroachment of the wolves in this manner: "The vermin steal our daughters and expose them to degenerate instincts. What possible value could a woman sustain in raising her own child when a wild animal threatens to usurp that fundamental role?"

To observe the regrettable aftereffects of IPRA, one only need visit the San Francisco Academy of Sciences, nestled in a grid of severely trimmed sycamore trees inside Golden Gate Park. In the building's atrium, adjacent to the albino alligator pit, is a glass enclosure containing an unusually large stuffed she-wolf. Her coat has been sun faded from dark black to reddish brown and the fur of her muzzle has been completely worn away, as though rubbed by numberless hands. Her blackened lips are curled over a pink-resin tongue—a benign pant. The long brass plaque at the display's base reads: *ATALANTA*. Her provenance is supplied on a tilted information sign in front of the case:

> Atalanta was captured in 1924 by newspaper reporter Clark Woodward at the request of William Randolph Hearst. At that time, Atalanta was assumed to be the last wild wolf in California, though there were six other wolf sightings over the next eighteen years. For close to a decade, she howled within Golden Gate Park's wolf enclosure. Field biologists, hoping to restore this noble predator to the state, are working diligently on a plan to create a wolf sanctuary in the Mono Basin.

The sign omits Atalanta's pedigree as a Wolf Interval as well as the startling information that she was euthanized in 1963. To this day, the Academy of Sciences has still not acknowledged the extraordinarily prolonged life of this animal or that of the young woman who was undoubtedly wrested from the wolf's body.

A majority of Atalanta's life continued out of the public eye and her interval organ was tested, but not without several men of small build sustaining severe injuries to their forearms, necks, and waists. Taxidermists, while preserving Atalanta's pelt, stuffed a chimpanzee skeleton into her interval organ as a private joke. No one found the skeleton or believed Atalanta to be an authentic Wolf Interval until the Loma

Prieta earthquake of 1989 severely damaged the Academy of Sciences. Her pelt split open and the hardened gray sack slipped out, rattling with the chimpanzee's bones.

REUNION

By the time Lotte was approximately twenty, her Wolf Interval had crossed the borders of twelve western states. Following a configuration of scents back to the Northwest, the animal and the woman returned to the outskirts of the town of R. Lotte recognized R. after her extended absence, due in part to a "greenish-brown color, opaque at the edges and lemon yellow at its transparent center" low in her esophagus.

At the time, Lotte had not been turned out in countless months, the need to do so having become especially rare given her petite and stable stature. In the woods at the edge of R., a feeling close to hunger wavered in her throat, though it certainly could have been a growl. For the first time in her travels, she wished to leave the boundaries of her vehicle. With great effort, she moved her hand from its position in front of her chest up to the sensitive and rough-textured aperture above her head. The Wolf Interval heaved and Lotte emerged, slick with saliva, her skin tan from the enzymes of her home. The wolf, feeling emptied and irritable, snapped at the air as though it were full of flies.

Lotte waited for her Wolf Interval to dote on her, to burrow her snout into the crook of her elbow, sniff the crown of her head, or lick her cold and shuddering muscles, but the animal did not deign to soothe her. With high-pricked ears and a wrinkled brow, she stared at Lotte squarely before she stood and advanced into a glade. Lotte tried to follow on hand and knee. She found her limbs too aching even in the soft mud and wet grass.

As dusk advanced, Lotte tried to warm herself within a rotting log. She was timorous in that pulseless space, her skin raw against the roughness of the bark, the erratic twitch of insect legs. Drawn to the smell of nearby R., she rolled in the mud to affect a mottled garment. There had been a half-constructed house; there had been a warm, upright woman. Lotte's memories of R. manifested as an eddy of burgundy flinders.

She found the house dramatically changed. The front porch was now enclosed and a new large room clung awkwardly to the back of the structure. Without knocking, she opened the screen door and passed from the sunroom into the living room. The furniture was new; she rubbed a striped couch in gold velvet with her fingertips and licked the high polish of a highboy constructed in a fine dark wood.

"*Mother,*" a young girl called from the stairs. "A stranger is in our house!"

Adeline came from the kitchen with the lid of a Dutch oven in her hand, but dropped it to the floor when she saw her lost daughter hiding behind the potted ferns.

"Daughter?" she said.

Lotte kept her eyes on the chandelier, its swaying red-glass droplets.

"I am over here, Mother," said the girl on the stairs.

Repeating, "Oh my girl," Adeline small-stepped toward Lotte and clasped her by her wrists. Thinking of the rosy color of the word "family," Lotte opened her mouth and bit her mother on the stomach through a layer of beaded gray silk.

> I had forgotten the fundamental direction of speech—I thought all expression was digestible. Because I experienced so little pain within the interval organ, I did not understand the meaning of my mother's tears and screams. I did not let go of the cloth of her dress and the fold of her flesh until my teeth hurt and my half sister started pulling out handfuls of my thin, coarse hair.

REEDUCATION

> *Helena Coates, age thirty-two: Had I succumbed to the savagery of my situation, I would have been no better than an inessential organ within the beast. These wolves steal your youth. That is why they live so long; they absorb the passenger. May my young daughters be spared the temptation of lustful wandering.*

> *Lorraine Thompson, age fourteen: I could not read inside the wolf. Now that I can read, I intend to read many books. I would like to see a city. I would like to ride in the subway. I sew very well and my stitches are very straight. My favorite meal is beef stew.*

*Beth Englander, age twenty-two: The adjustment was
hard, but now I am a telephone operator. I am indeed
grateful to serve my country in these trying times.*

*Lotte Pfeiffer, age twenty-nine: If I had grown old and
died within the wolf, I would have never known my
sister, Emily. One wishes to die accompanied, but this is
best with one's original family. I am learning how to be a
nurse and care for wounds.*

—Excerpts from IPRA handbook of 1933

ADDENDUM

How do I read this book?
Carefully, as though you are about to enter the mouth of the wolf.

For those who have forgotten, the wolf interval is a mobile dwelling.
How does a nomad dwell?

Dwell. From the Old English *dwellen*, "lead astray, hinder, delay." Of
Germanic origin; related to Middle Dutch *dwellen*, "stun, perplex,"
and Old Norse *dvelja*, "delay, tarry, stay."

* * *

A TRUTH

I would like to explain why I never bought a mobile dwelling, why I
decided to spend the money I had saved on a Vandercook letterpress
instead. Why did I choose a dying profession? To explain myself, I
wish I could reprint the last illustration of C. R. Bailey's booklet, but
in moves across the country in search of cities hospitable to the book,
I have lost a number of treasured papers. Let me instead try to con-
centrate on the sensation of Bailey's book, the intention of its pages.
     I opened the last folded illustration and saw two hands at the edge
of the paper, two hands so similar to my own. The hands on the page
pulled back the lips of a wolf into the shape of an inverted V, ex-
posing her teeth and the black circle of her throat. That is why all my
books have spaces like ribs, like throats. The book is an interval organ.
     If you are ready to fold your sheet into the initial folio, remember

the pleasure of this task. Align your corners and crease your sheet, first with your thumb, then with your bone folder. Admire the spine you've created—the backbone of the word. But in creating a book, there is always the need to reduce. Slide your pallet knife inside the crease and tear it in half. The paper will pant if your movements are circular. The new edge won't be perfect—it will have its teeth. This is a mark of your work, your hands. You are making a mouth for an author. You are reproducing your own mouth. The contentment of this task should feel like an expanding white mass on your tongue, lacy at the edges.

Circumstantial Evidence
Lynne Tillman

A SUNNY TIME

ALL OF A SUDDEN I liked birds, their shapes and colors, downy coats, and fluffy, rounded chests. I had, as a child, liked parakeets, had one or two, always ice blue, but it turned into childish love. Maybe now it had returned in a grown-up form. I don't know when birds on the street or flying around outside or in parks, or nesting in branches of trees began to call to me, attract my attention, attract in the sense that I was unable not to watch them as they bathed in dirt or sang to each other, but they did.

It might have been around the time I was walking on Lafayette Street, walking home from the Time Café on Lafayette, where I spent many hours at lunch or dinner for about ten years. The Time Café had high ceilings and an open space, and during the day, a lot of sun came through its windows. It was a sunny place to sit, and there was also an outdoor patio for drinks or brunch. In the evening, in the cellar or basement, there was a lounge and below that a nightclub called Fez, which I went to often, to give a reading, hear one, hear music, watch performance.

I was walking along Lafayette, going uptown, going home, when I saw a man and a little girl, maybe eight, standing on the sidewalk, looking intently at a fire escape. The man, probably her father, held a shoe box. This excited my curiosity—a man, girl, shoe box, the two looking up, concentrating—and I looked too. They were watching a small, brightly colored bird, one usually seen, in Manhattan, in pet stores. The bird sat on the rail of the fire escape. I watched also for a while, then walked on, past the Colonnades, the beautiful apartments built in the eighteenth century, where Edmund White once lived, and where I visited him seconds before the AIDS epidemic, so, in retrospect, everything seemed good and sunny then.

As I walked on, I saw a doorman standing at the entrance to a building. The bird had alighted on his broad left shoulder, just sitting there. I called out to the man, Grab that bird on your shoulder, and

151

in an instant he scooped it up. I don't think he knew it was there, it was so little and light. I asked him for the bird, for the father and daughter I'd seen trying to catch it up the road, and he handed it to me, without a word. I would call the moment dreamlike, but it wasn't, it was something else, and I carried the colorful bird in the palm of my hand back down Lafayette to the girl and her father, still standing at that spot.

I strode up to them, and said, Here's the bird. I handed it to them. They took it, astonishment almost on their faces, but not really that, and they said nothing. They just looked at me, and I walked away. When I think about this absurd incident, I wonder at the silence of it, even the silence of the bird in my hand.

BASIE'S DISAPPOINTMENT

He was seven weeks old and just two pounds, when David and I rescued him from the New York City kill shelter. The woman taking care of the kittens warned us against him, because he was wild. He's crazy, she said. They called him José.

(Later I tried calling him José. But the name didn't work, because my first association to "José" was José Feliciano and his cover of the Doors' "Light My Fire.")

The woman brought in "José" for me to hold, and he squirmed. But then, when I held him more firmly, he looked into my eyes. We gazed at each other long enough, and he kept still long enough, that we really looked into each other's eyes.

We'll take him, I told the doubting woman.

We called him Basie, after the Count, and because the recently dead cat that Basie followed, Louis, had been named after Louis Armstrong. Louis was only eight when he died of a heart attack. He supposedly had lymphoma when he was five, but he probably hadn't. He was born with a very bad heart.

Louis looked like an Egyptian blue, with a sleek blue-gray coat and a long, narrow face and nose. He was very elegant. Basie was a tuxedo gray kitten, with a white belly. I had wanted another gray cat.

Basie came home the next day, after he was fixed, and we needed to introduce him to Chester, our ten-year-old cat. David had said we could adopt a kitten only if we did it quickly, before Chester became used to living alone. Chester probably would have liked to live alone.

He was a long-suffering cat. First he had to put up with Louis, whom he mothered from when Louis was an eight-week-old kitten. Then Louis grew up and dominated Chester, he bullied him, even terrorized him. He would scare Chester off the spot on our bed where he liked to nap.

Also, Chester's beginnings were brutal. He was rescued from a Bronx vacant lot. When we adopted him at four months old, he had a sore foot wrapped in bandages. The shelter people said he would recover fully. But Chester still often holds that hurt paw up in the air, just above the floor, because he learned, or was conditioned, not to put it down when he was a kitten.

Chester was a classic tabby kitten, and beautiful. But he seemed to have less and less energy every day. It wasn't normal for a kitten not to play. He was soon diagnosed with distemper, which kills many cats. Chester was shot full of antibiotics by a determined vet. It was over a long, sad weekend in the vet's office, the same weekend John F. Kennedy Jr.'s plane was lost, but Chester survived. I believe his lonely hospitalization increased his fear of humans. But Chester is another story.

When we brought Basie home, Chester sniffed him in his carrier, and when we let him out of his carrier, Basie instantly, fearlessly, ran over to Chester. Chester was startled, and hurried away.

Two days later, Chester accepted Basie, as he had Louis, and started licking and mothering him, the "good-enough mother." Then, like Louis, Basie grew up to dominate Chester, though Basie still wants Chester to love him, lick him, and even shares some wet food with him at night. Louis didn't care.

Basie had looked into my eyes that first time I held him, and when we brought him home, and he sat by me on the bed, a tiny little kitten, he continued to look into my eyes, and I looked into his. For many moments, he and I would stare at each other. One day, to my surprise, little Basie reached out, with a tiny paw, but tentatively, to touch my eye. No other cat I've encountered had ever wanted to touch my eye. I stopped him, gently. But Basie was very curious about the eyes he was looking into. He wanted to know what they were. So it happened again and again, for two months at least. He'd reach out and try to touch my eye. To pat it. Nothing aggressive.

During this time, I felt Basie wanted to communicate with me. I spoke to him, and he appeared to listen. I talked. He didn't understand but he tried. It was in his eyes. He was so young. He'd cock his head to one side and listen.

When he was around six months old, Basie changed. He stopped trying to talk to me. Or he realized he couldn't understand. That was when he stopped trying to touch my eye. Basie still likes to stare and look into people's eyes. He will look in whatever direction David and I point. When we talk about some mischief Basie's gotten into, he will go right to the area where he misbehaved. But it's different. He's different. I once thought he was disappointed at the limits between us, between him and people, but if he was, I think he's forgotten.

Conversion Testimony
Rick Moody

IT WAS A ROUTINE DAY, the day of my conversion. I was at an artists' retreat in Peterborough, New Hampshire, the MacDowell Colony. I was lucky to be there, and in an ambitious moment in my career, working on finishing my novel *Purple America*, falling in love with someone on the premises, taking in spring in New Hampshire, hiking Mount Monadnock, meeting and greeting, full of dreams. It was seven years since my last drink. I would call my approach to what I put in my body—excepting the injunction against drugs and alcohol—*unenlightened*. I ate what I wanted to eat, and while I took seriously the suggestion (among my community of sober friends) that I have a spiritual life, I wasn't yet preoccupied with the resolution of that question. I took the spiritual stuff in stride. I'd read a book on Zen and then toss it aside and read a book on the Quakers. It was the semi-examined life. As regards the evening in question: I always hated the moments before dinners at the artists' colonies, those awkward quarter hours where you had to talk about what you had done that day. And so: There was no reason to suspect that this particular quarter hour would usher in a complete change in my life. And the chef who cooked dinner that night had no reason to suspect she would change my life. But she did. She changed my life when she decided that that night's dinner was going to consist of *meat loaf*.

I have always kind of hated *meat loaf*. The presence of the word *loaf* in the phrase *meat loaf* seems to be part of the problem. That phrase *meat loaf* has always been repellent to me, even when I was a child, and even though I ate meat (*flesh*, as vegetarians sometimes call it), I always thought there was something highly suspect about *meat loaf*. I have the same feeling about *pot roast*. Somehow these words weren't meant to go together: *pot* and *roast*, *meat* and *loaf*, and the idea of *meat* being packaged like a bread product is inappropriate to me. Then as now. In my thirties, I made my peace with the phrase, and had been known to eat *meat loaf* on occasion, especially in my penniless twenties, because I didn't have the money to make sure the next meal would be as good as the one in front of me.

Rick Moody

Nevertheless, when the cart of meat loaf was wheeled out of the kitchen at MacDowell, I felt some dark stirrings. This was not entirely unusual. Though I was not a finicky eater (I would eat, for example, almost any kind of hamburger, no matter how dingy the precinct in which it was assembled), I had, as well, a tendency to find *mac and cheese* totally nauseating, and had heaved it up once as a child, never to eat it willingly again. It was not, at first, disturbing to me to find the *meat loaf* at MacDowell was nauseating. What was novel was *why* it was nauseating. I remember the platter of *meat loaf* having a crimson hue, almost like it was a red velvet cake. My further recollection is of a kind of gray/tan base material over which some ketchup had been drizzled, nouvelle cuisine style, to create a lively and animated plate of gore. I had a thought about the *meat loaf* I will never forget. I thought: *car crash.*

That is, the meat loaf did not look like food, but rather like somebody's femur and quadriceps at a car crash or at a crime scene or in one of those preposterously violent war scenes that you might see in a film, when the film is attempting to be *realistic*. The meat loaf was disgusting to me, utterly abject, and just as abject was the proposition that I was meant to *eat* this gore that had been shoveled up from a soft shoulder. That I should eat it and engage in conversation with the other colonists, that I should pretend nothing was wrong: These obstacles were, suddenly, insurmountable. I can remember no more of the night, except that I didn't eat the *meat loaf,* and probably ate five extra pieces of bread and an extra helping of salad, and I didn't give the experience of abjection a second thought, really, because I had in no way prepared for abjection that night; it had overcome me, which I suppose is how *conversions* take place. Not because of persuasion (I have known a great number of vegetarians in my life), but because of an alignment of circumstances. I did not consider the possibility of renouncing *meat* that night. I imagined, simply, that I would never again eat *meat loaf.*

However, the feeling of abjection quickly extended itself to all *beef products.* As I say: I had no thought initially about the cow, the animal, who provided the *meat* in the *meat loaf.* As with most philosophical regeneration in my life, I could not make the journey until the old way of thinking was completely emptied of relevance. And so it seemed to me in this transitional period that *beef* was a constituent element in *meat loaf,* and probably, therefore, I should avoid *beef.* This was not, as I recall it, a difficult thing to give up, and there was no real cost to doing so. Every right-thinking person recognizes

156

that there are reasonable health-related criteria for avoiding beef. Hamburgers are petri dishes for listeria and salmonella, all manner of bacteria, and high cholesterol is a likely outcome after a lifetime of red meat, and I have heart disease in my family. Even worse, there is bovine growth hormone to contend with, excessive use of antibiotics in the food chain, etc. People approaching middle age, these days, often come to rethink *red meat*, unless they are ranchers or reactionaries who feel that there is some kind of pride inherent in red meat. I gave it up easily, and I don't remember regretting it.

There things stood for a while. I came to think I'd had an inexplicable reaction to the *meat loaf*, a bodily one, like Franny Glass passing out while saying the Jesus Prayer. A conversion experience. I did not care to look deeply into my own motives. Abjection is powerfully physical. One does not want to drink blood, one does not want to touch the excremental wastes of the human body, one avoids maggoty strongholds. Such was my experience of *beef*. I didn't *want* to think of a steak as the thigh of any animal, but I could not, it seemed, avoid doing so. As it happens, for eight or nine years in the nineties I taught at a summer program at Bennington College, and Bennington College, for reasons that are not hard to fathom (alternative culture! students! environmental consciousness!), had vegetarian fare in abundance in the cafeteria. One summer while I was teaching there (1998, I think) I decided to see if I could go a week without eating any *meat*.

Those Bennington vegetarians sure were lucky. Not a meal went by during my week of vegetarian experiment in which there was not some rather delicious mushroom item next pan over to the sinews of animal body that were laid out in charming fillets for those who were still that way inclined. I chose the vegetarian fare, and I also became an adept at odd configurations of salad at the salad bar (just beets and chickpeas! only things that are yellow! extra helpings of hot pepper!), and quickly the week was at an end, and it was a welcome surprise. I decided to go for another week. This was not a hard decision to make, then, because I was just biting off a little bit at a time. There were two qualifications, though. I was not ready to renounce *bacon*, though I had not eaten any recently, and I was not ready to renounce fish.

It seems to me I have gotten this far into this account without thinking through the symbolism of abjection, without looking for the ideas underneath abjection in my own case. It's one thing to say that you are phobic about certain meat products. This describes a truth up to a point. It's irrefutable, as long as you have physical symptoms. In a way, bodily symptoms of abjection are powerful precisely because there is no rhetoric attached to them. But that doesn't mean you aren't operating in a symbolic field, in the same way a dream ushers in its symbols. (I have a long-standing and pretty well-documented phobia of telephones, and I have spent many years trying to describe the origin, meaning, and purpose of my refusal to talk on the telephone. The reason to bring up this phobia now is simply to say that my telephone phobia is self-evidently full of meaning for me personally. There are historical and symbolically freighted reasons why I hate the telephone. So why not ask the same things about my feelings of disgust about *meat*?) Julia Kristeva created a blueprint for discussions of abjection in her essay on the subject, *Powers of Horror*, with results that were startling and important to me back in the time when I read a lot of theory. If abjection happens in your *whole body*, and its message there is complete, that doesn't mean it is not philosophical and intellectual. What does disgust about *meat* tell us about who we are?

So: When I was a child, we used to go shooting, right near where I now live (in Amenia, New York), on a dairy farm. Some friends of the family stocked their considerable acreage there with pheasant, and during the fall, when the fields were about to be plowed up, and the feed corn siloed, we traveled north and blasted away at the birds. The shooting part was bad, I agree, though since my earliest childhood there were dead pheasant nailed up in the garage of my house, and I was somehow used to it. My mother's father shot (and *trophy fished*), and my father shot, and our dog, a black Labrador retriever, was field trained in the traditional way. The hunt was a ritual in our family. Mercifully, I was a horrible shot. Apparently, I am just not meant to have a gun in my hands, and could never hit anything with either rifle or shotgun. Not even a clay pigeon was ever prey to me, nor ever shall be, now that I have renounced guns. But just the same I loved it out on the shooting trips. I loved the gray days, and the blustery days, and the threat that the Jeep was going to get stuck in the ruts of mud. I loved autumn. And yet the lessons of the dairy farm were more profound than this. I felt bad about the birds getting shot down, and I felt bad about the dog carrying the dead birds around in her mouth, and I felt bad about the cows on the dairy farm, who mainly seemed to stand around in their own wastes and moan plangently. And I felt bad for the dairy farmers themselves. They seemed dusty, weary, overburdened, and poor.

One day, we were running through the long, beautiful files of corn in autumn, and we—my sister, my brother, and I—came out by a mound near the river that ran through the valley there. The mound, it became apparent, had a bunch of hooves and parts of cows reaching out of it. This is my memory of the events, at any rate. A burial mound for whatever was left over of the cows, the sick cows, the last of the cows, the cow leavings. They came to this place, after they were useful no longer, and the farmer or his employees plowed up some dirt, and covered over the cow parts with a glaze of dirt and blood, and then left the whole infernal mess to rot. I had a profound sense, as a child, of the evil of that mound, the carnage of it, and of the loneliness of it. I felt, actually, as though not all the cattle were deceased. As though they were restless because of the way they were sacrificed. As though the bovine ghosts necessarily ambled around those environs, pawing at the ground and snorting with disquiet. In a kind of shock, we ran back to the shack where we were going to spend the night. Away from the burial mound. It was one of those moments of insight, one of those profound *bodily* insights: into the origin and end of all flesh.

In some way, the abjection of *meat*, for me, dates back to the sacrifice of the animals at the dairy farm. Lots of people, it seems to me now, are able to have this experience, the experience of learning about farming, *without* identifying with the animals, and without feeling compunction about eating animals, and I applaud them for their serenity. For whatever reason, I was not able, after a time, to go along with this cultural *blinding*. Perhaps part of the reason for the horror of the dairy farm, and the burial mound, was the problem of class. My class, the upper middle class, glorified narratives of subjection, the subjection of people and animals, but without ever explaining how the privilege came to be, at least to me. It was part of the aristocracy in those days that privilege came with the acreage. So of course there were dairy farmers who let us blast away at pheasant on their property, and of course there were dead cattle piled in one corner of the property. My having stumbled on this narrative of woe in the course of running around in the cornfields was a recognition of class, and it was hard not to feel, even if subject to delay, my eventual surfeiting of nausea.

I let go of bacon in 1999, but I think there was no wealth of bacon beforehand, in any event. With bacon it's mostly the curing agents that are the attractive part. *Simulated bacon* tastes great to me these days. I hung on to fish for a few more years. I let go of fish not because of conviction about the psychology of fish, but more because of dwindling fish stocks, the crisis of overfishing, the profound stupidity of the way we manage the oceans, the fact of Icelandic whaling, etc. Once I had renounced beef, chicken, poultry of any kind, pig, and lamb, fish was easy, and then there were not really any meats left that I was eating. It was hard not to conclude that I was a vegetarian, that the conversion had taken place without preparation. Upon concluding that I was a vegetarian, however, it seemed important, in some way, to have a *theory* of vegetarianism. Besides simply that *meat* disgusted me. Eventually, I came to believe that my idea of vegetarianism was this: It was wrong that nonhuman animals had been unable to consent to their being eaten. In the same way that I felt bad for the dead pheasant with the buckshot in them, coaxed out of their cages into the open expanses of the dairy farm, given an hour to wander off, then chased down and slaughtered, there was a feeling of injustice about the *eaten* that I couldn't and can't square with the civilized delicacy of mealtime. I couldn't and can't, somehow, eat the meal if the basic food group represented there is the food group called *injustice*.

Moreover: I feel powerfully that nonhuman animals have inner lives, senses of self, for which I have no demonstrable evidence of a scientific sort, but merely anecdotal evidence and firsthand experience. I base this idea on the fact that I am myself an animal and I have an inner life, and the only difference between me and a dog, for example, is computing power. I don't actually believe that computing power counts for much. This feeling about animals is an *effect* of the process in my life of abjection, vegetarianism, pacifism, religious and spiritual practice. And the end point of this thought about animals and their inner lives is, inevitably, compassion for the animals. This is a not very pleasant feeling to have sometimes. Animals are routinely tortured. We are against the torture of other human beings, or most people are against torture, but then we torture animals routinely, every day even. And if we don't participate in their torture, we profit from their torture, and this is painful to think about. I wore a black-leather motorcycle jacket for many years, and I loved that jacket, and Peter Singer advises it is OK to continue wearing a leather jacket if it was *already purchased*, but after a point the jacket just made me *feel bad*, just as the eating fish was making me feel bad, and I had to put the leather jacket in the closet.

I don't eat a lot of dairy, but I eat a little bit of yogurt, and I have been known to eat an egg if I can be certain it came from a *cruelty-free farm*, though I am aware that these words, *cruelty-free*, are more ambiguous than they ought to be, and some farms get away with things. I have eaten lobster a few times, once a year or so, despite the commentary by my friend David Foster Wallace. I do kill hornets and yellow jackets if they get in the house. I have had a ladybug plague at my residence in the winter in recent years, and if I manually removed them all to the outside, which I have done many tens of times, I literally would do nothing else but remove ladybugs. I have therefore dispatched an army of ladybugs to the hereafter, with keen regrets. And so my vegetarian results are mixed, despite the power of my conversion.

The murderousness of human beings extends to me too, that is, but I try to do the least damage I can do and to let the animals be where the animals are. There was a bat in the dining room where I ate dinner just tonight, and people mobilized in an attempt to send the bat on its way. But the bat is just *being a bat*. There's a line in Ram Dass, which I am herewith recreating from memory: "I believe that faith can remove mountains. I literally believe this to be true. But upon reflection I have come to see that the mountains are exactly where they belong." If you take this thought too far, you will allow for murderous rage of humans. (Dante says something similar about this in *Paradiso*: "Thus it can be that, in the selfsame species, some trees bear better fruit and some bear worse, and men are born with different temperaments" (Allen Mandelbaum translation).) But in my interpretation of Ram Dass, what he's saying is: *Let the animals be who they are.*

The drama of conversion is to be found in the fact that even though it happens suddenly, or has its metaphorical white light, it can undo itself at any moment. And yet, despite the slightly impure condition of my conversion, it has now lasted for a full fifteen years. I offer these remarks on the lives of the nonhumans for those whose conversion might come soon.

Three Poems
Sandra Meek

FLIGHT CAGE

Aviculturalists prefer their birds in naturalistic
open-style aviaries unlike this hospital's
gift-store-Valentine's diorama I keep
looping back to, avoiding Surgical Waiting's
gregarious and *nest sleepers* stocked
with board games or pillows. Behind glass, a lone
Tri-Colored Nun Finch; two Frosted
Peach Canaries clutch frizzing fists of rope,
basket nests dangling at the apogee
of kissing Ceramic Hedgehogs. An aluminum tree
shivers the landing of Zebra and Star
Finches who settle among badges

of red-felt hearts. So tiny, these birds, nothing
like the only Bohemian Waxwing I've ever
spotted in my yard or yesterday's stains
left against the glass he'd
flung himself hard to death at, spatters inked
so darkly purple who would believe
a living heart had pumped them.
Ominous, one day before my father's last
presurgery recital for his bed's hem of interns
how the three-years-ago surgeon cracked
open his chest to discover the porcelain aorta that

couldn't be clamped. Lips lecture-pursed, my father's
right hand punctuates air in professorial
mudra, thumb pressed to index finger:
knowledge mudra, though he doesn't
know it. Pinky winged
ever skyward, touch middle fingers

to thumb, and you'd get *heart mudra*. No glossy
crimson card stock, the oldest
surviving Valentine's a poem that Charles, Duke
of Orléans, penned his wife from his
Tower of London chamber, imprisoned
since the Battle of Agincourt, famous for the first
mass use of the English longbow
made of yew so scarce by 1472 a Statute
of Westminster mandated every docking ship deliver
per tun of goods, four bowstaves yew. Four hours
post pre-op, Gloster Fancy Canaries

and European Goldfinches hold court
inches from the window buttressed
by tiny tin trays of birdseed rainbowed brightly
as sugar sprinkles on the Inaugural Day cake
giddy staff, paper flags cocked
from surgical caps, carry
away from the cafeteria across
the atrium from Pintail Whydahs and Red-Headed
Parrot Finches crisscrossing the glassed air
of Society Finches which do not occur

in the wild. Ditto this Stuffed Goose
and Gander in Wedding Veil and Tuxedo
Jacket centering the view you could enter
in a free-flight hall where bird-watchers
sail through curtains of cords and every door
is wire-netted. The door
through my father's ribs was wired
shut three years ago, bracing
that surgery's failure, the damaged valve left flailing like a tiny

broken wing. The world's largest aviary breaks
into thunder on the hour, sanctuary dome spattering
rain to cordate leaves which twitch like the necks
of perching birds, listening: Blue-Faced
Parrot Finches, Blue-Capped Cordon
Bleu Finches—Blue Babies' formerly
fatally flawed hearts surgeons learned to resculpt
fifty years ago but it's my elderly

163

father floating above me in a surgical theater
undergoing *apico-aortic conduit implantation*, his heart to be
punched and stitched to a plastic stint tipped
with the pig valve that for years could very well
save his life. What makes this
experimental isn't the blood's
radical rerouting but the heart kept
continuously beating. The myth
about hummingbirds is perpetual

motion, that their wings
must never stall: Turtle doves the first aviaries
perpetually stilled were continuously fed
millet sweetened with wine, dried figs chewed to pulp
to plump them for market, but these bright,
slight birds flitting their hospital home are
not for sale, and caging may or may not
save them from the narrowing tunnel
of extinction that also holds the ancient
Egyptian belief if your heart weighs lighter
than the Feather of Maat, you will join
Osiris in the afterlife, but if you fail the scales
the demon Ammut will eat your heart and thus

vanish your soul. What percent of a feather
frames a passage for air? 1651, a freak accident leaves air
free-flowing the gaping chest
of an aristocrat's son; his pumping heart
could be directly observed, even
touched, as did King Charles the First
of England, that royal hand reaching through mystery's
swung-open cage. None of this hurt
the young man, who, history writes, lived out
a normal life span. The numbers

line up in the signage, but how do they measure
wingspan for these tiny blips
of turquoise or magenta, Gouldian Finches
in caps bright and variable as the surgeon team's
sharp relief to the puffy showerlike one
in spaceman silver the pre-op nurse

beknighted my father with as the lead doctor drew
a finger across his chest to show

where they would cut. When Hanuman tore open
his own chest it was to reveal how literal
his fidelity, the beloved faces of Ram
and Sita tattooed on his still-
beating heart, stamped indelibly as the ♥
first imprinted on coins of Cyrene in homage
to the Silphium seedpod, the plant, reliable
birth control, enriching that North African
city-state until harvested, yes,

to extinction. Layson Honeyeater, Black
Mamo, Passenger Pigeon, Crested
Sheldrake: How many species of birds
have gone missing since the 1904 St. Louis
World's Fair raised in wire the world's largest
flight cage, before aviaries evolved to glassed
miniature natural habitats or that of the latest
upcoming holiday for which loopy
cursive cards and small stuffed animals
are available at the hospital
gift store along with heart pillows
to cushion the hurt of a loved one's post-

surgical coughing? You never know
who will survive to the point
of that pain; my father may simply
walk out of this place with his name
still braceleting his wrist, IV bruises blooming
papery skin like pressed tea roses
pasted along this hall culminating
in a velvet ♥ encircled by several cherubs

on the wing. ♥ has two wings but
the human heart, four chambers,
no wings. *Chamber* in the sixteenth century
meant a certain ordnance to fire
salutes from guns that replaced
the longbow, thereby allowing the yew's

165

return to British forests
and Cupid's tiny arrow to appear
merely quaint centering the hospital's
main entry into this lobby I've wandered

back to where on a dozen televisions
the new president has just
sworn his oath; in the broadcast
small thunder of a 21-gun salute, departing visitors
paused before the screens move on
into their day, gleaming automatic doors
sliding open to the freshly manicured wing
of hedge flagging the hospital's
brick facade where an early spring's late morning lilts
into music, scattered chirpings
rising from the green.

RIVER HORSE (*HIPPOPOTAMUS AMPHIBIUS*),
OKAVANGO DELTA

What seemed a scattering of grass-torn seeds clarifies

as levitation, my lap's notebook
dusted with wings—midges both paper

and ink, breath and alphabet, as Shadrach releases us

from shore, poling the *mokoro*-trafficked clear-cut
Recalling the fossil of your longing

for elsewhere, what golden orb spiders, reed
to reed, have veiled with webs I can't help

but raze, my face both bow and blade,
an unhoused spider's dark filigree of amber pearls

briefly jeweling my hand. What's lost

most remains: Each spindled shadow's the stain
of a long-gone season's deeper green

fringing these waters my twenty-years-ago husband
scrubbed his wedding ring away to

with a frying pan's grit, only our guide urging return
to sift the shifting sand of those sweet shallows we'd

long since decamped. This much

I've learned—what's rinsed in flow
roots in sand; what rises from flood dries still

to a bristling hiss. *Hippo grass,* your food
and your shelter, can grow so rich it starves

the channel, and so itself, though

however beautifully balanced to clot
your every need, even the most perfect lagoon you'll

eventually abandon. Invisible,
mute, the current I trail my fingers to braids

an elaborate calligraphy: Lily stems snarled

to drowned bouquets beneath a leaf-fanned surface
undulating with midge-drenched blooms

as Shadrach names each aquatic grass
and flower—Vein Ink, Bullrush, Riverbed Tea, Magic

Quarri—before landing a half-swamped island
for game walking, a pack lunch we share, cigarettes he swears

he's giving up. No animals in sight, he names me

the trees—Jackal Berry, Leadwood, Rain—that fashioned a history
we both remember: dugouts his boat only mimics now

167

in fiberglass, no longer to feed the diminishing
of trees long lost to the shoulders

of tomorrow's sand road, *white tarmac* ashen as the view

I'll abandon, a room's mosquito net wound
to a gauze chandelier hovering above a still

made-up bed. Ashen as the museum's
glassed remains: *Hippopotamus amphibius*, fetus

decades bleaching. How far you've traveled, River

Horse, from Herodotus, from Job's Behemoth, *the first
of the works of God*, to this doll-perfect

stall, a half-formed smile's unlit wick
clipped before the first flare

of breath, before a single letting go
to sink to the safety of sand, river bottom you would

have so deftly run. Animated here only

in freeze: a diorama's painted background for birds
dangling in faux flight—Fishing Eagle,

Orange Hornbill, Red-Eyed Dove
whose call Shadrach echoed so I might know it

after, alone—when I would hear it, still unshored

by memory, his hand on my shoulder
to turn me not to him but

to you, River Horse, finally skating the pooled horizon
as if all you needed of world was water

and sky: not the halo of *blood sweat* that saves you
from burn; not the failing sun, the golden noose

of late afternoon light you rose through, that immersion
in warmth the ghost of a palm too briefly

lingering—Shadrach, the one who entered the flame
in faith, who embraced the fire,

who was not consumed.

STILL LIFE WITH ADOLESCENT POSSUM
AND MIDLIFE CRISIS

Midnight's staccato, the dog's warning bark, heralded
your backyard debut: bayed to the chain-
link curtain, in my flashlight's
spotlight, you, a perfect tableau
the dog's eager breath fogged but failed
to dampen, your throat sporting
the fur stole of its costumed
unbreathing, your limp tail's pink curl nearly
noosing your skull's bone Mohawk—sagittal crest
in spectacular stasis a nod
to your larger-than-life predecessor, role first
created by stone. Your unblinking eyes, a gold scrim—bourbon
and ground glass. A dream

artist's model, how you could hold
to gesture: You survived by convincing
survival was beyond you, death a diversion
you cued from your pores I'd chase
with drugstore perfumes.
Oh stacked vials of pills, oh sweet
rescue, razors beneath the tongue—melodrama
melded us but for your act's
one fatal flaw: youth
you hung to, thin hiss you couldn't resist
as I held you too close to breast
and bone, lifting your towel-swaddled, stiffened body
to safety's wreath

of long grass. What revived you to the serial
scatter of your kind wasn't
my light's lost audience, turning my back
to drag inside the dog now wildly
flinging himself at the gate
closed between you; any new moon
center-staging you, and you'd
hit asphalt, haunting the highway whose shoulder you live
to scavenge—dotted white line basting the abandoned
to *away*, fastest way out to the next

best thing. Your eyes' green-gold plates flashing
whose lonely headlights
this time, far from this yard's blackened
apron and the dog still
raking the fence for any
bitter lingering, dog I'm left calling
and calling from midnight's tar, your starry rain.

A Semi-Prehensile Lip
Edward Carey

THE MAN CALLED PAUL BUTTERBRODT filled his chair completely, which was a sofa. It was a giltwood sofa with double cane back and sides, and pale pink silk upholstery. Everything was oversized about Paul Butterbrodt—his boots, his breeches, his jacket, his cuffs, even his buttons. He had very thick hair that sat upon the top of his head like thatch. He was a very sensitive man, he cried often, at happy things as at sad. When he ate, his little fingers would stick out. He put seven lumps of sugar in his licorice water and stirred it with a long spoon, all the time kissing the air. He sometimes woke in a bad mood and on such days he spoke very little. Sometimes the wallpaper in his room disturbed him, it was of peacocks. All those eyes, from every corner, watching. He supposed, in his dark moods, that the peacocks might come to life, that there would be a terrible screeching, that he would be found on the floor scratched and pecked at, and the walls, once so colored with those birds and their staring feathers, would now be utterly blank, undecorated, they should have all flown away. Some days he did not like to be left alone, on other days he wished to see no one, and must be coaxed out at great effort.

Apart from the sofa, there were about the room, keeping him company, pieces of furniture of extraordinary delicacy and refinement, fragile, rare things, like him. There was a small writing desk of oak veneer and tulipwood, with Sèvres plaques. There was a D-shaped commode in carved walnut and two flanking side cabinets. An ebony Japanese lacquer secretary with a white marble top. There were twelve chestnut stools with needlepoint covers in two rows of six facing his sofa, which perhaps might originally have been an alcove bed. These stools were for his visitors.

Every evening, before the great unrest began, he would be seen in his excellently decorated room for six hours. Tickets were available at the door at a cost of three livres per person for a half-hour visit; elsewhere in the city Vaucanson's mechanical duck was two livres, Nicolet's tightrope walkers five. There were allowed to be twelve in his room at any time, but no more. The visitors were permitted to ask him questions but, typically, at least at first, they only looked. Everything he did was very novel to them. They viewed him as if he were not of their own species but some strange new animal gotten from far away, where perhaps all the natives were so excessive. As they looked at Paul Butterbrodt, the visitors considered size. They considered how some of us are very small and some not so, how some noses are grown considerable and some chins barely feature at all. Paul Butterbrodt made people think, some brains that were not accustomed to much deep thinking were jolted into activity at the sight of Paul Butterbrodt. He filled so much space, this one man, and they wondered, after a while, if that hurt him. They wondered which rooms, which doorways he would fit into, they wondered if he would fit into their familiar doorways and rooms, they wondered if he would fit into their lives. Generally they concluded that there was not room.

Since the visitors were sometimes too shy or too stunned before this titan to utter words themselves—whilst on contrary occasions they voiced rough and crude observations without a hint of shyness—he had learned to speak to them as they came in. He had discovered that for best results he should take the initiative. He greeted his visitors, no matter their looks or gestures, very graciously. Hoping it might be of interest to them, he told them about himself. And when he spoke, they considered, perhaps for the first time, what a miracle speech was, they were certainly a little impressed that this great achievement of flesh could talk, it was even shocking to them that he had a quiet, pleasant voice. His voice, they supposed, should have been as extraordinary as his body; it was disturbing to them that this great thing that had so much otherness about him should also have some sameness.

"Please do come in," he would say, "I am very glad to see you. My name is Paul Butterbrodt, how do you do? May I tell you, if it interests, if you were wondering, that I weigh 238 kilos. Do you care for hard facts? Or shall I tell you about an aunt I had who was fond of handkerchiefs? How are you all? How good of you to come to me. Indeed, perhaps you would not mind if I told you a little of myself. I hope you won't. Do, yes, do please sit down. Thank you so much."

He had been an eating prodigy since he was a baby, he had had a little sister who had not lasted, she had withered away, she was like a twist of sugar paper, so easily crumpled. Some things do not last. His parents, being Viennese confectioners, sugared him through his childhood and early adulthood. What years those were of lime-elderflower marzipan, of hazel krokant, of chamomile chocolate, how years later he would close his eyes and try very hard to recall the particular pleasure of a nougat waffle or rum bonfect, how he would love to place in his mouth a chocolate cat's tongue and as it dissolved feel the shades and tastes of his departed youth. The fatter he was the happier his parents were, the only way to keep him safe, they thought, was to endlessly feed him, but when the father had been blinded by an exploding vat of molasses and when his mother slipped on iced cherries and broke her head open upon the flagstones, poor Paul had fallen into new company. His girth being commented upon wherever he went, he at last came to the attention of traveling showmen.

"What do I have to do?" he asked.

"Eat," they said, "just eat. A good deal of eating."

Tearfully, he left his homeland forever. He toured then, he visited Prague, Lyon, Milan, Vilna, Riga, he had even seen the Coliseum of Rome—indeed he had been positioned in a tent outside it. He was not always well cared for, sometimes his clothes were not changed, but always he was fed. Paul would say, rubbing his eyes with his pudgy fists, "I am always very hungry, I am never full. The more I travel from home, the hungrier I feel. Nothing, no amount, can ever satisfy. When shall the hungry feeling leave?"

He arrived one afternoon in Paris, and even upon the Boulevard du Temple, where the entertainers are based. Suffering from indigestion and a running sore upon his left leg after toppling from his booth onto a wooden stake, hot and shivery as he was, a new showman had successfully bargained for him, and he changed hands. This new man, Monsieur Tallier, shaped like an owl with thick eyebrows and round head, was not unkind. He kept also two albinos from Guadeloupe, young, wide-eyed men who stuck to their own company, whom Paul Butterbrodt saw very rarely. Tallier was a soothing presence, he was very encouraging and complimentary. He touched Paul very lightly on his thigh, inquiring daily into how he felt. Slowly, many mouthfuls later, he was brought back to health and full girth by kindness, by gentleness, and by taking him on outings to other boulevard attractions. It was during one such excursion that Paul Butterbrodt saw something he had never thought possible before, something that moved him very deeply.

The rhinoceros that lived upon the boulevard very quickly became his very favorite excursion. For that leathery, wrinkled creature, Paul

Butterbrodt grew a great attachment. From the very beginning, from the intensity of its smell before he had even entered the beast's tent—for no amount of fresh juniper, thyme, or rosemary could extinguish the potent, musky aroma of the creature—Paul felt a great shifting inside him. He did not know that such a thing ever could be. He came back every day. He brought small gifts with him— some oats, some fruit, some pastries. The keeper, an overdressed, overscented creature, was very happy for this man to feed his rhinoceros for free. Paul Butterbrodt took to singing the beast some songs he had learned as a child back in Vienna, such as the "Song of the Three Holy Kings" and "I'm Not Tired, I'm Not Sleepy," and soon it seemed to him the animal reacted particularly when he appeared. In his turn, he heard the many noises of the rhinoceros. Paul Butterbrodt would say the great gray monster had a vocal range of considerable variety and mystery. Sometimes Louis, for that was the rhino's name, let out a high screech as of an animal a tenth of its size. Sometimes he made deafening noises similar to the sawing of wood— sounds that filled the tent and could be a little frightening, for you felt your very soul was being cut into. Sometimes he made a very deep gurgling noise that sounded as if it came from the bottom of a well, a distant booming of a beautiful voice caught deep within. "A strange melancholic singing," Paul called it. "Listen, Louis is singing back to me. It is such a song, a song of distant lands."

The history of the rhinoceros was well known. Louis had been taken from faraway Africa when only seven months old. He was to be presented to Louis XV from the Comte de Palet, who had hoped by this gift to return to court and to favor with his king, whom he had insulted by letting drop a careless remark about Madame de Pompadour. But Louis XV, unbeknownst to the crew of the *Dufferin* just set sail from the Côte d'Ivoire, bound for Bordeaux, had just been given a different rhinoceros by Monsieur Chevalier, the French governor of Chandernagor. When a second rhinoceros was offered, the king refused to accept. How many rhinoceroses did he need in his palace menagerie? Besides, it was said that the king did not like the beast, it seemed a caricature of himself, the Bourbon conk was mimicked in the creature's large snout, its stockiness, its lack of grace too painfully reminded the king of his own thickening body, of his own mortality. He would not accept de Palet's gift: One rhino was a splendid thing, two rhinos were a mockery. The Comte de Palet, his hopes of commissions in African diamond mines buried, his dreams of marble all broken, had staked his future and his fortune on the beast

and regarding the animal now he saw how absurd and ugly, how pre-
posterous and misshapen those hopes had been. For the rest of his
life, in his dreams, in his waking moments, rotting away in his family's sole surviving property in Normandy, little more than a piggery
with a turret, he saw horned monsters everywhere. He died of heart
failure brought on by terror, in the middle of the night, hiding in a
cupboard. The spurned rhinoceros was bought by a boulevard enter-
tainer and was named after the monarch he was intended for. So
Louis grew up upon the boulevard, and came, after a time, to be visited every day by a considerable man with sweet gifts. It seemed to
Paul that he and Louis understood one another very well. When he
felt he could get close, he looked into an eye of the great beast, and
he swore he could see Louis smiling at him. Sometimes, later on,
when he offered the sweet things, Paul found he was able to touch a
little piece of rhino skin, it was not as hard as he had thought, it was
the surface, he said, of a beautiful map.

"Do you like odd-toed ungulates?" he would ask his visitors, and
when the visitor looked confused, he would say authoritatively, "An
odd-toed ungulate is a rhinoceros. A horned cow. The upper lip of a
rhinoceros is semi-prehensile! There is a rhinoceros upon the boulevard only a few minutes' walk from here. I cost very nearly as much
to keep as the rhinoceros of the boulevard. The rhinoceros consumes
twenty livres' worth of bread, and fourteen buckets, each, of water
and of beer every single day. Whereas I have two roast chickens,
some veal or mutton, ten livres' worth of bread, three bottles of
wine, and five pints of beer. I am taken to him, once a day, we have a
regular appointment with each other. He and I. We are great friends,
we shouldn't like a day to go by without seeing each other. We are
the twin highlights of the boulevard."

But then came the great terrifying changes in the country, and
nothing for a long while was certain. From the very start, Paul Butterbrodt was inconvenienced. On the fourteenth of July 1789, the
boulevard was closed, shutters were latched, doors were locked. Paul
stayed in all day listening to the loud report of cannons, watching, he
believed, the peacocks' feathers rustling. Later he heard, very nearby,
shouting and screaming. He hoped very much that Louis was all
right. He could not visit him the entire day. He fretted so.

He found him the next day a little startled, needing some comfort.
He bought a cone of almond and pistachio cream, it seemed, he
thought, to help. Throughout the following weeks and months, Paul
was able to bring less extravagant gifts than he liked, sometimes he

came with lettuces, sometimes potatoes, a beetroot, a melon, some apples, some days-old bread, some straw, only straw. By then there were fewer objects in his room. One by one they had been taken away and sold—the writing desk, the commode, the secretary. Soon the twelve stools were no longer filled every evening. People across the city were finding different entertainment. Some of the stools were sold off. Monsieur Tallier, Paul's manager, was worried for his future. He was not so kind as he used to be, he spent less time with Paul, and could be short-tempered. Soon there were only three stools in the room. Then one day Paul Butterbrodt had to fend for himself, the man who fed him was no longer there, he had left the city without a word, taking his albinos with him; the albinos were cheaper than Paul, though there were two of them. What hungry days followed. Paul had some savings with which he was able to keep his own room, for a while he remained open for visitors in the evenings, but very few came. The peacock wallpaper fell away in places. By then Paul Butterbrodt was no longer the impressive spectacle of former days. It depressed him that he weighed now only 180 kilos, at his peak he had been 238, the times had reduced him, he could no longer be fed so much. His days were filled with hunger, from the moment he woke up his hunger would be beside him, wherever he went his hunger followed, when he slept his hunger shifted against him, grinding its teeth, but that mounting pain was often lessened by a visit to Louis, where he sat, his stomach making furious grumbles. He was so much thinner a Paul Butterbrodt than he had used to be that people no longer stopped at the sight of him. He was becoming an ordinary-looking fellow, he did not stick out so much, his clothes billowed about him. He looked big still, certainly very large, but no longer improbable.

So long as Louis the rhinoceros survived, Paul felt he could himself continue. He dreamed of the pair of them living together in some peaceful, rural landscape. He told Louis of these dreams and it seemed to him that Louis listened very carefully. They should have no worries, there would be no threat, those days would not be hungry days anymore. But by then, it could no longer be denied, there was something very wrong with Louis. Paul's poor friend was beginning to have foot problems. A sloughing of his hooves, they had a certain softness and flakiness about them, bits hung off. Louis no longer made the deep singing well sound, he barked rather, and made hoarse squeaks that could be heard from one end of the boulevard to the other, from the Temple to the remains of the Bastille, very nearly demolished. "I am," said Paul, before that building, holding his tummy, "a ruined castle myself."

At night back in his room at the end of the day he took off his own shoes and regarded his own feet, he stroked them and carefully washed them in some vinegar, all the time thinking of Louis.

On the day when King Louis XVI, grandson to the king who refused a second rhinoceros, was apprehended at a small village called Varennes, attempting to flee the country, Paul detected swellings on Louis's forelegs and neck.

Then there were cannons firing at the Tuileries Palace and people shot in the gardens and the palace stormed, and people hacked people to morsels, screaming servants plunged from high floors. In the morning there were thick clouds of flies.

Then there were skin ulcers. Small blisters around Louis's eyes and ears, under his belly also. Flies in his pen too. Paul looked into one of the rhinoceros's eyes, Louis was not smiling now but appeared to have a fog about him, he wondered what his friend was thinking, the beast was such a mystery in those days, so hard to read.

By the time France had declared war against Austria, and the king and his family had been imprisoned in the Temple, just a few minutes' walk from the rhino's pen, Paul noted with distress that Louis had difficulty breathing. Meanwhile Paul's own body was changing, it reduced, it thinned out, his skin hung loose in places, there were many more wrinkles than before, there were stretch marks all about him. He had more skin than he needed. But despite it all, despite the dangerous times, and the deaths that occurred almost daily on the streets, Paul was in those days healthier than he had been before. No one came to visit him in his room anymore, he was forced to abandon it, he cried at leaving the peacocks on the paper. He rented a room of sparse, ordinary furniture from a family on the Rue du Bac, it had plain whitewashed walls, but every day, without fail, he took the journey across the river to see his friend on the boulevard.

With this new family, Paul Butterbrodt entered a period of comparative domestic happiness. The family treated him as any other human creature and made no fuss. At first he was offended, but in time he grew used to it. The family were haberdashers and had found in those new days a business making tricolor cockades. From time to time Paul was invited to earn a little money, or reduce his rent, by working beside them. In the family there was a maiden aunt, a root of a woman in her late thirties with some hair on her upper lip and deep, dark eyes. There were many moles on her skin. She sat next to

Paul while he worked on the ribbons, she liked to listen to the stories of his tour around European cities, such stories as other members of the family called unpatriotic. She would be entranced by his description of the sweet things his parents had made, the rest of the family warned against such subjects and even, when Paul insisted on sharing these histories, shouted and threatened to report him. The maiden aunt, Charlotte she was called, said she would take it upon herself to make Paul a good citizen. They sometimes sat together on a bench by the Île Saint-Louis looking at the Seine, Charlotte tutoring Paul on what was appropriate.

Everyday she said to him, "Citizen Butterbrodt, what are you thinking now?"

She worried for him and told him so, she gave him extra food. The extra food that she gave him was in fact her own meager rations, she was starving herself for Paul. That extra food Paul in his turn brought to Louis.

Charlotte had always been the dependable person in the family. She was the one who looked after her parents when they became ill and useless, she was the one who never asked for anything for herself but kept quiet and serious and practical. The rest of the family came to Charlotte not with their secrets, never with their longings, but when they wanted something fixed, or when they had an illness, or when they had run out of money. She perhaps kept her money close to herself, hoarded it a little, but who could blame her, how else could she protect herself when the ailing elderly years came? No, if she was a little tight, she could hardly be blamed for that. Charlotte was simply Charlotte, a woman of no surprises, who had over the thirty-seven years of her life grown a little strange looking. A little bumpy here, a little hairy where hair did not generally grow on females, along the jaw line, on the upper lip, down her arms, private, soft hairs of a long-endured loneliness. She was just Charlotte, she never required thinking of very much, she took up little space. The world could change, France could turn itself upside down, but Charlotte, save for a little hair growth, or a sprouting of moles, would always remain Charlotte. Only then, quite suddenly, she wasn't. There was in the house this newer Charlotte, louder than before, asking for things, giving opinions. Even demanding. Ever since the new tenant had come to the house, Charlotte had become difficult. She had moods that she had never had before, she laughed. The other members of her family did not recall hearing that laugh before, what an oddly alarming noise it was, at first they could not tell where it was coming from. She cried, this new Charlotte, the old Charlotte did not cry, Charlotte was a dry husk, but there she was shedding wetness. Charlotte, in late 1791, had become a little moist.

Charlotte was often now not at her desk or in her tiny room, often she went out. She spent money. She went out with Paul Butterbrodt, sometimes even when there was much work to be done. Once, at her insistence, she had gone with Paul to visit the rhinoceros. Paul was very uncomfortable at the idea and put off the day as long as he could, but the woman would not let the matter drop. So she came along. Barely noticeably, she shook her head at Louis, Paul supposed she wanted to tidy him up, but she was thinking, "What a thing to love. That creature, so far from home, is ridiculous on Paris streets. It will die soon, surely it will die soon, for such a thing cannot live long, and then I will comfort him."

Louis in his turn was very restless, he struck the floor with his hurting hooves, he stayed in the corner, and would not be encouraged out of it. No, the visit had not been a success. Paul would not take her along another time, though she often asked, he did not like her sitting with Louis, it was not right, she did not belong there. So Charlotte stayed home and waited for him. Whenever Paul came back from Louis, Charlotte always found him distant and moody. Only after an hour or two did his looks soften, then, with her gentle encouragement, he might tell her again the story of his life, and, on rare miraculous moments, he might pick up her creased clawlike hand and pat it, with great and undoubted fondness. Once, oh once, he even kissed it. Paul Butterbrodt considered, looking at this gnawn woman, that if his hunger were to take human shape, and he felt the pain to be a person in its own right, then this woman was what his hunger should look like. And, indeed, sitting next to her he did feel a little fuller.

Throughout December of 1792 Paul, still feeding the unhappy creature, noted in his friend a terrible increased buildup of oral plaque. Struggling to help in any way he could, he gave Louis his own bed blankets, and, in turn, Charlotte gave Paul one of hers. On the twenty-first of January, 1793, while so many people had congregated on the Place de la Révolution, formerly the Place Louis XV, while the Rue Saint-Antoine was lined with soldiers, while drums were beaten, when suddenly there came a great deafening cheer, a roar that sounded as if it were made by some single creature of immense proportions bellowing at the earth, Paul was with Louis. Paul heard the crowd's exclamation at the beheading of Louis XVI while he sat in tears not for the king, but for his ungulate friend, who in reaction to the unusual wave of noise passed a profuse and watery diarrhea.

There followed a period of terrible respiratory problems, the sound of Louis's labored breathing was hard for Paul to bear, and then Charlotte waited long hours for Paul to come home. Paul too was suffering from a cold, he let his own nose drip, he did not look after himself, Charlotte often told him so, wrapping her shawl around his neck. The great creature on the boulevard, its skin hanging down, seemed to be suffocating under its own weight.

On the thirtieth of July, 1793, Paul Butterbrodt early in the afternoon lumbered happily off to the boulevard, it was a pleasant sunny day, with pollen in the air, he went as usual to his greatest friend in the world. But his friend was not there. He found only traces about the pen, thick puddles in the straw. A portion of the pen's fencing was badly dented. There was a terrible new smell.

Louis's keeper, no longer so pleasant smelling in those days, was not present, in fact he was getting himself considerably drunk at Café Robert around the corner and would not return to his property until he was certain that Paul was no longer there. A stable boy had been left all on his own to deliver the news.

"Where's Louis?" Paul asked.

"He's gone, Citizen."

"When will he be back?"

"He shan't be, Citizen."

"I must go to him. Tell me, quickly now, where he is? Is he very ill? Oh, poor Louis!"

"Well, he's not well, Citizen. I'm afraid, no, he's not."

"But where is he, boy?"

"He's all over the place, Citizen. Poor fellow. He's not in one location, but, sorry to say, many. He's come apart."

"Speak plainly, oh tell me! Tell me!"

"I hate to tell you, but I fear I must be the one, I must do it, they said. I was given extra for it, though I'd just the same not have the food. He's dead, sir, all dead. This morning it happened. Just here. They were quick about it, but he is big, and not easy to get to. That skin is very thick."

"LOUIS!"

"I am so sorry, sir. I am."

"LOUIS! LOUIS!"

"Please sit down, sir, gather yourself. You've had a shock."

"LOUIS! LOUIS! LOUIS!"

"You are so miserable, aren't you?"

"It is all too much to bear! Too much altogether!"

"We knew you'd take it bad."

"Oh! God!"

"Steady, steady!"

"I am burst."

"Please, please now, it had to be done."

"Had to? Had to? Why did it have to?"

"He wasn't making any money."

"Money! Oh! Money!"

"He was costing, you see, rather than making."

"Where, please, I beg you, tell me, where is he now?"

"I was trying to say before. He's, how to put it, not all together. He's in different places. He's been sold, sir, to different people. Believe me, sir, I am sorry. Meat, sir."

"MEAT!"

"They're calling it horse, sir. I should've said."

Paul, trying to catch his breath, reading the signs properly in the soiled hay now, looking with hopeless eyes, understanding the smears, reading the history in all the mess, could be heard wailing up and down the Boulevard du Temple, bawling, inconsolable. Huge bellowing sounds he made, more animal than human. He quietened after a while and sat on one of the old boulevard benches and would not be distracted by anyone, he just sat there in a stupor, looking ahead vaguely. After a half hour he stood up, and proceeded to march up and down the boulevard, repeating the same sentence over and over.

"Louis!" he cried. "Louis! Louis!"

Paul shouted his message, pausing only to fill his great lungs. People tried to shut him up, he wouldn't even look at them, he marched on, pounding the boulevard floor.

"Louis! Louis! Louis!"

Then everyone left him alone. Only Charlotte, who had been fetched by the stable boy, wept beside him, begging him to come home. He shrugged her off, to her entreaties he only replied, "Louis! Louis! Louis!"

They arrested him, only when Paul's wrists had been bound did he quieten a little. They took him to the prison of La Force, and there, until his trial and even until he was put on the slide beneath the guillotine blade, he was heard muttering to himself only ever the same word over and over. When he saw among the crowd a wraith of a woman, with moles and some little hairs on her top lip, a skeleton in a greasy dress, tears in her eyes, just before the final moment, he said only, "Louis. Louis. Louis."

When it was over, and the crowd dispersed, the woman stayed there, she stayed through the day, seemingly unable to move, people knocked into her, she did not appear to feel them. At last from deep inside her came a sound she had never made before, nor one she would ever make again. A strange broken scratch of a noise.

Happy Chicken 1942–1944: A Memoir

Joyce Carol Oates

I WAS HER PET CHICKEN. I was Happy Chicken.

Of all the chickens on the little farm on the Millersport Highway, in the northern edge of Erie County in western New York State in that long-ago time in the early 1940s, just one was Happy Chicken, who was the curly-haired little girl's *pet chicken*.

The little girl was urged to think that she'd been the first to call me Happy Chicken. In fact, this had to have been one of the adults and probably the Mother.

Probably too it was the Mother, and not the little girl, who'd been the first to discover that of all the chickens, I was the only one who came eagerly clucking to the little girl *as if to say hello.*

Oh look! It's Happy Chicken coming to *say hello.*

The little girl and the little girl's mother laughed in delight that, without being called, I would peck in the dirt around the little girl's feet and I would *seem to bow* when my back was lightly stroked as a dog or a cat might *seem to bow* when petted.

The little girl loved it, my feathers were *soft*. Not *scratchy* and *smelly* like the feathers of the other, older chickens.

The little girl loved hearing my soft, querying clucks.

Early in the morning the little girl ran outside.

Happy! Happy Chicken! the little girl cried through small cupped hands.

And there I came running! Out of the shadowy barn, or out of the bushes, or from somewhere in the barnyard amidst other, ordinary dark-red-feathered chickens. A flutter of feathers, *cluck-cluck-cluck* lifting in a bright staccato *Here I am! I am Happy Chicken!*

The Grandfather shook his head in disbelief. Never saw anything like this—*Damn little chicken thinks he's a dog.*

It was a sign of how special Happy Chicken was, the family referred to me as *he*. As if I were not a mere hen among many, a brainless egg layer like the others, but a lively little *boy-chicken.*

For the others were just ordinary *hens* and scarcely distinguishable from one another unless you looked closely at them, which no one would do (except the Grandmother, who examined hens suspected of being "sickly").

Truly I was Happy Chicken! Truly, there was no other chicken like *me.*

My red-gleaming feathers bristled and shone more brightly than the feathers of the hens because I didn't roll in the dust as frequently as they did, in their (mostly futile) effort to rid themselves of mites. It wasn't just that Happy Chicken was young (for there were other chickens as young as I was, hatched from eggs within the year) but I was also far more intelligent, and more handsome; your eye was drawn to me, and only to me, out of the flock; for you could see from the special glow in my eyes and the way in which I came running before the little girl called me that I was *a very special little chicken.*

The yard between the barn and the farmhouse was cratered with shallow indentations in which chickens rolled and fluttered their wings like large demented birds who'd lost the ability to fly. Sometimes as many as a dozen chickens would be rolling in the dirt at the same time as in a bizarre coordinated modern dance; but the chickens were not coordinated and indeed took little heed of one another except, from time to time, to lash out with a petulant peck and an irritated cluck. When not rolling in the dirt (and in their own black, liquidy droppings), these chickens spent their time jabbing beaks into the dirt in search of grubs, bugs. Stray seeds left over from feeding time, bits of rotted fruit. Their happiness was not the happiness of Happy Chicken but a very dim kind of happiness, for a chicken's brain is hardly the size of a pea; what else can you expect? This was why Happy Chicken—that is, I—was such a surprise to the family, and such a delight.

My comb was rosy with health, erect with blood. My eyes were unusually alert and clear. But each eye on each side of the beak, how'd you expect us to see *coherently*? We see double, and one side of our brain dims down so that the other side can see precisely. That's how we know which direction in which to run, to escape predators.

Most of the time, however, most chickens don't. Don't escape predators.

Sometimes, they're so dumb they *run toward predators.* They do this when the predator is smart enough to freeze. They can't detect immobility, and they can't detect something staring at *them.*

I was not really one of *them*. To be identified as special, and recognized as Happy Chicken, meant that, though I was a chicken I was not *one of them*. And particularly, I was not a *silly, stupid hen*.

Sometimes—at special times—under close adult scrutiny, and always held snug in the little girl's arms—Happy Chicken was allowed *inside the farmhouse*.

No other chicken, not even Mr. Rooster, was ever allowed *inside the farmhouse*.

Never upstairs but downstairs in the "washroom" at the rear of the house—a room with a linoleum floor that contained a washing machine with a hand wringer, and where coats and boots were kept—this is where the little girl Joyce could bring me. But always held gently-but-firmly in her arms, or set onto the floor and held in place, in the washroom or—a few special times—in the kitchen, which opened off the washroom, where the Grandmother spent most of her time. Here, the little girl was given scraps of bread to feed me, on the linoleum floor.

And here I was sometimes allowed up in the little girl's lap, to be fussed over and petted.

The other chickens would've been jealous of me—except they were too stupid. They didn't *know*. Even Mr. Rooster didn't understand how Happy Chicken was privileged. Sometimes Mr. Rooster stationed himself at the back door of the farmhouse, clucking and preening, complaining, fretting, fluttering his wings, insisting upon the attention of everyone who went inside the house, or came outside, shamelessly looking for a treat, and when he didn't get a treat, squawking indignantly and threatening to peck with his sharp beak.

The little girl was frightened of Mr. Rooster, and hurried past him. The Mother and the Grandmother shooed Mr. Rooster away, for they were frightened of him too. The Grandfather and the Father laughed at Mr. Rooster and gave him a kick. They thought it was very funny, a goddamn bird trying to intimidate *them*.

Sometimes Happy Chicken was allowed in the washroom overnight, in a little box filled with straw, like a nest. And little Joyce petted me, and fussed over me, and fed me special treats.

Happy Chicken! You are so pretty.

. . . you are so *nice*. I love you,

Happy Chicken. *I love you.*

The little girl whispered to me, that no one else could hear. The little girl had many things to tell me, all kinds of secrets to tell me, whispered against the side of my head where (the little girl supposed) I had "ears"—and when I made a clucking noise, the little girl spoke to me excitedly for it seemed to the little girl that I was *talking to her, and telling her secrets*.

What are you and Happy Chicken always talking about, the Mother asked the little girl, but the little girl shook her head defiantly, and would not tell.

(Sometimes, there was an egg or two discovered in Happy Chicken's little nest. The little girl took these eggs away to give to the Grandmother, for they were *special Happy Chicken eggs* not to be mixed with the eggs of the hens out in the coop.)

(Yet still, though Happy Chicken produced eggs, it seemed to be taken for granted that Happy Chicken was a *boy-chicken*. For always, Happy Chicken was *he, him*.)

The little girl was given a gift of Crayolas! At once the little girl began drawing pictures of me on sheets of tablet paper. *Russet brown* was the little girl's favorite Crayola crayon, for this was the color of my beautiful red-brown feathers. The little girl drew and colored many, many pictures of me, which were admired by everyone who saw them. With the help of the Mother, the little girl carefully printed, beneath the drawings,

HAPPY CHICKEN

Sometimes, visiting relatives would peer at the little girl and me from the kitchen doorway, as the little girl sat on the floor beside my box drawing me, and I was tilting my head blinking and clucking at *her*.

The little girl would overhear people saying, *Is that just a—chicken? Or some special kind of guinea hen, that's smarter?*

For it had not ever been known, that a chicken could be a pet, in such a way. At least, not in this part of Erie County, New York.

Between a chicken and a little girl there is not a shared language as "language" is known. Yet Happy Chicken always knew his name and a few other (secret) words uttered by the little girl and the little girl always knew what Happy Chicken's special clucks meant, that no one else could understand, and so when the Mother, or the Father, or any adult, asked the little girl what on earth she and the little red chicken were talking about, the little girl would repeat that it was a secret, she could not tell.

186

Sometimes, at unpredictable moments, I felt an urge to "kiss" the little girl—a quick, light jab of my beak against the girl's hands, arms, or face.

And the little girl had a special little kiss on the top of the head just for *me*.

I was a young chicken less than a year old at this time in the little girl's life when she hadn't yet learned to run on plump little-girl legs without tripping and falling and gasping for breath and *crying*.

If the Mother was near, the Mother hurried to pick up the little girl, and comfort her. If the Grandmother was near, the Grandmother was likely to cluck at the little girl like an indignant hen and tell her to get up, she wasn't *hurt bad*.

If the Father was near, the Father would pick up the girl at once, for the Father's heart was lacerated when he heard his little daughter cry, no matter that she hadn't been *hurt bad*. (But the Father was not often nearby for he worked in a factory seven miles away in Lockport, called Harrison's Radiator.)

But always if an adult wiped the little girl's eyes and nose the little girl soon forgot why she'd been crying even if she'd bruised or scratched her leg—the little girl cried easily but also forgot easily.

When you are a little girl you *cry easily and forget easily*.

Nor is it difficult to appear *happy* when you are a *young chicken* and as without memory as the smooth, blank inside of an egg.

The Mother had chosen the little girl's name *Joy-ce Carol* because this seemed to her a happy name, there was *joy* in the name; when people spoke the name they smiled.

The Mother was a happy person too. The Mother was not much older than a schoolgirl for the Mother was not yet twenty years old but the little girl had not the slightest notion of how old, or how young, her pretty curly-haired Mother was, no more than Happy Chicken had a notion of anyone's *age*.

This was the time when the little girl was an only child and so it was a happy time for the little girl, who had her own room (separated by just a walk-in closet from her parents' room) upstairs in the clapboard farmhouse. One day soon it would be revealed that the little girl was just the firstborn in the family. There would come another, a *baby brother with the special name Robin*, competing for attention and for love the way the squawking chickens competed for seed scattered in the barnyard at their feeding time.

187

The little girl had no notion of this amazing surprise to come. The little girl had no notion of anything that *was to come* except a promise of a drive to Pendleton for ice cream, or a visit with the Other Grandmother (the Father's mother) who lived in Lockport, or a holiday like Christmas or Easter, or the little girl's birthday, which was the most special day of all—June 16, when dark-red peonies bloomed in profusion along the side of the house as the little girl was told, *just for her.*

On her fourth birthday, the little girl was allowed to feed cake crumbs to me, while the adults looked on laughing. Happy Chicken was allowed to sit on the little girl's lap, if the little girl held me snug, and my wings tucked in, inside her arms.

Pictures were taken with the Father's Brownie Hawkeye camera. Pictures of *little Joyce Carol* and *Happy Chicken*, 1942.

With a frown of distaste the Grandmother would say, in her broken English, A chicken is *dirty*. A chicken should *stay on the floor.*

The Grandmother did not like me, though sometimes the Grandmother pretended to like me. In the Grandmother's eyes, a chicken was never anything more than a *chicken*. And a *chicken* was only of use, otherwise worthless.

Outdoors, when the little girl was nowhere near and the Grandmother approached, I knew to flee, and to hide. Always to flee and to hide away from the other chickens, so brainlessly scratching and pecking in the dirt, in the darkest corner of the barn or far away in the orchard.

A chicken is not *dirt-y*, the little girl protested. Happy Chicken is *nice and clean.*

And so when a small dollop of hot, wet mess came out of my anus, which I could not help, and onto the little girl's shorts, the adults pointed and laughed, and the Mother quickly cleaned it away with wadded tissues as the Grandmother made her clucking-tsking noise.

The little girl was embarrassed, and ashamed. But the little girl always forgave me. And soon forgot whatever it was I'd done, because she was such a little girl, and forgot so easily, and was soon again stroking and petting me, and kissing the bone-hard top of my head.

Happy Chicken—*I love you.*

Because she was such a little girl the little girl was always hoping that all the chickens would like her, and not just Happy Chicken, who was her pet. Naively the little girl hoped that the rooster—who was even more handsome than Happy Chicken, and much larger—would like her. And so the little girl was continually being surprised—and hurt—when the rooster ignored her or, worse yet, bristled his feathers indignantly and rushed to peck at her hands or bare knees sharp enough to draw blood.

Many times this happened, that the little girl cried *Oh!*—and ran away frightened, and sometimes Mr. Rooster would chase her, and if the Grandfather was watching he would double over in laughter as if he'd never seen anything so funny. The Grandfather had a loud, sharp laugh like bottles popping corks. His barrel chest would shake, his small, shrewd eyes would shrink in the fleshy ridges of his face, his laughter turned into snorts, wheezing, coughing. Such loud, protracted coughing. And still, the Grandfather was laughing. For nothing amused the Grandfather more than someone chased by *that goddamn bird* unless it was the sight of the Grandmother's white sheets billowing on the clothesline so hard, in such wind, clothespins slipped and a sheet sank to the ground and the Grandmother came running out of the house, furious, agitated, muttering in a strange guttural speech the little girl did not understand and that frightened her, like the loud shrieks and squawks of the chickens when something threw them into a panic, so the little girl stood very still and cringing and shutting her eyes, pressing her hands over her ears like one who is waiting for something distressing to *go away, stop.*

If the little girl was inside the farmhouse, and heard a sudden squabble outside, a sign that someone or something was agitating the chickens, the little girl would run outside immediately to search for me. Oh oh oh—where is Happy Chicken?

The little girl knew about foxes and raccoons and stray dogs that might drag away chickens and devour them—though it would be very unusual for any creature to make such a foray in daytime—and so the little girl had to find me amidst the commotion, scoop me up in her arms, and kiss the top of my head and smooth down my neatly folded wings and carry me quickly away promising that *nothing bad* would ever happen to Happy Chicken.

We were Rhode Island Reds. Three dozen hens and a single rooster.

Other male chickens in the flock had been squashed as soon as it was evident that they were *male.* Our rooster had not a clue that he'd come close to oblivion. Or, our rooster had not a care that he'd

189

come close to oblivion. Through the day Mr. Rooster strutted in the yard and roosted in the lowermost limbs of trees, showing off his spectacular tail feathers, and the ruff around his neck; bristling red-brown, dark-red, yellow-red feathers that shone in the sun. Yellow-scaly legs, and nasty-sharp spurs just above the talon claws. Though Mr. Rooster was as stupid as any hen pecking brainlessly in the dirt, he was fascinating to watch, for you never knew what Mr. Rooster would do next. (You never knew what any hen would do next, but anything a hen can do is of so little significance there is no point in observing her.) Mr. Rooster could leap into the air fluttering his wings, for instance, and devour a dragonfly three feet above the ground, and Mr. Rooster could rush in a blind rage at an unsuspecting hen, or two unsuspecting hens, or, as if he'd only just thought of it, and now that he was doing it, it was a significant thing to do, throw himself down and roll over vigorously in the dirt until his gaudy feathers were dull with dust like those of an ordinary chicken.

Mr. Rooster gave no sign of knowing who I was—who Happy Chicken was! Ridiculous how this stupid bird seemed not to notice even as the little girl singled me out for special attention and treats in his very presence. (I'd have liked to think that Mr. Rooster was jealous of me, but the fact was, Mr. Rooster was too vain and too stupid for jealousy.)

That is, Mr. Rooster was indifferent to me unless I stepped brashly in his way, or failed to get out of his way quickly enough when he charged forward into the midst of the chickens at feeding time. Sometimes, for a reason known only to Mr. Rooster's pea-sized brain, he crowed loudly and irritably and flapped his wings in a show of indignation and flew clumsily to alight on a rail fence, like a person clumsily hauling himself up by a rope.

At dawn, Mr. Rooster woke everyone with his crowing. He was the first rooster to wake in all of Millersport—soon after Mr. Rooster crowed, you would hear roosters crowing at neighboring farms. No other rooster at any neighboring farm woke earlier than Mr. Rooster, and no other rooster crowed as noisily.

The hens took for granted that Mr. Rooster's crowing tore a rent in the silence of the countryside-before-dawn that allowed the sun to appear. The little girl may have thought this also, but only when she was very little.

The Grandfather, who took little interest in the chickens—these were the Grandmother's responsibility—was still proud of his *goddamn bird*. The Grandfather liked it that Mr. Rooster chased away other chickens and barn cats who ventured too near and had to be disciplined.

How many dawns the little girl was wakened by Mr. Rooster's cries. Through her life to come, long after she'd grown up and gone away from the farmhouse on the Millersport Highway to live, she would wake to the faint, fading cry of a rooster just outside in the dark-before-dawn.

Is a rooster a harbinger of the Underworld? Does a rooster wake you so that you have no choice but to follow him into the Underworld?

After she'd become an adult older than the Mother and the Father of her early childhood, and the little scabs and scars caused by the rooster's beak had long faded from her knees, frequently she would find herself touching her knees like braille when she was alone. Very often, in bed. In the bright, pitiless light of a bathroom she would examine her knees, frowning and baffled; her childhood scars had vanished as if they had never been. . . . It is hard to disabuse yourself of the superstition that your skin is indelibly marked since childhood in a way known only to *you*.

Upsetting to remember how Mr. Rooster would single out a hen for no reason—had she disrespected him? taunted him? dared to eat something meant for him?—peck and jab at the terrified bird until she began to bleed, and chase her until she seemed to fall, or to kneel, before him. And then, Mr. Rooster might have mercy on her, and strut away. But a scab would form shiny and bright as a third eye on the hen's head, which would attract the attention of another hen, and so soon—for some reason (the little girl could not understand this, it frightened her very much)—this hen would peck at the afflicted hen, and soon another hen would hurry over to peck at the afflicted hen, and another, and another; and sometimes Mr. Rooster, attracted by the squawking, might return for the *coup de grâce*—a series of rapid beak stabs until the poor afflicted hen was bleeding, fallen over, and unable to right herself beneath the frenzy of stabbing beaks. . . . And hearing the barnyard commotion the Grandmother would hurry out of the house, scolding and shooing, with the intention of rescuing not the struggling live hen but the limp hen corpse for the Grandmother's own purposes.

In her harsh, guttural speech the Grandmother would curse the chickens and the rooster. Much of the Grandmother's speech had a sound of chiding and cursing. And the Grandmother would take up the limp, blood-dripping hen corpse into the kitchen and boil a pan

191

of water on the stove and drop the hen corpse into it, so that the feathers could be plucked more easily.

At these times the little girl had run away and hid her eyes.

The Mother would say to her, Don't pay any attention, help me in the kitchen, sweetie!

Mostly the little girl would not remember such things. The little girl's memory of the farm on the Millersport Highway was very selective, like the colander into which the Grandmother dumped boiling water containing her thin-cut noodles, made out of the Grandmother's noodle dough, that trapped just the noodles but strained away the liquid.

In later years she'd recall with a fond smile very little of the farm, the barnyard, the flock of Rhode Island Reds—just *me*.

The little girl was so excited! She was *five years old*.

This was the summer the little girl was allowed to help the Grandmother collect eggs from the hens' nests in the chicken coop (where the chicken droppings were so smelly you had to hold your breath especially after a rain) and soon the little girl was allowed to feed the chickens by herself, twice a day, their special chicken feed. Like tiny pebbles the chicken feed seemed to the little girl, seized in handfuls to toss to the chickens; to get the seed you lowered a tin pie pan deep into the feed sack, itself contained inside a larger canvas sack to keep out rats and mice.

So exciting! The little girl almost wet her panties with anticipation.

And when she began to call to the chickens in her high, quavering voice as the Grandmother had taught her—*CHICK!-chick-chick-chick-chick-CHI-ICK!*—chickens came rushing in her direction at once, and made the little girl feel very special—very *powerful*. It was not ever the case that the little girl felt *powerful*—nor could the little girl have defined the sensation, at the time—but calling *CHICK!-chick-chick-chick-chick-CHI-ICK* provoked such a feeling in her, set her heart to pumping and a warm, rich sensation coursing through her veins; the little girl felt very special, and very proud.

Oh, she could see—for she was a quick-witted, smart little girl— that the chickens were oblivious of her, in their greed to devour seed they took not the slightest interest in her or in their surroundings; yet still it seemed to the little girl that the chickens *must like* her, and *knew who she was*, for they came so quickly to her, colliding with one another, scolding and fretting, pecking one another in a frenzy to get to the seed the little girl tossed in a wide, wavering circle.

The Grandmother had instructed the little girl to distribute the seed as evenly as she could. You did not want all the chickens rushing together in a tight, compressed spot and injuring themselves. The little girl understood that she had to be fair to all the chickens, not just a few. But the largest and most aggressive chickens rushed and pecked and beat away the others no matter how hard the girl *tried*.

Of course, Joyce Carol always fed *me*, specially. In a safe, confined area, by the side of the house. This was Happy Chicken's special meal, which was served ahead of the general feeding. If other chickens noticed, and ran clucking to this meal, the little girl stamped her feet and shooed them away.

Though he might have been prowling out in the orchard soon there came Mr. Rooster running on his long, sinewy legs. Mr. Rooster could hear the *Chick-chick-chick!* call from a considerable distance. He pushed through the throng of clucking chickens, knocking the silly hens aside, and gobbled up as much seed as he could from the ground. Sometimes then pausing, looking up with a squint in his yellow eyes, and making a decision—who knows why?—to rush at the little girl and jab her bare knee with his beak.

So quickly this assault came, when it came, the little girl never had time to draw back and escape.

Ohhh! Why was Mr. Rooster so *mean!*

The little girl was always astonished, the rooster was so *mean.*

The rooster's beak was so *swift, so sharp, and so mean.*

Worse yet, the rooster sometimes chased the little girl, trying to peck her legs. If the Grandmother saw, she shooed the rooster away by flapping her apron at him and cursing him in Hungarian. If the Grandfather saw, he gave the rooster a kick hard enough to lift the indignant bird into the air, squawking and kicking.

It was one of the mysteries of the little girl's life, why, when the other chickens seemed to like her so much, and her pet chicken adored her, Mr. Rooster continued to be so mean. It did not make sense to the little girl that Mr. Rooster devoured the seed she gave him, then turned on her as if he hated her. Shouldn't Mr. Rooster be grateful?

The Mother kissed and cuddled her and said, Oh!—that's just the way roosters are, sweetie!

193

Plaintively the little girl asked the Grandmother why did the rooster peck her and make her bleed and the Grandmother did not cuddle her but said, with an air of impatience, in her broken, guttural English, Because he is a rooster. You should not always be surprised, how roosters are.

The little girl wandered the farm. The little girl was forbidden to *step off the property.*

There was the big barn, and there was the silo, and there was the chicken coop, and there were the storage sheds, and there was the barnyard, and there was the backyard, and there were the fields planted in potatoes and corn, and there was the orchard and beyond the orchard a quarter-mile lane back to the Weidenbachs' farm, where there were dogs that barked and bit and the little girl did not dare to go. In these places chickens wandered, and also Mr. Rooster, in their ceaseless scratching-and-pecking for food, though it was rare to see a chicken in one of the farther fields or in the lane. Happy Chicken only accompanied the little girl if she called him to these places, or carried him snug and firm in her arms.

The little girl placed me on the lowermost limb of a tree, so that I could "roost." The little girl urged me to try to "fly—like a bird." But if the little girl nudged me, and I lost my balance on the tree limb, my wings flapped uselessly, and I fell to the ground and did not always land on my feet.

At such a time I picked myself up and tottered away, clucking loudly, complaining like any disgruntled hen, and the little girl hurried after me, saying how sorry she was, and promised not to do it again.

Happy Chicken! *Don't be mad at me, I love you.*

(It was taken for granted, it was never contested or wondered at, that our wings were useless. We could "flap" our wings and "fly" for a few feet—even Mr. Rooster could not fly farther than a few yards; though there were wild turkeys, fatter and heavier than Rhode Island Reds, who could manage to "fly" into the higher limbs of a tree, and there "roost.")

*

Not just the chicken coop and much of the barnyard but the grassy lawn behind the house—"lawn" was a fancy name given to the patch of rough, short-cropped crabgrass that extended from the barnyard and the driveway to the pear orchard—was mottled with chicken droppings. Runny black-and-white glistening smudges that gradually hardened into little stones and lost their sharp smell.

You would not want to run barefoot in the backyard, in the scrubby grass.

And there was the ugly tree stump along the side of the barn, stained with something dark.

And surrounding the stained block, chicken feathers. Sticky-stained feathers in dark, clotted clumps.

No chickens scratched and pecked in the dirt here. Even Mr. Rooster kept his distance. And the little girl.

Grandma was the one, you know. The one who killed the chickens.

No! I did not know.

Of course you must have known, Joyce. You must have seen— many times. . . .

No. I didn't know. I never saw.

But . . .

I never saw.

In later years she would recall little of her Hungarian grandparents. Her mother's (step)parents. For few snapshots remained of those years. She did know that the Grandfather and the Grandmother were something that was called *Hungarian*. They'd come on a "big boat" from Budapest years before the little girl was born and so this was not of much interest to the little girl since it had happened long ago. The grandparents seemed to the little girl to be *very old*. The big-breasted, big-hipped Grandmother had never cut her hair, which was silvery gray streaked and fell past her waist if she let it down from the tight-braided bun. The Grandmother had been eighteen when she'd come to the United States on a boat and at age eighteen it had seemed to her too late for her to learn English, as the Grandfather had learned English well enough to speak in it haltingly and to run his finger haltingly beneath printed words in a newspaper or maga-zine. The Grandfather was a tall, big-bellied man with scratchy whiskers and rough, calloused fingers that caught in the little girl's curly hair when he was *just teasing*.

Worse yet was *tickling*. When the Grandfather's breath smelled harsh and fiery like gasoline from the cider he drank out of a crock. But the Mother insisted, Grandpa loves you; if you cry you will make Grandpa feel bad.

The farm was the Grandfather's farm. Of the farms on the Millersport Highway, it was one of the smallest. Much of the acreage was a pear orchard. Pears were the primary crop of the farm, and eggs were second. The little girl and her parents lived on the Grandfather's farm upstairs in the house. The little girl understood that the Father was not so happy living there, for the Father had been born in Lockport and preferred the city over the country, absolutely. The Father had tried his hand at farming and "hated" it. The little girl often overheard her parents speak of wanting to move away, to live in Lockport, where the Father's mother, who was the little girl's Other Grandmother, lived. Except years would pass, all the years of their lives would pass, and somehow they did not ever move away.

The Grandfather and the Grandmother were not the Mother's actual parents but her (step)parents because the Mother had been *given to* the couple, a long time ago when the Mother had not been a year old.

The Mother had relatives—a mother of her own, who lived some miles away and spoke only Hungarian and refused to see her.

They were all Hungarians: immigrants from the countryside outside Budapest, Hungary. After the Mother's father had been killed in a drunken fight, the family was so poor, so many children, the Mother had had to be given away to the childless Hungarian couple on the Millersport Highway—there was shame to this, and so it was not spoken of. But it had had to be done.

The little girl knew virtually nothing of this. The little girl could not conceive of a time before herself any more than Happy Chicken could conceive of such a time.

The little girl ran away to hide sometimes. When the adults were speaking sharply to one another. When the Grandfather cursed in Hungarian, and the Grandmother cursed in Hungarian.

The little girl was breathless and frightened often but why the little girl would not recall.

The little girl often took me with her. Happy Chicken in the little girl's arms, held tight.

My quivering body. My quick-beating heart. Smooth, warm beautiful chicken feathers! The little girl held me and whispered to me where we were hiding in the old silo beside the barn, which wasn't used so much any longer now that the farm didn't have cows or pigs or horses. Smells were strong inside the silo, like something that has fermented, or rotted. The little girl's mother warned her never to play in the silo, it was dangerous inside the silo. The smells can choke you. If corncobs fall onto you, you might suffocate. But the little girl brought me with her to hide in the silo, for the little girl did not believe that anything bad could happen to *her*.

Except the little girl began more frequently to observe that if a chicken weakened, or fell sick, or had lost feathers, other chickens turned on her. So quickly—who could understand why? Even Happy Chicken sometimes pecked at another, weaker chicken—the little girl scolded, and carried me away.

No, no, Happy Chicken—that is bad.

We did not know why we did this. Happy Chicken did not know.

It was like *laying eggs*. Like releasing a hot little dollop of excrement from the anus, something that *happened*.

Hearing a commotion in the barnyard, the little girl ran to see what was happening, always anxious that the wounded hen might be *me*—but this did not happen.

Though sometimes my beak was glistening with blood, and when the little girl called me, I did not seem to hear. *Peck peck peck* is the action of the beak, like a great wave that sweeps over you, and cannot be resisted.

The little girl grew up, and grew away, but never forgot her Happy Chicken.

The little girl forgot much else, but not Happy Chicken.

The little girl became an adult woman, and at the sight of chickens she felt an overwhelming sense of nostalgia, sharp as pain. Especially red-feathered chickens. And roosters! Her eyes mist over, her heart beats quick enough to hurt. *So happy then. So long ago. . . .*

Still, she would claim she'd never seen a chicken slaughtered. Never seen a single one of the Rhode Island Reds seized by the legs, struggling fiercely, more fiercely than any human being might struggle, thrown down onto the chopping block to be decapitated with a single swift blow of the blood-stained ax, wielded by a muscled arm.

It was the Grandmother's arm, usually. For the Grandmother was the chicken slaughterer.

Which the girl had not seen. The girl *had not seen*.

The girl did recall a time when Grandfather was not so big bellied and confident as he'd been. When the Grandfather began to cough all

the time. And to cough up blood. The Grandfather no longer teased
the little girl, or caused her to run from him crying as she'd run from
Mr. Rooster. The little girl stared in horror as the Grandfather
coughed, coughed, coughed, doubled over in pain, scarcely able to
breathe. The Grandfather would scrape phlegm up from his throat,
with great effort, and spit it into a rag. And the little girl would want
to hide her face, this was so terrible to see.

It was explained that the Grandfather was sick with something in
his lungs. Steel filings, it was said, from the foundry in Tonawanda.
The Grandfather had hated his factory job in Tonawanda but the
Grandfather had had to work there, to support the farm. For the farm
would not support itself and the people who lived on it.

Selling eggs, sitting out by the roadside. Sitting, dreaming, waiting
for a vehicle to slow to a stop. Customers.

How much? One dozen?

Oh that's too much. I can get them cheaper just up the road.

Always there were eggs for sale. And, at the end of the summer,
pears in bushel baskets. Sweet corn, tomatoes, cucumbers, potatoes.
Apples, cherries. Pumpkins.

With a faint sensation of anxiety the little girl would recall sitting
at the roadside at the front of the house behind a narrow bench.
When sometimes the Mother had to go inside for a short while and
the little girl was left alone at the roadside.

Hoping that no one would stop. Hoping not to see a vehicle slow
down and park on the shoulder of the highway.

Some of the anxiety was over chickens, which made their blind-
seeming way down the driveway, to the highway. Chickens oblivious
of vehicles speeding by on the road, only a few yards from where they
scratched and pecked in the dirt.

Carefully the little girl watched to see that no chickens drifted out
onto the road. The little girl knew, though she wasn't altogether certain how she knew, for she'd never *seen*, that from time to time
chickens had been killed on the road.

It was one of the constant anxieties of the little girl's life that
Happy Chicken might be hit on the highway, for the little girl could
not watch me all of the time.

Each morning running outside breathless and eager to call to me—
Happy! Happy Chicken!

And I came running, out of the coop, or out of the barn, or out of
a patch of grass beside the back door, hurrying on my scrawny chick-
en legs to be stroked and petted.

198

*

The laughter was kindly, and yet cruel.

Of course you ate chicken when you were a little girl, Joyce! You ate everything we ate.

No. She didn't think so.

You'd have had to eat whatever was served. Whatever everybody else was eating. You wouldn't have been allowed to *not eat* anything on the table.

No! This was not true.

You hated fatty meat, and you hated things like gizzards, but you ate chicken white meat. Of course you did.

No. That was—that was not true. . . .

Children ate what they were given in those days. Children ate, or went hungry. Your father would have spanked the daylights out of you if you'd tried to refuse chicken, or anything that your mother or grandmother prepared.

But *no*. She did not believe this.

It's true—she does remember her Hungarian grandmother preparing noodles in the kitchen. Wide swaths of soft-floury ghost-white dough on the circular kitchen table, which was covered in oilcloth, and over the oilcloth strips of waxed paper. She recalls her grandmother, a heavyset woman with hair plaited and fastened tight against her head, wielding a long, sharp-glittering knife, rapidly cutting dough into thin strips of noodle. The surprise was, sometimes you could see a pleading girl's face inside the soft, flaccid old-woman face. And the little girl remembers something, an object, pale skinned, headless, in a large pan simmering on the stove, the surface of the liquid bubbling with yellow fat.

You loved chicken noodle soup! You don't remember?

She hides her eyes. She hides her face. She is sickened, that terrible smell of wet feathers, plucked-pale chicken flesh.

Protesting, I had nothing to do with *that*.

Trying to recall in a sudden panic—what had happened to her pet chicken she'd loved so?

Our memories are what remains on a wall that has been washed down. Old billboards advertising MAIL POUCH TOBACCO, in shreds. The faintest letters remaining that, even as you stare at them, fade. The Hungarian grandfather who'd been so gruff, so loud, so confident, and had so loved his little granddaughter he'd been unable to keep his calloused fingers out of her curls, had died at the age of

199

fifty-three, his lungs riddled with steel filings from the foundry in Tonawanda. When he'd died, the Catholic priest said, *It was his time. It was John Bush's time.* The Hungarian grandmother lived for many years afterward and never learned to speak English, still less to read English. The Grandmother died in a nursing home in Lockport to which the granddaughter was never once taken, nor was the grand-daughter told the name of the nursing home or its specific location.

What happened to *me*? What happened to Happy Chicken?

Oh, the little girl did not know!

The little girl *did not know.* Just that one terrible day—Happy Chicken was not *there.*

She mouths the words aloud: "Happy Chicken."

There is something about the very word "happy" that is unnerving. Happy happy happy *happy.*

A terrible word. A terrifying word. *Hap-py.*

Waking in the night, tangled in bedsheets, shivering in such fright you'd think she was about to misstep and fall into an abyss.

Happy. Hap-py. We were so hap-py. . . .

In the cold terror of the night she counts her dead. Like a rosary counting her dead. The Grandfather who died first and after whom the door was opened, that Death might come through to seize them all. The Grandmother who died somewhere far away, though close by. The Mother who died of a stroke when she was in her mideighties, overnight. The Father who died over several years, also in his mid-eighties, in the new twenty-first century, shrinking, baffled, and yet alert, in yearning wonderment.

Wanted you kids to have the best you could have, but that didn't happen. We were just too poor. I worked like hell, but it wasn't enough. Things got better later, but those early years—! The only good thing was, we lived in Millersport. We lived on the old man's farm. You loved those animals. Remember your pet chicken—Happy Chicken? God, you loved that little red chicken.

Daddy brushing tears from his eyes. Daddy laughing, he wasn't the kind to be sentimental, Jesus!

She was thinking of how they'd found the rooster—not Mr. Rooster then, but just a limp, slain bird—beautiful feathers smudged and broken—out back of the barn where something, possibly a fox, or a neighbor's dog, had seized him, shaken him, and broken his neck, threw him down and left him for dead. Poor Mr. Rooster!

Seeing the rooster in the dirt, horribly still, the little girl had cried and cried and cried.

And several hens, limp and bloody, eyes open and sightless. Flung down in the dirt like trash.

And there came the time, not long after this, or maybe it had been this time, when Happy Chicken disappeared.

The girl was stunned and disbelieving and did not cry, at first.

So frightened, the little girl could not cry.

For it seemed terrifying to her, that Happy Chicken might be—somehow—*gone.*

She'd run screaming to her mother, upstairs in the farmhouse. Her mother, who claimed to have no idea where the little chicken might be. Together they searched in the chicken coop, and in the barn, and out in the fields, and in the pear orchard. Calling, *Happy Chicken! Happy Chicken!* Wildly calling, *Chick-chick-chick-chick-CHICK!*

Other chickens came, blinking and clucking. Yellow eyes staring.

And not one of these was *me.*

That morning the Mother had taken the little girl into Lockport to visit with the Other Grandmother, who was her father's mother, who lived upstairs in a clapboard house on Grand Street just across the railroad tracks. The Other Grandmother read books from the Lockport library, never less than three books each week. And these books smelling of the library in plastic covers. And these books smartly stamped in dark green ink LOCKPORT PUBLIC LIBRARY. The Other Grandmother took the little girl hand in hand into the children's entrance of the library, to secure a library card for the little girl. For now the little girl was old enough for a children's library card: six. And the little girl was allowed to take out children's books, picture books. Such beautiful books! The little girl could barely speak, to thank the Other Grandmother. And the little girl and the Other Grandmother read these books together sitting on a swing on the front veranda of the gunmetal-gray clapboard house on Grand Street.

In all that day, the little girl did not once think of me.

Those many hours, blinking and staring at the beautiful brightly colored illustrations in the books, turning the pages slowly, as the Other Grandmother read the words on each page, and encouraged the little girl to read too—the little girl did not once think of Happy Chicken.

But when the Mother took the little girl home again to Millersport, in the late afternoon of that day, and the little girl ran out into the barnyard to call for me, there was no Happy Chicken anywhere.

They went to search the chicken coop, the barn, the orchard. . . . Where was Happy Chicken? The little girl was crying, sobbing.

The Grandmother insisted she had not seen Happy Chicken.

The Grandmother had never distinguished Happy Chicken from any other chicken. How ridiculous, to pretend that one chicken was any different from any other chicken!

The Grandfather too insisted he hadn't seen Happy Chicken! Wouldn't have known what the damned chicken looked like, in fact.

Anything that had to do with the chickens—these were the Grandmother's chores, and of no interest to the Grandfather, who was worn out from the foundry in Tonawanda and couldn't give a damn, so much fuss over a goddamn chicken.

When the father returned from his factory work in Lockport in the early evening, he was in no mood either to hear of Happy Chicken. He was in no mood to hear his little daughter's crying, which grated on his nerves. But seeing his little girl's reddened eyes, and the terror in those eyes, the Father had stooped to kiss her cheek. The Father had not laughed.

*She is calling him—*Happy Chicken! *Her throat is raw with calling him—*Happy Chicken!

She has wakened in a sick, cold sweat tangled in bedclothes. The little red chicken is somewhere in the room—is he? But which room is this, and when?

But here I am—suddenly—crouching at her feet. Eager, quivering little red-feathered chicken at the little girl's feet. The little girl kneels to pet me, and kisses the top of my hard little head, and holds me in her arms, my wings pressed gently against my sides. And the little chicken head lowered. And the eyelids quivering. Red-burnished feathers stroked gently by a little girl's fingers.

Where did I go, Joyce Carol? I flew away.

One day that summer, my wings were strong enough to lift me. And once my wings began to beat, I rose into the air, astonished and elated; and the air buoyed and buffeted me, and I flew high above the tallest peak of the old clapboard farmhouse on the Millersport Highway.

So high, once the wind lifted me, I could see the flock of red-feathered chickens below scratching and pecking in the dirt as always, and I could see the roof of the old hay barn, and I could see

202

the top of the silo; I could see the farthest potato field, and the farthest edge of the pear orchard, and the rutted dirt lane that bordered the orchard leading back to the Weidenbachs' farm.

For it was time for Happy Chicken to fly away.

Animal Care and Control
Paul Lisicky

WARNING BEWARE OF ALLIGATOR

I'D GIVE YOU A SWAMP if I could, but I have no swamp to give. Do not assume I will bite you just because I've let you feed me fish. Who would you be if everyone thought you'd want to eat them? You don't want to know that I differ from the crocodile, with his narrow snout and taste for human flesh. I have no taste for humans, but please don't take that personally. Your little dog will do just fine. I'll drag him down to my house of muck. I'll kill him with such tenderness that he'll wonder why I haven't done it sooner. How wonderful he'll be inside me, a house inside a house inside a house. You think that's where you want to be. That's why you go behind the fish shed and pick up the bucket of remains. If you'll let me commune with Snoopy and see you once every Tuesday, I'll be just fine. Controlling? I beg to differ. I only ask that you look fondly at the top of my head, see my snout and my beady eyes and know I'm not going to destroy you. Could you say the same? Don't you think it's awful to watch you waiting for my jaw to spring open? The mechanical is no fun. I was just kidding about Fido, or whatever it is you want to call him. You make me feel irreverent and I'm as holy as they come. Jesus had a thing or two to say about that, but let's keep him out of it for now. Too hungry for sacrifice, I fear, and you miss the finer points. Your attention is so heavy on me right now it's a wonder I can open my eyes. I want to take the world in just like you. I want to sun myself on the dock, though I fear you're going to flinch if I take one of my famous steps. This is not about what you think it is.

GRIEG

Grieg's back leg was sore, but he kept pace beside his human, because she thought he needed his seven o'clock walk. He looked up at her bewildered face, her frowsed hair, her nicked-up glasses. He knew she'd have preferred to sit down with a glass of wine after work, the laptop open on the blue stool beside her, but she wanted to be a good mother, which was why she was out here on the marsh's fire road, walking two times faster than he could possibly walk. Blackbirds sprang from tree to tree. Grieg didn't have the sounds to tell his human he needed to turn back. To cry would be to seem weak, and he'd known of another dog who had seemed weak, shunned by the other cocker spaniels in the dog park because she'd started peeing on human laps. He would never be that weak. He'd keep trudging through the world war in his leg before he'd let it come to that. Grieg's human needed to think of herself as a good person, but no one wanted a weak dog, no one.

Grieg did not shake on the examining table. He kept his gaze up on the lights, and when the vet announced that Grieg did not have cancer, that he'd merely been suffering the consequences of too much enthusiasm, he did not feel his relief right away, nor did his human. They stumped out into the day, a little stunned and queasy, in need of breakfast, and walked for a while past the cedars. Up ahead they saw a church and animals. There was a priest in walnut-colored robes amid the animals, a bullmastiff, a hen, a cat held over the shoulder like a baby, a ferret, and instantly Grieg felt relief warm his sore leg, though not as much relief as his human obviously felt. She walked faster, and tugged Grieg along until his leash was taut at his neck.

"The blessing of the animals," she cried. "God be with us!" And dropped to her knees, and raised her hands to the sincere discomfort of all the animals assembled. The hen staggered to the periphery, as did the bullmastiff, even though the priest's hand had just been upon their heads. The priest himself looked down at Grieg with a kind of mercy that said, Pity to those for whom God's love was ever in doubt, and Grieg looked back up at him with a face that said, I've never seen this nutjob in my life, and joined the circle of the other animals until he returned to her.

HOUSE SITTER

On the final night of his ten-month stint as a house sitter, Asher lay on the sofa, the heat of the reading lamp working into his lips and brows. The question that had been goading him all day, through the hauling out and the cleaning up, needed to be spoken: What message do you have for me? He looked over at the boxes taped tight with maps and cups and weather instruments, his precious things. He'd lie up all night for an answer if that was what was being required of him. He'd stayed up all night before.

The report did not come right away—reports rarely do. It came at the point when he felt himself going under. The smell of catbox, pungent and dusty, up from the cushions of the sofa. The smell was not constant. It came and went like a pulse. He'd never smelled catbox before, not in this house, where no one took care of a cat, not even the owners, who coughed at weeds and trees and animals, most things that were alive. He did not know what to do with this message, as he did not know why he was moving on to another house where there wouldn't be room for his furniture, not that he had any. He'd lived so lightly on the earth. Even when he'd tried to leave a stain of himself—in the tub, just as an experiment—the walls wouldn't hold him. He could barely see his hands.

The Snow Leopard's Realm
Vint Virga

*As we reach for the stars we neglect the flowers at
our feet. . . . For epochs to come the peaks will still
pierce the lonely vistas, but when the last snow
leopard has stalked among the crags . . . a spark of
life will have gone, turning the mountains into
stones of silence.*

—George B. Schaller, *Mountain Monarchs*

A SNOW SQUALL IS HEADING our way. The bank of dark clouds
presses closer. But for now the morning is impassively still—blue
skies with the sharp chill of December dawn, which bites through
my gloves at the tips of my fingers and slips under my scarf to the
nape of my neck. My breath drifts before me in foggy, warm eddies
that rest and then freeze on my eyebrows and lashes.

The first blaze of sunrise hits the boulders above in a burst of burnt
orange poised in a beam on the uppermost ledge that then swells,
washing down the weatherworn faces of granite. With thick drifts of
snow piled behind and beside me, I can almost believe that the path
where I stand climbs eastward into the Nepalese mountains retrac-
ing Peter Matthiessen's steps in search of the snow leopard he never
found. Just as he did over four decades earlier, I catch traces of paw
prints left in the snowbank, wandering up to the lowest rocks. Yet
in spite of my training as a veterinary behaviorist and all my years
working with leopards in zoos, my search at this moment is no more
rewarding. I know all too well they most likely are perched right
under my nose on the uppermost ledge, somewhere between all the
fir trees and boulders, surveying the boundaries of their domain. As
in the wild, Himalayan ghost cats.

In this modern age with man's untamed expansion and unbridled
craving for more and more land, snow leopards remain one of earth's
most mysterious, elusive creatures. For though they roam freely in
perhaps thirteen countries, from Afghanistan eastward to the Great
Gobi Desert, only a handful of humans have seen one in the wild. In
the lonely mountain ranges of Central and South Asia—amidst an
unrelenting and frigid terrain of snowcapped pinnacles and secluded,

craggy bluffs—with their smoky gray coats and softly blurred charcoal markings, snow leopards can vanish right within your gaze to nothing more than another rock, a scraggly shrub, a lifeless shadow.

A purple finch flutters from the small grove of firs, and at the base of the trees I sense two shadows stir, alert to each detail of the tiny bird's movements. Then, in a synchronized streak of sleek black and gray forms, both cats spring from cover out onto the rockfall—Bashur in the lead by a nose before Willow—vaulting a good thirty feet from the firs, just as the bird comes to rest on a boulder. Sharpened claws in a swipe reach to seize tail feathers as the finch flaps its wings once again to take flight, and for a moment I'm breathless in anticipation (wishing almost as much for Bashur's success as for the finch in escaping its fate). Then, astonishingly, the bird soars up higher, far out of reach of the snow leopard's grasp—from a halfhearted effort by Bashur, I am certain.

The cats track the finch in its flight for a moment, then both pairs of eyes turn toward the trail where I stand. Notwithstanding the time I have spent with each leopard, I lose track of my thoughts in their calm, studied gaze. Looking into their world from my human perspective, I find mindfulness in their quiet contemplation, remarkable awareness in their sensitivity, and wisdom in their feline capability to exquisitely adapt to our endlessly changing world. As my breath matches theirs with each heave of their chests, it's as if for an instant the glass wall has melted and I'm standing alone—just a mere leap away—held as if I were prey by my own fascination.

The cloud bank rolls closer and an icy breeze stirs the leaves of the shrubs at the base of the boulders, and Willow turns her gaze to face into the wind. Her broad nostrils widen and twitch with piqued curiosity while a gust brushes through the long locks of her fur to reveal the thick down of her paler gray undercoat. She considers the news that the blast of air brings her—whiffs of the red pandas and Indian rhino swept from their habitats and carried downwind, their keeper approaching with fresh meat in her arms, the strength of the storm that is building above us and first whirl of snowflakes beginning to fall—then she stretches and wanders head into the wind. While Bashur stays in place to consider me longer, I catch Willow behind him a dozen yards off, pawing then rolling in a thick bed of straw that their keeper no doubt has laced with fresh scents of antelope, zebra, or elephant. Then Bashur turns, pads off, and joins Willow upwind.

As the storm comes upon us, the snow drives down with fury, stinging my eyes and cheeks with small, icy flakes that quickly envelop the landscape around me. Through the thick veil of white, I can make out the leopards—Bashur standing by Willow as she rolls in the straw and its blanket of snow. And in spite of the bitter wind numbing my body, I smile at the chance to be out in this blizzard alone with the leopards.

By this time most mornings, I can watch zoo guests strolling along the bend in the trail just above where I stand. Mothers meander with newborns in strollers. Young children excitedly tug at their daddies' arms. Students with notebooks race in teams on scavenger hunts, hoping to answer all of their teachers' questions. I see them rushing up to the windows to catch sight of the leopards, chatting and giggling while craning their necks, scanning the rock wall, the bushes, the pond.

All the while, Willow and Bashur lie in hiding—sometimes in the fir grove concealed by the shadows, other times in the open, blending in with the rocks—camouflaged from all but the most discerning eyes. Avoiding the babble and hubbub of humans, just as their cousins do out in the wild. Even researchers who have devoted their lives to snow leopards, spending years in the mountains at the top of the world on the trail of their paw prints, scratch marks, and scats, tell tales of nearly stumbling over them—not a hiss, not a growl, frozen in utter silence—before the large cats betray their disguise and bolt off reclusively into the distance. Never once has a snow leopard attacked a human in the wild. Instead, they retreat farther into the mountains, no matter how fervently we search for them, a vestige of nature untouched and unspoiled. Ghosts of the mountains in their last lonely vistas.

Loose Lion
Terese Svoboda

THEY PITCHFORKED OLD GRAY ON account of his sleeping in the dark part of the barn.

Don't blame them. I would've thought it was a lion too.

News like that makes the telephone here worthwhile. I was over at the Tickles' last yesterday, the Tickle Tickles, not Avery's bunch, when I heard that the lion was loose. Mabel Tickle tried to hush the operator but it was no good, she screeched and screeched, like the lion was on her lap.

Creeping through the jungle like a golden track, boomalaya, boomalaya, boomalaya, boom.

I don't care for poetry but Vachel Lindsay has it beat.

The boom makes all the little kids scream for mercy.

Likely. They got a posse making noise in the cornfield now. They'll find the lion and make mincemeat out of him, you'll see.

Mmmmm, lion sandwiches. I'll bet you could make a good-looking lion purse with what's left over from a rug. You know the governor's going to want the rug.

I paid twenty-five cents to see that circus show and they went on without the lion. They didn't give us a penny back. I guess the tamer had better look for a new job.

He better look for his old one.

Maybe it actually is a man-eater like what it says on the poster is what the lion tamer is thinking. The little ladies who hardly even scream Oh! go to church to see lions curled up with lambs, they never had a pig as nice as pie turn on them and try to bite off their hands. But the lion-tamer's lion was as nice as pie. The tamer whacks at the cornstalks with the gun barrel, trying to scare it out. It's still too light to see the fires inside the houses over which such nice pie might be cooking, the settlements being close to the fields because a man can't farm much farther than he can keep going with the plow. Which is a blessing because it's not much farther than a person could call out Lion!

Over eight feet tall is what he shouted out when the lion stood on its legs in the show to dance with him, husband to wife. He said maybe the townspeople should play the show music to get the lion to stand up again and somebody volunteered to hitch up a mare to lug the gramophone over rather than walk the field with the rest of them. Cowards. Why it was only two shows ago sticking his head inside the lion's mouth that he'd seen that bad tooth, black and yellow, going green.

Aunt Flo's second boy, supposed to be home for supper, gets shot first off. Hardly grazed him, but still. Then Hanrahan's hat fills with holes— it was dangling from the end of his rifle, thank God. A right jittery bunch, most of them. Colonel Horst the worst, the Civil War on his shoulder, each of the leaves on the cornstalk like a flag to him if there's any blow at all. He claims he surprised the lion and shot it in the leg but nobody saw him do it, but nobody goes into the field or the brush adjacent to look.

The circus says they want the lion back alive and the townsfolk too. They hire horses so they can see over the tops of the corn, and bring in the aerialist's nets so as to flush the lion out into them. But after a week they pack up and move on.

The tamer stays put, out of a job without an animal, and boards with some woman known as Aunt Flo for the time being. He says the other circus was getting too close to theirs in the revenue department and there is nothing like a loose lion for publicity. Good? Flo asks, or bad? Listen to me, he says, last year six circus trains got wrecked and the animals all ran off. Now how would six of them wreck? No other kind of train wrecks so easy as that. It's just part of the act. He just says he would have switched to contortionist if he'd known about the racket, or trained up a horse. A loose lion!

A week after the first search is called off, a horse goes missing, and parts of another.

I'm going to leave what's left out for bait, says the fuming owner. He lays it, bleeding, on a circle of hay. It's not fresh but maybe the lion isn't so fussy.

Not far away lie two lovers, one of them against the killing of the lion enough that she keeps the other away from "the hunt of your life," as advertised for two weeks in the local newspaper, keeps him away by the oldest means possible. These two lovers are not married except to other people so each spouse assumed the other's elsewhere. They have found the McHenrys' good for them, a farmhouse abandoned in a battle between heirs. Since she is one of the heirs, she can keep the battle going. No one from either side is allowed entrance until it's settled. She has her alibis and since she is still so young and so newlywed, she hardly has to use them, and since he's a man he has places to go whereas his bride doesn't. He is beating his way back to his own homestead, tra-la.

The bait is took is the news of the week.

The lion isn't that big sitting down. The lover steps closer. It's not like a snake is what he thinks, you want to put out your hand and call it. He doesn't yell or they'll know where he is and why he is in the wrong place at the wrong time, but he doesn't turn his back to it in a run. It's been shot in the leg, it doesn't move when it sees him, its eyes narrow. He stares, he thinks he's casting his power over it, that it is paralyzed by his might. He has been drinking.

The lion wrangles its head and a halo of dust rises, then it limps off.

He tells everybody it sat somewhere else.

The Summers' boy out calling their good trained dog that is running in the dark drops his torch too close to a hay bale and it catches. Volunteers take all night to put out the fire. After it's over they find big bones all burnt. They say they saw the lion raise itself up and jump through the fire like at a circus hoop but that the fire jumped higher.

The tamer isn't so sure about the bones. Could be a big badger or a cow's, he says. Did you find teeth?

Nobody finds teeth.

Does the lion eat underwear since Mame lost two skivvies from the line? is the kind of question they pepper the tamer with. He doesn't tell them how the lion scares the bejesus out of him, always has. He never could figure out, he swears, how the lion got past the bars of its cage, must've been some voodoo. In fact he was drunk when the first alarm got out, then he closed the cage quick where he had forgotten the latch. He had sung to the lion all week giving it its dinner, making it turn its head where he put down its food, a bit short that week. The revenues had slipped since he'd been refusing to put his head inside on account of that rotting tooth. But he did put his head inside that last time. He had to or lose his job. People would come back again and again to see his head inside that lion. Maybe he left that door open because he was finished even thinking about his head inside that lion.

He is swinging a hammer for Kolste on the days the Kolste boy has to help at the post office.

She married into the region, leaving Chicago and Papa behind as most girls do. Church-held suppers, as innocent as that, is where the new wives did the dishes while the new husbands dried. That's how the two lovers met when it didn't seem that she would ever meet anyone ever again. For her loneliness, her father had bought her a radio. Sometimes it picked up the Chicago symphony, which she sits and listens to without moving or else dances with her broom to the melodies. It is hardly dance music, and she weeps. Not so anyone can see, not in the open but in the kitchen just after the broadcast when she is making her new husband coffee. Sometimes her husband does see and catches her by the arm and asks if the floor is that dirty.

A new fellow feeling sweeps the town in its fame of having a lion lost in its whereabouts: Beers are raised in toasts to the town's bravery, a newborn is named Tiger despite its being a lion that is lost, and the women's auxiliary draws up a coat of arms with the lion as a sort of human.

He is dolling himself up for her again, even a tinch of that scented talcum the city boys wear, and he is putting on his best shoes—*Off to church?* asks Ellie, his wife, bending over laundry she's been refusing to do unless he makes peace with her in the bedroom way, which he has, he has done his duty, as hard as it is with her so pregnant, he is taking the shortcut to the McHenrys' about a mile out of the way of his stated destination, he is passing the slate fall and the ashy quarter section and the fence nobody yet fixed at the bottom because there's a washout so close, a kind of natural fence the way he looked at it, he is leaning hard into the door where it is warped from no woman to look after it properly, he hears her moving in the back room where they like to go and he stops in the foyer, adjusts his wardrobe in anticipation, his face showing red in the ratty old mirror, he pulls the bedroom door toward him.

She's in the corner in the half-light of the old curtains rotted and torn, she's in the corner lying there with someone else.

No.

The man steps forward the way he didn't before. The lion rises, an arm falling to one side. Because of its hurt leg, it doesn't lunge, the man lunges, and the powerful stench of the lion's mouth and its paw flatten him. Scrabbling up, he pulls at her body, which is not the thing to do.

Afterward, the lion jumps out the window they left open.

What is left over of the woman her husband has a hole dug for and weeps beside her radio. How did Ellie's fella know where to look? And in his best clothes? The telephone operator knows why and says so.

When a moose wanders into town the very next year, someone shoots it right off. They are not going to wait for trouble.

The tamer runs for sheriff. Vote for me, he says. I'll protect you. Nobody else wants the job, too dangerous, and having him stay on means that if the cat comes back, they can put him out as bait. What he does is take all that he saves from sheriffing and puts it into stocks. Everybody else who has two cents to his name is doing that, never mind paying for a new planter. The Roaring Twenties may be just about over but this time he's not going to be left behind.

An Interview with William S. Burroughs

Conducted by Bradford Morrow

WILLIAM BURROUGHS AND I were friends for nearly a decade before I flew out to visit him at his home in Lawrence, Kansas, from April 3–6, 1987. We had gotten to know each other when, in my twenties, I published a variant passage from *The Naked Lunch* as a small press book, *Doctor Benway*, with an introduction he wrote for the occasion. In the years following, we mostly met for long afternoons into the night with James Grauerholz and others at my old apartment on West Ninth Street, conversing about everything imaginable. And in *Conjunctions:9*, I was honored to run an excerpt from William's amazing tribute to felines, "The Cat Inside," which includes one of my favorite—of many—Burroughs lines: "Workers are paid in cats and cat food."

Anyone I have ever known who met William unvaryingly found him to be a true gentleman, gracious and sharp-witted, an irrepressible, knowledgeable raconteur of the first order. During my stay with him in Lawrence he was in fine form, introducing me to a man who made walking sticks from bull pizzles and teaching me how to throw knives into the wooden siding of his backyard garage. I hadn't intended to interview him or made any preparations to do so, but as a person who has always loved animals, I noticed over the course of the first couple of days out there that our conversation kept returning to lemurs and a host of other beasts.

Not unexpectedly, William had a large posse of cats. One basement window of his house was left open so that this tribe of neighborhood kitties could come and go as they pleased, eat the food and drink the water William left downstairs for them. Some were feral, others were moochers from down the block, yet others were official residents with names, but all were in one way or another as devoted to William as he was to them. He was a born animal behaviorist. *Cat Fancy* magazines were stacked on the coffee table in the living room and the only television shows I saw William watch (with the sound off, as I recall) were nature programs. In short, the man was as devoted to animals as I was. Without giving it much thought, I asked if we could do an

215

impromptu talk about the subject.

Why was our dialogue never published before now? Quick answer is, when I got back home to New York, I listened to the tape in horror. The audio quality was so poor that transcription seemed impossible. The project, if one could call it a project, was set aside and the tape itself went missing for a number of years. It wasn't until we decided to do an issue of *Conjunctions* devoted to animals that I set about searching around in earnest for the cassette and found it. I asked my friend Dan Grigsby, a sound engineer and expert at audio restoration, if he would try to improve the sound quality enough that we could transcribe it. To say we are deeply grateful for Dan's painstaking work would be a serious understatement. I want also to thank Micaela Morrissette, Nicole Nyhan, Joss Lake, Zappa Graham, Emma Horwitz, and Pat Sims for their combined efforts with me to transcribe this talk. Alas, even with all these attentive ears at work, a few words remain too elusive to include with confidence, so pardon us a couple of lacunae.

I must express great gratitude to my dear friend of so many years, James Grauerholz, Burroughs's secretary and now literary executor, for taking the time to read the transcript for accuracy and generously granting permission for its publication here. As the reader will see, the conversation is freewheeling and extemporaneous, but William's elemental genius, the distinctive way he viewed the world around him and all the beasts in it, humans included, shines through.

BRADFORD MORROW: Let's talk about animals. When did you first fall in love with lemurs?

WILLIAM BURROUGHS: Oh, well, I'd heard about them, I didn't know much about them. I had a very good impression of them, marvelous creatures. It was stirred since I got into cats. I see lemurs as marvelous animals. See, they were at one time widely distributed all across the world. And now they've shrunk back so that they're only now found in Madagascar, true lemurs. I know there are creatures similar to lemurs found in Borneo. Gliding lemurs, flying lemurs, found in Borneo.

MORROW: So, the lemurs came out of your interest in cats.

BURROUGHS: Yes. They're kind of a combination of monkey and cat and they're humans.

MORROW: But lemurs, they're not in the cat family.

BURROUGHS: They're not in the cat family nor are they in the monkey family. They call them prosimians. They're not monkeys. There are no monkeys in Madagascar. And also there are no predators.

MORROW: You mentioned you can see lemurs somewhere in the United States.

BURROUGHS: Oh, yes. There's the prosimian center at Duke University. I've corresponded with them. They've got three hundred lemurs in a natural habitat. I showed you the pictures. Yes, and I'm going down there to talk to them and see their lemurs. Apparently lemurs tame very readily. The pictures show the lemurs climbing all over people. Beautiful creatures. They'll just jump up on their shoulders.

MORROW: Those are ring-tailed?

BURROUGHS: Ring-tailed, yes. Those are also known as cat lemurs . . .

MORROW: Cat lemurs.

BURROUGHS: Because they purr, like a cat. They are the easiest to tame. Some of the larger lemurs like the spotted and the black lemurs are not so easy to tame. It takes time.

MORROW: Cats, you've always loved cats?

BURROUGHS: My whole life, oh yes. When I moved here, I was out in the country and that's when I think a mess of cats came around and I formed an attachment to this one who would keep coming over. We had a stone house at the top of the hill where we had all these cats.

MORROW: And you told me about a snake, when we were together last in New York, that you liked too.

BURROUGHS: Oh, I don't judge the snakes.

MORROW: What are your favorite animals?

BURROUGHS: Lemurs.

MORROW: Lemurs are your favorite—you like them even better than cats?

BURROUGHS: Well, we don't have to draw a line. I like cats, I like lemurs, I like raccoons, I like—skunks are marvelous animals. When

I was a kid, we used to have descented skunks as pets. They make great pets. But now the vet says it's practically illegal for him to treat a skunk or a raccoon because of rabies. The ordinary vaccination doesn't always take with lemurs, with humans, with skunks, or raccoons. People are discouraged from making pets out of them—they make very gentle pets. But skunks are great. Skunks are like ferrets, weasels, raccoons. Some of them are called ringtail cats, but it isn't a cat. It's essentially a raccoon but it's much smaller than a raccoon. It's like a miniature raccoon; they only weigh about four or five pounds. But in the wild, the wild cats, there's lots of cats, wild cats, that are much smaller than house cats. There's one, the rusty spotted cat that only weighs four pounds at maturity. A miniature cat. . . .

MORROW: You were telling me yesterday about this project for an animal center in Lawrence of some sort.

BURROUGHS: Well, a no-kill animal shelter.

MORROW: I think that would be a great idea.

BURROUGHS: Well, yes, they have two in New York, outside of New York City. Also there's one in Chicago called Tree House. There's one outside of New York, in Bronxville or somewhere, called the Elmsford Shelter. I got a list of them somewhere in my *Cat Fancy*, and there are about ten of them scattered around.

MORROW: If you had your way, how would you run a shelter, how would somebody do that?

BURROUGHS: Well, I'd write to Tree House to find out how they do it. But what you do is, well you have to enclose animals and monitor them, photo them, get them spayed and neutered. Some get stopped from breeding, get put up for adoption and all that. It's no big trick nor is it necessarily very expensive. They have these food dispensers. These need to be filled, every day and week.

MORROW: There are stray dogs in Lawrence.

BURROUGHS: Well, naturally, yes, there are. I'm not interested in dogs.

MORROW: (*Laughs.*) I won't ask. Birds, you have a bird feeder.

BURROUGHS: I have a feeder. Well, I just don't care for them all that very much, about birds. I like crows. I had a pet crow for a while. Crows are more intelligent than birds. It was a long time ago, about sixteen

218

years, I had a pet crow. I had its wings fixed. But whenever it heard one of the other crows, it would just go nuts, go flapping out there.

MORROW: Where was that?

BURROUGHS: Outside of St. Louis. This crow would eat bananas out of my hand very eagerly and then it pecked viciously at my fingers.

MORROW: When the banana was there?

BURROUGHS: No, no, anytime. He wanted to eat but didn't like me, so I let the wings grow back.

MORROW: Was he a lame crow? Well, you don't go to a pet shop and buy one.

BURROUGHS: No, you don't. Someone brought him when he was very young. But he just wanted to be with the other crows, so I let his wings grow out.

MORROW: And that's how that story ended?

BURROUGHS: He flew away with the other crows.

MORROW: Be hard to keep a crow and cats at the same time.

BURROUGHS: Well, I didn't have cats then.

MORROW: What other animals have you kept?

BURROUGHS: Oh, I've had a ferret. And I had an angora goat. It was a little goat. Little goats are the cutest things. Put out your fist and they don't budge. Cute little thing.

MORROW: Long-legged. Kind of wobbly.

BURROUGHS: Well, I guess.

MORROW: You seem to be an expert on snakes too, and spiders.

BURROUGHS: Well, snakes I don't care about—well, not always. The relative potency of the venoms—the most, I suppose, drop to drop, is between a krait and a sea snake, a yellow-bellied sea snake. All sea snakes are poisonous. And some of them are deadly poisonous. The fatal dose of a sea snake or a krait is about one or two milligrams, it's a thirty-second of a grain, a tiny amount. But a krait, it's about—you can almost never pick them up; sea snakes, it just doesn't happen. People are bitten by the kraits. And even with immediate antivenom, your chances are only fifty-fifty. Without antivenom, they're nil. Get

219

the table lamp, I've got a snake book here somewhere, it shows the number of people bitten and their deaths.... (*Looking at book.*) You've got, like, people bitten by a cobra, 150 deaths ... ten or twelve, this was with antivenom, of course. Now we get to the krait. Number of people bitten, nine; deaths, eight.

MORROW: This is where?

BURROUGHS: India. It shows the relative potency of the venom. Now, the bushmaster, which is a huge snake, it's got to be twelve, fifteen feet long and as big around as that. (*Gesturing.*) But they have a very weak venom. It's two hundred milligrams is the fatal dose—imagine, two hundred milligrams as opposed to one milligram. But they've got a hell of a lot of it. That's their ... They can shoot in a jigger full of their venom. The shock of that, without a doubt, leaves you dead in a few minutes. If they had a potent venom like the krait they'd really be a terror. Probably the most dangerous of all the snakes, well, the most dangerous snake, is probably the black mamba.

MORROW: Where is that?

BURROUGHS: In Africa. They're very potent. I think fifteen milligrams is the fatal dose. They've got a lot of it. They get to be eleven feet long.

MORROW: How did you gather up all this information?

BURROUGHS: Various places, like in books.

MORROW: Any idea why you would be interested in snakes? It's not like you keep snakes.

BURROUGHS: No, I don't keep snakes.

MORROW: Any idea why?

BURROUGHS: Never ask anyone "why." (*Laughter.*) Never ask anyone "why." They've got a little bladder of poisonous venoms. Of course, the black widow has a very potent venom, you can [*inaudible*] a tiny amount, it'll make people deathly sick. It's not fatal for a healthy adult but it makes you very, very sick indeed. Gives you terrible stomach cramps.

MORROW: What kind of snakes do you have around here?

BURROUGHS: We have a team this year, they've caught about fifteen hundred dollars' worth of snakes. We've caught copperheads. They have quite a weak venom. These snake handlers get their reputation handling copperheads. It's about the same potency as the bushmaster. That is, two hundred milligrams is the fatal dose. But no copperhead would have anywhere near that much. They probably have fifty milligrams at the most so people very rarely die from a copperhead bite. So they got copperheads, and they got a [*inaudible*]. Small, about that big (*Gesturing.*), but Dean milked it for me just to show me how it's done. He's not into the venom business. He got a fatal dose: Sixty milligrams is the fatal dose for that kind of snake.

MORROW: What is the venom used for?

BURROUGHS: To make antivenom. That's a large-scale operation.

MORROW: You have to have the exact same snake venom to get the antivenom?

BURROUGHS: Sure, well, there are classes of venom. The two main classes are neuro- and hemotoxic venom. Neurotoxin is a nerve venom. That's the cobras. Cobras, kraits, sea snakes, mambas. This is quite painless. People may not even know they've been bitten right away with a mamba until they start to slur their words, their speech gets slurred like they're drunk, and then they're—boom— dead. Dean brought in a black mamba and a green mamba. When he was here he had a green mamba and he wouldn't let it out, they're too quick. Another thing about the mambas is they're very quick, they're very hysterical, and they will attack without provocation.

MORROW: They're arboreal?

BURROUGHS: They're arboreal, so they come slipping down out of the tree and they'll whack you. They can make ten miles on the level. That's fast.

MORROW: That's quick.

BURROUGHS: One of the quickest snakes. Quick and very aggressive and very dangerous. If I let it out, it would get up on something and I'd have a hell of a time getting it down. We let a cobra out in this room once—Dean had a cobra, thirteen feet long.

MORROW: In this room?

BURROUGHS: Yeah. It went all around the room. He had a special trick to control it with, though. He came out with a hook.

MORROW: Who is this?

BURROUGHS: Dean Ripa. He's a real professional snake catcher, he's been bitten three or four times.

MORROW: You don't go in for the big zoo-type animals then, you're not crazy about them, elephants or . . . ?

BURROUGHS: Oh, well, no, I don't have the facilities. (*Laughter.*) He had the Gaboon viper, he had one of those and laid it down on the couch here. Now this thing is about *that* big around and *that* long, weighed thirty pounds. Had a head like a small shovel. That's a hell of a thing to be bitten by. They have both neuro- and hemotoxic venom and a lot of it. Fangs about an inch long. It just lay there and growled. They growl, like a dog.

MORROW: On your couch here?

BURROUGHS: Yes. He growled, like a dog. Another thing about them, see, most snakes do this. (*Makes a slithering gesture.*) The viper walks on its ribs like a caterpillar. It looks very sluggish, but they can move very, very rapidly, they can catch a rat in the air. Very dangerous. . . .

MORROW: How did this Gaboon move?

BURROUGHS: Crawls on its ribs, eyes straight ahead.

MORROW: Ripa was just showing off his snakes?

BURROUGHS: He had eight of them that he had to offer. I said I couldn't have them in the house because of the cats. . . . There's very little money in this. I said, How much do you get for this Gaboon viper that you brought back from Ghana? Well, six hundred dollars. I said, That's ridiculous. I thought five thousand.

MORROW: What's the life expectancy of a Gaboon?

BURROUGHS: Oh, like most snakes they live quite a long while. I don't know just how long, but years. Ten, twenty, thirty years. They live a long time.

MORROW: You were talking about going to Madagascar, right?

BURROUGHS: Yes. Well, I don't know, I'm going to go down and talk to these people at Duke and find out all the details, you know, the visas and all that.

MORROW: That would be a great trip.

BURROUGHS: Yeah, very expensive to get there and back because it's so far. It's about five thousand dollars round-trip.

MORROW: That would be to go to see the lemurs?

BURROUGHS: Well, I'm going to see the lemurs here. Well, listen: that, and I want to see the whole of Madagascar, you know, the different plants, everything they got there. They've got all kinds of quite unique plants and animals.

MORROW: Have you been to the Galápagos?

BURROUGHS: No, I haven't, but I'm not so interested in that as I am in Madagascar. I'd also like to go to Easter Island, to see the giant heads.

> (*Morrow turns off the tape recorder for a break. When he turns it back on, the dialogue recommences with discussion about Central and South American environmental issues, particularly the denuding of rain forests in the Amazon, the Iran-Contra affair, American education, and political apathy among youth.*)

MORROW: I can imagine an argument, though, where it's not any worse now than it's ever been. It's just, it's the same kind of shit you must have complained about thirty years ago.

BURROUGHS: I wonder. I wonder. No, I think—

MORROW: You think it's gotten worse?

BURROUGHS: Oh, yes, I think the young people now are politically more ignorant than they were in my day. Jesus Christ, we at least looked at maps of the world, and I don't think there was anyone in the high school that I went to—of course, this was way before the war—but certainly they would all have been able to place France and England and Germany on a map of Europe.

MORROW: They would have been able to tell you who fought in World War I.

BURROUGHS: Yes, they probably would, and they would also know when the Civil War was fought.

MORROW: How do you turn something like this around?

BURROUGHS: I don't think you can, and I don't know the point in bothering with it.

MORROW: Why do you say that?

BURROUGHS: I'm not concerned about these stupid people. I'm more concerned with animals than with people now. There are too many people! They're not endangered *enough*.

Gavage

H. G. *Carrillo*

WHAT HE WOULDN'T DO to be higher than God about now, running with his boys, free in the sun, on the streets, knuckling rocks at the windows in the abandoned building down from his Moms'. Instead, he wakes to find the same sleety rain, his head ringing as it is drummed from nodding against the window, and he is still on the bus with the same raging hard-on.

They don't call it Juvey anymore—don't lock them up like he's heard they used to—and he isn't shut up in the house like his primo, Fredo, with an ankle bracelet and a mess of video games. No, he is on his way to being reformed. Re-formed, he has overheard his new social worker tell his Moms, in a new style in a new way, he'll learn skills, he'll learn a new way to look at the world.

Two years down of the four years he's to do. His Moms counts the days with Xs on a calendar in their kitchen like the new social worker told her would be best for showing how far he has come since the morning he was picked up with a gun and a Marlboro Reds box with half a blunt in his coat pocket.

Though he had been trying to tell them from the beginning that there was nothing to remember—look upon; reflect on—from that day when all he had done was get dressed, go out in the alley behind his Moms' to get high, and head toward school. The next thing he knew he was being thrown up against an unmarked.

The part he never told, would never tell, was how he had heard his boys yelling, running up behind him—he had no idea how many there were, or who was there for sure—and how as they passed he was spun a full 180 on the ice. The blunt was the only thing he could explain, the Reds box he had found in the trash outside the currency exchange down from his Moms', and he didn't smoke cigarettes.

Possession—of a handgun, of a *controlled substance*—at thirteen meant for the first time he could remember he was always under watch, was sent to a school with surveillance cameras in the classroom, they tested his pee weekly—sometimes twice a week—and he wasn't allowed to hang out with anyone, except his Moms, who still

225

called him Mateo or Teo or Spooky.

His whole body now responded to shouts of Ungarte! though only the Latin teachers or supervisor get it right, but it doesn't matter, he spends most of his time hiding the fact that whatever even comes close now—Ungarty! Ungrateful! Unguentino!—tears through him the same, from head to foot, like an open box cutter.

His dick won't let up, each bump the bus takes runs a white-hot electric current from his balls that oozes out of the tip and makes him wonder what will keep him from screaming his head off like the big Mexican kid just this past summer who lost it on the way back to the city, lost it so bad they had to stop the bus. Rolling on the floor screaming so much their supervisor that day had to call in, screaming that took three boys to hold the boy down he was thrashing about so. Gnashing his teeth, screaming until the kid had lost his voice but kept on screaming anyway, screaming until just a girlish rubber toy squeak was coming out when the paramedics came and put a needle in his arm.

They had been out picking cabbage that day. Sweaty and foul as they were from work, they had to stand in line on the side of the highway in the sun, while cars passed and honked, a carful of girls blew them kisses while the paramedics lifted the boy, who by then was no longer screaming but was making gurgling—head and eyes rolling—pigeon-like sounds, as he was carried on a stretcher out of the bus and shoved—like bread into an oven—into the back of an ambulance.

And as much as he tries to remember being taken out the next week, to the same fields, the same farm, bent over for hours multiplying rows of cabbages, remembering that even though they had all seen the screaming kid but said nothing about it and instead complained how much their backs ached at the end of the day, how they thought their arms would fall off, Ungarte can't help but touch himself. At the same time that he rolls his body away from the boy sleeping in the seat next to him toward the window, he forces his thumb into the top seam of his left trouser pocket until it gives way and he has his hand around it, can huddle into himself and slowly stroke.

He had lost the right to have weekends he could call his own and just roll out of bed when he wanted to, head to the park, to the basketball court, eat what he wanted when he wanted and where he wanted. The first year, he and his group of boys were taken to the city's parks daily where they had to pick up garbage. The supervisors broke rules, beat boys, swore at them, once he had even seen a boy get spit on.

226

But there was nothing they could do about it and nobody to tell. The new way, his new social worker told his Moms, is an experiment they are trying that takes a few selected boys out of the city each weekend to redirect their energies. And his Moms trusts her and signed the papers because his new social worker is pretty and white, and somewhere along the way learned to speak Spanish with the clean, clipped, clear precision of a newscaster. His Moms wants to trust her, like in a movie wants to be the brown woman who comes to trust a white woman without having it somehow come flying back in her face.

Often, when he strokes he thinks of his new social worker's tetas and what the powder he sometimes sees between them smells like. Even though he isn't supposed to have a girlfriend or anything like that, he sometimes kicks it in the laundry room with a girl—older, probably about twenty-five, who presses her lips against his neck, tells him *to pretend a teacher is about to walk in*, says to call her Kai, even though he knows her name to be María and he has seen her with her husband and three children—and sometimes it's the way she unzips him, pushes the crotch of her panties to the side, and, with an insistence that feels like a mix of anger and hatred, shoves him into her, and the way—when she's done—she just walks away leaving him unsatisfied, hanging out.

Though right now he strokes to nothing at all, a black hole, a still, warm, wet, shapeless place.

Since the year Ungarte picked up trash in the parks, he and groups of boys have been taken out of the city, for country air, for the experience, for whole weekends, his new social worker said, so they would have some sense of how they were to organize their time once their time was their own again.

Before the cabbage farm he had spent every weekend for three months at a dairy, mucking stalls, three hours from the city, and since then he had picked apples, pears, and melons. They raked and shoveled and lifted and loaded, ate, washed, and took care of their bladders when they had permission, slept in barracks built for migrants with a supervisor or two who rotated, keeping watch over them in the night. No hats or caps, hoodies or chains, no jewelry or personal items. They wear security tags that are scanned by the supervisors as they are shifted from place to place, but they should leave wallets, IDs, and money at home. They were free to choose whatever shirt they wanted, as long as it was blue or brown or green or khaki and had no writing or pictures on it and was versatile

227

enough—most wore sweatshirts over T-shirts—for shifts in weather;
as long as it was not a sports shoe, they were free to choose whatever
they wanted as long as it was a work boot—preferably steel-toed in
brown, not black—and appeared to be utilitarian rather than fashion-
able. They were all issued a jacket in the spring they exchanged for
fall/winter ones. It is not really a uniform, his new social worker told
his Moms, they get four pairs of khakis and she should let him take
care of the cleaning and repairing of them himself.

Sewn tough by prisoners upstate, new, fresh out of the packages,
the pants fell like a double-sided drop cloth. Double-stitched at the
seams and all sized larger than they are marked. There is no give at
all in them except for the pockets—flimsy in their construction,
something men who made them predicted boys who wore them would
need: a relay of secret hands—opening into a dark, damp, focusless
universe of sparks that connected to no real woman, but to thousands,
the smell of dank, of fingers and upper lips, a mouthful of unwashed
hair, the burn of salt in the corners of his mouth. And just when he
is close to letting loose against the back of the zipper, a tear of sunlight jags the sleet and gray outside and bounces him back upright
and blinking.

The Hudson rolls black and green opposite the direction they are
headed, and through the bare trees it is as if they are being raked
through the icy water. To ease the queasy in his stomach he begins
to count the heads on either side of the aisle in the rows ahead of
him. And it is at fourteen that he gets to the white boy.

Light reddish-brown hair, pale greenish-pale spotted skin, he is
called Mueller, but even the supervisors, as though they've never seen
one before either—wide-set, nearly colorless eyes that first make
him appear blind—call him White Boy. White Boy, come here! White
Boy, I'm talking to you! Over the last three weeks when they have
been sent out to dig, cut, and stack roots into trucks, only once did
Ungarte hear one of them call out Mueller!, and it is only by chance
that he saw the white boy turn his greasy head toward the sound and
walk in its direction.

Sixteen, Seventeen, Eighteen, Ungarte counts. There had never
been one before; most looked like he did or some variation of him.
Brown boys, black boys, there had even been an Indian from some-
place in India that had wanted a girl so much, said he couldn't speak
English too well at the time, so he let her know by pissing outside of
her door like a dog until someone in the building caught him. And
where Ungarte saw a logic rise out of what the Indian told him—how

poor his family was; how they all lived in a one-room; how they needed to come to the US to find out just how dark they were— Ungarte found he couldn't care and couldn't appreciate what a white boy could do to get himself put on one of these buses once a week. Twenty. Twenty-One, no reason he could think of why a white boy should have been there. They played golf, they were loved by girls who smelled like cream, they lived in houses like the one the bus turns off the main highway and heads for, houses with gables, rolling lawns, white fences, gardens, trees all around, and the nearest neighbor miles away at another farm. They lived in high-rises with doormen, they took cabs all the time, they drove expensive cars or hired them, they drank scotch and fucked the women in *Playboy* magazine and married the ones that wore head scarves and dark sunglasses and shopped one store for olive oil and another one that only sold cheese.

Twenty-Eight! the supervisor calls out as he scans Ungarte's pass and pushes him to line up with the others on the grass.

Not like the military, his new social worker had told his Moms, just something to teach him we live in a world that has rules and a certain order. Hands at his sides, spine straight, eyes forward, despite the wind, the razory specks of sleet that take bites out of his face, nearly twelve heads in front of him, he can see the only one not shivering in the cold is the white boy. He noticed when it was still hot out the white boy didn't sweat as much as the rest of them, the white boy carried less, took more breaks, required more water, he needed more breaks to go to the bathroom, ate less, took up less space, and now, apparently, handled the cold better. It's how they do, Ungarte thinks.

Welcome! Gentlemen! the farmer shouts as he walks across the field toward them in a pair of black rubber boots that come up to his knees. It is the first time Ungarte has actually seen the farmer, or the owner of any of the places they've worked. He is a white guy, of course, bald and bright as an egg with a great heft of belly underneath a brand-new Carhartt. His hands are as big and pink as raw catcher's mitts and he throws them into the air, tells them he is happy they've come to work with him the next two months, that he wants them to feel comfortable. And then he stops and says as comfortable as they can within the rules and regulations set up by their supervisors. Nearly a hundred and twenty-five years ago, he tells them, Hudson River Farms had been an impossible dream his Dublin-born great-grandfather had of a tiny place he could raise enough food to keep his family of ten alive

229

on, and now with a hundred and eighty acres, over fifty products in a world market, a tiny wish has returned a thousandfold.

Boys, the farmer starts, and he begins to tell them about what a simple dream can do—how far it can take you; where it can lead—and Ungarte can see that White Boy is the only one who seems to be listening. His blind-looking eyes are on the farmer; he nods his head up and down as though it were tied by a string to one of the man's big pink fingers. Neither of them—unlike everyone else, even the supervisors—is pounding his feet against the ground and clapping his hands against the cold. And maybe it is because he can—despite the bitterness of the wind, the rush of gooseflesh that runs from his calves up to his neck—just by pushing his hips forward, Ungarte thinks his dick hard again, pushes it forward and up toward the tag on his zipper until it aches to poke out over his waistband, tents the front of his pants so that anyone who looked could see, and he finds himself unable to give a fuck.

Instead of going to work straightaway, they are taken into a white building smaller than the main house that the farmer calls the little barn, though it looks more like a church to Ungarte. The echo from their boots against the concrete floor rises toward the exposed ceiling beams of the vast, mostly empty room. There are rows of white folding chairs set up in front of a screen, and even though the room is heated by a woodstove in a far corner, after standing in the cold, the blast of heat that meets them as they file in is enough to force most of them to take their jackets off while they line up against the wall and wait for their next instruction. No, no, no, the farmer says, no, I want you all to take seats, feel comfortable.

The front remains empty. Ungarte sees most have seats in between the screen and the back, and a hulking figure at the far end of the row to his right slouches and immediately begins to snore once the lights are lowered. And as the screen begins to flicker with hundreds of ducks—white feathered, white billed, streaked with black—he slips his hand in his pocket and his cock instantly bucks and stretches as though it will never stop blooming, turn his breath inside out, force his lungs to work backward.

He sucks his lips into a tight circle as the farmer says, We hatch over five thousand ducklings per year, the farm processes eleven thousand pounds—that's five thousand kilos—of foie gras. Fa-Wah Gra-ah, he pronounces it for them over and over again and he then begins waving his hands in rhythm for Ungarte and the other boys to repeat. Some catch on, but most continue to look at the screen. The farmer tells them it is the best foie gras outside of France. Some, he says, grinning all toothy and wide as if he is taking them all into his confidence, consider it better, and he raises his hands, Fa-Wah Grah!, to conduct them again. And the fact that Ungarte can hear the white boy's voice—clearly, over the muttering of all the boys around him—believes he can smell his rotten breath, see his crusty, uneven teeth, causes him to lose it, so as the lights come up he pulls his hand out of his pants without busting a nut.

Even then, instead of going to work, they are lined up and sent crunching across an icy field and into another dining hall. Before the farmer can announce that, here on Hudson River Farms, the help, the management, and the owners all eat together, Ungarte finds himself wishing for a time just months ago when lunch meant a box with a sandwich with orange cheese and wilted lettuce; he wants the two bottles of warm apple juice, the dried-out orange or the over-ripened apple they are used to eating on the side of the road or in the middle of a field. Bright and noisy with the clattering of plastic trays and the low growl of men's voices, the dining-room smells make him suddenly hungry, a deep-to-the-middle-of-his-stomach hungry that makes him want to knock people in the aisles over, stomp them down, kick them out of the way to get to the hairnetted women passing out trays.

Foie gras, the farmer announces when the trays are placed in front of them, but says they shouldn't expect it at every meal; this is a one-time special occasion. And the smile he throws is so wide and grinny, proud and self-satisfied, it is only that Ungarte is so hungry he can taste the bottom of his stomach and that he hasn't asked them to pray that keeps him from getting up and kicking all the man's teeth down his throat.

He is caught off guard. All he can recall of the film they were shown, all he remembers, is the ducklings, trampling all over each other, and the feathers and the drone of the farmer's voice. In front of him there is a green salad, some peach slices swimming in a clear-ish juice, and what looks to him like torrejas or buñelos—sweet, like the kind his tía Rachel makes—and it smells like lechón, like Christmas, like waking cold mornings warm, safe and sound alone in his bed with nowhere to go and nothing to do. And it is what promised to be warm on his tongue, go down savory, fill his belly in ways that will make him feel all-over sexy and sleepy, that suddenly turns to shit in his teeth. Exactly what he would think shit would taste like—gritty and warm, as if it was coming directly from the source—with the consistency of clay.

And it is precisely as he realizes he has no idea where to spit, Ungarte turns his head and sees the white boy, grinning like a fool—shit all stuck to his teeth like he's been lapping at the farmer's ass—and it makes Ungarte wonder what the boy would look like with his head split open, brains spilling out like a cracked egg, dangled out a window by his heels, submerged underwater, eyes all bulging.

By the clock, they'll get to work in less than twenty minutes. The supervisors will dole out, show how to do their tasks, and like always, right before the hard work starts, the white boy will complain about his stomach and need to spend the first half hour—when everyone else is breaking his back—locked away in the toilet. He'll come back, grabbing his belly, complaining. He might get to lie down for a half hour halfway through the day, while everyone else is aching, stinking—ready to pack it in, readied, primed to shove his fist into the first person that says anything—because there were enough supervisors out there who never seemed to see the bullshit in the white boy's batting lashes, or know enough to know when he was telling a white-boy lie.

Lining up in the hallway, a shoulder against the wall, they wait. Permission, they are supposed to say, and one of the supervisors will tap him ahead to form another line in front of the men's room. And it is possible that Ungarte is hard just because he manages to call out Permission before the white boy, hard—Permission, he hears the white boy's voice behind him—because he can hear the white boy's feet shuffling on the floor the way he does when he's trying to tell them all his stomach is giving him trouble. Permission, Permission, Ungarte hears behind him, and where it may be any number of the other boys, it only sounds like the white boy begging—Permission, Permission—like the white boy whimpering as if he were being wrung for the last drop of blood. Hard, so deliciously, pearly, shiny hard, with the white boy the next to go in behind him, Ungarte nearly kicks the door open, before ripping at his zipper and blowing his load all over the seat—the back—the rim of the toilet, and the wall directly above it.

He is the best, he is the strongest, the fastest, the smartest, Ungarte tells himself, and between the fifth and sixth weeks of going out to the farm, his new social worker tells his Moms that the reports from his supervisors are all glowing. Always on time, Always takes the initiative, Never complains, Never swears, Never gets in fights, she says, and as she checks each one of his praises off he notices her creamy tetas bounce.

Though when the social worker leaves, his Moms tells him that she didn't need that immodest woman to tell her that she needs to be proud. She was always proud of him, what she needed was to know that he was safe.

Cuídate hijo, she says each time he's off to play with the ducks.

Their first day in, the farmer had shown them the difference between ducks and geese, which soon became crystalline to Ungarte when a lone duck dove through the air to catch a goose behind the back of the head. The bird turned its head and within seconds had the duck's leg in its beak. Within seconds, there had been a skirmish of feathers and squawking when, as if from nowhere, one goose turned into fifty or more, and the farmhands ran toward them, crying out with rakes and hoes in hand, and when it was all cleared, had it not been for the blood, what was left would have been indistinguishable from the feathers, grit, and bird shit in the dirty snow.

This hardly ever happens, the farmer told them, nearly never, he said. Watching the man who had talked about owning everything they could see, standing on land that had belonged to his family forever—that was his to give to his sons—with his mouth wide open, had made Ungarte hard all over again. Never, the farmer had said like he might cry, which made Ungarte all the harder. Never, the farmer said, he couldn't figure how this had happened. Though the only one of them who asked why was the white boy.

Then again, White Boy was the only one who later asked why they had to muck out the stalls and clean cages when the ducks would only come and shit all over them later. He wanted to know why they needed to use gloves when they were raking up hay if what they were doing was safe, if they weren't going to get anything from touching duck shit all day long.

White Boy throws long sighs into the air anytime he's asked to do anything; outside, in the cold, his hate for nearly anything said— any distance they are asked to walk, any new chore they are asked to do, anytime they are told to stand, sit, haul, or shovel—is spit up as icy vapor. Even though the foie gras they had had the first day made him sick—sent him retching into the corners of the barn until he was sweaty with the dry heaves—so sick, he was unable to work—he complains about the orange cheese and bologna sandwiches they get—he's barely able to stomach an apple—he calls out to the farmer every time they see him, when are they going to get some more of that stuff they had when they first got here. That brown stuff! White Boy screams after the farmer as if the man would

233

somehow not know what he meant.

Hey, Mueller, the farmer will call out, raising a hand in the air as he passes. He knows White Boy's name. It's just how they do, someone will mutter around him, but Ungarte lets it slide off him, lets nearly everything the other boys say while they are working slide off him. Like grease on a duck's ass, he would say if anyone was to ask, but they don't and he's pretty sure he's the only one who would think it was funny, laugh so hard at shit like that his dick goes hard and he can taste blood in his mouth.

He keeps his nose pretty clean, his new social worker tries to translate from the report his supervisors submit for his Moms. But the young woman quickly gives up, and just tells her that he does everything that he is told and more. He wonders how much more is more.

Ungarty! the farmer will call out to him the same way he calls Mueller when he wants to get White Boy's attention; however, Ungarte is the only boy that he will go up and talk to. Through the supervisors he gives Ungarte what he calls special assignments— Give it to Ungarty, he tells them, he'll get it done—and when White Boy howls, why is it always Ungarty, the farmer just calls over his shoulder as he walks away, Be more like Ungarty. He's the most trusted member on his crew, his new social worker tells his Moms, he sets an example for all the other boys, the farmer is placing Mateo in charge of the most important chore that they have, he'll be the leader for all the boys.

Cuídate hijo, his Moms says before she goes out. When he overhears her talking on the phone to his tía—and to the man she flirts with who runs the bodega at the corner—she now says things like, Teo works weekends, and, While Teo is off at his job. His new social worker now says things like, It has had an overall good effect on him, There is marked improvement in his schoolwork, He has no problems getting on with his teachers or his classmates. Although, as if yanked upright by the flowered housedress his Moms wears before she goes out to clean other people's floors and feed their babies, it is as if she suddenly remembers there is no paycheck attached to what he is doing. It's just payment of a debt that will eventually claim more debt. And she loses her smile as she says it again—Cuídate hijo—before she heads out.

Both hands shoved deep into his pockets—each of them bottomless: Full of himself—as he follows the farmer, he counts each crunch of his boots—two to one—against those of the farmer as they cross the icy field. I want to tell you something, the farmer says without turning to see if Ungarte is there or not, you're going to be in charge of, well more or less semi-in-charge-of, one of the most important functions on this farm. Without this we're nothing, the farmer yells as he slides the door on a barn none of them has ever worked in before.

This is what we call the twenty-day barn, the farmer says.

It's the sound that hits him first—the screeching, piercing Help-HelpHelpHelpHelp! of birds and the growl of machine engines—that deafens him, and then it's the smell. For weeks he and the other boys have been around thousands of birds. They had spent time learning to count the days from lay to hatch; they learned to turn the birds and the bins that separated males from females; they threw seed and filled feeders; they had dug up, buried, and hosed away mountains and mountains of shit, though suddenly there is something in the air in the barn that knots his stomach over onto itself and forces it toward his throat, and it's the sudden shock of the farmer's voice— Come on, Ungratey, let's get started—that makes the boy swallow hard and keeps him from shaming himself.

This is where we bring them at six months, the farmer yells over the din. Unlike in France where they're kept twisted up in pens, he says, pulling the boy closer to him to yell in his ear, we let them walk around, well, as long as they're able.

Like beetles scurrying in the light, the four women and one man working in the barn are dark and small and quick between what at first to Ungarte looks like a chaos of Mulards, but he soon can see each woman is seated on a slotted wooden box between two corrals. From one corral, they grab a duck by the neck, turn it upside down, and scan the tag on its foot before shoving it into the box.

Show the boy, the farmer tells the man.

Although the man is not all that old—not as old as Ungarte's Moms—his face is drawn up like an apple that has sat around too long. His two front teeth are brown and look as though they have been cut in half, and even over the bird stink, he gives off a steamy, stale mixture of tobacco and BO. Ungarte can feel the man's eyes look him up and down before he spits out ¿Hablas niño?

And Ungarte imagines that it is because Spanish to the farmer is a stream of sounds like the screeching of the birds or the grind of the machines he continues to yell at him while the instructions are given. Don't worry if you don't get this right the first time, the farmer tells him, it took me a while, it takes everyone a while.

When the birds get so heavy they can no longer stand in the corrals they need to be put here, the man tells Ungarte as he points to the wall; while at the same time the farmer says, They really don't feel anything, it's not as if they have the same kind of gag reflexes we have. They hardly feel it, they don't know what's happening, the farmer yells over the man's instructions of how to shove a duck or goose into the wooden box—feet first, hold the neck tight, push the middle down hard—and the farmer tells him there is no need to be nervous, none at all.

Don't worry, the farmer cautions as the man shows Ungarte how to stroke the bird's neck—tells him to hum, so it feels comfortable, but be firm so it knows to be a little bit afraid of you—as he inserts the feeder into its throat. Don't let the bird pull away from you, the man says, the bird—it's a bird—it don't know when it's full. You're waiting for the machine to kick off like a rifle, then you pull it out.

Don't be afraid to make a mistake or two, the farmer says as the man relinquishes and makes way for Ungarte, when I was a boy my first dozen or so were failures, colossal failures. Killed off a dozen and a half of my father's prime geese in between getting it right.

Ungarte spreads his legs wide as he straddles the wooden box that is still warm from the rump before his. It's all about getting the right angle the first time in, the farmer tells him, there's no undoing it once you've gone in at the wrong angle, and you just end up goring them anyway if you pull out and try again.

We've tried other ways, the farmer tells him as the man wheels the machine in front of Ungarte. For years we've tried to develop a bird through training or inbreeding or crossbreeding—whatever they call it—so all they do all day long is eat, but the damn birds forget everything else they need to know about survival, and the fuckers start laying eggs anywhere, the males won't rut, or whatever it is they do, females won't brood—they hardly even eat, none of them—and they lay all over the lawn, on the roof, everywhere.

By the time Ungarte reaches for the first bird, he realizes the farmer is no longer talking to him. Over the noise of the machines and the honking and quaking of birds, over the instructions of the man in Spanish, the farmer is just talking. And it is when the man shouts ¡Bueno! that the farmer looks down to see Ungarte grab and successfully feed his third bird. That's it! That's it! the farmer is yelling, he slaps the man on his shoulders, That's it, he's got it, to which the man says, Yes. That's it—as Ungarte goes on to feed the fourth then the twelfth then the twentieth bird in a row—like you were born to do this, the farmer says. And he's all teeth, the man who showed him says as he throws a hand in the air and walks away, and Ungarte is pleased, not because he is good at what he has been chosen to do, but because he's hard, hard hard hard, so close—so close—hard.

That afternoon, at lunch, the farmer names Ungarte Head of Special Projects. At first none of the other boys can be bothered to lift their eyes from their plates to care, but when the farmer announces that Ungarte will be choosing four of them to work with him on the project, suddenly all but White Boy throw a hand up.

He picks Fulton and Andres because they are both strong and silent and push through heat and cold and sweat and ache like it's nothing. Villarreal, because he's smart and quick and never cuts corners and always gets the work out of the way. And, of course, he chooses White Boy, who he knows will whine and complain and cry and clutch his stomach and spit up his lunch and act like a bitch all day long.

There was no way he was going to do that, White Boy insists as the five of them—now named The Feeding Team by the farmer—go back to the barn. No way, no way in hell am I doing no fucking special project, White Boy mutters to himself, though he comes along anyway. Perhaps he realizes he would have spent the rest of the day wet and covered with mud or imagines there will be less work where they are headed.

The barn is warmer and damper than Ungarte remembered it earlier. A sheen rises on the faces of the other boys, and they shed hoodies and sweaters and stand in sweat-marked T-shirts, watching the man give the same instructions. And as Ungarte watches, something strangley lets go in him—even though he is unsure of what it is—he knows he knows what he needs to know before he needs to know, perhaps for the first time ever, before he needs to know it. So, when the man calls out—Fulton, then Andres and then Villarreal as trained and ready to go—and he asks about White Boy, who has begun wearing a trench as he paces four or five feet of dirt littering the air with what he can't do—how he'll be sick all over the place if they try to make him, how he had a condition—Ungarte tells the man to leave him be.

Just let him go, he tells them when the other boys complain that White Boy should at least be asked to rake up the shit and cart out the ducks that accidentally die in the middle of feeding. He puts White Boy on keeping the feeders filled to the top—not allowing any of them to go less than halfway full—which allows him to go on complaining. And by the next afternoon, White Boy believes that he has a fever, isn't sure he can hold his lunch down. He needs to lie down every half hour or so, then every ten or fifteen minutes, and then he just spends the rest of the day arms curled around his belly, trudging between the bathroom at the far end of the barn and a hay pallet he has raked up for himself nearby.

It doesn't seem to matter which of the supervisors comes through, each kicks the boy's boots and screams for him to get his ass up and get back to work, but the moment they leave, White Boy starts to complain again and Ungarte chooses to ignore him. The other boys eventually begin to fill their own feeders when they go empty, they rake for themselves and carry the dead birds to the grinder, and at the end of the weekend—when they are all shaking and their muscles are knotted up with ache—as they are counted and scanned back onto the bus headed back to the city, the farmer comes out to say he has never seen workers like Ungarte and his team, never before has he had a group of workers—even the ones we pay—do as much in as little time.

And even though it doesn't seem to do anything for the other boys—none of them even turn in the direction of the farmer's voice—Ungarte notices that White Boy turns and waves back at the sound of his own name, his face is shiny and his chest is pushed out. The farmer is waving as their bus heads toward the road, and White Boy is the only one who looks, the only one who turns and waves back. And sitting directly behind him, Ungarte is hard—up and down in his pocket the entire way back.

They are the best group, the most efficient, the most on the job, the famer says over the next couple of weeks as he stops by the boys' tables while they are eating, when he brings visitors to the farm. He hauls troops of men in suits out to the feeding barn, who tiptoe around bird droppings and puddles of White Boy puke, to take a look at a group the likes of which, the farmer says, he has never seen.

Open wide, Villarreal tells the goose he is feeding as he stops and throws on a grin so wide and forced Ungarte imagines it burns the inside of his ears when the farmer comes around with two photographers. They also take pictures of Fulton and Andres, and the other workers. They get shots of the rafters, the geese, the ducks, the cages, the feeders, the boxes the feeders sit on, the bleeds of gray daylight through the dirty windows high along the top of the barn. The muck, the slush drain, the gutter that runs the perimeter, and then they leave without taking a single picture of White Boy.

What the hell? White Boy yells out the door after them. What the hell? echoes across the field as the photographers head toward the main house without turning to hear where it came from. What the hell? as he looks to the other boys who keep working. He looks to the man who had shown them all how to feed, who simply responds, No que hablo, as he walks away from the boy.

Throughout the rest of the morning, White Boy complains of stomach problems, he asks the others if they can hear the ringing in his ears, see how blurry his vision is, but eventually reclaims his job filling the feeders with a cursing, slamming, angry vengeance. And for hours as he mutters fuck thems—fuck yous, fuck anyone who ever walked up in heres—into the air without any particular target in sight, he makes sure to top each feeder as soon as it is three or four inches down. The next morning, they can all kiss his ass—kiss his shiny pink ass—as he rakes piles of dirt and droppings into another pile of dirt and droppings only to do it and rake it all up again and again. They can kiss it—kiss it, kiss it—kiss my ass all of them until their lips get chapped, and Ungarte recognizes it is just the thought of him spending the rest of the assignment this way, just the thought of White Boy folding and refolding himself in a pile of droppings and dust for the next five weeks that makes him so hard and heady he drops the goose he has just fed and instead of reaching for the next bird he shoves his hand deep in his pocket.

He has wrapped his ankles around the base of the box, presses his thighs into its edges, and thinks he could watch White Boy sweep the same pile of dirt forever when suddenly White Boy stops, drops the rake, and announces he is bored. Never been so bored in my entire life! he yells as he opens the door, and it is as if, caught up short by all the light and cold air he is letting in—he turns two full circles—he realizes he has nowhere to go and there is no one to hear him.

He wanders around a while until one of the supervisors walks through and he lies back down on the pallet, holds his stomach, and scrunches his eyes as he always has. Though, I'm bored! he pops up again when he hears the door slam behind the man. Show me how, he pulls at Villarreal's shirtsleeve, I'm bored, show me how! But he is shaken off as Villarreal drops the duck he has finished feeding and goes for a goose in one of the cages. Show me, come on, man, show me, White Boy follows him. And just at the moment when Ungarte is certain Villarreal looks as though he is about to send White Boy through a wall, he grabs the bird he was after and pushes past the boy.

No que hablo, says the man who had shown Ungarte how; No que hablo, the man who had shown them all how says as White Boy goes to grab for him, pleading, Show me. Come on, man, show me! when Ungarte comes up and separates the two of them by shoving White Boy away. But it only causes White Boy to turn toward and follow Ungarte, Show me, come on, man, it ain't going to hurt you to show me. And to his surprise, Ungarte finds White Boy backs up like a dog—You do what you always do! he yells at the boy—as he advances toward him. You do what you always do, he says in a lower tone— one that doesn't part his teeth and comes out of the center of his chest—and even though the boy keeps talking, he takes a step back for each of Ungarte's toward him until he falls backward onto his hay pallet in the corner.

Though it isn't seconds after Ungarte is back to work—has inserted the feeder deep into a mallard throat—that White Boy is up pestering whoever is closest. I'm bored, show me how, I'm bored. And it is not until the duck goes limp in his hands—he feels it collapse; the bottom split out of it—and he feels the sloppy wet plop of innards and the rattling spill of feed on the tops of his boots that he realizes he has gone hard all over again.

Across the barn White Boy goes nearly faceless as an egg, and even though his mouth is open and moving—a red wet vibrating circle in the air in front of him—whatever the boy is saying it is the birds' screeches, the roar of machines, and a numb thump that floods Ungarte's ears. Not a sound, but a stream of feathers, bills, wide-open throats that seems to be coming from the top of White Boy's head, out the back of his neck, that tells him he is actually headed toward the boy through the sea of birds, past the cages and machines.

He hears the squeal of the wire catch on the toilet and the door slam shut, he hears himself counting to ten the way his new social worker has told him he needs to, but it is only as he hears himself counting—one forty-seven, one forty-eight, one forty-nine—under his breath that he realizes he has passed it. And where he hears the wire catch and the door slam again, hears himself throwing the lock, if White Boy says, Don't, You can't come in here, I'm sick, My stomach, Leave me alone, he has no idea. He hears himself count seven fifty-two, seven eighty-nine, nine hundred as he lifts White Boy off the toilet, and flips him around. Through the forearm he has wrapped around the boy's throat—his fist nearly fits in the boy's mouth—he can feel the quickness of the boy's pulse. Through the door he can make out the sounds of birds and machines, the occasional yelled instruction, he hears the rhythmic banging of the boy's head against the back wall, he hears himself reach eleven hundred and fifteen, and his pace slacken before he recognizes he has been muttering, You'll do what you always do, under his breath.

He doesn't bother to shower or clean his boots over the rest of the weekend. As if posting a dare, he wears whatever has splashed on him while he waits.

And it is the shift in light that he first notices during the last few weeks of their assignment. Shorter shadows as the days grow longer open sudden golden jags quick as falling stars or lightning-bug flashes of opportunity in the otherwise muddy Hudson. He is awake, increasingly awake with each trip up. Each time the farmer sees him— Ungartey is the best of the best; Never seen anybody get a group to work like he does, that Ungartey!—sets something fiercely animal off in his chest, pricks his hearing to things like the low snore coming out of a boy three seats in front of him, things like the faint smell reminiscent of the undercoat on a goat that comes up in the air when there are twenty or so of them loaded on the bus in the mornings, perch him on the edge of his seat, clear his eyesight toward the slightest movement out of the ordinary. He is primed, readied, and hard.

I've never seen anything quite like it, his new social worker tells his Moms earlier in the week, he's a new man, becoming a model student, dependable—getting stronger every day, taking advantage of everything that the program has to offer. Hold on, mijo, his Moms tells him after the woman leaves, hold on, with each day she takes off the calendar.

Last night in the laundry room, he had turned the stroller with the sleeping baby in it away and bent Kai over the dryer. As they eased into the warm vibration of the machine, deep deep inside her he had found he wanted to tell her there will be no miracles here as much as he wants to tell her a duck's heart can reach up to a thousand beats per second in flight—he knows, he has looked it up—but to worry about either is a waste of imagination. But when he started to he accidentally slipped and called her María, which in a second caused her to push him off her, tell him she had to go. She collected her panties off the floor and dropped them into the machine she had going and rolled the baby onto the elevator. It's a big place, he said, even though he knew she was probably at her front door by then, with the kind of logic that wastes a whole duck they've bred and tended just for its liver. He thinks she needs to know it is the kind of logic that makes it impossible for a boy to just be holding a gun. He thinks she should know things like that as well as the ways around it. He wants to tell her it is possible to make a white boy— now when he walks around him, looks at him, blows his breath onto his neck—go pink and very, very silent. But he would need to tell a woman who, because her mamá named her María, calls herself María.

Three Poems
Kevin Holden

SIMULIIDAE

that would
ever on the surface
ever expanding / of the world—
black fly horse fly
star black & prismatic
eye, that would
be a code
ever inturning move to
the animal moving
unthought, on the surface—
fly out in exponential hum
rattle out
the brain cup
green metal
sheen at the splitting
discus, for cold
skeletal drink at the warm
body, & buzz in the rotating
hollow of the instant
& see ultraviolet
wings tesseracting the spectra
beyond
to unfollow
green variations, buffalo
gnat lying fallow to unfold
the brain
or hover—
in some air

Kevin Holden

MIRROR

that would be
humans moving
& what, to be human?
& what, to see that or care
the difference spreading
that is, dot variations pixels
in zirconia
no one would say to watch that
other humans moving on a screen
they
interest us
or, bodies / language
that would be, a memory
of that place
nonhuman row through the trees
following the
other animals
to hold a green object
moving through the north
& up & up
towns & ice
the poor, the railroad, the wood, the lakes
dark animals
& move under glass pieces
how much, say down shaft blond
the jay curving in, meanly
phoning
string code farther for a green window
& hold the wire
a talking bird

URSUS ARCTOS

& black glass
reflection
in snow's bank, hedged in—
to think
the animal's thought
unthought—bear in the blizzard
tracks immediately
covered by snow, endlessly thickening—
not-you to say
or feeling, outside the
horizon of time &
the colored lights aurora
mind to unravel the cave of winds
shadow the city in the bear's mind
glyph pattern 2-D hunter
fall falling fall
sinking in 20 names
to touch
the lens of the
boundary inside the boundaries
& stagger unaware
under hexagons

The C————s[1,2]
Monica Datta

25 JANUARY 2013

THESE WERE NEITHER the velvety spaces of his childhood Januaries with nineteen hours of malamute sky, nor the crepuscular glows of the Parisian winter, cloaking tree skeletons in rosy-golden inky sheets through April. Winter daylight in New York should have been crass and efficient, nine to five, but this year a hurricane blew out the greenish autumn, and now it was always dark.

This morning half asleep—again, with the lights on—Neal saw a set of unblinking, beady yellow marbles nestled in Saul-scaly chromium-oxide lids, pebbled and dappled and mean.

A zoological society in Michigan had contacted his temp agency in search of an illustrator. The assignment was overdue. Neal left a raw, creamy paper wound at the bottom of the brochure's front cover to accommodate the beast. The fee was the three months' rent owed to the landlord. Neal asked if he could draw a snake instead. Not that there was ever any *good* news about c————s; they weren't tiger kittens. He turned on the radio.[3]

Yikes! said the newscaster jovially. There was heavy rain in South Africa. Flooding, which had already killed six people, was about to destroy a c———— farm at the border with Botswana. This odious farmer saved the hotbed of shoes and handbags and murder by letting *all fifteen thousand of them into the Limpopo River.*

---

[1]For some reason Neal was slightly more comfortable with c———— than a————.

[2]Annotations by Jean-Louis Katz.

[3]Or paintings, drawings, sculpture. Comics, animations, political cartoons. Children's stuffed toys. Children's wooden toys. Carvings. Etchings. Scratchings. Clawings. Puppets. Dragon puppets. Toad puppets. Lizard puppets. Inflatable rafts in their likeness. Or metal clothespins. Wooden clothespins.

31 MARCH 1983

It was rare for a four-year-old boy to feel his heart was being boiled in acid when he saw the word *a———* but so it had been. Neal's pop-up animal alphabet book had, on the first page, a monster with gaping jaws and huge teeth and gleaming jelly tongue. Rough with sores, it roared its name: *A———!* He always skipped that page.[4]

One day after school his mother was not home. At night on the telephone she said they gave her a little boy. His name was Rabindranath. Rabi for short.

Like Neal, his father had some afternoons off from school. They went to visit the next day, but Neal was not allowed to see Rabi. *You're too dirty,* his father explained on the way home, because Neal had not washed his hands.

That night in the hospital he took a moving staircase and saw them basking on the beams in fluorescent slime, mouths propped agape by natural levers. They lay on their sides revealing tiled bellies of celadon and their jaws hung open sideways like the lifts. They told Neal that if he took the lift he would turn to poured concrete.

At home, when he was about to go to sleep, Neal pressed against hard armor *because they were about to eat him!* He woke screaming next to a heap of books in his bed. Nina hit the shared bedroom wall and told him to shut up.

The *a———*s were everywhere. At school Sister Mary gave lessons about tooth brushing with Nessie, a squishy, high-voiced *a———* puppet who lived on her hand during the day and in the loch at night. There were wooden splinter-scaled *a———*s called dinosaurs on the ledges and in the toy box. In the afternoon he used up all the green paint (there was no more blue, the favorite) and had to use gray, and everything he did—cars, flowers, Rabi—looked like *a———*s. On the way home he saw their swampy homes in moss; their backs, buried in mud, in tire marks in the ground.[5]

---

[4] *A———* resembled other words with mechanistic and hostile qualities: aggressive, agrarian, allegorical, agate, algae, profligate, ligature, Ligeti, litigator, alleged, allegation, alley, agility, Rigoletto. Elevators. Escalators. Percolators. Insulators. Refrigerators. Incinerators. Liberators. Aviators. Radiators. Validators. Instigators. Carburetors. Dilators. Flagellators. Aggravated, agrestic, acrostic. Accelerate. Aggregate.

[5] Handbags of *a———* skin, but really all handbags. Leather of *a———* skin but really all leather. Shoes. Belts. Zippers. His father's toenails. His father's calves. The teeth of Stuart MacKenzie. The teeth of Sister Mary. The teeth of his dentist. His own teeth. Horses. Carrots placed at certain angles. *Haricots verts* split open. Green scrubbing sponges. Steel wool. Dinosaurs. Rats. Mice. Pigeons. Birds. Eels. Snakes. Lizards. Turtles. Frogs. Dogs. Tongs.

While his mother was in the hospital, dinner was, alternately, Weetabix, take-out curry and pizza (that night). He sat with his father and Nina in front of the television and watched John Humphrys on the BBC: Rebel crickets were back from matches.

Daddy, asked Neal, *what do a———s think about?*

Eating, he said. Nina snickered.[6]

The next day at school there was still no blue paint, so he read all the animal books. The United States had the highest population of a———s: They were in the bathtubs and washbasins and in swimming pools and the streets and Americans kept baby ones and when they grew up they ate you unless you put them on the subway by flushing them. In New York there was a friendly c——— on East Eighty-Eighth Street called Lyle. Babar sometimes fought c———s but also valued their advice in running the country. Otherwise they would eat him. Napoleon brought them to France from Egypt. There was an awful, cackling family of a———s, dapper in fur-lined wool, squabbling, plowing through crowds, breaking balloons. A———s *all around*.

8 FEBRUARY 1993

In the weeks between sentencing and his mother's fourteen-year incarceration, there was cold, black howling.

His mother built a shrine for Rabi in the coat closet and would close the door, several times a day, to wail. At first the neighbors would call the police. But she was already going to prison.

When the day came, he didn't see her. The front door clicked behind him and he heard the howling again. Neal turned back. Then he ran to the subway. The 1, 2, 3, and 9 lines spilled south like ribbons of blood, and the A, C, and E tangled like veins downtown, and when he considered the corporeal possibility of other lines' other colors his eyes fluttered open.

He was almost late. Sister Agatha pulled him into her office, which, with wainscoted walls and myrrhish funk, looked and smelled like *The Sound of Music*.

Sister Catherine told me your mother left today. Are you all right?

Yes.

---

[6]As a child, his sister had been overweight and wore a brace of Barbara Hepworth sculpture bands and brackets that made her look like an a———, rationalizing her satisfaction that one was likely to eat Neal.

And your family? How are they?
Neal knew the answer but said: *I want to become a nun.*
Excuse me?
I've—
Are you even Catholic?
No. I asked my dad once if I could convert and he said no. Besides, roles for men in the Catholic Church are so limited.
If he had said such a thing before the incident, she would have laughed, but her face darkened, and her breath caught fire like a dragon's.
Neal, she said, *you cannot be a nun. You might find a way to be one, and won't like what happens.*
By day's end, the nuns began to resemble c————s: Their habits were very dark blue, which could as easily be very dark green, and hid their necks—c————s had no necks—and most in advanced age had the tendency to walk with their shoulders leading, which lent the appearance of hind legs.[7]

25 JANUARY 2013

Neal rented studio space in an ex–bus garage in Bushwick. He was freezing in four layers and winter jacket. The flat, taupe space had comforting, creaky floors, and glimmering white[8] noise from the machinery. There was free coffee. He filled the paper cup with only a couple of ounces so the acrid, dark potato water wouldn't get cold, and got up for refills.
People trained to look were watching him, again. Despite Neal's cinereous costumes of moth holes, his beauty offered some protection. In France a drunk Bavarian told him he was the bastard son of Helen of Troy and Vitruvian Man, which lent Neal the comforting notion that his grandfathers were Zeus in swan form and the Doric column. Nevertheless he received mostly the disadvantages of optimal geometry. Strangers poked him like a piece of public art or missing pound of flesh. He was a silent muse, never listened to—*yes* and *no* were similar words, he thought, black and white in their affect—

---

[7]Holders for floppy and compact discs, especially in green. Books. Anything that opened and shut. Doors. Pinking shears. Gardening shears. Scissors. Knives. Paper shredders. Binder clips. Staplers. Lobsters. Langoustines. Avocados.
[8]Neal has mild cases of both grapheme-color synesthesia, in which letters and numbers are perceived as color, and chromesthesia, in which sounds are perceived as color.

and had a muscular memory so underdeveloped that, on mornings after, he couldn't tell whether there had been a man or woman and had to look for clues.[9]

Neal secured vellum with rulers to his drawing board, inhaled, and uncapped a marker.

He tried to caricature the a————. Whimsical fun! He could change the rest of the illustration, which was much easier than drawing a single c———— in the style of the current piece. Then he added one scale too many, and the whole thing fell apart.

Neal tried to make a wash of green, soft and laurel. He eyedropped water as if the whole thing weren't unsalvageable.

Then he tried parts. One tooth. One eye. The blank space between the tail and hind legs. Each shocked him off the page.

He threw away everything and almost regretted not asking whether the client preferred a————s or c————s but they would have asked him for pictures of both.

Despite the morning's promise, Neal took out the painting in question and couldn't decide whether to scrape out a Phthalo-black road. He was running out of paint, except for a birthday gift of handmade Italian and French earths, still unopened. He sliced his knife across the canvas like a Roman barber.

3 DECEMBER 1998

In college Neal was failing cognitive psychology. The professor, a Zen Buddhist, gave him a meditation guide and a one-year-old a————, eighteen inches long, sweet and grassy and delightful as a watercolor jungle.

He took the wriggling baby a———— back to the dormitory and set it on the sofa. It began tearing and gnawing the sofa, tossing about its foam flesh, ripping the spines from books, soiling his bed scarlet with the sofa's body. (It had been alive?)

Neal used a calling card to reach his mother in prison. *It's ruining everything.*

Send it here, she said.

---

[9]People with beady eyes. With sharp teeth. With dry skin. With sharp noses. With no ears. With no necks. With red eyes. With long nails and untrimmed cuticles. With short nails gnawed to stubs. With defined abdominal muscles. With fatty bellies. With short legs. With steel whips for legs and arms, etc. Growling. Groaning. Cackling. Smug smiling. Blank stares.

Neal took the a—————— on the bus downtown. He heard whispering and grumbling and soon the bus was empty. Even the driver left. He walked the rest of the way.

In the rush to send away the a—————— he forgot to put on shoes. They found a shoe store, which glowed boiled-yolk sulfur from skeletal shelves and was, like everything else downtown, going out of business. Neal shoved his feet into a pair of Pyongyang metro-gray Velcro sneakers without unfastening anything and shouted to the salesman that they were too small, but the a—————— was tearing up what remained of the shop. Neal sighed and picked up the a——————.

He tiptoed in geisha-bound feet to the post office, a—————— under his arm.

Hi, Neal told the postal worker. *I would like to mail this a——————
to the women's prison in Plattsburgh, New York. How much will it cost?*

You can't mail a——————s, sir. No animals are allowed in the postal mail, said the postal worker.

Could I please buy a box? Neal asked. *The medium-large one. Priority Mail.*[10]

The postal worker groaned and brought him the box. Neal wrestled the a—————— into the carton, flapped it shut, and stood over it with crossed elbows so that it couldn't escape. It was scratching open the cardboard, growling, poking out mother-of-pearl claws.

Hi, Neal told the postal worker from the same place in his throat. *I would like to mail this box to the women's prison in Plattsburgh, New York.*

I said you can't mail a——————s!

He watched the a—————— run round and round, forming a tire of kudzu.

25 JANUARY 2013

Neal was congratulated for securing representation from a well-known commercial gallery, but had been avoiding it: Despite his advancing age, painting was to Neal a childish way of understanding why humans had so many ear bones. Dealers plied him with boxed

---

[10]The egg-hatching queue. The metal machinery. The cold-blooded worker. The metal grates. The *do not attack* signs. The shoulder-sloping uniforms. Corrugated cardboard. The edge used to cut mailing tape. The cut edge of mailing tape. The USPS eagle with the long, sharp frame.

Prosecco and asked about his ceramics, of which he had none.

He squinted at the newly painted walls, which had the glacial quality of octogenarian hair. Sarah, an old friend, was a gingery ex-modern dancer from Cornwall. When the gallery hired her, she was allowed to bring two artists, one of whom was Neal. He recognized the directors from a previous boxed-wine incident but agreed anyway.

We're so excited! Sarah said, embracing him.

Yes, said Neal. *But it's not quite . . . I was hoping for your advice.*

All right. Neal followed Sarah to her office, which seemed to function, for now, as storage. He cleared a table of boxes. She perfunctorily offered tea. He slid open the portfolio. She winced. He, generous with paint, suspected smudging.

Sarah put on her reading glasses and knotted her delicate brow. *I wanted to ensure you were, you know, seen.*

We're not selling it for parts, right.

We liked your . . . what was it, Hippocrates series.

That stuff was a bit naive, said Neal. *It's from grad school.*

We discussed this in November.

It's not unrelated to the humorism series, said Neal.

I didn't expect something so literal, Sarah sighed. This *is naive.*

Perhaps that's the humor of humors, I just . . .

She stepped back and put her hands together. *All right. So it's a river of bile and phlegm with c———s and a———s and snakes and things. In the style of Courbet.*[11]

Neal gasped. *Oh my God.*

18 MAY 2003

Neal's French was immaculate, a talent he attributed to being denied Bengali by his naturalized Scottish father: *We don't wants you to sounds likes them wogs and Pakis, innit laddie.* He rented a *chambre de bonne* from a Vietnamese doctor, found a job at a garage and soon had a robust knowledge of argot that led many to think he was a thug, work in group shows, and a healthy addiction to walks in the Bois de Boulogne. Still, after three years, he was beginning to feel uneasy. His friend Zoë referred him to Jean-Louis Katz.

---

[11]Hidden places. Tall grasses. Things that were wet. The marsh of the palette. The tracks of the brush. The texture of canvas. The watery murk from rinsing brushes. The assault of paint thinner. The smarminess of linseed oil.

The sprightly, bespectacled Katz, a Lacanian psychoanalyst from southern Ontario, enjoyed rocking back and forth in brightly colored sneakers. Today they were the chemical orange of gas fires, the sun, hazardous waste, apocalypse, raw carrots. Incongruously, Katz smoked cigarillos, but not around Neal, who was sensitive to smoke. Still he absorbed the vanillic odor, soothing and fetid.

So at the dep, *when you were ringing up the groceries, a man's presence reminded you of a c————.*

It's a garage. Actually his car *reminded me of an* iguana.

Thus the car reminded you of a c————.

Neal said, *Most reptiles are too primitive to experience any kind of affection. They only express fear and anger. But iguanas can develop qualities of trust and calm in order to get along with others.*

Like your mother.

My mother is not a reptile. It's my amygdala.[12]

Oh-ho, I don't think so. How about your brother?

I've always had the a———— phobia.

You mentioned that your brother had force brute *and a skin condition. And your phobia began around the time of his birth.*

I don't think of him anymore, said Neal. *You speak as if I killed him.*

Katz paused. *That's interesting. Let's stop there.*

The session had been eighteen minutes long. Katz charged Neal forty-two euros a week for three sessions, a steep discount for which he received a subsidy. Neal muttered, *Thanks* when he handed Katz fifty, to which Katz said, *OK.*

When told *OK* in response to *thank you* Neal felt rejected, another thing from his father, who thought *OK, you're welcome, it's nothing, no worries,* or anything other than *no, thank YOU* were all extremely rude.

Hey, you got a toonie? asked Katz. Neal shook his head.

---

[12]Jean-Louis Katz doesn't remember asserting that Neal's mother was a c————, but instead that she was not one. That she was not one of those refrigerator mothers who induced autism. In fact, he was thinking of his own mother, Outaouaise novelist Paulette Leduc, and Lacan's interpretation of the c———— mother, and the disappearance of the protection his father had offered back in Guelph. Still, Jean-Louis Katz knew what psychoanalysis had to say about *not.*

25 JUNE 2009

Nebraska was not on the way to anywhere. One summer Neal received a grant to attend a residency outside Omaha. The most exciting images were from the map: He was impressed by how many right angles there were. He saw bluffs and windmills and sunflowers and soft, blond straw. Flat land, flat green, flat sun, flat sky.[13]

A sculptor dropped him off on the way to see her daughter in Kansas. He expected 1970s cop-show staircases, but the building was a former secondary school. *Three-F*, his mother had said. The interior had the same coffee-bleach stench he remembered from grade school and the same faux-terrazzo linoleum in brown and green.

Neal rang the doorbell and heard the metal shuffle of four locks. His mother, in aging, had become her inverse. Everything about her that had been lush was dry, everything black was white, everything plump was thin, everything soft was hard. And vice versa. She had been Lakshmi round, creamy, cow-buttered peonies, but now her beauty was taut and sphinx-like, all armor and needles, and alien, like a temple carving.

Her accent had been evolving in prison and was broadening to suit the plains. She offered tea and microwaved a Tetley bag with a sugary shower and milk of chalk.

She asked what he was doing in Nebraska. He said he was at an artists' residency. Michael Jackson was dead, of anesthesia and displaced longing. His mother used to love Michael Jackson. She said she was going to go out for a while, and if he wanted food she could take him to the diner across the highway. He declined. The apartment had two bedrooms, but the spare was full of large boxes.

He fell asleep on the sofa and had a horrible dream. Neal worked at a hockey rink in Guelph, Ontario, and was instructed to prepare the arena for the evening match. A team of a————s had challenged a team of sharks to a hockey game. The blood match of the century, his colleagues enthused.

The a————s had many requests. They presented detailed instructions in ghoulish maroon a———— calligraphy, which Neal guessed wasn't really ink.

---

[13]He avoided all countries—except, unfortunately, for his adopted one—known to harbor c————s in the wild, i.e., 51 percent of countries, and all continents except Europe and Antarctica. New Zealand supposedly didn't have any, but he didn't believe that one, or Tunisia. It was the national animal of Iran, Lesotho, and Timor-Leste. He refused to visit Florida, Louisiana, Alabama, North Carolina, Texas, South Carolina, Mississippi, or Georgia, where they roamed free.

1. Please keep players frozen at –3,000 degrees Celsius until match time.

2. Dead pucks/models/human beings will be discarded at the side of the rink.

When he woke at 6:00 a.m. his face was wet. Neal inhaled sharply. His mother had still not returned home. He smoothed the sofa cushion and walked out, locking the door to the best of his abilities without a key. He ran through the corridors and walked north, hoping to hitchhike to the nearest bus station.

25 JANUARY 2013

Cosmos and his wife, Laura—pronounced the Petrarchan way, *Lahoora*—last year bought a house. They had only moved in a month ago: Laura, from a small town in the Spanish Pyrenees, found brownstones to be of poor quality. She decided to demolish and rebuild the interior. When Neal asked why she bought the house in the first place, Cosmos offered, *We have problems with our architect.*

Neal saw a bell but decided it wouldn't ring. He opened the door and saw tarpaulins and drop cloths suspended from what once were floors and ceilings. It was large enough to be livable anyway.

Hey, said Cosmos. *Would you knock down the dining room and kitchen walls?*

Right now?

No, dummy. I want to liberate the space.

What *do you want to do with it?* Neal asked.

Cosmos chortled. *Just kidding. How's things?*

Emma, Cosmos's four-year-old daughter, bounded into the room. Initially Neal didn't understand her, but now that she was older they had things in common, like a fear of wild animals. *We got the pictures!*

Neal was queasy. Laura had commissioned twenty-six animal alphabet cards in watercolor from a renowned commercial children's painter. Emma began to take out the cards, protected from themselves by an exotic polymer he didn't recognize.

Look at the letter A!

Leave him alone, darling, said Laura, walking in with crossed arms. *He's hungry.*

She took off Fridays not because she was underemployed, but because she was partner in an international branding consultancy (Neal still didn't know what that was) and did as she wished. Six months earlier, Laura and Cosmos had had a son named Xavier. Neal had met the baby twice and found him boring: Xavier lacked a reasonable command of French and was insufficiently excited about having a name that began with the letter *X*.

Laura clicked against the soon-to-be-excavated parquet floor on low-heeled ankle boots to kiss Neal on both cheeks. *Hello,* she said, dropping him in a device used to purify nappies.

Come join us, Cosmos told her. *I made dhal and green beans.*[14] Laura leaned in to him and mumbled something in her native tongue. Neal stared at Emma's paintings. *S—sloth. T—tortoise. U—unicorn.*

Unicorns aren't animals, you know, said Neal.

I have a lot of work to do, said Laura. *It was nice to see you, Neal,* she said, clicking out of the room.

Neal, said Emma.

Not now, said Neal.

She already ate, said Cosmos. *I can't give her dhal. The FBI designed her palate. Overreacts to everything. Give me twenty minutes to clean up. Baby, go show Neal your paintings.*

Emma led Neal to her bedroom on the second floor. She owned many reptile representations, including a wooden c——— hanging from Kenya and squishy puppets. The rug was the perfect hideous chromium-oxide shade.

Ready? she said, standing at ease.

Let's go backward, said Neal.

Emma took out the cards and flipped them over. *Zebra. Yak. X-ray fish. Wallaby . . .*

Neal leaned back on the carpet; he was at once afraid of its touch and seduced by its texture, from the downy bellies of newborn goats from Asia Minor. Perhaps he could snip a bit and use it in something. This meant he was thinking of soft things, and of his work. This meant he wasn't thinking of a———s, and as soon as he realized he wasn't thinking about them, he would start thinking about them again.

Actually, Emma, I have a headache.

We're halfway. She frowned. *Ibis. Hyena. Giraffe . . .*

---

[14]Fluted tart pans. The edge used to cut Cling Film. The edge used to cut aluminum foil. Calculators. Perambulators. When someone told him *see you later.* When someone told him *after a while.* Broken eggshells. Broken glass. Broken dishes. Spinach. Kale. Chard. Cavolo nero. Broccolini. Collard greens. Cabbage. Blindness, scurvy, and rickets from lack of vitamins.

No, Emma. Please. Please stop.

Flamingo. Elephant. Dove. Chameleon—Neal snatched the cards away from Emma.

Emma's face flushed as if she had been slapped. She began to tear, silently, gazing.

Emma, said Neal, *I'm sorry. Can you please accept my apology?*

She gave him the *what the hell* look he got so often, and ran out of the room past Cosmos, who was coming to join them.

Did she hurt herself?

Neal sighed. *I was thinking about a———s again. Today fifteen thousand c———s escaped into the Limpopo River.*[15]

Did Emma talk about a———s? Cosmos addressed Neal and Emma in the same tone.

No, but she had those cards, and A *was obviously a———.*

That's the only one you could imagine.

Neal nodded.

Cosmos sighed. *They're c———s, not a———s, right? So why were you afraid of a———s? Why didn't* C *bother you?* He sat on the floor and took off his glasses. *Neal. This must stop. Your infantile imagination cannot hijack your life. You can't attack my daughter like you're on drugs.*

God, I didn't attack her.

Are you on drugs?

No!

Then you're an asshole. I can't do this right now. We'll talk about this later.

Can I talk to her?

Get the fuck out of my house!

Neal stood up and opened the door. On the way out he saw that *A* was *antelope.*

---

[15]Hedges. Bushes. Clouds. Binding materials with teeth. Spiral notebooks. Open books. Thorns on roses. Leaves on dandelions. Algae. Grass. Ponds. Bogs. Humidity.

Greta and Her Creatures
Michael Parrish Lee

CROC

LOUNGING IN THE SUNSHINE for much of the afternoon, this creature possesses large white glass eyes that shake in a manner at once fearsome and friendly when Greta's hand is put inside him. Croc chats and jokes with the other creatures, but if they come too close he snaps his teeth. Although his teeth are made of felt, the other creatures try to keep their distance.

MONKEY

Monkey is the oldest creature but not the most familiar. The origins of Monkey are uncertain to Greta. Monkey seems to have always just been there. Monkey is very friendly, but he is not the friendliest of the creatures. As Monkey chatters, Greta senses something distant in Monkey, something almost sad. "Where did you come from, Monkey?" Greta sometimes asks. But Monkey pretends not to hear. Greta thinks that one day Monkey will tell his story, and she is quite happy to wait. As with Croc, Greta's hand can be put inside. However, Greta does not do this with Monkey as often as she does with Croc, and Monkey's vitality does not seem to depend as much on it.

SANDRA

Sandra is a small, stout bear who cares deeply for the other creatures. Her long fur is very soft and obscures her black eyes. The way her fur obscures her eyes plays a part in the way that Sandra cares deeply for the others.

TEDDO

A small, slim bear, whose fur is much shorter than Sandra's, Teddo has large eyes and a white belly. Teddo is fun and friendly and well liked by all. However, Greta contains one inner location in which Teddo does not matter as much as the other creatures.

GRETA'S MOM (A.)

Greta's Mom is a shadow.

BILLY BLOCK

Carved from wood and adorned on six sides with a red number 4, Billy Block hops rapidly up and down, wishing to speak but unable to do so. Billy Block's parents and siblings—each painted on six sides with a number of his or her own—live in a forest, Greta knows. Do they haves mouths with which to speak? Was it only Billy who was forgotten when a woodsman carved their facial features? Or do they communicate with each other through their numbers or by hopping up and down, having no need for mouths—meaning that it is not the case that Billy Block cannot speak but rather that Greta either cannot understand or cannot speak correctly?

Billy Block might not look like much, but he has the heart of a kangaroo.

JUNIPER

Even though Juniper is a small cotton pig, his name is not Pigly. That is the name of a different creature. Juniper was once a girl but is now a boy. He likes to eat slops and sleep in the mud produced by taking the folded blanket at the foot of the bed and reorganizing it in the crack where the side of the bed meets the wall. However, Juniper is not strictly lazy. He likes to dance (especially with Percilily) and amble through low, green hills and pick wildflowers with the other creatures. Greta predicts that Juniper will marry Sandra. She also predicts that Juniper will one day be a girl again.

GRETA'S MOM (B.)

Greta's door is very tall. The door opens and a long shadow enters.

PERCILILY

Percilily is a beautiful hippopotamus. She wears a tutu and enjoys swimming in the blue waterways that crisscross Greta's bed. Percilily has very long eyelashes. We estimate, through data obtained from Greta, that the eyelashes are as long as the hair of a human princess. Croc harbors romantic affection for Percilily—as do Teddo, Juniper, and, perhaps, My Bird. However, we are able to estimate that Percilily harbors romantic affection exclusively for Juniper, and, perhaps, My Bird.

GRAY #2

Gray #2 is a brave, handsome dog, sporting a fine, short, gray coat that, despite its shortness, keeps him warm through the winter. Gray #2 is a guardian but not the main guardian. He can smell anything and so detect intruders. He likes to eat sausages and porridge with syrup and sliced bananas. Sometimes, if the others have not bathed or accidentally emit gas, Gray #2's nose twitches and he becomes annoyed.

Gray #2 came after Gray. Gray was a wise gray owl who disappeared. Greta has made inquiries into the disappearance of this creature, but these inquiries were met only with a denial that such a creature ever existed and with the appearance of Gray #2.

GRETA'S BROTHER (A.)

He runs into Greta's room and bounces on her bed, disturbing the pile of creatures convening there. Gray #2 sniffs and growls, Croc snaps at his bottom, and Monkey bonks his head, so Greta's Brother—after a final bounce—runs screaming out of her room.

PIGLY

Pigly is a tiny, brown, furry creature—perhaps a small rodent. Greta has not yet determined its species or dwelt on the matter at length. Pigly hides in a log and makes a high-pitched sound. Greta does not know whether Pigly is a boy or a girl. To Greta, Pigly matters even less than Teddo.

GRETA'S DAD

Greta's Dad is composed of three elements: a. The Face, b. The Ground, c. The Laugh.
   a. The Face is the largest face in the world. It contains a red complexion and a very wide smile.
   b. When Greta elevates, she no longer sees The Face. Instead she sees The Ground far below. She holds on tight and hollers loudly. It is now that she hears c. The Laugh.

SUZY (A.)

Suzy is the small three-dimensional likeness of a human female. Suzy does not sit on Greta's bed with the creatures but lives instead in the back corner of Greta's closet. At one point Suzy could speak, but she can no longer do so. Greta does not think about Suzy, except in rare moments when she wakes from sleep and remembers, with a cold, nauseous sensation, that Suzy still lives in her closet.

FLOPSAM

Flopsam is zany and fun! While his physiology might not appear amenable to vigorous activity, Flopsam is perhaps the most energetic of the creatures. His flat, square, floppy body is ideal for sailing through the air, like a kite, only faster. And despite the small, floppy arms that sprout from his corners, Flopsam has no difficulty racing through the low, green hills with Juniper, hopping rapidly up and down with Billy Block, playing tug-of-war with Monkey, and even, on two occasions, spanking Croc for misbehaving. When Flopsam needs to relax, he floats down from the sky like a parachute. But Flopsam rarely needs to relax.

Greta remembers how she found Flopsam on the ground outside, just lying there without a home. She remembers holding him tightly in her bed and crying as voices argued outside her door, an angry woman's voice saying loudly, *Another one, garbage,* and then Flopsam's name.

MY BIRD

The best and favorite of the creatures, My Bird has been saved for last. My Bird bears a physical resemblance to a large bird on television; however, My Bird is not that bird. My Bird is the Guardian of Greta and occupies a place of distinction among the creatures. When at night Greta sleeps under the covers with Croc, Monkey, Sandra, Teddo, Billy Block, Juniper, Percilily, Gray #2, Pigly, and Flopsam piled on top of her, My Bird lies at Greta's side, his beak facing out to peck away any monsters or bad things that might come in the night. Greta holds tightly My Bird's long, floppy neck, which has grown threadbare from Younger Chewing that Greta does not recall. At the back of My Bird there is a string that can be pulled to make him speak, but Greta is also able to make him speak without using the string. My Bird is separate from the other creatures, but he loves them and they love him.

SUZY (B.)

Two long, shadowy arms push forth the small three-dimensional likeness of a female.
   "Here you go—a lovely dolly."

HOW PIGLY WAS ONE DAY KILLED

One day something terrible happened. Something terribly large fell on Pigly and crushed the life out of it. None of the other creatures saw this happen or could figure out what fell. Greta and her creatures attended a funeral presided over by a somber Croc. The one time that Croc told a joke, Monkey bonked his head as a reminder to be somber. Greta felt strange.

CROC AND MONKEY GO ON AN ADVENTURE

The creatures have become suspicious. How did Pigly really die? Did someone kill it? The creatures begin fighting and some are seriously injured.

Everything has gone wrong.

After consulting with My Bird and Greta, Croc and Monkey decide to go on an adventure in order to locate the Amber Potion and use it to bring Pigly back to life.

Croc swims through the river, carrying Monkey on his back. Croc eats fish and Monkey picks bananas and coconuts from the branches that hang low over the water.

Finally they come to a cave, but there is something horrible inside. However, they are brave; they enter the darkness despite the danger. They feel as though they are being watched. They move quickly deep into the cave until they discover the Amber Potion shining like treasure. They take the potion and run as quickly as they can. They feel something following them. Something horrible happens in the cave. But they manage to escape and return with the Amber Potion.

As the other creatures gather around, Sandra takes the potion from Monkey and pours it into Pigly's small mouth.

Pigly comes back to life. Everyone cheers and celebrates. Now there is no more fighting.

However, something strange occurs. Almost as soon as they begin to celebrate and dance, the creatures realize that they didn't really miss Pigly after all. Pigly makes its high-pitched sound and scurries away to the log that it hides in.

The next day, Pigly is found killed again.

JUNIPER SHARES A KISS

After dancing, Juniper pulls Percilily behind a pillow and they kiss romantically.

But something is wrong.

Sandra has seen them. She saw them dancing together and followed as Juniper pulled Percilily away from the celebration in case he was going to beat her up. But when she saw them kiss, Sandra became jealous and let out a cry.

"It's OK," Juniper says. "Kisses can be shared."

"That's silly," Sandra says, but she is amazed to see the kiss float up from between Juniper and Percilily like a beautiful pink butterfly. The Kisserfly (as it's called) floats over to Sandra and lands on her lips romantically, and she knows that one day things will be different and she and Juniper will be married.

GRETA'S MOM (C.)

A long shadow pushes forth two dresses. One is large and one is small, one for Greta and one for her dolly.

"You're a big girl now. You don't need to play with all those silly *things* anymore. Be a good girl. Be a doll for mommy."

Once the shadow has gone away, Greta pushes the dresses into the corner of her closet.

HOW TEDDO IS KILLED BY ACCIDENT

On a fine summer's day, Teddo and Gray #2 are walking by the river, discussing the finer points of growing cabbages for making into ice cream, when suddenly something terrible happens. Croc, being tickled by Monkey, leaps up into the air with laughter and accidentally lands on Teddo. Earlier that morning Croc had a large breakfast of fish and snails, making him heavier than usual, so now when he lands on Teddo he crushes the life out of him.

THE CREATURES GO TO WAR

Everyone is very upset. And since all the Amber Potion was used up on Pigly, there is none left for bringing Teddo back to life. Gray #2 barks angrily at Croc for being so careless. Monkey steps in front of Croc and says, "It was an accident."

"It didn't look like one to me," says Flopsam, coming to Gray #2's side, his small floppy hands curled into fists.

"Not so fast," Monkey says, holding his banana like a pistol.

Flopsam takes a floppy piece of string and whips the banana out of Monkey's hand.

"Why you!" Croc says and snaps at Flopsam very hard.

Other creatures come running to see what all the commotion is about, and very soon there is a War.

Croc has bitten onto Flopsam's floppy leg and is spinning him in the air like a helicopter. Billy Block, hopping mad, bounces onto Monkey's head. Juniper throws slops over Billy Block so that the latter's painted numbers are obscured. Sandra feels sorry for Billy Block, but she wants to help Juniper, so she kicks Billy Block into the river. Gray #2 bites Sandra's neck. The tall door opens and a long shadow peeks in. Percilily does an elegant belly flop onto Gray #2 in order to break his bones. Croc has begun to make explosions with powder he has dug up from under the pillow. The creatures are badly hurt— missing teeth, eyes oozing black goo, skin fluffing and peeling away— but they continue to fight and bite and blow up and hit one another until Monkey, who is old and wise, crawls away from the War to look for My Bird and ask for help.

"It has to stop," My Bird agrees, and together My Bird and Monkey go on a journey to look for Greta.

Together, My Bird, Monkey, and Greta agree that the creatures will continue to fight and argue until Teddo is brought back to life, so Greta journeys to the Battleground. When she arrives, big as a giant, My Bird and Monkey on either side, the creatures stop fighting and fall silent. They feel very ashamed, and they move aside so that Greta can inspect Teddo's body. She lifts it up and feels that it is dead. There is no Amber Potion, the creatures say, but Greta hushes them. She takes Teddo in her arms like a baby and breathes into his mouth. He is alive, the creatures can see. Her breath has brought him back to life. The creatures cheer. The long shadow shuts the door.

HOW IT HAPPENS AGAIN

Greta is playing. She is making Teddo and Percilily go ice-skating together. There is, however, a spot on the river where the ice is broken. Teddo loses his grip on Percilily's hand and goes flying toward the broken ice. He cannot stop. He looks behind with wet, pleading eyes, but something is pushing him forward—he is going too fast and cannot stop. He falls through the broken ice and the water is so cold that he cannot swim properly. Percilily tries to skate over to help him, but she trips on something and it is too late, too late. Teddo has drowned in the cold water.

Greta reaches down and pulls him out. She takes him in her arms like a baby and tries to bring him back to life with her breath. But it doesn't work anymore; it only worked once. Teddo is dead for good, she decides, her eyes wet and her throat painful. It is so sad: He is really dead.

GRETA'S BROTHER (B.)

He runs into Greta's room and bounces on her bed. He has made a bow and arrow and asks her if she wants to play. But Greta is sad. Teddo is dead and won't ever come back again. Greta's Brother offers to kill her so that it won't matter. My Bird kindly pecks his eyes, and he runs off to go live with the Indians.

MONKEY FIGHTS THE INDIANS

Now there are Indians all over the place, riding horses and shooting buffalo. They disturb the creatures with their noise and their dancing. One falls off his horse and tries to hitch a ride on Flopsam. Another uses his feather to tickle Sandra, who hates to be tickled.

Monkey has an idea. He puts banana peels on the ground in places where the Indians, riding their horses, are likely to slip and die.

Monkey is a hero. The Indians are gone and things are back to normal.

However, one banana peel has been forgotten, and on the way to the ceremony where Monkey will receive his Hero's Cape, Juniper slips and breaks his neck. Greta tries to fix him, but it too late; he is dead and she can't bring him back. Who will Sandra marry now?

THE TWILIGHT OF THE CREATURES

The creatures are now very sad. They pull each other's hair and say evil words to one another. Gray #2 becomes very angry and foam fizzes from his mouth. He is no longer a guardian. He runs around and barks and bites. Percilily tries to stop him, so he eats her face off. She runs and screams, without her face, and drowns herself in the river. Sandra is so angry at Gray #2 that she grabs him by the tail and turns him inside out. Inside out, Gray #2 can no longer breathe the air that he requires, and so he slowly suffocates. Flopsam and Billy Block cannot believe that Sandra has killed Gray #2. They find a pair of scissors and cut her into many pieces.

Greta needs to scold the creatures so that they will learn to behave. She takes Flopsam aside and tells him that he is bad. Flopsam feels so ashamed that he runs away to the place on the ground outside where Greta found him, and there he sets himself on fire.

Greta cannot believe what is happening. She cannot believe that the creatures are dying. Her face is very red and wet. The door keeps opening, but Greta doesn't care.

Billy Block pushes Monkey, so Monkey throws Billy Block against the closet door. There is a loud bang and a crack, and Billy Block's brains spill out and he falls to the floor and can no longer hop up and down and will never get to go on a journey into the forest to find his parents and siblings. Croc loves Monkey very much. However, Croc cannot forgive him for throwing Billy Block against the closet door.

"But you killed Teddo," Monkey says.

"That was different," says Croc. "That was an accident. And besides, Teddo wasn't as important."

Monkey puts a stick in Croc's mouth to keep his jaws pried open so that Croc can't kill him. But Croc crawls forward and grabs Monkey's neck and strangles him, both of them making gurgling sounds. Now Greta will never know where Monkey came from. She is making loud noises. She watches two white shaking hands take Croc by the jaws and pull them apart until there is a cracking sound.

Greta, eyes and nose leaking great quantities of fluid, takes My Bird into her lap and holds him very tightly. She pulls the string at the back and My Bird says that he hopes they will remain friends forever. She pulls the string again and My Bird says he wants to die.

"I'll never kill you, My Bird." But My Bird insists, and, with stinging eyes and a terrible pain in the muscles of her face, Greta holds tightly his long, floppy neck and snaps it. Soon the sun goes away and everything is covered in shadow.

THE NEXT DAY, PLAYING

On the following day the creatures have all come back to life. Even though they were permanently dead, Greta has made them alive again. She plays with them and has fun. But there is something different now, some new thing inside her, because even though the creatures move and speak, Greta cannot forget that they are really dead. Greta plays and no one bothers her, except for the bones that are buried beneath her, and Suzy, who waits in the corner of the closet.

Pond Animals
Martine Bellen

He brushes the Heart Sutra onto seashells and tosses them into the
pond. "Form is no other than emptiness, emptiness no other than
form." The waving, wielding, yielding, booming fluid that is
puddle, companion of moon, compassion of moon;
    Heartbreaking atmosphere swallows seashells in the perfect
Wisdom of the moment, of the moon, in the ancient pond beyond,
        To the other shore . . .
    Though it is frozen, melting, dripping, Animals Animals
Dripping from within . . . Pond without end . . .

Something is swimming across her, and then there's the swooping,
The shimmying.

In every Japanese garden, there is a pond. Weeping willows
And black pines.
        Water's edge. Darting turtles, daring.

In every human being, there is a pond. Weeping and pining. Her
Edge. Her ledge.
        Her daring.

Jorge Luis Borges recognized that his inner animal had nearly
expired. While in his younger years, he was a monkey, now he had
turned into a tired old moose. The first sign of the metamorphosis

268

was his losing his black, then the reds; his last color was yellow.
And one day, our hero awoke to realize he had become
His mother's dream.
                    It was her eyes that kept him.

Wittgenstein's *Remarks on Colour* was written while he
was dying of stomach cancer. Stalked by death, he was a sheep cat.
Little sleep cat. The lame one. The lamb.

Fading colors, farming colors

Kafka asked for his work to be exsanguinated upon his
death. Defenestrated. The waning breath of his words to be bled
out, tossed, singed, torched, not humiliated by bylaws and red tape.

Once the growl is gone. A soft resting place. Elephant
Intelligence. The grief.

She spots the cup of pond on the night table. The table has slipped
into a dream, and she buries her nose into the lovely pond and,
with her paw, sends ripples deep into her animal. A guttural noise
in the forest, yonder, that's buried in the body on the bed, in the
bed of her body. The ground rolls over, and, as she leaps to safety,
the pond follows her onto the floor,

So the dead can ride over rivers . . . into the sun,
Wearing their horse bone suits

Her death closet filled with ancient helmeted heads,
                                        Water monsters

A body of standing water, a standing body. Water gardens are ponds
as are solar gardens of thermal water. Vernal ponds spend some of
the dry season not as ponds. Though even when waterless, they

might be referred to as a basket of fluid,
>   They might be referred to as ponds.
The ones that are most deeply hidden are touched by sunlight or a
Person
>   Walking through them without being submerged. Ponds as
>   Ponds and ponds not as ponds but as puddles reached into
>   And turned into ponds
>   By light and life
>   Ponds turned inside out.

Once ponds sculpted the moon, the moon of his eyes filled
With jellified orbs—He saw
Amoebas and seahorses and starfish and multiverses
Singing above and beyond this shore . . .
>   Animals Animals without end. . . .

Aerie

Emily Anderson

THE EMBROIDERED TOWELS rub it in my face. *Aerie at Eagle's Rest: You're Home to Roost.* Home. The point of a nest is to fly it. But there is no getting outside of this place; it's shaped like a doughnut. The wind hoots over the courtyard like a hillbilly over a jug. They call it the nest. I call it a hole.

Yesterday I got caught in a draft and rolled right past my suite. Had to cat the loop again, including the special-care crescent they call the Hatchery, where the demented get left out like a carton of eggs, lolling their bald, white heads, forgetting to blink their invisible eyelids.

The staff refer to them as Memory Birds or Hatchlings. As in, "I found this little Memory Bird trying to make a break for it. Where does she belong?"

"Oh, put her with the other Hatchlings."

* * *

Their loony logic seems to be that if they give me enough bird helpers, I may start to think I am Cinderella.

An orderly wearing seagull-print scrubs tries to run her mop under my Philadelphia highboy. "You're going to have to get on your hands and knees for that one," I tell her, and she does. I ask her why they call them Hatchlings and she says, "Who? They do?"

A tech in wren-print scrubs takes my blood pressure. I ask her about the Hatchery. She gets frustrated and beaky and overinflates the cuff, squeezing until I cry aloud.

Two big men in turkey-print scrubs install a 150-inch flat-screen television on the wall above the credenza. It's from Stu, naturally. I look at it for a while. I press the help button and demand those turkeys de-install.

* * *

Emily Anderson

Aerie at Eagle's Rest: An American Fairy Tale. So says the bald eagle on the binder where the hawk nurse logs all my intakes, outputs, and opinions. Apparently my insides are an affair of state. And my mistakes. "What are you, trying to read your future?" I ask, as she peers into the commode. She laughs. I feel like the golden goose.

* * *

The president held both my hands in one of his. *Your disregard for human life is a credit to us all.* Pepsi, the first canary, swooped through the trees, dive-bombing us with cherry blossoms. *Pink snow,* Mr. President.

* * *

Two turkeys lift me onto the examining table. I have never liked big men to touch me. Especially not big men who are big birds. But I am a positive person, a Daughter of the American Revolution, so I lie there, waiting for the nurse with the hawk scrubs, thinking that it's better than childbirth. Better than spread-eagling into icy stirrups. I always told my children, If I could have just laid an egg and flown away! Sure as shot wouldn't be here if I had flown.

* * *

I wear emeralds and my fingernails are dirty. They've fished up a string of so-called Reasons to Roost and clamped them into my binder. Campaign contributions to the calibrated malaprop. Vertigo at galas. Spicules. Enlarged pupils. A scare at the house in Scottsdale.
  Me. Here. Confined. Me. A bird of the air.
  Is it a crime to be afraid?

* * *

Wouldn't *not* pressing "panic" on my Lifelink have been the true evidence of incapacity? I subscribed to the surface so I could use it. And where is the accountability, I want to know, of the Private Emergency Services Team who took fifteen minutes, *fifteen minutes*, to show up. I could have been dead. Dead.
  The irony. Me. A woman perfectly capable of defending her property.

I'm a good shot with a snub-nose .38 special. I'm a good shot with an 870 Wingmaster.

Apparently I'm not who I think I am. I'm a raven lunatic with the towels to prove it.

* * *

The leaves are flailing. I can look out my window and see clear to the road. The bulldozers circle around our hill, digging and digging. I know what they are up to. They're making our hill seem taller. They're building a dramatic approach to the Aerie. So says the Forefeathers for Our Future folder. "Take a dramatic approach." They asked me for a contribution.

Why do you care what happens outside of America?

Every day the bulldozers look a little smaller.

The approach is working.

I think the American people trust me.

* * *

"How's the flexibility in your fingers?"

"Enough of this hawk talk! All I hear is *cak-cak-cak-cak-cak!* I want to know about the Hatchery."

"The Hatchery?" The hawk wraps each of my fingers with yellow tape.

"The Hatchery. I demand to know why you call it that."

She smiles and asks me if I remember Gil Hatchery. "May he rest in peace," she cheeps and rips a piece of tape with her teeth.

"RIP indeed. My late husband respected him, until he became so forgetful. He said he was a good golfer for a debt collector. He used to say, 'That Gil could squeeze blood out of a stone and—something— out of a golf ball.'" I tap my yellow talons against my chin. My husband's thinking gesture. I always liked his big mouth.

"Mr. Hatchery was not only a good golfer. He was a good man. He left Aerie at Eagle's Rest a very generous bequest."

"Was that so-called beak-quest before or *after* the egg timers?"

"Egg timers?"

"Alzheimer's. Do I have to make cuckoo noises to get at the truth?"

"Because of his generosity, the Hatchery Crescent has become a state-of-the-art crescent, a national—no, an international—leader in long-term transitional *cak-cak-cak-cak!*"

273

"That's what you call it?"
"I'm just going to palpate your gizzard here; any sensitivity?"
"*Cak-cak-cak-cak!*"
"Very good. Deep breath, please."
"And the Hatchlings?"
"Who?"
"The Hatchlings. Isn't that what you call them?"
"Why do you call them that?"
"Why do *you*?"
She pulls a camouflage pen out from behind her ear and begins to scratch.

* * *

That pigeon nurse with the foreign twitter-twatter! Today she poked me five times, out for blood: Jab! Jab! Jab! Jab! Jab! No wonder she's still wearing Rat of the Sky scrubs. When I defended my poor arm, she squawked, "I get Eagle!"

The doctor came in, looking like Steve Martin with his white hair and useful complexion. I admired his platinum bald-eagle tiepin. He smiled and said, "Young lady, I hear you're quite a tough egg to crack."

His name is Lawrence Eagle, and he was in my son Chip's class at Harvard. I didn't even feel a pinch when he took my blood. He'll give that Pigeon the what-for. I have every confidence.

* * *

We get a different engraved fork at every meal in the Rookery Refectory. Today at lunch my salad fork said, *Aerie: Fly with the Best* and my dinner fork said, *Aerie: The City on a Hill.*

Fly with the best. City on a hill. What a hoot.
We're not flying. We're dying.
It's just an approach.

* * *

Is this still America is what I'd like to know.

* * *

So our salmon flies here on a plane.

So? Sew buttons on a balloon!

Up here Dr. Eagle makes the rules and gives the forks.

Do something that man doesn't like and the flatware will scold you. For instance, I most certainly do not know where Mrs. Rockwald's legs are. The old coot suspects I've taken them. The seagulls just tell her, "Oh, I'm sure they'll turn up." The woman's a double amputee, frankly. You'd think they might have the integrity to remind her.

But, as it turns out, *I'm* the one that gets the Birds of a Feather fork at breakfast. I know what it is. Be nice or you'll get Eat Crow.

Dr. Eagle kept his eye on me all day. I hope his tiepin sticks him.

* * *

I'm pushed out into the Nest to "enjoy Indian summer." The walls of the Nest are covered with plastic thatching. It looks like Papua New Guinea and smells like Barbie dolls taking a tan. "I don't *like* to enjoy," I tell the young training wren who pushes me around.

I knock my nectar out of my cup holder. The trainee whistles "Hail to the Chief" through her buckteeth. She wheels me to the Vista to watch the Approach grow.

The bulldozers circle in their track, tiny and pathetic. One day the hill will be so tall I won't even be able to see them. Already their beeps are sad and ragged.

"Please don't stop whistling," I tell the trainee.

But she's *not* listening.

I press my Lifelink.

* * *

"Were you frightened?" asks Dr. Eagle, looking less like Steve Martin and more like Lloyd Bridges, who once goosed me in Maui.

"Did you hear about Chip?" A mother can't help crowing a little.

The doctor goes for my hand but I pull it away in the nick of time. "Then you know he's a champion skier. And shooter. Does biathlons. He's in the running for the Word Cup, did you hear?"

"In fact, I did, and I'm sorry—"

You can't expect a doctor not to envy a young man like Chip. Fresh powder. A helicopter. Those medals. Those models. "Did you read about him in the alumni magazine? Because I don't imagine you get to Bessans or St. Moritz much."

275

"Doctor?" says the hawk nurse. He shakes his head. Men shouldn't opt for feathered hairstyles. It's unprofessional.

"I'M VERY HAPPY FOR HIS SUCCESS," the doctor shouts.

"I hear you, I hear you. I couldn't be prouder of Chip, Chip—"

"It's a very dangerous sport, isn't it," interrupts the hawk. "Skiing. Not to mention shooting. Guns can be very dangerous. Accidents happen so easily and home is statistically the most dangerous—" The doctor puts her in her place: "Not now, Elizabeth."

I let him touch my hand. "Why were you frightened?" he asks.

"Frightened? Why? Why would I be frightened?"

* * *

After I get the flock fork again, I decide to take a gander at our Constitution. It's engraved in gold on a floor-to-ceiling plaque behind the glass aviary, which the Eagle stocks with macaws. Their long feather tails look dipped in rainbows. I peer through all these bright birds and read the golden rules, and I endorse most of them.

Aerie at Eagle's Rest: A Nonsmoking Facility. Thus Mr. Ars Rockwald, financier, smokes a steel kazoo, pacing, cock of the walk, just like my late husband. Except in Mr. Rockwald's case, a flock of ducklings follow the sound of his smoke. Here at Aerie, an adorable dozen of fuzzy water fools consistently mistake a former congressman and military hero for their mother.

I like also: *Aerie at Eagle's Rest: Soar Above and Grow Wings.* Dignity is imperative. We are God's noblest creatures. A macaw turns the red side of his face to the glass, the better to see me with. His eye glitters. I'd like to pop it in my mouth like an olive. He makes a sound like a Lifelink alarm until his blue girlfriend swoops over to comb his feathers with her beak.

* * *

I have no clue what happened to Eugenie Rockwald's legs. She's got a terminal case of the they've-got-to-be-somewheres.

"I haven't a clue; may I pass you the caviar?" I tell her politely from the far side of a pink pile of salmon. Our president says we have an advantage here in America—we can feed ourselves—and he's right. But I'd tell her to shut it if those damn nitpicking macaws would cut their cackle.

Tell a truth, an honest truth, and those birds repeat it, repeat it right back to the Eagle. "Let me spread a little carrion on this cracker for you, Mrs. Rockwald."

* * *

We were spooning up our crème brûlées and drinking our decafs. Mr. Rockwald was smoking his ducklings when Mrs. Rockwald began flapping her arms, fish eggs all around her mouse.

She pointed straight at her husband—financier, congressman, veterinarian—and howled, "Son of a bitch, I know where my legs are! They're in the broom closet with him, writhing around in lust!"

Lust, lust, lust, trilled the macaws in their dinnertime cage.

Quack quack, said the ducklings.

"Fancy that. A congressman a leg man," I said. But I had custard in my crop and my words came out yellow and honky. The hawk passed me a *Sweetly Sing* napkin and I upended the toothpick dispenser. This is *still* a city on a hill.

* * *

A Bill pertaining to Soar Above has been passed to resolve the issue of lunatic spousal accusation. Dr. Eagle etched it right into the Constitution—*Aerie at Eagle's Rest: Mate for Life.* The legless harpy has been found in violation of same and has been assigned to knitting.

And since Mrs. Rockwald, having no legs, has hardly any lap, she has no place to hold her ball of red yarn except her mouth.

Democracy works.

Still. No system is perfect. Sometimes Mrs. Rockwald loses a stitch and when she goes looking for it she finds no lap and no legs and gasps. Then the yarn falls like a line of blood to the floor.

* * *

Nobody told me Stu and Marlena were invited.

I'd been hoping to pick the Eagle's brain about some new legislation, but here was Stu, coffee stains on his polo, frowning the way he does when he tries to smile. And Marlena, piping right in about "advance planning."

"Advance planning, huh? You know, it's possible I'll leave it all to the macaws."

277

"The McWho?" said Stu.

"I'm especially fond of Little Blue."

"Your mother very much enjoys our aviary," said the hawk.

"We're not talking about financial planning," said Dr. Eagle, "only about how to make you comfortable here."

"Is this about the Approach?"

"No," said Dr. Eagle, "it's about Revolution."

"Pardon me?" I said.

"Your body is going through many changes," said Dr. Eagle. Marlena was all thumbs on her cell phone and Stu was halfway through a French cruller. The doctor leaned close and said, "The eagle retreats to its hidden aerie, plucks all his feathers, and reemerges victorious."

"Victory?" I said. "*Victory?*" Stu was dribbling. I passed him an *Eat like a Bird* napkin.

"Transformation," said the doctor, taking an amber fish-oil capsule from his jacket pocket and popping it in his mouth.

"Transition," said the hawk, scratching with her pen.

"Preparation," said Stu, glaze stuck in the corners of his mouth.

"An advance plan, an action plan," said Marlena, looking at her phone.

"Victory," said the doctor and winked at me.

* * *

The president held both my hands in one of his. *Rebirth is traditionally represented by the sacred number of thirteen. Thirteen stars on the seal. Thirteen arrows in the eagle's right talon; thirteen olive branches in his left. Ours is a magical country. Our forefathers embedded their magic in our money.*

Hand to hand, hand to talon, talon to talon to dollar.

Oh e pluribus, e pluribus.

Could it be *her* talon, Mr. President? With the arrows?

I appreciate your disregard for human life.

* * *

When I tell Sophie, the poor girl who cleans me, about the lip gloss gummed to the mouthpiece of Marlena's cell phone, she tells me about her cousin who does permanent makeup. "Like tattoos," she says, "only classy."

Emily Anderson

"Never have children." I look down at my Lifelink button, desperately bored.

* * *

I find feathers in my bed.

The hawk suggests a change to hypoallergenic bedding. Even my thread count is bound up in the eagle binder. This is all news to Sophie, who does her best to get away without reading. "You're a keeper," I tell her, as she moistens a Q-tip with pink gel.

* * *

I'm oftentimes asked what difference it makes to America if people are dying of malaria in a place like Ghana.

* * *

While Sophie swabs, I make a mess of Birds of a Feather.

Still, Sophie doesn't mind if I make an occasional jab at Mrs. Rockwald. I can't always be growing wings. Mrs. Rockwald once parked her motorized chair on top of Sophie's foot, then stabbed her thigh with a knitting needle. Sophie screeched and flailed, stuck like a rotisserie chicken.

I'm not saying she wasn't in part asking for it; it's true she wears nothing but shorts and knee pads under her smocks. There is plenty of dark meat to needle.

"That's for kissing up my husband's ducklings," said Mrs. Rockwald (and it's true—Sophie sometimes squats to gobble them up).

"Sophie, you ought to poison the old bitch," I tell her; her flutter strokes give me palpitations. "What difference does it make to America if people are dying in a place?"

Sophie beeps for the Wren to come and get me and hops on her good foot toward the door.

"Don't forget your legs!" I point to her crutches.

Sophie's crutches are unforgettable.

Sophie, of course, forgets them.

* * *

279

I remember meeting a mother of a child who was abducted by the North Koreans right here in the Oval Office, the president said. *It was a heart-wrenching moment to listen to the mother talk about what it was like to lose her daughter.*

Mrs. Rockwald snaps up a fish in the Rookery. She holds it in one swiveled claw and rips it to shreds with the other.

* * *

Sophie's crutches belonged to the late Frau Monschgeier, a lady of the last regeneration. Dr. Eagle loaned them to her. Herr Monschgeier used every ounce of his diplomatic savoir faire to obtain from a cagey vizier crutches said to have magical properties not otherwise pacified.

They looked like human legs and likely were. Herr Monschgeier spent his life filling his good lady's crippled lap with such gems. He was a Duesenberg of a man, a man of a real time, a man of a real place: Zanzibar, I think.

"Sophie," I said, while the fat Wren pushed me around, fondling a Snickers bar in the pocket of her scrubs, "Sophie, you're too young; the world was lost before you even arrived; you've never even seen a real man, have you; never even dreamt of Zanzibar."

"Zanzibar," munched the Wren, or perhaps "Snickers bar."

Because my Sophie was gone.

* * *

I've started sleeping with my eyes open so I woke right up when a man came into my room.

He was smoking, and very loudly too. It had to be Rockwald.

He picked up Sophie's gleaming bone crutches, put them under his arm, and started to make away with them. When he caught my eye on him, he got right in my face and winked.

"Mr. Rockwald! Those are somebody's legs!"

Rockwald pressed a fluttering finger to his yellow lips.

I shrieked like the wind cresting the Nest. To shut me up, Rockwald scooped up one of the ducklings and put it on my face, where it smoot.

Later that night, I lost the rest of my hair.

Don't Like It? Grow Wings.

* * *

Pink snow very much, croaked my late husband, a twist of my hair for a boutonniere, exactly how we buried him. *Duckworth, I'm going to make a wish, the president said. I wish the Bald Eagle had not been chosen the representative of our country. He is a bird of a bad moral character, Duckworth. He does not get his living honestly. You may have seen him perched on some dead tree near the river, where, too lazy to fish for himself, he watches the labor of the fishing hawk, and when that diligent bird has at length taken a fish, and is bearing it to his nest for the support of his mate and young ones, the bald eagle pursues him and takes it from him.*

* * *

We'll let our friends be the peacekeepers and the great country called America will be the pacemakers. "I've got your z-score," says the hawk. Turkeys put me through a bone scan and now they've got my insides. The hawk clips my scans into my binder and snaps it shut. "Hollow," she announces. "Perfectly hollow. Be careful you don't get caught in an updraft."

* * *

"Why do they call you Hatchlings?"

"Sushi, darling?"

"Hatchlings. Why do they call you that?"

"Why? It's a diminutive. In other words, a nickname. For citizens, a synonym, it means the same as citizens." My daughter has a sixth-grade vocabulary; *you* try getting her to talk about anything other than *Duck Tales*.

Her nose starts to whistle, like it does when she's about to cry. Like it does when she's about to make amends.

Aerie at Eagle's Rest: Giving Family a Capital F.

"I'm sorry for what happened." She means the Christmas in Aspen she passed out with a lit cigarette. Her neck bobs like a toy duck's, a wooden duck's. The hands over her face don't belong to her. They look like my mother's hands, veiny and pinched at the fingertips. "I brought you this," she says, clawing up a heap of red wool and waving it at me like a flag.

* * *

I cut the jacket's scarlet threads with my teeth—which are still all mine, every one of them—and scatter the golden buttons onto the floor for Sophie to get her dinner with.

* * *

These days, I sleep as lightly as I did when I was expecting. It's like a dream when Rockwald tiptoes into my room carrying a sprig of purple mayflower stuck in a mason jar. "Where did you get that?"

"Why, Tennessee, ma'am." The mayflower smells scissory, like bourbon.

"Ma'am, I'll admit it. My family may be old, but we're a bunch of bootlegging sons of bitches."

When he takes his pants off, his legs are white and skinny. His black socks go up past his knees, like an egret's. "In Tennessee, ma'am, we have a thing called hospitality."

I scoot over and let the old buzzard into my bed. He knows every verse of "My Country, 'Tis of Thee." "My heart with rapture thrills," he sings through his steel cigar, "thy woods and"—he gives my bed jacket the eye—"templed hills."

When Ars puffs "The Star-Spangled Banner," the room fills with flapping ducks.

I look at up at the fat, full-grown ducks. "Oh, God, for a Wingmaster 870."

"A tomboy," he says, "an apex predator." When he slaps my flank I know just how it feels to be a crème brûlée. My shell cracks and inside I'm six kinds of softness: pudding, feathers, blossoms, cotton, seed, etc. Ars says, "Happy is a man with a flock of ducks and no gun."

I don't know about that. But I notice he wears a real eagle feather behind his ear. Which noble bird dropped that? He spreads his arms the width of the pillow. What a wingspan. A long time since I've rested my head on anybody's snowy breast.

"Now listen here, my chickadee. You keep your beak *shut.*" He pinches my nose closed. He has quite a grip for someone so arthritic. "If you tell anyone about any of this, they won't believe you." He gives my nose a wrench. As if I were a squawking pigeon, a soiled dove, a broken-record macaw.

"Birds of a feather!" I squeak.

He lets me go and reclines, smoking his crippled kazoo. "So long as you heard me."

"Oh, I know you better than you know yourself, you old duck-sucker." I roll away from him. I keep rolling until I hit the floor.

Something cracks.

A red curtain falls between me and mine. My electronic bed, my smoking financier, my flock of ducks, my Sophie's legs, my eagle binder, my emeralds.

"A great fall, a great fall," says Rockwald. Then: "My people were all the king's men." He presses the Lifelink and starts humming "My Country, 'Tis of Thee" quickly, quickly.

Sweet land of liberty, where's Sophie?

I remember meeting a mother of a child who was abducted by the North Koreans right here in the Oval Office.

In my breast a lantern clatters like a ride through the night.

* * *

Dodos finally got something right. The letters are now the proper size on the hawk's name tag. *Betsy R.* Sharp fingernails for such a historic figure. She wraps a white cloth around me. I stripe it fast and red. "My stars," she says. "I'd better get—"

"So soon," says Dr. Eagle, feathery from all the arrows he's administrating.

"I know, Doctor," says Betsy Ross.

"I thought—surely not before Christmas."

"I've got the olive branches, right here in my smock."

The wicker walls of the Nest rise up like mountains, crested with snow. The stars swell.

"Ah! The stars of progress," says the Eagle.

"Grow wings," says Betsy Ross.

I can see all the way into the valley, past the approach and through the blinking snowplows to the curve of river. The little town three miles out is waking up; our flag slides up into the dawning sky above the flat-roofed school and my heart pitches powerfully at the succulent sight of a rabbit's pale tracks in the snow.

"It's too cold," says Betsy Ross. "Doctor?"

My wet feathers. My four fathers.

Me, a bird of the air.

Emily Anderson

I cut my name in the crusted snow with my talons. Each flake sparkles. Betsy Ross's shadow surges toward me from behind. "Don't you think we'd better put this one in the aviary until spring? Doctor? Doctor?"

The Snow on Tompkins Square Park
Frederic Tuten

A MAN LIMPED into a bar. He folded his stubby hands on the counter. The bartender, Aloysius, a blue horse, said, "What will you have?"

"A glass of water, please."

"We serve horses here, and people who look horsey. You aren't and you don't."

"I'm waiting for my girlfriend, she's very horsey."

"Well, in that case," the bartender said, "cool your heels."

The man waited a few minutes, checked his watch, looked out the window. Freezing rain fell outside. He nursed his water and then, twenty-seven minutes later, when the glass was dry, he said, "I guess she's not coming. Or she got stuck in the rain."

"Wait a while longer," the bartender said. "You don't want her to come and find you gone."

He had been thinking the same thing but he also thought he would leave and give her a lesson for always being late and expecting him to be waiting. Or if she did not come at all, he could pretend he was never there. But the icy rain decided him to stay. It gave him a good excuse to tarry.

"Thanks," the man said. He wanted to give weight to his "thanks" and added, "Very sporting of you."

He moved to the edge of the bar to make space for other customers but none seemed to be coming. He looked about the room. A table of three horses. They looked at him not unfriendly but not friendly, looked at him in a dispassionate way, he thought. One horse, a red filly, gave him a warm smile, showing him all her teeth. Some were drinking a dark beer in glass buckets and there were bowls of oats set on each table but no one was eating.

The bar had no TV and no radio. The woman he was waiting for made him unhappy. She had always made him unhappy, she would always make him unhappy. That thought made him say: "I'd like a scotch."

"Sure," the bartender said.

"And make it a double, neat." He had heard that word "neat" in movies and liked its ring.

"We have all kinds of scotches," the bartender said.

The man looked into his wallet and said, "Nothing too expensive and nothing too cheap, if you have."

The horse gave him a long stare with one eye. "That's OK, you don't need to order anything. I'll bring you another glass of water, with a lemon twist this time if you want."

"Yes, I'd like that," the man said. "And the scotch too, please." He looked at his stubby, hairy fingers, counting each one twice. He looked in the mirror behind the rows of glowing, friendly bottles, and saw that nothing of him looked horsey but that he looked, rather, like a flounder.

After silently counting his fingers again and letting his thoughts roam, he heard a voice from one of the tables.

"Hey! If you're alone, come over and join us, why don't you," the red filly said.

He glanced at the bartender, who said, "That's fine. I'll bring over your drink."

The man introduced himself. The others did the same. One, who looked like he had a thoughtful life, was named "Jake." The other, with a black patch over his eye, was named "Patch," and the red filly said her name was "Red."

"Someone stand you up?" she asked.

He stood up and sat down again. "It seems like it. Yes, someone."

"What brings you to these parts, Louie?"

"I live up the street, on the park."

"Never seen you here," the filly said.

"I heard we weren't welcome."

"Everyone's welcome who looks a little horsey or is sympathetic to horses or hasn't injured them. Have you?"

"No, I like horses. Thought I would like to be one. But I guess I can't because I look like a flounder."

They laughed. "That's very funny," Jake, the wise-looking horse, said. "But you don't look like a flounder, you look more like a, like a codfish!"

Then Patch said, "Doesn't matter what fish you look like, you look like a fish out of water."

"Yes, I'm a fish out of water. I don't know where the water is."

"I think you need to be cheered up a bit," the filly said. "Have another drink."

"That's a good idea," Louie said. "One's on the way." He called out to the bartender.

Two horses walked in, one very large, broad and meaty, with a cocky walk; the other lean and shy, with his head down. They came to the table. The cocky one said, "Who's this fella?"

"A friend," the filly said.

The large horse gave him an intimidating look. Then said to the filly, "Whatya doing later?"

"I don't know, Harry," she said. "It's not later yet."

"OK, OK," he laughed it off. "I'll be here a while and catch you later. You too, fella," he said. He took his time getting to the bar, the shy one trailing behind.

"Don't mind him," Red said. "He used to be a police horse. He was very proud of himself when he was younger. He was big in the Macy's Day Parade and the Easter Day parade and the Columbus Day parade and all the important parades and now he's retired with a nice pension."

"I didn't mind him," Louie said.

Patch, who had been silent until then, said: "Don't mind him but watch out when he starts backing into you because soon he'll have you squeezed against a wall and you'll wonder what happened to your breath. He learned lots of nasty tricks for all kinds of occasions."

The bartender brought over a half–filled tall glass of scotch and a glass of water with a twist of lemon. "Be anything else?"

"Not right now," Louie said, looking about him. He smiled and raised his glass in toast to his new companions. "To horses," he said.

The wise horse tapped his hoof on the table and said to the bartender: "Bring him a bag of oats—no, make it a bowl. And don't forget a spoon."

A yellow horse with long eyelashes sauntered into the bar solo. She came to the table and daintily made her hellos.

"Hello, Sally," Red said. "Haven't see you in a while."

"Well, I've been here and there," she said. "Mostly there, if you get my drift." She gave the man a long, friendly look and smiled, showing a row of large, white teeth.

"Introduce me to your friend, why don't ya?"

"This is Louie," Red said. "He owns a few banks and a string of polo ponies."

"Hey! That's great," Sally said. "See you later, Mr. Banker."

She left and brushed up to the police horse. They chattered amiably. Affably. The police horse said loudly, "Bring Sally a Kir Royale."

Red turned to the man and, sotto voce, said: "She had her teeth done, can't you tell? Anyway, she used to be a circus horse. Very

287

famous and loved by persons from six to sixty! She had the riders stand on her bare back, and she'd circle faster and faster but no one ever fell off."

"That's wonderful," Louie said, his thoughts traveling elsewhere. "Fish out of water," he said dreamily. "What's the water I belong to? The Atlantic, the Pacific, the Mediterranean, the Nile, the Amazon, the Hudson?"

"You could swim in the East River," Jake said. "It's so close you could walk right over and dive in."

"Cod don't swim in the East River," Patch said.

"Well, they used to swim in the Hudson two hundred years ago," the wise horse said. "It's an estuary, you know."

Everyone nodded. Aloysius called out, "A river drowned in an ocean."

"You know, the longer you sit here, the less you look like a fish and the more you look like a horse," Red said.

"How kind," Louie said.

"Yes," the wise horse said, "that's true. I see equine features emerging. Maybe because I see Red, our friend here, likes you."

"Oh! Go on," she said, with a huff.

"I'm sorry, think I have intruded on something here," said Louie.

"But nothing that can't be resolved, right, Red?" the wise horse said.

The filly tossed her head and said, "Look! It's stopped raining." And, turning to Louie, "Maybe you'd like to go for a walk?"

"Think I could use one. Think I'm getting a little tipsy." He let his head fall to one side. He laughed. He called out to the bartender, "If a woman comes in looking for me, offer her a drink and ask her to wait, OK? A Kir Royale, maybe."

The bartender nodded. The police horse turned swiftly and said, "That's my signature drink. Go find another, chum."

"Don't even answer him," the filly said. "Let's just go."

And they went into the day.

The day was gray. A chilled gray. The sky was thickening with crystals of gray light. He was gray.

Tompkins Square Park was empty but for a lone policeman, statue-like, in a glistening rain slicker.

"Let's cut through here," she said, stepping into the walk on Eighth and Avenue B.

"I never knew they let horses in the park," he said, stopping short.

"They don't," she said, "but the cop's a friend."

"How ya doing, Red?" the cop said. "Still looking for work?"

"Not anymore," she said. "My horse came in."

The cop looked at the man, up and down.

"Who's this?"

"A friend. He lives here."

The cop mused on this and said: "Never seen you before."

"I swim mostly in the East River, by the fire boat."

"That's why," the cop said. Then, turning to the filly, he said, "What you doing later, Red?"

"Later than when?" she asked.

"OK," the cop said. "I get it. See you around."

They walked. Red said, "You seem to have trouble dragging that leg. Wanna sit down a minute?"

They did, on a slatted bench still wet from the rain. After a while, he said, "I'm a dull man. I'm a very dull one."

"That's true," she said. "And colorless."

"I always wanted to be colorless and not bother anyone."

"Well, you don't bother me!" she said, in a voice that cheered him, just as the rain began to turn to snow.

"I used," he said, "to love to read about famous horses. That's how I came to like them. Like the Lone Ranger's horse, Silver, or King Alexander's horse, Bucephalus, or Quixote's horse, Rocinante."

"I don't read much," she said. "I'm not for the life of the mind, like Aloysius or Jake, who's always reading—and I don't mean for the odds."

"I never knew that horses liked to read."

"That's sad. Sad that you don't know a thing!"

He was afraid he had hurt her feelings, his not knowing this about horses, so he said, "I always wanted a life without misfortune. So it's been a life without much range."

She said nothing. He the same. The snow fell on them and around them and whitened the black branches of the naked trees and the black tops of the park's iron railings. Red said, "I always like the snow and the way it tells us new things."

"I like the way it makes everything quiet for awhile," Louie said, wanting to add to the conversation.

It was darkening, the snow deepening and swirling like little white tornadoes.

"It's getting cold now, I'm going back to the bar," she said. "I can enjoy the snow through the window."

He was cold but didn't want to leave. He didn't want to go home.

The stairs, the climb, dragging his leg, the same door, the same key, the same turning on the hall light, the same hundred and twenty-five watts.

"I'll walk you back, if you like," Louie said.

"Don't you have a cane?" Red asked.

He did, but he had left his house without it, not wanting to seem old.

"I have three for decoration but forgot them at home."

"Well then, get ahold of me because I don't want you to slip and fall."

The pathway was heaping up with snow and the tree branches bent under its wet weight. He could hear the rumble of the snow trucks sent out to do their work, and the cries of the snowball fighters far down Avenue B. They walked cautiously, he gripping the snow-topped park rail until his hand went numb.

Red stopped. "Louie, why don't you climb aboard and I'll give you a ride home. Then I can walk back to the bar myself."

"Not possible. I never let a lady walk alone at night." It was not true but he felt heroic saying this and he wanted her to feel his heroism.

She shook off the snow in gentle, slow sways. He brushed away the little white ridge left on her head and spine.

"I could come to your place," Red said carefully, "but I suppose you don't have an elevator."

Louie imagined her standing in his living room, her hooves leaving little puddles of snow, making the fading roses on the carpet bloom, the steam from her body and breath painting the walls with tropical color.

"No elevator," he said, "but maybe now I'll move where there is one."

They heard a voice through the snow.

"Hey, Red, wondering if you lost your way in this blizzard." It was the police horse.

Then, seeing Louie, he said, "Still here, chum?"

"Thanks for looking after me," Red said. "But we're copacetic."

The horse said, "Oh! Sure, Red," and wedged himself between the filly and the man, shouldering him against the rail and slowly pressing the wind out of him.

"Don't be a jerk, Harry. Stop or you'll never see me again."

"Come on, it's just a friendly shove," the police horse said.

"Stop or I'll get you eighty-sixed from the bar forever."

Harry stopped and in a small, childish voice said, "I'm sorry, Red, and you, too, mister."

He backed away into the curtaining snow and darkness and called out from a distance, "I'm not sorry at all."

"Louie, you don't look so good," Red said.

His ribs hurt and he spoke with a wheeze. "I'm all right, Red, I just need to catch my wind."

They stood for a moment, he wavering against her, while the snow tumbled down on them in clumps.

"I think you should come back to the bar, Louie. You're going blue. You could use a drink," she said.

"Sure, Red, let's go then." Louie gave her his bravest smile.

They slowly made their way to the bar, where Aloysius greeted them and Jake said, "Back from the South Pole already?"

"Aloysius, let's fix up Louie here with a drink. Something special," Red said. "He's going soft under the gills."

They sat at the table, Louie sunk weakly in the chair.

Jake said, "He's all wet and going green."

The bartender thought about it and said, "I have something here, something very old, from the days when the Greeks fermented their wine with grapes from a sacred mountain grove, grapes that sucked iron power from the sun."

"That mountain," Jake said, "where Plato threw dice with the gods."

"Oh! That wild man in love with horses," Patch said. "Did he ever know we horses dreamed him his ideas?"

"We read and we write and we dream. We dream the books that all the books in the world come from. We dreamed books before the earth got cool. We dreamed books before the invention of Time," Jake said.

Sally, her head on the bar counter, looked up and said in a sloppy voice, "It's always life in the past you talk about but where are we now, tell me?"

Then she gave a long look over to the table and said: "Hello, Mr. Banker, buy a lady a drink?"

"Yes," Louie said.

"Bring me the best," Sally said to the bartender, but then she put her head back on the counter and fell asleep.

"It's hard not being young and a star of the ring," Red said. "You didn't have to buy her a drink but it was sweet of you."

"You know," Jake said, "now I see that you don't look like a fish of any kind at all."

"Like a beached whale?" Louie asked. "Like a whale in the snow?"

"No, not at all," Patch said.

"You look like something in the becoming," Jake said, tilting his head.

Aloysius brought over a golden drink glowing with the drowned light of an old sun.

Louie sipped until color came back to his face. "Feeling better," he said, but then he shivered in the cold of his wet clothes.

"You should go home and get into bed," Red said, "before you catch the pneumonia."

"Oh! Not right now," the man said, his cheeks flushed. "I like it here, my friends," he said, raising his glass.

Aloysius went to the door and opened it to a wall of mounting snow. A wind of flakes swarmed through the room.

"Sorry, but I doubt if you can leave now anyway," he said to Louie. "You can't walk in these drifts, and there's nothing moving in sight."

"Wonderful, I'll stay a while, I'll stay till spring," Louie said.

"You can stay the night," Aloysius said, "just as long as you don't have another drop."

"He's not drunk," Red said. "He's pleased."

"Not drunk at all," Louie said, rising, glass in hand. "I drink to you all and to this retreat, to this cave, to this glade of dreamers. I drink to becoming."

"He's feverish," Jake said, "his face is sending off sparks."

"It's hot in here," Louie said, "even though I'm freezing."

Aloysius and Red led him to a back room with three stalls of hay. Louie undressed to his shorts and stretched himself out in the straw.

"Take this," Aloysius said, covering him with a thick horse blanket. And turning to Red, the bartender said, "I think we're all glued here till morning."

"Don't use that word, it give me the chills," Red said.

"What's the difference," Aloysius said, "the glue or the ashes? The soul is immortal."

"I always wondered," Louie said, suddenly raising his head.

He could not sleep and wished they would return, all of them, and talk about the immortality of the soul, how the body died but the soul went on its way—to where? The straw smelled of spring and sun and the blanket of the thick steam of horses. The street lamp shone faintly through the window, glazing the room silver. He thought of the woman whom he had waited for and was glad she had not come. She had not made him happy and would never make him happy. He had never before been happy.

He closed his eyes and felt himself happy. And he soon slid into sleep. He was on a snow-tipped mountain in a glade surrounded by snow. The sun warmed the glade but left the mountain frozen in snow and ice. Horses grazed and drank from a pure stream. Some had wings. Some spoke nervously about the world below the mountain and of the dangers waiting there. But others said they never intended to leave the glen and did not care for the world below and for those foolish enough to have gone there. The young ones pranced and splashed in the stream and nipped at each other in amorous play but no one minded and let them be. Some horses came to speak to him. They wanted to know—as he had lived below and had visited among them—his thoughts of the world. Was the visible world the terminal end or the edge of another, invisible world? they asked. He did not know, he said. They laughed in a friendly way. And then asked: Was his body the edge of his world or just a perishable form of an invisible self that had no boundaries in time and space, that had no beginning and no end? He said he did not know, but added that he was indifferent to the answer, happy as he now was among them in the glade. He was wise, they said. He was not sure if they were just being polite. A great golden horse with golden wings circled them, saying nothing. But then he came close, and, bending low for Louie to mount, he said, "Come, join me, if you will."

"Yes," he said, "I gladly will." They rose above the glen and flew high above the world until it shrank into a speck among specks and then they sped away toward the sun.

Louie woke to the clatter of life and voices in the bar and quickly dressed; his clothes were dry. All the horses of the previous evening surrounded a table heaped with buckets of grain and bowls of water. They had set aside a place for him with a plate of cooked oatmeal and a napkin and wooden spoon.

He nodded; they did the same. Then, silently, they all began to eat as the first true light of day came through the window.

—For David Salle

Four Poems
Rebecca Bridge

(SOME LUCKY)

—*For Paul Hoover*

Skip to the howls and the cows
will come home, hear the beating
of the tacks into the walls?
Nailed in like multiplication tables,
drilled into these tiny mahogany-headed
pupils dropping leaves to fall through minds,

drift across the autumns and,
thick-skulled, there go those dogs again
howling and squeaking (like some lucky beds),
or brand-new shoes on linoleum spit shined
(like some lucky lips), or lips reading
when the signs don't flash language

and the records spin music in treetops,
scratched over and over scratched
(like some lucky backs), with thighs wrapped
around them, decorative as tutus, and
the active volcanoes are dressed for a fight,
throwing the towels in the hampers and

the cows sleep at night.

WHAT WONDER

The dark had descended, nighttime was
a velvety hat, sat well upon all the heads
of field mice. Where? Well, they were
hidden underneath the davenport of course.

The world was in childish verses, deafened and sick
from the wonderful night animals, oh, be-
witched world! The world was under me whispering
nasty and soft, saying: You seem *taller* lately.

IN THE EVENING, EVEN DEEPENING IS PRETTY

Somewhere deep in the cheese fields of the
Great Midwest, upon the bough of an old
cheese tree, we sat and sat and we told stories.
It was a pleasant time, with fruits ripening
and other things ripening and the sun shining
just so how it shines in the Midwest and other
things shining. It was past quitting time for the
migrants and so they had gone and migrated
home. It is a beautiful day for most people
either he said or I said and then one of us agreed
with the other. It is always nice to be agreed with and
we both felt so. We both felt deeply and we told
stories about other times when we had also felt
deeply. One of us lied but I do not know which.
The sun was drunk on its shining and so drunk drunk
that it made a fool of itself. We pretended not to notice.
It went to bed. Most things went to bed. We too
were tired but we did not go to bed. We were the
owls watching over the night critters. We
would not sleep and how could we? There were
so many, many stories still scuttling and about.

BECAUSE THE WORLD CAN'T CONTINUE IF THE BEES DIE

My heart was alone and having
what might have been a tender moment.
I could not tell. It seemed so still
and I asked, "Are you all right?"
but it did not answer me. It does this now
and often. I say, "So the weather's nice."
I say, "Haven't heard much from you lately."
I say, "Would you like a coffee?" I have grown
used to the silence although I cannot
say that it has grown used to me. I can
only guess at my heart's moods
by the tiny clues it leaves. They are like
boot prints left out in a dust storm.

Before this quiet started, my heart
treated me differently. I was a friend to it,
a best friend to it, and it would tell me all about
all everything. It would just be an afternoon and
my heart would burst out with "I am a pogo stick!"
And then we might laugh until our bellies ached
because I would sigh something like,
"I am a tub of chocolate pudding."
The whole wide world seemed
just like a whole wide world of afternoons.
Everything was pleasing to me and
I had not known that I was required to answer then.
Then when my heart had so quietly whispered,
"Rebecca, sometimes I am so scared that
I'll suddenly forget what to do with this air."

Today would feel so different if we were still speaking,
saying, "We are swarms of bees!"

Becoming Human
Janis E. *Rodgers*

SAVANNA CHIMPANZEES AT DAWN

WE TREKKED INTO THE BLACKENED bush under a blurred crescent moon. The scent of smoke and ash lingered in the air and the simple mud-hut compound Dr. Jill Pruetz calls home in Senegal disappeared as if it never had existed, as if I never had gone to sleep fitfully under my mosquito net, but had been walking all night by the light of stars.

Down a barely distinguishable path, we made our way toward the plateau where Jill knew the group of thirty-two chimpanzees she studies have built nests and spent the night. I tried to imagine them at dusk, a blood-orange sun sinking below the red-rock plateau as they climbed up trees to build nests where they would sleep, safe from prowling hyenas. Headlamps on the trail, there was utter silence—partly out of exhaustion, but for me, it felt like a reverence for the forest, for the species of nonhuman primate I would shortly encounter for the first time. I was filled with both awe and fear as charred branches rubbed up against my legs, leaving streaked imprints on my quick-dry field pants, like the forest's fingers, examining me.

At 4:45 a.m., Jill had anxiously waited at the opening of the fenced compound of her base camp, Fongoli, while I groggily laced up my boots. She wore a baggy, ripped T-shirt (beige—chimps don't like bright colors), and well-worn boots stained orange by Senegal's phosphate-rich earth. Her brown hair was tied in a ponytail, and her backpack contained the day's supplies—water, binoculars, a waterproof notebook and pen, cookies, a bag of peanuts, and a couple of hard-boiled eggs from a boutique in Kédougou, the nearest town. The boutiques and hotels had just cropped up in the last couple of years due to the influx of gold and iron mining. When Jill first started working in Senegal over ten years ago, there wasn't even electricity in Kédougou. Now, Le Bedik hotel offers not only a stunning dining-room balcony overlooking the Gambia River, but a swimming pool and Wi-Fi.

The region of Kédougou in southeastern Senegal, a place home to both chimpanzees and gold, shimmers like a green gem in an arid country dominated by sand and flat, orange earth. Parc National du Niokolo-Koba is a UNESCO World Heritage Site, and some of the only forests and mountains in Senegal are located here. Most of the country is only slightly above sea level, but in the southeast, the foothills of Guinea's Fouta Djallon Mountains reach elevations of 1,640 feet. Kédougou is also one of the poorest regions in the country, and the place where savanna chimpanzees (*Pan troglodytes verus*) use tools to hunt.

Jill (or Le Patron, as she is called by many here in Senegal), an intrepid primatologist from Texas, started her field site to study the unique behaviors of these western chimpanzees who eke out an existence in a parched mosaic of savanna and woodlands with limited water sources. A PhD student of Jill's, Kelly Boyer, focuses more on the conservation end of primatology, as the reality of threats to great ape habitat, like mining and human encroachment, become more exigent. "Based on birth and death rates at my site, the group of chimps there will be extinct in sixty years, and that's an optimistic estimate," Jill said.

As corporate gold- and iron-mining companies bombard Senegal's lush forests with bulldozers and gaping pits in the earth, chimpanzee habitat disappears. Truck corridors and mining concessions raze mountaintop forests where chimps once spent the night in nests built of tree branches. The largest company, ArcelorMittal, known for its global steel-production initiatives, now mines for iron ore in the mountains of Bofeto, an area where Kelly has documented the presence of chimps. Kelly attempts to measure the effect of iron-ore mining on chimp habitat through line transects and nest-count surveys. With this information she estimates population densities in areas destined to become large-scale iron-ore mines. Her goal at this early stage of research is to assess chimpanzee populations and their habitat, as well as existing human disturbances, prior to the construction of mines.

Despite the challenges she faces, Kelly appears undaunted by her task of working toward conserving an endangered species. Strong and blonde, her face wrinkled by the West African sun, her energy levels and optimism are extraordinary. She has salsa danced in Houston, worked at a chimp sanctuary in Guinea, and now, in her early thirties, she is pursuing her PhD at Iowa State University. We met in a conservation biology class and quickly became friends and yoga buddies. At a workshop in Iowa City, we listened to a well-respected yogi, Desirée Rumbaugh, discuss nonattachment and regaining joy after loss. *Vairagya*, or nonattachment, is a key component of yoga. Everything changes and everything will eventually end, Desirée chanted, as we inverted our bodies into headstands, testing ourselves to see how long we could hold the pose.

While still in Iowa, we had sat on the floor of Kelly's office with a huge US Geological Survey map of Kédougou spread out like a treasure scroll. It was only a field copy, meaning it could get dirty or marked up, but it was the most beautiful map I'd ever seen. The glossy *région de Kédougou* boasted deep purple gallery forests and sweeping green mountains I could journey through with the trace of my finger. I marveled over the cartographer's skill and precision, the satellite imagery laid out beneath our fingertips. This little jewel at the bottom of Senegal's great sandy expanse represented a last sanctuary for a dwindling population of savanna chimpanzees. The minimal swath of green I could cover with my palm was about to be swallowed by bridges, mines, and paved roads. Silver elephants on Kelly's ring seemed to dance off into veins of *galerie forestière*. She ran her finger across the base of mountains between her two study sites—Kharakhena and Bofeto—places she had found evidence: nests and scat and pant-hoots. Her finger stopped, pressed into the top of the Fouta Djallon.

"If ArcelorMittal has its way, these mountains will be destroyed."

The abrupt sound of a pant-hoot flew into my heart like bats fleeing light—the breathy, low-pitched "hoots" became quicker and quicker until they climaxed in higher-pitched "pants"—hoo, hoo, hoo, hoo . . . ah ah ah ah ah! A sudden stillness pervaded our party. I looked at the back of Jill's head, expectant of her next move.

"It got light fifteen minutes earlier than yesterday," she noted. "They're already down from their nests."

With that we quickened our pace. I turned off my headlamp as the palest of lights crept onto the plateau. The chimpanzees' presence in the forest, in the world, in this tiny nook of a West African country nearly buckled my knees as I struggled to follow Jill's footsteps even more closely now. My entire being became sublimely concentrated on hearing the next call, seeing my first glimpse of wild chimpanzee. It wasn't long before a flash of fur-covered blackness darted through the trees before us. I saw the wrinkled, brown face and steady, mahogany eyes of a savanna chimpanzee—a mother with a pink-eared

299

infant clutched to her chest, tiny fingers just visible through the fur on the sides of her stomach.

"That's Natasha; she's a little nervous with her newborn," Jill said, as Natasha walked swiftly away from us, cupping a hand over her baby's fuzzy head.

Natasha was quite gray for a female of twenty. The average life span of chimps in the wild is forty-five, but they can live into their sixties in captivity. Jill described Natasha as one of the shyest females among humans, but with other females in the group, she was tough.

"The first time I saw Natasha she was fighting with another adult female, Lingua. It was a throw down up on the plateau, and they both had babies! She's pretty scrappy," Jill said, "but she's very protective of her daughters."

Jill named Natasha, and Natasha's first daughter, Sonya, after the characters in *War and Peace*.

"Natasha may have a droopy lower lip, and not be the prettiest of chimps, but she's full of life," Jill said.

Natasha held her baby protectively, a gesture I imagine any human mother could empathize with. Chimpanzees form long-term bonds with family members that may persist throughout a lifetime. Having the opportunity to observe these bonds and interactions in their natural habitat was not a privilege I took lightly. Even as I write these words it still astounds me that after only seven hours in a plane from New York City, and a day's long drive across Senegal, I was here, *dans la brousse*, amid wild chimpanzees.

When I told Kelly I wanted to document the work of primatologists in the field as they attempt to study and conserve a dwindling great ape population, she was my most ardent supporter. "That's fabulous!" she said, and found some grant money to get me a ticket to Senegal, to witness the struggles and joys of a primatologist in the bush. Instead of studying wild primates systematically, like I'd done in the past in Kenya, I planned to write about them. I wanted to document not only the existence of both chimpanzees and field researchers in Africa, but to try to better understand what it means to be human. I wanted to write poetry about these stunning creatures who have inspired fear, repulsion, awe, and love in humanity.

Two summers ago, in the coastal province of Kenya, I had worked as a research assistant watching mangabey monkeys glide through colossal palm fronds. Their small, furry bodies made monumental echoes through the open forest as they clutched hard, red fruit under their chins like miniature football players and leaped strategically from palm to palm. The Tana River mangabeys (*Cercocebus galeritus*) are not only an endangered species, endemic to the highly fragmented Tana riverine forests of the coastal province, they are an extraordinarily elegant monkey—with dark, stoic faces, heavy eyelids, graceful tufts of gray-white fur—but scientific journals don't want to hear about things like that. Those journals want methodologies and procedures, figures, tables, results, and peer reviews. Hard data is important for quantifying behaviors, but what can it tell us about beauty, empathy, love, and mortality? Does poetry have a place beside science, or will it continue to be relegated to the humanities, to the Unnecessary and Unimportant? I cannot begin to understand or appreciate the complexities of science without love's betrayal of it, and the poetry that allows me to see it this way. Poet and scientist Katherine Larson addresses science directly on this issue: "Science— / beyond pheromones, hormones, aesthetics of bone, / every time I make love for love's sake alone, / I betray you."

One of the many things that makes chimpanzees at Fongoli special is that early hominids are thought to have inhabited a similar type of savanna environment, and the selective pressures associated with such a harsh, arid habitat may be comparable. This means that hominids evolving in the early Plio-Pleistocene, 2.5 to 1.5 million years ago, may have lived similarly to the way these chimps do now—perhaps they had similar home ranges, diets, and maybe, like chimps, our early ancestors cooled off in caves during extremely hot weather.

The vision of what chimpanzees could tell us about human evolution propelled Louis Leakey to send a young Jane Goodall to Tanzania to conduct the first long-term study of chimpanzees in the wild. In 1960, Goodall was the first field primatologist to introduce the public to how incredibly human-like chimpanzees can be. The same year she arrived in Gombe, Goodall observed a chimp named David Greybeard pick up a twig, pull off the leaves, and stick it in a termite mound. He then proceeded to slowly pull out the twig covered in termites, and pluck them off with his lips. Protein. David Greybeard caused our notion of "man the toolmaker" to be forever vanquished.

The chimps had already come down from their nests when we arrived, and were pant-hooting their good mornings to each other.

Next, they started to eat. Between May and June is the season for a green fruit with fleshy orange seeds called *Saba senegalensis*, or simply saba, as the locals say. These bitter fruits are a main food source for chimps, but also popular with humans. Saba has evolved into a cash crop and is collected by local people and sold to buyers for the market in Dakar and other large cities. Jill's concern is that the harvest of saba by humans, which has increased fivefold over the past several years, will drastically reduce the availability of the fruit for chimps, and have a serious impact on their survival.

Later in the summer, Jill followed the Fongoli chimps toward a creek bed where they seasonally voyage to feast on what is locally known as "minkone" fruit. The site, called Gingi, after an adjacent village, is home to a dozen or so of these fruit trees, a staple part of chimp diet in the late rainy season after saba has stopped growing. When Jill got to the creek one damp July morning, she recalled, all the trees had been cut down for cultivation.

"You couldn't even recognize it," she said, describing an absence in the forest that, for the last ten years at least, had been an integral secondary food source.

Two adult females in the group, Bandit and Lucille, sat next to a termite mound and stared for over an hour at what had once been a major nesting and feeding site they frequented. Jill does not have a way to evaluate this behavior scientifically, but cannot help but wonder: "Were they taking it all in? Were they shocked at the devastation? Or were they waiting to see what activity was going on?"

A male squatted at the top of a tree. A hooked white scar the shape of a slim crescent moon was exposed on his lower back as he reached to pull a branch of fruit to his mouth.

"That's David," Jill said quietly. "He's my study subject."

She pulled a small, curled notebook from her ripped pants pocket and began taking notes. I could immediately tell that she cared deeply for this stunning fellow, perhaps the same way Jane Goodall had felt for her own David.

"I'm going to follow him."

Jill descended a steep, leaf-littered bank into a tangle of saba trees.

We had walked past castellate termite mounds, over metamorphic rock plateaus and through tangled lianas. We struggled through tough potato vines and trees that strangled each other. And here some of the chimps were resting under a cool, viny thicket. An old chimp leaned back on a rock and closed his eyes, his lips slightly parted in a grin. He had a sparse, white beard and pink scars on his chin. The side of his face was bathed in sunlight, the thick fur on his back covered in dead leaves. He crossed his arms and looked down at a companion sleeping next to him. In that moment I was just a voyeur observing another human being, simply "people watching" as my mother and I used to do in Manhattan, seated on the library steps. There was something in their faces that I had not seen in the mangabeys.

When Goodall first discovered chimps making "fishing poles" to retrieve termites, the idea of "man the toolmaker" was dispelled, but man was still considered the only creature who hunted with tools. This hallmark behavior created a distinct boundary between humans and chimpanzees that exalted humanity and stuck nonhuman primates definitively into the animal-kingdom mix, or so we thought.

The Fongoli chimps proved us wrong once again. Jill observed ten different chimps use "spears" to hunt prosimian prey in twenty-two documented cases. Tool construction involves five steps that include trimming the tool, a tree branch, to a point, in attempts to extract little nocturnal prosimians called bush babies (*Galago senegalensis*) from cavities in hollow branches and tree trunks. Bush babies emerge from their slumber at dusk and communicate through what sounds like language—cries or squeaks. They are agile leapers with large, thin ears like bats; huge, saucer-shaped eyes; and silvery fur coats. Even though in only one of twenty-two recorded cases was the chimpanzee successful, Jill insists that the toolmaking and hunting behaviors were both systematic and consistent. The tools were not used as probes or for rousing, she asserts, but instead these handcrafted tools were forcibly jabbed toward their prey multiple times and smelled and/or licked upon extraction. The discovery of chimps using tools to hunt, a behavior never before recorded in a group of wild chimps, landed Jill in *National Geographic* and put the Fongoli chimps in the media spotlight. Jill now asks us to rethink not only theories about tool use and hunting, but what it means to be human.

Local people such as the Malinke and Bedik tell stories about chimpanzees and monkeys. They believe that humans turn into monkeys if they are somehow outcast from society, and also that chimpanzees are their ancient ancestors and must be protected. Monkeys may be hunted and eaten for bush meat here, but not chimps. Using this traditional knowledge as a conservation tool is key. As folklorist Gregory Schrempp wrote in 2011: "Science can enrich its perspective through a sympathetic attitude toward myth and other forms of traditional wisdom." Gathering and documenting stories about people's interactions and beliefs about primates will also be valuable when there are no primates left.

How will we describe the great apes to our grandchildren or great-grandchildren when these creatures are no longer around, except maybe in zoos? How will we explain to them that hairy creatures whose expressions resembled those of humans once lived in the wild, but then went extinct? We won't read them scientific papers. We'll tell them stories, and hopefully, read them poems.

GOLD DIGGERS

Kelly and I entered Le Bedik on a Friday night in Kédougou and were greeted by an international coalition of mining-company employees, many still in their field clothes—geologists from Nigeria, a South African mine manager, a driller from Hungary with a round, sweating face, who was quite drunk. There were representatives from China and Australia, and a lanky fellow from Lebanon with charcoal-rimmed eyes who stumbled outside after he was refused another drink.

Le Bedik, the only locale in Kédougou with Wi-Fi, is usually our first stop when we come into town for supplies. Wealthy businesspeople, like the mining-company executives, typically reserve rooms. The president's wife, Viviane, stays here when she comes to check on the regional hospital she helped to fund a few years ago. Carved-wood elephant murals adorn the back wall of the bar and rustic village scenes color the concrete walls. From the restaurant balcony we could hear the echo of children's voices, the sound of women smacking clothing against rocks in the Gambia River. The mountains of Guinea were just visible in the distance, shrouded in a white sky, hazy from smoke lingering after a recent bush fire.

Like the miners, we were not quite clean after a week in the bush studying savanna chimpanzees, though we'd washed our hair and put on earrings. I chatted with a shaggy-haired geologist from Cape Town who sat at the end of the bar blowing cigarette smoke out into the fading sky. He was utterly baffled by a writer who had come to this uncomfortably hot country to study chimps.

"What do we need besides statistics and data?" He crinkled up his sunburned face and poured himself another whiskey.

"What will numbers tell us about chimps when they go extinct in the wild?" I said.

"What can you write about monkeys?" he asked. "They eat, they shit, they sleep."

"Apes," I corrected him.

At the other side of the bar, Kelly struck up a conversation with a reserved South African mine manager. He told her about a gold-prospecting expedition in Kharakhena, the field site where we had conducted transects and set up reconnaissance cameras to learn about the area's local chimp populations.

"I've been working here for months and I've never seen a chimp," he said.

"They're very silent when they want to be. You don't see them, but they're definitely around Kharakhena. We can tell based on nests they build at night to sleep in. . . ."

"They build nests?"

"Yes, they push down branches and leaves."

"Wow."

"Chimps are so resilient, but only to a point. When it comes to mining, we don't know what they'll be able to handle and what they won't. Obviously the loss of habitat will be an issue, but will the noise of bulldozers and other large machinery be a problem?"

"It won't be a problem," he assured her, his face stoic.

Kelly eagerly pulled up a vegetation map on her Toughbook that showed all the areas in Kharakhena where she'd documented the presence of chimps. The map abounded with rich blue circles that predicted home ranges. Blue meant gallery forests—habitat with fruiting and nesting trees used by chimps.

"We just have a small prospecting plant," the mine manager said. "That area, we just use the water source, we only put the plant up for exploration, but we're not going to do anything there."

"What do you mean, the water source?"

"We're building a dam. There's no other way to work in the dry season."

"A dam?!"

"There will be plenty of water for the chimps. It will help them."

"How could a dam possibly help the chimps?"

"It will! Why not? We'll have a camp with fresh fruit for them every day! They eat fruit, right?"

Images of chimps fighting over bananas surely made Kelly cringe, even though she kept a smile on her face. Provisioning wild chimps is forbidden at most research sites, as it has a strong influence on their behavior. When Jane Goodall first started working in Gombe

National Park, she provisioned the population with bananas to speed up the habituation process, so that she could observe and record behaviors before her funding ran out. When they got accustomed to provisioned food, their natural patterns of behavior changed. Habituated primates that lose their fear of people are more prone to death by hunters and other predators, and can also be dangerous to people. Because primates are genetically closely related to humans, they are susceptible to many of our diseases and, like us, can get a common cold or pneumonia.

We were all drunk and famished, so the mine manager bought some Pringles, a delicacy here, and paid one of the waiters to reopen the kitchen and have some steak and fries made up for us, on his tab. He ordered a bottle of white wine and filled our glasses, while the geologist polished off his own supply of Jameson and told us stories from his days in Angola, how he had left half-smoked cigarettes and water for the local diamond miners who were often beaten to death and thrown in the river, their bodies fished out in the morning. The world will turn a blind eye to unjust deaths for things like precious metals and gems.

"There would be blood coming from their ears, nose, mouth, and the supervisors would just say, 'They've drowned. They've drowned.' They didn't drown. Those buggers had been robbed blind."

He shook his head and rolled the last bits of ice in his glass. I imagined the Angolan workers, killed for pocketing a diamond. I imagined the poor working conditions, the small red glow of a half-smoked cigarette that would be waiting for them at the end of the day.

"We are all stakeholders," Kelly pointed out when our food arrived. "I'm going to be working here for the next several years, and so are you," she said to the mine manager. "We should collaborate."

"There are no chimps where my mine's going in."

"Yes, there are."

Kelly continued trying to convince him that chimps do indeed exist in areas where his company wanted to build mines, at the base of several mountains, where local people believe that chimps are the spirits of their ancient ancestors. Kelly knew she had to pick her battles. The mine manager has only a small-scale concession compared to other companies in the vicinity, namely ArcelorMittal. As she argued, I felt the mist of a heavy rain on my face at the onset of a seasonal downpour.

THE STARRY-EYED YOUTH

The rainy season was just beginning when we arrived in Bofeto village, which was green and glistening against the forest after a midday shower. Mud-slick mountain roads sent our Land Rover fishtailing through fields of Djakore cattle with their long, fine horns and fulvous coats. We slid past bicyclists and into the neon-green savanna, just sprouting new grasses that seemed to glow. After the dry season had left the country barren and thirsty, the rain added fresh color to the once-dusty landscape.

Rustic wooden fences, cattle enclosures, and mud-hut compounds with thatched roofs lined the roadsides. This seemed like an idyllic village, a pristine place that had been untouched by Western influence, until Kelly pointed to the hills. They looked lumpy and shaved in places, like they'd gotten a bad haircut. The hills—which contain caves where chimps rest when temperatures rise in the dry season—had been mangled by mining roads.

We crossed a bridge wide enough for construction equipment that leaned heavily to one side over the murky river. A hand-carved wooden canoe tied loosely to a tree on the shore looked as though it would be swept away if the current picked up. Bulldozed roads replaced vague dirt trails, and once-pristine forest was infiltrated by heavy machinery and mining camps. I thought of the lesson on nonattachment and loss we'd received from yogi Desirée Rumbaugh back in Iowa. More and more chimp habitat is destroyed each time Kelly returns to Senegal to conduct her research, and there is seemingly little she can do about it. Everything changes and everything will come to an end. Can I accept this yogic philosophy but still care about conservation?

The impacts of mining in Senegal, and throughout West Africa in general, became a reality to me not only when I saw large-scale mining operations that left gaping holes in the earth, but also when we dined with the people who worked for these companies. When a mining company wants to start a new mine in Senegal, it makes a contract with the government, typically declaring that after the mine has been exploited, it will be responsible for reclamation. Mine reclamation is supposed to mean that the hole will be filled in and the landscape rehabilitated—topsoil put down and trees planted. As the geologist disclosed to us at the bar, this step is often overlooked, and mining companies say they've surpassed their budget, pay a fine to the government, and quietly leave the country. The

ArcelorMittal mining camp is adjacent to Kelly's field site. Due to the rains, the chain-link-fenced compound seemed deserted aside from a few guards and their dogs. Dump trucks would get stuck in these muddy roads.

Kelly monitors this distinct nook of Senegal in an attempt to determine the effects of mining on chimp habitat. Here, the forests are not only home to chimps and other wildlife, but to some of the world's most desired minerals. ArcelorMittal is the largest steel-producing company in the world, and in the Faléme region of Senegal, they've made a contract to mine for iron ore, a key ingredient of steel. On *Forbes* magazine's "Most Powerful People" list, Lakshmi Mittal, the chief executive officer of the company, is number forty-seven of the seventy people named. His daughter's wedding was the most expensive in recorded history, a $60 million affair.

Mineral mining is a key aspect of economic growth, as Mr. Mittal and the company website advocate, but it is also extremely danger-ous and destructive. ArcelorMittal's website claims that it is con-cerned with sustainability and safe working conditions, but what it doesn't show is pictures of the open pit mines left to erode and mar the earth. It doesn't show pictures of children washing gold in mer-cury with their bare hands. It doesn't show mines long since aban-doned or resources vanished from the African earth.

In the village, we were greeted by our host, Smiti Damfakha, his four wives, and eighteen children. One wife was displaced from her hut at the center of the compound, and our bags were shuttled in-side assembly-line style by the children. Donald Duck sheets were tucked into the two wooden beds, worn linoleum covered the dirt floor, stacks of metal and plastic bowls were kept on a small table, and there was even a motorcycle out front: all indicators of the small amounts of wealth local people make mining. Damfakha was ex-tremely proud of his moto and always asked Kelly for gas.

Most local people work artisanal gold mines, small-scale mining that often relies on rudimentary and toxic methods, like mercury wash-ing, to extract metals. Despite Damfakha's efforts as a cattle herder, hunter, and part-time miner, all of which makes him rather affluent in his community, none of his daughters will ever have a wedding that costs anywhere near $60 million. Most often, he won't even have enough gas to ride his moto out into the bush to hunt for dinner.

Damfakha welcomed us with bowls of sour milk and sugar, a deli-cacy in the village, the consistency of thin yogurt with cottage cheese chunks. The children peered shyly into the narrow hut opening.

They examined our backpacks and equipment—Toughbook computers, GPSs, camera traps—and shooed chickens trying to enter. It felt absurd, all that we had brought for only a few weeks. Despite the rains, it was still extraordinarily hot, and animals that were kept in the housing compound attracted a plague of flies. We fanned ourselves with thatched mats and greeted Damfakha's large family. They gathered into the crowded hut, eager to see why the "toubabs" (white people) were here. This is the village Kelly calls home during her stay.

The next morning, I pulled a mosquito net off the rickety wooden bed Kelly and I shared, and, looking for my boots, found two dead rabbits on the doorstep. Their thick, amber eyes had gone expressionless. Damfakha's first wife came inside the hut and smiled at me. She gathered some cooking utensils and lifted the rabbits by their ears. The sky was still dark with a few lingering stars as I watched her light a fire outside the hut and start to boil water.

Kelly and I quickly dressed by the light of our headlamps and prepared our packs for a day out in the bush. We filled our extra water bottles, put sunscreen on our faces, and made coffee. Kelly checked the batteries on her GPS and decided on a few nesting sites she wanted to visit from the year before. One site she listed was *la place du baobab géant*, the place of the giant baobab. There she had found over forty chimp nests, old and new, and determined that this was a nesting site they had been coming back to for years.

Damfakha arrived in a sweat-worn button-up shirt and knit cap and took us into patches of woodland forests below the shaved mountains. We shared handfuls of peanuts and little bags of biscuits for breakfast as the sun rode up over the mountains and washed through the savanna, making the grass appear translucent. Dew from the rainy season's quick-growing grasses soaked through our boots and socks within minutes.

We navigated stretches of savanna pocked with mushroom-shaped termite mounds and clusters of white flowers, petals long like lilies. Every so often we stopped for water or a bathroom break, but Kelly was eager to get to *la place du baobab géant* before lunch and the heat of midday. We spoke little, but occasionally Damfakha would ask for new boots (he only had sandals), or new linoleum floors for his wives' huts. Kelly agreed to bring him work boots the next time she visited, but demurred about the new floors.

"You know that stream near Dakar?" Damfakha asked in his minimal French.

At first we were stumped.
"The big one," he said.
"You mean the ocean?" Kelly asked.
"Do you have to pass over that to get here?"
"Yes. In an airplane."
"I didn't know there were villages on the other side."
Kelly spotted the giant baobab—the thick trunk was wide and buttressed, the sparse limbs like an intricate root system secured into the sky. Male chimps will pound their fists on tree buttresses like these to get the attention of the group. However, beside the giant, no other trees remained. The earth surrounding the baobab was scorched and ashy. Chimp nests, and all the trees that contained them, were gone. What was once a forest that chimps utilized for food and sleeping trees had been cut down and burned for cultivation. Kelly's mouth dropped open as she stopped in her tracks and scanned the desiccated earth. She threw her backpack to the ground and ran through the field.

A bare-breasted woman in a long, blue warp skirt adorned with fish bones planted peanuts amid blackened tree stumps. The woman glanced over at us briefly before resuming her work. Kelly started to cry.

"There were forty nests here last summer," she whispered, hiding her face so Damfakha wouldn't see her tears.

Chimps returned to this place often, a sanctuary guarded by the baobab, now the lone survivor in what will become a field of peanuts local people use to make a traditional sauce.

"I know people need land to cultivate, but why did they have to choose this spot? Why here?" Kelly asked.

There were still a few trees left on the periphery, and a number of old nests, but Kelly figured that the chimps had been forced to find a new place to go.

She wiped her eyes with her shirtsleeve and pulled out her field notebook. She lifted her chin and diligently wrote down the GPS coordinates and time, then simply: "forest gone." We were seeing firsthand the effects of human encroachment on what was previously considered wildlife habitat. Can chimps viably share space with humans? How long can their displacement go on before there is simply no room left on the planet for them?

"They've found somewhere else," Kelly decided, examining the blue swaths of forest on her GPS. "I want to check out the gallery forests to the north. I haven't been there yet, but I'm sure there're chimps."

Despite setbacks, Kelly remains dedicated and inspired, and most importantly, she truly believes that chimpanzees have a place in the future of our planet. On the back of Kelly's business card is the famous quote from Baba Dioum, an environmentalist from Senegal: "In the end, we will conserve only what we love, we will love only what we understand, we will understand only what we are taught." Kelly is working toward conservation education programs in local schools to teach children the value of protecting forests and the animals that reside there.

"There are losses we just have to let go of," Kelly said, turning away from the giant baobab. "This year there will be peanuts instead of chimp nests, but many years from now, the forest will start to come back."

And with the forest will come fruit, and with fruit, chimpanzees.

Another day in Bofeto, I got on the back of Kelly's moto and we rode through the bush, over the ArcelorMittal bridge, and into gallery forests to the north. The USGS map promised stretches of dense forest. We hiked through savanna-woodland mosaics not looking for chimpanzees, only evidence of their presence. As Kelly taught me, habituating primates could put them in danger. Besides, we can learn all we need to know about the unique behaviors of West African savanna chimps from the group Jill habituated at Fongoli. Also, Kelly had recently begun putting camera traps in places where she'd documented feeding activity, and has some wonderful footage of chimps bringing fruit into caves. These wildlife-surveillance systems take pictures at even the slightest of movements, and allow Kelly to observe behaviors she otherwise would have missed. She's even gotten footage of a curious lion sniffing the camera lens.

As we crossed the savanna into gallery forest, baboons barked in alarm, those in the foreground statuesque as they watched us stumble through vines and twisted lianas.

"There have to be nests here," Kelly said as we turned on our GPSs, wrote down our coordinates, and began looking.

In waterproof field notebooks we recorded the time, latitude, longitude, number of nests in one place, how old they were, and what habitat they'd been found in. Kelly considers nests fresh if they were built the previous night, old if they appeared to be from a few weeks ago, and ancient if they were made months or even years ago. Instead of trying to see chimps, we sought out remnants of their existence—nests, feces, places they'd left discarded fruit, caves they'd rested in.

We descended dense, wet, green hills, and sound seemed to drown away. All I heard was our footsteps, water falling from leaves, birds chirping. A flash of orange antelope crossed our path, and immediately we found nests. Many of them were fresh. Kelly spotted footprints on the edge of a termite mound, and we searched the ground for feces, which were filled with saba seeds.

"They were here eating just this morning," Kelly said, poking a pile of dung with a stick.

We left the bush late that afternoon with notebooks full of fresh nest counts. On the back of Kelly's moto, wind dried the sweat on my face. We traversed rock-studded mining roads that cut through stretches of savanna and forest, making accessible land that had been known only to local hunters a few years ago.

"Stop! Stop! Stop!" Kelly yelled suddenly. Damfakha's moto in front of us had swerved into the grass, and a few yards away, a series of hulking black masses knuckle-walked through a patch of termite mounds.

"There they are! It's a whole group of them!" Damfakha pointed excitedly.

Kelly and I both jumped off our moto and let it fall into the road.

"Come on! Let's go!" Damfakha motioned for us to follow him, but Kelly begged him to come back.

She frantically grasped for her binoculars in attempts to get a group count. How many males and females, how many adults and juveniles? How many mothers with infants? Eight black chimpanzees, muscled shoulders poised above the neon grass, walked single file away from us. A juvenile sprinted to the front of the group.

"It would be so easy to follow them," Kelly said, "but we just can't."

Her hands shook as she held the binoculars to her face. I grabbed for mine and got a brief glimpse of the backside of an adult male at the end of the line before they disappeared into the forest. We stood at the edge of the road, silent and breathless, our boots toeing the grass as if some invisible wall were keeping us out of the bush. It's best they remain afraid of humans, I told myself, particularly now that their forests are being replaced by mines. As much as Kelly would have loved to find out where they were going, she was satisfied just to know that they were still here.

Back in the village, I was too tired to write. My boots were muddy and soaked through with condensation, my stomach rumbled, and my legs felt like Jell-O. My desires were primal—all I wanted was food. I ate a prized apple I'd been stowing away at the bottom of my backpack, an import from South Africa sold at a boutique in Kédougou. I swept away pieces of bone from the rabbit we'd had for breakfast, and sprayed insect repellent everywhere. It was no match for the fly population, and the day was still too hot to get underneath my mosquito net to read or nap.

While Kelly entered data into her Toughbook before dinner, I hiked a cow path to a rock plateau above the village. No one is ever alone in a village—I still heard roosters, women pounding millet. I listened to children running home from the fields, trailed by their mothers, who were carrying buckets of peanuts and cabbage. The hunting dogs came to bark at me as the sky lowered its purple gaze onto rocks still warm with sun. Rocks that harbor gold. A child threw stones at the dogs, and I noticed that his jersey, torn at the shoulder, featured Barack Obama's smiling face.

The dogs yelped and ran down the cow path. I listened to a generator's whir. I found a sense of solitude and stillness here, and felt myself a part of the landscape, a white bipedal creature sitting on metamorphic rock, a rock perhaps filled with precious metals. This landscape has been vastly modified by time, animals, weather, people, agriculture, and mining companies, but it felt ancient and knowing. The wind moved easily and intimately through the grass, welcoming another wet season. The sky was a bare lavender, and I could see every indent, every contour and carved space of the moon. Damfakha approached in a loose, button-up shirt covered in yellow and red butterflies to tell me that dinner was ready. There would be antelope, rolled into balls by his wives, fried in palm oil, and served over rice. Once, there were volcanoes here. Who knows what tomorrow will bring?

Three Poems
Dan Rosenberg

SERVAL

Our bed is elevated. The serval hunts
on wires. Breaks open a butterfly. Dust
crushed in a vertical pounce. Lovemaking

on the proscenium. And lovemaking
in the hardware section. Our bed,
strung on wires. Our serval makes

a proscenium of love. We break
open the butterfly with a vertical
crush. Our eyes closed in deep grass

for up to fifteen minutes, the stillness
before the leap. Your paws clamp down.
Break open our lovemaking: the dust

crushes out. What else so honestly
powders itself to our paws? Butterflies,
hunted. Make do with the wares

we have offered each other. We receive
a proscenium closed in deep grass.
Your serval breaks open her hardware,

dusts our bed. And at my pounce
a proscenium closes. Your paws clamp
our bed: a lovemaking. The hunter

sleeps a hunt in our bed. The feline
twitch and flex of hardware. We elevate
our hands, the bed, we hunt the butterfly,

a vertical pounce. This lovemaking
breaks open. What dust crushes out
from us. What dust on wires we are.

What dust so honestly itself in deep grass
for up to fifteen minutes. The eyes clamp
on wires. The butterfly, dust-hunting.

The proscenium closes our lovemaking.
What else on wires, what else breaks
open: the hunter the hunted loves making.

SAFARI

stuck long unbuckled in the middle seat sweating—
we buzz toward the black and blue sails—tsetse flies
(—vectors carry disease—mark the path
of force)—sterilized—sails keep the population
down—a shared design—the lion stands
on a giraffe's head and chews—the family has
a thirst—a vision—imagining through lenses
bent—maggots nest in zebras' nostrils
when they're still—alive—it takes just a quick
imitation—of corpse—watching—nothing
we've done surprises—the space from mind
to eye—the lively socket what's in there—
clockwork—motion but—not dance—the vulture's
black wings spread still—not death—the drying after

DON'T LET ME INTERRUPT

The garden-party feline flexes his paws.
Tremor and tremble, swat the thimble.
Rust skitters over bricks. The box
on her belt keeps her blood sugared. He bats
the wire, bolts, she shivers, under her chair

a screw unthreads itself. Hunted
from the begonias, she holds it together.
Bunch of pleats dramatic in a thin-veined fist.
Acne arm, colored frames askew—but just so.
Thumping in temples her blood is a slow-
dance beat. Her delicate ankle bound
in a strappy number, she stands, teeters,
the feline scrounges the corners for spillage.
Buds unfurl, a nub sprouts to thorn, we
congregate in the cat's domain with our pastries
and time. What can't we celebrate? A plane
shifts the clouds, the wall garbles the traffic,
the news, our empathy condenses, these
mason jars of booze, some suffering, the claw
streak left white down her calf, and what else
shall we call to sacrifice? The ice is vapid
in our glasses, chittering over muddled mint.
Her dress is covered with flowers but is not
made of flowers. I slouch down to eclipse
the sun with her head. She's an angel,
the light strikes from her head, a liberty
crown, the box beeps, I feel the tug
of claw and fang upon my shoelace knot.

Cat and Bird

Kyoko Mori

ON THE CONCRETE FLOOR of the boiler room, the small, dark bird resembles a fan knocked out of a flamenco dancer's hand. Its curved wings, folded, cross over the tail feathers. The bird—a chimney swift—is about five inches from head to tail. Up in the sky, its wings would span twelve inches as it soars and glides, catching and holding two hundred midges or mosquitoes in its mouth. Chimney swifts cannot perch. They spend the whole day flying and rest at night by clinging vertically to a rough surface, such as the bricks inside a chimney. Their hooked feet can support their weight for hours in that position, but if a swift falls from its roost, as this one must have during the unseasonably cold night, it is unable to stand or hop.

In our brownstone, the bottom of the chimney is in the locked boiler room in the basement. Any other day, a trapped bird would have weakened and perished, but I'm here with the pest control guy to monitor our co-op's mouse and roach situation.

The pest control guy, Roosevelt, is over six feet tall. He can take down wasps' nests and move dishwashers out of the way to check for roaches underneath. He's cheerful and talkative, so when he goes quiet, I know that a bird trapped indoors makes him nervous.

The bird flutters up to the window, slides down, and falls on the floor, where it sits flat on its chest. The boiler room is separated from the outdoors by two double-locked metal doors I don't want to open with a bird cradled in one hand. "I'll go find a bag," I tell Roosevelt.

When I return with a small paper bag from my apartment, Roosevelt and the bird are exactly where I left them. I kneel on the floor and close my fingers around the bird's back. The swift doesn't resist being picked up; it makes no sound at all. But the moment I drop it into the bag and close my fist around the top, it spreads its wings and begins to flap. Through the heavy doors, up the stairs, along the side of the building to the backyard, I can hear the wings beating like Chinese firecrackers inside the bag.

I tip the bag and slide the swift out onto the picnic table behind our building. In the morning light, the feathers look sooty brown.

317

The swift pushes itself up off the table and ascends the clearing in widening circles. I count the spirals—three, four, five—until the bird rises over the treetops and disappears into the sky above our building, where every evening for the last couple of weeks, a small flock has appeared at dusk to circle, forage, and dive into our chimney.

It's the last week of May. Chimney swifts have left their wintering grounds in the upper Amazon basin of Peru, Chile, and Brazil to disperse through their breeding range. Some will nest here in Washington, DC, while others will continue up the coast to Maine or southern Canada. If the bird I held in my hand returns tonight, or if it becomes one of a mating pair and spends the summer raising its young in our chimney, just on the other side of my bedroom wall, I won't know it. All full-grown chimney swifts look identical, male or female, one-year-old or four-year-old. Still, any swift in North America this time of year, before breeding has started, is at least a year old, born the previous summer, migrated to the Amazon, and returned, so the bird I just released has traveled ten thousand miles at least.

In my apartment on the top floor of the building, on the bed adjacent to the chimney shaft, my two cats are sleeping with their light brown and dark brown legs tangled together. They've never been outside except in my car. Though the three of us run around the apartment several times a day with feather toys on strings, and Miles the Siamese loves to fetch his orange chew toy, the combined distance Miles and Jackson have traveled on foot isn't likely to add up to a mile.

In the small Wisconsin town where I lived in the 1990s, I raised the baby birds people brought to the wildlife sanctuary after storms or tree trimmers or their dogs had knocked down the nests. I was on the list of trained rehabilitators on call who took the birds home, cared for them, and released them back into the wild. I kept the nestlings in the spare bedroom, away from my cat, and fed them every fifteen minutes with a soupy mixture of protein and fruits in a needleless syringe. There were robins, house finches, waxwings, chipping sparrows, kingbirds, each kept with its own kind in a makeshift nest of a paper-lined berry box inside a plastic laundry basket. Most of them stretched their necks, opened their mouths, and clamored for food with little prompting.

I became a volunteer because, unlike my friends who had grown up on farms, I couldn't look at the barely feathered birds lying on my lawn and say, "For every bird that dies, hundreds will survive." After taking several birds to the sanctuary, I wanted to be one of the people who came to pick them up, who knew what to do beyond lifting the poor things off the ground and sticking them in a shoe box.

I kept a daily log of what each bird had eaten and how it was developing, when it learned to fly around the room and was transferred to the large outdoor cage in my backyard to learn to forage on its own. There were pretty birds—cedar waxwings, Eastern kingbirds—I felt lucky to see up close and there were common birds I liked all the same because each had a distinct personality. Some robins were bent on trusting me too much and had to be discouraged from following me around; others screeched and backed into a corner, only to open their beaks, flutter their wings, and beg to be fed. The fear of intimacy and the tendency to give mixed messages, I could only surmise, weren't the sole province of humans.

At about two weeks old, a nestling would stand up in the berry box for the first time and climb onto its edge. There, it would lean first on one leg and then the other to open and preen its wings before hopping down to explore the paper-lined floor of the basket. Birds that left the nest never returned to sit in it. I let them fly around the room and peeled them off the woven tapestry, where they landed and clung. In the controlled environment of my spare room, more birds survived than might have in the wild, with parents who wouldn't have been able to feed their young if the weather was uncooperative or predators were prowling their feeding sites. The birds that died usually had something obviously wrong, like deformed legs or wings. Even I could say, then, that for every bird that died, hundreds would survive. The moment their nests got knocked to the ground, the nestlings had nothing more to lose: Any day they lived in my care was time they didn't have otherwise.

I gave up volunteering after my first book was published and I started teaching workshops at summer writing conferences. Eventually I moved to the East Coast to live in a one-bedroom apartment with two cats. The care of migratory birds is strictly regulated by the US Fish and Wildlife Service. The license I had in Wisconsin, through the sanctuary where I was trained, isn't valid in Washington, DC. I'm not likely to spend another summer with birds clamoring for food inside laundry baskets in a spare bedroom. I regret the lost chance the way other people sigh over never seeing Paris again or having forgotten how to play the violin.

*

319

The main ingredient of the soupy formula I mixed for the birds was dry cat food soaked in warm water. "Veterinarian-recommended cat food with high protein content, such as Science Diet," our rehab manual—a huge black binder of mimeographed sheets—specified. Science Diet dry food was what my cat, Dorian, ate, so he contributed to Operation Bird Rescue by sharing his food. Dorian was an old-fashioned seal-point Siamese born in 1979, stockier and more violently committed to his one human than the cats that would follow him. He bit my friends and drew blood but sat calmly on my lap while I brushed his teeth and trimmed his claws. I could hold him upside down by his hind legs and swing him back and forth, or sling him over my shoulder like a sack of potatoes and carry him around the house. Somehow, though, I assumed all this was about him and not about me. That cat would have let me do anything to him to spite everyone else.

But when Ernest and Algernon, the two Siamese cats who lived with me in Boston and then in DC, turned out to have serious stomach problems—feline inflammatory bowel disease, which is akin to Crohn's disease in people—and required daily medication, I remembered the knack I'd discovered I had through my care of birds. Every year, there had been a few birds that didn't open their mouths when I approached with the feeding syringe. I'd learned to hold each of these birds in my hand, insert the tips of my thumb and forefinger into the rubbery corners of its mouth, and press till the beak popped open, slide the syringe in before the bird could snap its beak shut, and shoot the food down its throat, careful to avoid the trachea. Both the rehab manual and the volunteer demonstrator at the training session had warned that too much force could break the bird's beak.

Feeding a reluctant bird required dexterity, timing, and concentration, a combination that came surprisingly naturally to me. I had never before thought of myself as competent or capable. I broke knickknacks while cleaning the house and couldn't hang pictures on the wall without hitting my fingers with the hammer. In cities I visited regularly, I got lost by failing to remember, or notice, some landmark that was obvious to everyone else (the bronze dome of the state capitol building, for example). I was flummoxed by tools, gadgets, and a host of inanimate objects large and small, but when an animal in need was involved, it was a different story. All the distractions fell away, and I found myself in a quiet space where every detail I noticed was larger-than-life and relevant: Together, the animal and I had entered a magic circle where I could perform any complicated task with as little effort as would be required to thread a needle under a magnifying lamp.

Like Dorian, Ernest and Algernon followed me around all day demanding to be petted and picked up, so holding them on my lap and prying open their mouths was easy. A cat's mouth is huge and strong, with sharp teeth and a sandpaper tongue. I found it almost comical to stick my thumb and finger in, drop the pill, close their mouths, and stroke their silky throats to make them swallow. The whole procedure only took a minute for each cat. Ernest, the slender blue-point who was the picture of dignity and elegance, bolted if he sensed that I was about to give him the pill, but there was really nowhere for him to go in our small apartment, and as soon as I caught him, he went limp in my arms and assumed a resigned posture and expression on my lap. Algernon, the seal-point whose black face made him look like a little monkey, sat at my feet and watched while I pilled Ernest. Either he was more accepting or else, every night, he believed that only Ernest was getting the pill. Algernon never led me on a chase, but once I put him belly up on my lap and picked up his pill, he raised one chocolate-colored paw in protest. His claws were retracted and he didn't push my hand away; the gesture resembled the benign, desultory wave of the Japanese Maneki-Neko mascot in a store window.

The pill routine, which started when they were seven, became a docility demonstration my cats and I sometimes performed in front of our guests. By the time their inflammatory bowel disease worsened, the cats were ten years old. When first Algernon, then Ernest, started throwing up every day and losing weight, I gave them subcutaneous fluids and Vitamin D shots. Even though I had chosen to drive myself to the emergency room after a bee sting instead of sticking my leg with the EpiPen as instructed (I did put the pen on the passenger's seat, within easy reach, in case I started choking for breath while stopped at a traffic light), I had no problem putting first one cat, then the other, on my lap, pinching his skin, and inserting the hydration needle. When the tip went in correctly, the slight resistance felt right, like an embroidery needle sliding into a thick linen fabric. As the water began to flow, the cat on my lap closed his eyes and purred. Unlike the birds, Ernest and Algernon understood that I was only trying to help. If they could have lived ten more years, I would have sat with them every morning to watch the line of water descending the clear tube.

*

321

The birds that clamored for food had instinctively associated the beak-like shape of the feeding syringe—and through it, me—with their parents. These birds gained weight more steadily, left the nest, and learned to fly sooner than those that had to be force-fed. In the outdoor cage, where I visited them a few times a day with the syringe of food, they lined up on one of the branches I had rigged up to flutter their wings and open their mouths. I had to make sure that everyone was eating enough to stay strong though hungry enough to start investigating the seeds, fruits, grains, and worms I'd left around. The birds that continued to come to me were easier to monitor than those that hid. Still, it's not natural for a bird to grow up perceiving a human as nurturing or benign. Rehabilitators who raise birds that are likely to be harmed by people wear disguises or use hand puppets.

The small songbirds in my care, however, had no value as food, illegal pets, or trophies, so they had less to fear from humans. The most important lesson a house finch needed to learn before being released, in fact, was how to feed itself from the ubiquitous cylindrical seed feeders in our town's backyards. I taught my finches by using the syringe of food to lure them to the feeder I'd hung inside the cage, getting them to perch on its metal rungs, and tempting them to peck at the seed ports by smearing the formula there. Throughout the summer, there were always six or seven finches in the outdoor cage. In each group, one finch figured out the feeder first and the others followed suit. I stopped going to the cage with the formula and watched the birds through binoculars. In a few days, every bird was eating from the feeder and the flock was ready to go. Not one finch came back to beg food from me, though more than thirty were released every summer in my backyard and, for all I knew, some were eating from the cylinder outside the kitchen window.

The finches in the outdoor cage learned through imitation, just as they would have in the wild from their parents, who flew with them for a week or two, showing them the food sources and roosting sites. Then the first-year birds would have dispersed among the larger flock, leaving the parents to lay the next clutch of eggs. Birds don't stay with their parents or siblings once they know how to feed themselves. A few species mate for life and many flock with their own kind, but not with their original family.

The summers I volunteered at the sanctuary, I was in my midthirties and married for nearly ten years. People were finally beginning to believe my husband and me when we said we didn't plan to have children.

"I spend the whole day with other people's children," Chuck explained. "I don't have to come home to raise 'my own.'"

Chuck taught first-graders at an elementary school. He was good with children. If he had married someone else, he would have become a father. My job was at a college, where I taught mostly juniors and seniors.

"I'm the one who doesn't want kids," I said. "I'm uncomfortable with young children. I can't imagine becoming a mother."

I couldn't have been more explicit, but most people assumed that I was forgoing motherhood in favor of my writing. Only a few women, themselves childless, understood that human babies didn't appeal to me. These women laughed with recognition when I told them, "When I look at babies, I just think, *Why can't they be furry?* I don't get why people make such a fuss over them."

The presence of fur, though, wasn't the deciding factor. Dorian had been eight weeks old when I met him at his breeder's house. Like most Siamese kittens, he scarcely had any fur; his long pinkish tail resembled a rat's. In the spare bedroom where he was being raised, Dorian left his sleeping siblings, sauntered over to me, and began to rub his mouth against my finger. His lips were parted just enough to reveal his tiny teeth, sharp as dressmakers' pins, but he was purring. His whiskers vibrated as his wet gum slid back and forth. Though I didn't know as much about cats then as I would later, I realized that he was marking me with his scent and claiming me for his own. He was mine, I was his, and there was no going back. When I pulled back my hand in order to pet him, he bumped his forehead against my palm over and over and wouldn't stop. He wanted to be the one to pet me, not the other way around. I was amazed by the sense of recognition and inevitability that came over me. A few minutes into our first meeting, he was already my cat or, to put it his way, I was his human.

My devotion to Dorian was instantaneous, all-exclusive, and everlasting—the way I imagined a mother's love would be for her children. No one else had a claim to that same bond with me, but sometimes, the nearly naked, lizard-like nestlings in the laundry baskets opened their mouths, fluttered their bony wings, and caused me to believe that satisfying their hunger was the most important thing in the world. With the birds, I knew that our bond was temporary, that loving them, or respecting their essential nature, meant letting them go in the end.

I didn't experience a fraction of my bird-nurturing urge—let alone my total obsession with Dorian—with any human child. Babies repulsed me with their faintly sour odor; when they cried, I wanted to run screaming from the room. I was keyed to respond only to the wrong babies, animal babies. Left alone with the young of my own kind, I panicked the way other people did when a bird flapped around the house and threw itself repeatedly against a closed window.

I didn't know that Chuck was afraid of birds until, a few months after we moved in together in our twenties when we were students, a starling and its fledgling fell through a hole in the siding of the house we were renting and ended up behind our dining-room wall. I came home from my morning class just in time to see the adult bird fly out of the space where the pocket door that separated the dining room and the living room slid in. Dorian, who had been sitting nearby, remained in his spot, too stunned to chase a live toy. I picked him up, carried him to the bedroom, put him on the bed, and shut the door. By then, Chuck was chasing the bird from the dining room to the kitchen and back, his head covered with an afghan that was usually draped on our couch. He had opened the windows of the dining room and was trying to direct the bird to them.

Our apartment was on the second floor of the house, with large sliding doors that led from the living room to the balcony. I ran to the living room to open those doors; the starling came soaring across the house, flew through one of the doors, and disappeared. We couldn't see where it went, which meant that the chirping that began a few seconds later and got louder and louder was coming from behind the wall.

We were afraid to move the pocket door and crush the bird by mistake, so we borrowed our downstairs neighbor's saw and cut a hole in one of the wooden panels on the wall. We shone a flashlight into the opening and glimpsed a fledgling with peach fuzz on its head. It was hopping between the exterior and the interior walls, chirping loudly. I tried to coax it out with sunflower seeds from our pantry, but every time I reached in, the bird hopped farther back toward the exterior wall. Soon, I had to return to school for another class.

"Dorian can stay in the bedroom till I come back," I said to Chuck. "Maybe the bird will come out and you can catch him." Chuck had gone canoeing in the Boundary Waters and spent a week sleeping in a tent. He had lived in the country, where he once helped a friend kill some chickens because he didn't believe he was entitled to eat meat unless he knew where his food came from. It never occurred to me that someone who did all that would be afraid of a bird that was small and clumsy enough to fall through a hole in the wall.

Three hours later, when I returned, Chuck was sitting in a chair a few feet away from the opening we'd cut out, holding his tennis racket.

"The bird keeps coming out and then hopping back in. The next time he comes out, I'm going to block the hole with this."

Almost as soon as he said that, the bird emerged. Chuck sprang up and slammed the racket over the hole.

Startled, the bird fled across the dining room toward the kitchen, hopping, then flying low, landing, hopping, flying again. "Great, he knows how to fly," I said. "You can put him out on the balcony where the other one went. That must have been his mother."

When I went to the living room and opened the balcony doors, I was astonished by the loud clamoring—like a chorus of squeaky violins—of the starlings that had gathered in the trees.

I ran back through the house, relieved that the fledgling wouldn't be lost on its own. Though this was a decade before I became a re-habilitator, I knew that birds didn't abandon their young just because a human had touched it. Here was a whole flock gathered to take care of its own.

In the hallway outside our kitchen, the fledgling was crouched in the corner, rocking on its feet and screeching at Chuck, who was holding a broom.

"Come on, Buddy," Chuck said, reaching gingerly toward the bird with the bristles of the broom. "Let's go. I'm only trying to help." The bird lunged at the broom, causing Chuck to stagger backward, and flew into the kitchen, where it landed next to the stove. All its feathers were puffed up; its beak was wide open as it screeched. If that bird had been a cat, Chuck would have understood that the poor thing was hissing and growling and getting ready to pounce in des-peration because it perceived the broom as a weapon rather than the helpful tool—similar to a traffic-cop's baton—that Chuck intended it to be.

Chuck was eventually able to get the bird to turn around, to hop-fly through the house onto the balcony. As soon as we closed the doors, several starlings landed next to the fledgling and flew with it into a nearby tree. Dozens of others were waiting. The fledgling hop-flew to the higher branches and disappeared among the leaves.

"You should have told me you were afraid to touch that bird," I said to Chuck. "I thought you wanted to be the one to let it out, after waiting all those hours while I was at school."

"I don't like handling little animals," he said. "I'm afraid they're going to bite me and I'm going to freak out and squeeze them to death by mistake."

For years afterward, Dorian and I played a game called "Chuck and the Bird"—in which I chased Dorian around the house with a broom, calling out, "Take it easy, Buddy. Don't bite me. I'm only trying to help you."

I occasionally play "Chuck and the Bird" with Miles and Jackson, though Chuck and I have been divorced for eighteen years and he hasn't met the current loves of my life.

We got divorced because after thirteen years of marriage, I decided I was happiest alone. I didn't want to live with anyone, not even Chuck, who was easygoing and accommodating, willing to give me all the time and space I needed. I moved to a small apartment across town with Dorian, who was by then fifteen.

That's how I wrote about my divorce in one of my books, making it sound like Dorian was a colorful minor character in the story of Chuck and me: I was married to a schoolteacher from a small town in Wisconsin and we didn't have any children but we had a Siamese cat who terrorized everyone who stepped foot in our house; the cat became a mascot, a symbol of the choices my husband and I made to be different from the people around us; when even this childless marriage began to seem oppressive, I decided to live alone.

The truth is more like this: Between the ages of twenty-two and forty, I lived with a Siamese cat who loved me and hated everyone else; for thirteen years in the middle of his reign, I was married and the cat came to tolerate my husband, enough to sit on his lap if I wasn't home or sleep on his chest till I too retired for the night, at which time the cat walked across the bed, crawled under the covers into my arms, and put his head on my pillow; in the last two years of the cat's life, we were alone together—as we had been at the beginning—and he and I were at our happiest. The cat in this revised story is no mascot. He is both the symbol and the partner of my solitude. What he gave me was fortified solitude, not a distraction from it.

When Dorian finally died, I cried so much for weeks that the man I was dating then—who was hoping that I might move in with him and his three well-mannered felines once I didn't have to worry about Dorian—said, "Maybe you should get another cat, a cat of your own." We were crossing the street in front of my favorite restaurant in town, where he was taking me out to eat. I had stopped in the middle of the road to remark, "If a big truck came and hit me now, it would be no loss." There was no vehicle in sight. What I'd said was utterly ludicrous and a total insult to my date. No matter how many cats I had in the future, I would never again be with Dorian. All the same, I couldn't go on the way I had been.

"If I get my own cat," I said, "I'm never going to move in with you. I probably won't even stay at your house overnight because I'll be busy trying to bond with the kitten."

"That's OK," he said. "I just want you to be happy."

He was letting me go. By the time we got across the street and entered the restaurant, my move to Boston two years later was a foregone conclusion. Dorian had guarded my solitude until a successor could be found. The second half of my life would be a cat relay, with me as a baton passed from paw to paw. I would learn in time that if I had two cats, I would never again have to be catless.

The Joint Reign of Miles and Jackson began with twice-a-week baths and daily pills because the bald spot that Jackson, the Burmese, had on his head turned out to be ringworm, a highly contagious fungal infection. Jackson came to me in January of 2011, at twelve weeks old. Miles, six months old by then, had been with me since July. The veterinarian said I could keep the cats separated for sixteen weeks—the length of a semester—or treat them both. Even if there had been space in my apartment to quarantine Jackson, I wouldn't have. The cats were getting along well. Separating them for so long would have ruined their relationship.

I had been brushing Miles's teeth every night since he was eight weeks old, so opening his mouth and cramming a pill into his throat was only a minor adjustment. Like Ernest—whom he resembles, though, in addition to his blue-gray "points," Miles was developing shadowy ripples of lynx-point stripes on his cream-colored coat— Miles ran if he sensed that the toothpaste and the pill were in the offing but relaxed as soon as I caught him. Jackson, glossy brown like a little prince dressed in a mink coat, had been raised in a house piled with old photographs, magazines, fabric scraps, and unopened boxes of cat-food samples—I suspected his breeder, a retired middle-school teacher, was a hoarder though, thankfully, not of animals—nursing from whichever mother cat happened to be nearby. He was the mellowest, most confident cat I'd ever met. Whenever he wanted attention, he clawed his way up my legs onto my lap and demanded to be petted. The pill regimen didn't faze him a bit.

For the baths, I carried both cats into the bathroom and shut the door. It seemed prudent to start with Miles, the older and more cautious. "Wet the fur thoroughly," the directions on the medicated shampoo bottle said. "Apply and lather, being careful to avoid the eyes and the mouth. Leave on for ten minutes and rinse." I dunked Miles in a dishpan full of warm water, doused him with the shampoo I'd shaken to a full "lather" inside a plastic bottle made for squirting barbecue sauce on spare ribs or chicken wings, then wrapped him in a towel and held him on my lap for ten minutes. He only started squirming and meowing about eight minutes in. By the time he was being dunked again for the rinse, he was yowling, but he never bit or scratched me. I towel-dried him, put him on the bath mat, and repeated the process with Jackson, who was so small that he resembled a hamster when wet. I'd have to be an idiot, I thought, not to be able to handle him. The cats scampered out as soon as I opened the door but within ten minutes, they came up to me, purring. I petted their still-damp fur and told them that the whole ordeal was a team-building exercise. Unlike the pills, which had to be given for sixteen weeks ("A semester of pills," I said), the baths could stop after six weeks, when Jackson had had three consecutive "negative" readings on his skin test. Miles and I never developed ringworm. After caring for Ernest and Algernon, who had gotten sicker as time went on, it was a relief, even a pleasure, to bathe and pill these young cats at the beginning of our time together.

On the wall opposite the door in my foyer is the black-and-white photograph that Chuck took of Dorian in 1986. Dorian is sitting on the bed, mouth open to expose his pointed teeth like a vampire's. He was actually yawning but he could easily have been roaring. The quilt billowing around him has patterns of lion heads.

"That's my first cat, Dorian," I tell my guests. "He's my household god."

Dorian is my One God of Solitude, though his successors too have fortified the happiness I discovered in living without a human partner. My favorite day is one on which I don't go anywhere except to run in the morning: I can spend hours afterward reading with the cats on my lap, writing with them by my side, or puttering around the apartment with one of them on my shoulder. Like Chuck, or the man I was dating when Dorian died, my current boyfriend understands that I am more like the archetypical cat than my cats actually are: finicky and independent, needing to be left alone until I decide it's time for company. The cats like him enough but they keep him at an ideal distance, three and a half hours by Amtrak: He has to come to us since pets aren't allowed on the train.

The difference from the Reign of Dorian is that Miles and Jackson—as did Ernest and Algernon—enjoy occasional entertaining. Because Dorian hissed, growled, and lunged at everyone from the meter reader to my in-laws, Chuck and I seldom had any guests. We believed that only boring people got all dressed up to make small talk around a dinner table, so we didn't care. With Chuck and later without, I went to the movies, concerts, restaurants, and parties with a group of friends I'd known for years, some of whom liked to organize outings and get-togethers so the rest of us didn't have to. Although, or perhaps because, I didn't intend to move through life partnered, I valued having a close-knit group of friends.

When I moved east for a new teaching job, I suddenly had no one to call me every week with plans for movies and dinners. My new colleagues and neighbors were always saying how busy they were. In the brief conversations we had by the mailboxes or in the laundry room, they expressed strong, even heated, opinions about what they liked or—more often—what they couldn't stand. Inviting these people to dinner in my apartment seemed less daunting than asking them to a cultural event or an eating establishment. Many seemed to soften, or at least be amused, when I said, "I live with two amazing cats. I'd love for you to meet them. We'll make you dinner." I started announcing that the cats and I liked making rhubarb pies (a Wisconsin specialty), that they'd mastered a repertoire of vegetarian recipes, and took turns baking to keep our sourdough starter going.

Food preparation has turned out to be another exception, besides caring for animals, to my general ineptitude. Last August, I spent the whole morning failing to learn the computer program the colleague who'd volunteered to teach me had assumed I would master in ten minutes and was relieved to stay in my kitchen all afternoon assembling a trifle, for which the cats and I first prepared an angel food cake, lemon custard, raspberry jam, and whipped cream. We'd volunteered for the dessert portion of our co-op's backyard cookout. Instead of carrying the heavy glass dish down to the yard, I invited my neighbors to my apartment so the cats could host the finale. About twenty people sat in our living room eating the trifle and drinking sherry.

I had been "clicker-training" Miles and Jackson. Cats respond more to hand gestures than to voice commands; there are dog tricks you can never teach a cat, such as "Wait" (look longingly at the offered treat but refrain from eating it till the trainer says, "OK"). Still, it had taken Miles and Jackson only a few minutes to understand the basic concept: A "click" from the clicker I wore around my neck meant they would get a treat; to cause me to "click" and toss them a treat (dehydrated shrimp, recommended by our vet), they had to do something. They learned to come, sit, stay, stand up like a bear, shake hands, high-five, and even jump over a pole.

Jackson was eager to show off in front of the guests in our living room. By far, the pole jumping earned the loudest applause, but people were amazed just to see him jump up on a chair on command, sit, and raise his left paw (my fault: I got confused which hand was which when I was teaching him and, rather than retrain him, decided that feline handshakes should be the reversal of the human version). Miles waited until only a handful of our close friends from the building were left, but he did his routine too. He's shy with strangers and clings to me. He can jump straight from the floor to perch on my shoulder like a pirate's parrot, Athena emerging from Zeus's forehead, or, for that matter, my conjoined twin ("My True Siamese," I call him: "Two heads are better than one."). My friend Pamela Petro, who stayed with us to give a reading at my school last fall, took a photograph of Miles on my shoulder and me slicing apples at the kitchen counter and e-mailed it to me under the title "Sous-chef." I'm pretty sure she meant that Miles was my helper, but since I was doing the prep work and he was watching, the title should, more logically, refer to me.

At the peak of their migration in early October, five hundred chimney swifts circle our building every evening at dusk. Over the loud chattering, clicking calls they make, you can hear their wings slapping together as several birds hover above the chimney's opening, maneuvering around one another as they wait their turn. They dive in one at a time while hundreds swirl above like smoke blowing into the chimney instead of out. I don't know how far down the chimney shaft the birds go to roost. The chimney rises above the building's roof and there is a crawl space between the roof and my ceiling. If the swifts filled up all that space, then some would have to cling to the bricks next to my bed.

In their sleep, I've read, swifts continue to chatter. Some nights, I stand on my bed and put my ear to the wall. So far, I haven't heard anything. I've held my cats—Ernest, Algernon, Miles, then Jackson—aloft in my arms and pressed their ears to the wall, hoping their keener sense of hearing might detect a faint bird chatter. Each cat has looked down at me in total incomprehension.

Chimney swifts were once called "North American swifts." They roosted in tree hollows across the eastern United States until the European settlers cleared acres of forests to build houses—at which point the birds started using the bricks inside their chimneys. It's a story of adaptation, of wildlife managing to live at close quarters with humans, but only a few ornithologists with special mirrors and cameras have been able to observe their nesting and roosting habits inside chimneys. Although the swifts' general migration pattern is known, how far south they travel in the winter is up for debate. Swifts eat flying insects in the air, so—unlike birds that can be fed on seeds, grains, or mealworms from a dish—they cannot be kept in captivity to be studied. They nest and sleep practically inside our houses and yet they remain mysterious and elusive.

That's the traditional view of cats too: aloof, independent, mysterious. Recently, when some indoor-outdoor cats were outfitted with cameras around their necks to assess their environmental impact, many owners were surprised by the distance their pets traveled daily, the frequency of the skirmishes they got into with other cats or predators, and the number of birds, rodents, insects, and lizards they hunted. Some people also discovered that their cats had another family who fed them, let them sleep in the bed, and considered them their own. Apparently, a cat can have two of his proverbial nine lives simultaneously.

The owners in the study let their cats out believing it's cruel to keep these natural predators from following their instinct. Most were not convinced, even afterward, that their pets should remain indoors. It must be that the appeal of an indoor-outdoor cat is precisely its freedom: The cat goes to places we cannot follow, does something wild and dangerous, and still comes back to us—like a kite that soars above the trees and power lines and returns in one piece.

Still, cats are products of ninety-five hundred years of domestication. Miles and Jackson shouldn't have to fulfill themselves by roaming

331

the neighborhood, any more than I have to go wilderness camping to realize my human potential. In some areas of the United States, indoor-outdoor cats pose a significant threat to ground-nesting birds whose numbers are diminishing. I wouldn't let Miles and Jackson loose to eat even the common, abundant birds that frequent our yard, but more than that, I don't want my cats to *be* birds.

I released the birds I'd raised, knowing that most would not survive their first migration. To care too much about their individual fates would have been unnatural, even unkind; kindness to wildlife means respecting their freedom. Every summer, chimney swifts return to the chimney and hummingbirds sip sugar water from my window feeder. Cardinals and woodpeckers frequent the sunflower-seed feeder year-round, but I cannot tell if the same individuals are at my window from hour to hour or season to season. Birds are ephemeral, and our encounters with them are fleeting. That's the essence of their beauty. The goal of conservation is to save the species, not each individual bird.

Living with a pet, by contrast, is all about caring for a specific individual. Before the word *pet* became popular in the late nineteenth century, a companion animal was referred to more often as a *favorite*. A favorite dog or cat was an animal set apart from all others of its kind by being given a name and being invited to live in the house as a member of the family. I'm not sure when people started making a huge distinction between dogs and cats, when pet owners became polarized between dog people and cat people. We don't have to clicker-train our cats to understand that a favorite cat and a favorite dog are more similar than different. They are two types of music, classical and jazz, say, the opera and zydeco. With each pet, we make a commitment to the individual: We love this dog and no other; this cat is mine.

Unlike the chimney swifts beyond our bedroom wall, my cats are only as mysterious or unknowable as people are. Miles and Jackson haven't learned to speak with words, but I grew up in Japan and spent two decades in the American Midwest. No one says what he or she means in either place; that kind of disclosure is simply not expected. Here on the East Coast, people express their opinions and feelings more readily, only to insist later that at the time of their previous comments, they hadn't known all the relevant facts or they hadn't been fully aware of their own motives and intentions. No matter where you live, it seems, understanding another human being requires both a leap of faith and the act of imagination. At least with my cats,

I know everything about them already. In our 660-square-foot apartment, not much happens to Miles and Jackson that I don't witness firsthand; due to the guilty choice I made to acquire them from breeders instead of from a shelter, I was able to learn where and how they were born and raised. It's not difficult to observe their behavior and deduce their intentions or feelings.

How freely we should ascribe human motives and characteristics to animals—anthropomorphizing them—is an interesting philosophical question. But in practice, we anthropomorphize other people, in a manner of speaking, every time we ask ourselves, *What would we do in their place? If I said or did that, what would I really be trying to communicate?* We routinely fail to understand others because they are not us, and yet we have no other tool besides observation and imagination to bridge the gap between the self and the world.

Our sunflower-seed feeder is in the window next to my writing desk. The cats like to sit between the window and the desk, on the shelf my boyfriend—who is very handy—built for them. The feeder hangs from a flower pot a few inches outside the window, but the birds either don't see the cats and me or else they understand something about the windowpane's impenetrability. Though prettier birds often perch on the flower pot and the feeder, mourning doves are Jackson's favorite. They are big and fat, move slowly and sit in one place for minutes at a time, and make a lot of noise when three or four crowd the feeder, jockeying for position. Jackson, no longer hamster sized, sits with his face pressed to the glass, his muscular body compressed like a torpedo ready to be launched. His eyes, the color of gooseberries, register the doves' every move.

Miles lounges next to him, with his back to the window, his blue eyes on me. Sometimes, he falls asleep while watching my fingers on the keyboard. He's just beginning to doze off again when Jackson rears up on his hind legs and thumps the window with his front paw. The doves scatter; Miles startles awake but doesn't look back. I don't think I'm committing a flagrant act of anthropomorphism to say that Jackson studies the birds, ever hopeful he might catch one to eat, and Miles could care less about birds because he'd rather watch me.

The doves don't return right away. Instead, a single chickadee lights on the mesh tray and picks up one seed in its beak—a seed it will crack against tree bark, to eat only the kernel at its center—and takes off. Some abstract longing or regret flutters up into the air with that bird. I think of the chimney swift in my hand and the dozens of other birds released in the garden that is no longer mine. No matter how hard I tried not to get attached, of course I felt sadness and worry when I let those birds go, as though a part of me would disappear with their flight and eventual demise.

Jackson crouches down on his perch. A thousand miles away, a few descendants of the birds who learned to fly in my spare room might be building their nests. Miles settles back on his post too to resume his scrutiny of his favorite subject: me. Jackson is my sentry, my outward eye; he watches the world for me. Miles is my twin, my familiar, the one whose inward gaze gives me back to myself. Anchored between them, I am exactly where I should be, alone at home.

The Re'em
Adam McOmber

UPON THE DEATH OF GERMAN MONK Ulrich Gottard, a manuscript was delivered to the Roman Curia in a sealed oaken box for consideration by the Holy See. The lord protector of Cromberg Cloister, Father Benedict, wrote in his letter of submittal that he deemed the document a "significant and distressing epistle" due, in part, to the impossible and quasi-heretical nature of its narrative. What was perhaps even more troubling, though, was the reaction the letter produced among younger initiates of the German cloister. These men, like Ulrich Gottard himself, were said to be of a delicate and Romantic nature. "Troublesome searchers," Benedict called them. The followers of Gottard began to meet secretly in a dimly lit room beneath the cloister's chapter hall. It was there they attempted an interpretation of the letter—as if its passages were some kind of holy writ. The group began referring to itself as the Re'em and eventually claimed to have discovered that Gottard's letter contained a message that would soon deliver them all from earthly constraint. When the members of the Re'em began to suggest a pilgrimage to Egypt, Father Benedict was forced to intercede.

Gottard's narrative—now well known in higher echelons of the Roman Church—unfolds over a series of days during a visit to the Holy Land, soon after his taking of First Orders. An amateur geologist as well as a man of God, Gottard begins his writings with a description of certain curious formations of volcanic alkaline rock in the arid landscape surrounding Mount Sinai in Egypt. Gottard notes that the rocks had, in places, fused together and formed what looked like the arches of a "black and imposing architecture that lay crumbling on the stony hillside, as if left there by some ancient and unknown race."

It was in one such glittering temple of blackish stone Gottard encountered the animal that would soon overwhelm his thoughts. "The creature stood upon its four legs," he writes, "and was the size and approximate shape of a Calabrese stallion. Its coat was pale in color, and the hair of its pelt was longish and matted in places. Clearly

335

not a domesticated beast." Other elements of the animal's appearance, he continues, were entirely unique. For, unlike a horse, the creature was possessed of cloven hooves and a short, leathery tail. In temperament, it behaved nobly, regarding Gottard as he approached, much as one man might carefully regard a stranger. The creature's most striking feature was the single braided horn that protruded from the center of its head. "The horn," Gottard writes, "in certain light, appeared semitranslucent, and at other times looked as though it was nothing more than a piece of twined bone." The monk soon begins referring to the creature as a "re'em"—an animal mentioned in the Vulgate of St. Jerome (*Canst thou bind the horned re'em with his band in the furrow. Or will he harrow the valley after thee?*).

Upon returning to the village near the mountain, Gottard ascertained that such creatures, though not common, were at times found in the area. Their home—a valley some miles from Mount Sinai—was accessible if accompanied by a suitable guide. Gottard, unable to banish the encounter with the creature from his mind, produced coins from his purse, and a guide was brought forth—a young man, dressed in white, introduced as Chaths.

Gottard writes that, upon seeing the young man for the first time, he felt a sense of recognition. It was not that Gottard had met the young man before, but in Chaths, he saw something of himself. "As if the villagers had produced not a guide but a mirror," he writes.

On the following morning, the two set out to locate the valley of the re'em. And as they they walked, Gottard found the guide unresponsive to his questioning. Chaths would do no more than mumble a phrase or two in his own language, of which Gottard knew little. The journey was longer than the monk expected, and soon the guide indicated they should make camp for the night. This would allow them to arrive at the valley by morning light. "It would be unwise to approach after nightfall," Chaths said in words finally plain enough for Gottard to understand.

The monk found he could not sleep. There was a wind that made a strange sound in the hills. And small animals seemed to scuttle in the darkness beyond the reach of the firelight. He spent much of the night considering the fire itself, imagining he saw within its flames the re'em, walking in circles. Where the re'em trod, black formations of stone appeared to rise. Horns that pierced the earth. Gottard turned from these visions in the fire to regard his guide again. There was something in the young man's features that was not handsomeness exactly, but a quality more like beauty. The sort of beauty that radiated from an ancient sculpture or a stone made smooth by the sea. Gottard felt drawn to Chaths and troubled in his heart because of it. As the sun began to rise, the monk went to the edge of firelight to kneel and pray. "It was then," he writes, "that a most distressing event occurred. I felt as though a hand were suddenly pressed against not only my mouth but also the surface of my very soul. My prayers would not leave me. They were trapped. God would not hear."

This disturbance of spirit caused Gottard to call out, waking Chaths, who brought water and sat with the monk. In order to calm Gottard, Chaths finally relented and told him more about the creature they sought.

"It's not an animal," Chaths said. "Not as you believe."

"What then?" Gottard asked.

The guide shook his head. "It does not exist. Not as other things do. The sight of it is thought to be caused by a fissure that develops in the brain. A fever is said to cause the fissure."

Gottard remembered feeling ill a few nights before he encountered the re'em. He'd attributed the sickness merely to the sort of malaise that often came on during travel. "So you're saying the animal is some sort of hallucination?" Gottard asked.

Chaths shook his head. "The fissure—it allows a man to see crossways. The animal walks there in that light."

"I don't understand—crossways in the light?"

Chaths offered more water to the monk.

"You've been afflicted with the fever too?" Gottard asked.

Chaths nodded. "That's why I'm your guide."

The idea that sickness had caused him to see the re'em troubled Gottard. Perhaps there was no point in any of this. He was chasing a mirage. Chaths indicated they should begin walking before the sun rose too high. Soon enough the two men came upon not a valley but a kind of hole in the wall of a rocky outcropping. The hole was surrounded by more of the same black volcanic stones that Gottard had seen upon his original encounter with the re'em. The hole seemed to waver slightly, to fluctuate. And Gottard wondered if this too was a symptom of the supposed fissure in the brain.

Chaths indicated that Gottard must be silent once inside the tunnel. The horned creatures were not easily disturbed, but there were other things that lived in the valley beyond. Things that did not appreciate the presence of men. The young guide seemed troubled as he spoke, as if he could see some future the monk could not. Gottard attempted to provide comfort. But Chaths pulled away, indicating that Gottard was not to touch him.

It is in Gottard's description of the "valley" that the sense of his letter begins to falter. What he saw after emerging from the other side of the tunnel does not correlate to any known topography in the vicinity of Mount Sinai. It was a landscape, verdant and lush. "Like a garden allowed to run wild for years," he writes. Farther along, the landscape began to change and the earth became covered with what Gottard describes as a new variety of rock. The monk posits that the pressure of ancient volcanic activity had caused crystals to form. The large crystals protruded from the earth and were of varying colors: deep vermilion, saffron, and azure. The sunlight, which streamed into the valley at an odd angle (crosswise, thought Gottard), struck the crystals and caused a prismatic effect.

Gottard and Chaths appeared to be walking on the floor of a strange sea. The waters of the sea were composed of wildly contrasting colors, so utterly immersive that Gottard soon began to feel as though he were drowning. He fell to his knees, and Chaths came to support him. Gathered in the guide's arms, Gottard forgot he'd been warned not to touch Chaths, and he put his hand on the young man's face and then on his neck. Thinking again how beautiful Chaths was. Not like a mirror or a sculpture, but more like water. Chaths was a still lake in this ocean of shifting color.

It was then that Gottard heard the sound of hoof on stone and turned to look out into the valley. Standing between two of the great crystalline forms was the horse with the single horn. The re'em, in its own environment, was contemplative, more circumspect than it had been on the mountainside. As it approached, the colors that rose from the surrounding crystals appeared to intensify. They shifted to paint the body of the pale horse. Gottard, in his delirium, writes that the braided bone of the re'em's horn seemed to pour color from its tip. As if the horn were bleeding. And the bright, colorful material that issued forth ran in streams down the horse's forehead and into its black eyes.

As Gottard reached out to touch the braided horn (for the re'em was now close enough for him to do just that), he sensed the approach of a vast form. Chaths had said the re'em were not alone in the valley, and Gottard suddenly realized this was true. The monk writes: "The being—for it was a sort of being that approached—was too large to actually be perceived by my eye. It seemed instead that the atmosphere, the very air of the valley, grew denser. And it also seemed that the being sang in a voice that was too loud to be heard by my ear. Yet I could sense the sound of it nonetheless."

"You aren't permitted here," Chaths said. "I'm sorry, Brother Gottard."

"What do you mean?" the monk asked, turning to look at the guide. The young man was alive with bleeding color. It swam across his body, as he stood with his palm against the neck of the re'em.

"You are not permitted," Chaths said again.

"It was then," Gottard writes, "that the approaching form—the great being—enclosed me. I felt as if I were drawn up into the palm of a vast hand—a hand too large for me to see. Chaths watched from the ground. As did the re'em. I was lifted high enough that I could perceive the entirety of the valley. All of it was alive with maddening color. I saw a whole herd of re'em running—making rivers in the shifting light. I was drawn higher still, until I felt that I was being pulled out into the heavenly spheres. I could hear the spheres singing; they joined their voices with the voice of the great being. And still, I was drawn upward, toward the cold empyrean itself. And then finally I awoke on the hillside where I'd first encountered the beast. I lay beneath the crumbling architecture, already forgetting the colors I'd seen. Such was the dullness of our world. I called out for Chaths. But my call went unanswered. The guide had remained in the valley. Likely he'd known all along he would stay. Perhaps that was the fate of all guides. And there beneath the black rock, I dreamed that I too would one day guide someone to the valley. And then I would finally be permitted."

Cardinal
Nora Khan

I WALKED JEREMIAH OUT OF CLASS, down the hall, out to the yard, and let him scream into a square yellow pillow. I watched the veins in his neck fill with blood then contract as though his blood had drained out with his sound. If he'd forgotten his pillow, I put my hand over his mouth. My hand wet with his phlegm as he screamed into my palm.

We would stand shaking, looking out into the woods around the school for a few spaces of breath. I held my right hand away from my side and his face flooded with relief. It was December in Connecticut, and the weatherman said we had remarkable apricity, a warm sun in winter.

I'm a class aide to Mrs. Albrecht, third-grade teacher at Franklin Arts Charter. I take the children to the nurse to get their medication and I step in to manage them when they're out of line. Jeremiah had been put on another pill, an orange one, and his psychiatrist said he would act out this way for a while. Albrecht and I came up with plans for him. Letting him scream outside was one of our more bizarre routines, but it worked. It was extreme, but not that crazy. Crazy was the amount of medication he was on. Craziest was pure Jeremiah, no medication. Something had to give.

After one particular session, we headed back into Classroom West, where he cut quick past the group tables to the long windows. He knelt at the sill and watched for birds, for their numinous quicksilver presence in the thick of white oak edging the yard.

He turned to me. Dark-brown hair, yolky eyes, a thick eyelash fringe that made him look like an exiled prince. "Where is he? When will he come back? Will he come close to the window?"

None of us knew. He meant the cardinal, the one that lit on a tree that lined up with the center of our room. That winter the small red king took an interest in our class. When he lit high up, he turned to look back down at us, at all the children, their small necks straining, full of blood and more blood, looking up at his brighter body's blood on the leaves.

And so the children caught the fever to see the bird. Whether he flashed diagonal or lingered on a branch for a minute, his presence lit up the room and turned them ecstatic. All the lighter, bilious males had cleared out months before, and he remained. Throughout the day, the children waited for Jeremiah to see the cardinal, because he always saw the bird first, caught him, and then cried out, There, there, there. Look.

The second week into this bird-watching, Albrecht paused at the window. "How fantastic," she said, leaning over Jeremiah to watch. "A red animal! A bright red animal. And it's so gray and cold outside. Isn't it nice to see some color?"

Jeremiah took up most of my days at Franklin. I gave him his pills in the morning and afternoon. He was seven. He needed them all. His whites, his oranges, his yellows, his blues. White and yellow for focus, blue for happiness, orange for calm and impulse control. He rarely ate; he traded parts of his lunch away throughout the day. During gym, he ran and ran. Large heavy head and swollen stomach.

Carolina Tearstone, his mother, explained that the pills brought him down to speed. As she spoke, she flattened the air before her with her hands. Carolina was a spindly lawyer with bloodshot eyes and she lived in a townhouse in the historic district. I had once heard her staccato on the phone as she walked the length of the halls.

"Then we send him away. Send him to a boarding school or a special school and they can deal with him there," she snipped. "He's a boy. He can handle it. Let him handle it. Throw him in cold water and make him learn. That's how I learned! He's been a nightmare, Jeremy, you aren't here to know—"

Hang on tightly, I told him, as he swung from my arm, dragging me down with each step down the hall. The halls dwarfed us on that long walk to the nurse's office. The auditorium was locked. Pipes exposed, roofs leaking, rooms that changed from hot to cold on a dime.

The school nurse cut the big pills with a small knife then slid them across the counter toward me. Five, six, three, and two. Two, one half, three, and three. I turned each pill in the light. In college, my roommate, a Gold Coast princess, had been on the same pills since she was eight years old. Thirty minutes after taking her dose, when their effect was heaviest, she would talk about how her parents had abandoned her. I thought of all the kids in college taking triple rounds to bang through finals, then going on to become doctors, lawyers, and bankers. Ritalin, Concerta, Adderall, Dexedrine.

Nora Khan

Hang on tightly, let go lightly. I picked up the phrase from a movie. I also had read, in a poem, Lose something every day. I tried to learn how to lose everything in my life with a little less pain each time. I lost my parents, pop, pop, two soup cans filled with water knocked off a railing into the grass. My mother, that was last winter. I saw her body wheeled briskly out our front door in the middle of the night. The toxicology report noted no foul. Clearly, it had all gone foul. I hadn't been able to help her. I didn't even know she was ill, or where all the medication in the bathroom had even come from. What had I been doing but building a brick wall around my selfish life? Rich tapestry we weave.

Over the past year I let the loss sink into my flesh, learned to pass it through me as slow waste. That job was the twine holding my life together. I was twenty-four years old. I sat in the corner of West and watched the children and felt fear, hope, longing for each of them. I was afraid for their delicacy, their heads filling with all the images and stories they'd carry for life.

Emil Jones, Lisa Taliaferro, Leah Thompson, Gwendolyn Rael, Jeremiah Tearstone, Julian Squire, Amy Wadsworth, Tessa Hansen, J. P. Lilly.

We taught them how to call things by their names. School, temple, bird, snow, god. Some days, I could see my own edges blur. I was Jeremiah, I was Emil, I was Leah. I was all of their mothers and I was all and I was in each of them.

I thought about Jeremiah's brain, the synapses cleared by cold blue fire, cotton balls shoved in the spark plugs. A few glass layers snapped into the gel of the optic nerve, his gaze contracting. I thought about him waking one day and wanting his mind back, wanting his singular disturbances all to himself. Wanting reparation for all the time he could have spent in the woods, ears open to its silent music.

On a class trip to the carnival, he told Albrecht that he heard a violin playing in a tent on the edge of the grounds. We didn't believe him, but then, leaving the carnival, I saw him, a man facing the train tracks, tuning his violin.

I watched for the cardinal with Jeremiah. I didn't know what he wanted. The more I saw it, the more unlikely its existence seemed. Red! The audacity!

The cardinal's black pebble eye held all of us within it. A perfect siren set off in the middle of a white-sun day, like a wild and blessed emergency. Brilliant, imperious, cresting, black masked throat all full. It chirred and shook a fall of powder off its branch.

342

Jeremiah, sentinel, marshal, held on with both hands. His body shook with the effort of not flailing and not shouting. I hoped there was a place in him that I could reach. This seemed possible, because imagining him older was easy, longing all built up into something so much more vast and uncontrollable than one ever imagined it could be. You started to see it as a large spinning phantom on the horizon, receding, your longing.

I saw words—dysfunctional, impulsive, lazy—words he heard at home, at school, every day, entering his ears and sliding on down into his blood, stamped toxic in his cells. Words distilling his future selves. I saw him at fourteen climbing down a fire escape, clambering into a car with other boys in search of better pills. I saw him shuttled from high school to high school, then resisting his way through college in a funk of stimulants and downers. A smart, creative kid, but not a truly ambitious one. Not a closer.

Albrecht asked the class, "Who do you want to be? What do you want to learn along the way?" Each day she wore a blazer and taught grammar from a lectern. She believed in each child's passion and talent, in the genius in each tiny creator's heart. "Your children will learn to look at the world with open hearts, with minds attuned to beauty," she'd told their parents.

"Boring!" Jeremiah rolled his head back to gaze out the window upside down. The children tittered. Later that day, I saw his assignment. He'd written, I want to be red.

Surely, I saw him first slip a pill in his pocket that second week of January. He pretended to swallow it, then showed me the pill in his hand and I smiled and didn't say a word. I felt true, thrilling fear passing from my neck down through me in a wave. I saw him do it the next day, and I felt less. Then each day, effortless, quick, I let him put his oranges away. He slammed open the boy's bathroom door to flush them. Accretive, small, splinters lodging deep.

Snow fell relentless over the bay, the lighthouse, the streets long winding into town. The children had cabin fever and couldn't focus. They drew birds in quiz borders, on their hands. They took their lead from Jeremiah, who tracked the king's halting flight in a composition book: the tree it landed on that day, whether it let out its full-body sonar chirp and how many times it did.

I paged through his book. Page after page of trees with cardinals colored in as ornaments. I'd loved horses that much, once, when I was ten. But I couldn't remember a time since when my every thought and breath were sunk into another living thing.

When I saw our cardinal, I felt fear. I felt him catch in me, arrest me, disrupt my hard-won peace. I saw him and thought, Today a mother lost a child, and today, in some far corner of the earth, yesterday's skirmish broke into a massacre. The king flipped, on to the next oak; a train skipped on its tracks in the middle of the night.

Come February, Albrecht and I managed to get the children out on to the playground. Jeremiah practiced his cardinal calls at the wire fence.

And there it came, and we held our breath, let its fist of heartsong strain and beat against our silence. Its song alternated between a searing, warning intensity and a frenetic, small chucking, back into a coppery stream of whistled chirring. Somewhere, salmon-gray wings shuddered in response. A song honed over fifty generations to earn the queen's ear.

It turned on its tail and looked at Jeremiah, and then it looked at me. I thought, He's mad. His black full eye is mad. He comes from dinosaurs. He moves the winter to burn. He careened off and the snow swallowed up his place and we were left alone, listening to his fading call and somehow, there was nothing right in any of it.

After it took off, Jeremiah crumpled against the fence. I held his hand as he got the look that said he'd throw himself on the ground in a paroxysm of violent, incoherent need. His eyes sealed up as he gulped for air. He writhed in his green ski jacket, kicked my shins, and howled.

"No! No! No! No!" He wept.

Albrecht swooped in, windmilling her arms. "Jeremiah!" she boomed.

He crouched in the dirt and continued to wail quietly. He squinted, as though spotlit.

"I hate this," he said. His hands slipped against the fence. He looked into the trees. Leah began to weep too.

"What do you want?" I asked.

He crawled under a bench and lay on his back on the freezing concrete. I was afraid of the wildness in me, but I wasn't afraid of that in him. He asked me for a hug and I knelt down and held him. Counted to three, released. He smelled like dry leaves and glue.

*

The teaching unit that month was on art history and the South, and the children were supposed to make face vessels. Artisan slaves in the Southern pottery trade made face vessels in their free time, built faces into jugs and pitchers. The faces were their real selves, the hidden, triumphant selves that lived through and despite all destruction.

Albrecht slid trays of cold, heavy clay from a deep fridge. Her white silk hair was clipped straight across her forehead. The class put on their smocks weakly, early as it was that morning. Albrecht struggled to explain the task.

"If you were a slave and this was your secret, what would you make? Does everyone understand what I mean?"

The children cut the slabs with white plastic knives, kneaded the clay. Jeremiah frowned and picked up his chopsticks and poked holes into his slab. He dug in his thumbs deep and pressed with his full weight into the holes.

The children were always teaching us. Make something where there was nothing. You had to take your pain and work it like the clay, press and stretch it with relentless force. You had to master your love and turn it outward, like the Mars rover, if your love was the Mars rover, smooth and clean in a new direction. Retract the legs and turn steady east and clamber forward. Soar high, wide, south, into the red stone sea.

They held up their masks when done. A laughing man, an old-timey pilot in goggles. Their little bodies shivered behind their masks. Leah had sculpted her own face but with fuller cheeks. J. P. had made the face of Benjamin Franklin from a poster of the Great Inventors.

Albrecht held Jeremiah's mask under its chin and no one could say a thing, it was so real, its cheeks and brows and lips shaped around a grotesque happiness. Albrecht looked delighted and disturbed that Jeremiah had it in him, to make such an awful thing. The ropes of eyebrows and lips had been massaged into the flesh of the face. The eyes were human.

A shattered mug, the small bookshelf overturned, Julian with a pink slap stripe across the nose and out the window we could see Jeremiah running past the swings. I watched him watching the trees, his eyes separating and scanning each leaf, his small whorl ears combing the whole aviary's calls, pinpointing, seeing his bird at the moment it made itself known. The first nomad who peeled off the group in search of water and food had the same restless eye gene.

I was in over my head and I couldn't tell a soul. On our hall walks, I pleaded with Jeremiah to take all his pills but he said no.

His mother didn't arrive one afternoon and I had to walk him home. Their town house had fig trees in a front garden sunk beneath high walls.

The front red door was open, and Jeremiah pushed his way in before I could speak. The kitchen was decorative and unused. In the narrow, dark living room, a cleaning lady had her back to me as she vacuumed with headphones on. The air was thick with dust.

I walked after his sound, up the narrow stairs. He knelt before a television in a small room.

In a large workroom filled with drafting tables and shelves, Carolina looked up at me. She had a phone in one hand. She waggled the other hand by her temple.

"You brought Jeremiah?"

"He's in the next room." I waited for her to speak. She looked back down at the phone.

"I'm so sorry," she said. "I was calling the school. I need to come in to talk about him. I'm taking him to a new doctor tomorrow. We have to try and get this figured out."

I wondered if Carolina wasn't on something. She seemed to be unwilling to get up from the chair. As I left the house, I turned to see Jeremiah leaning in a window, watching me go. These were other people's lives, their families, their unhappiness, not mine.

They were jumping because he was jumping and then he began to dance and punch the air, seized by a hundred small demons peeling him in every direction, and as he leapt they leapt in time, the air filling with quivering, precious bodies. Are they possessed, Albrecht asked, the floor shaking, and they laughed, whipped their heads about to see each other's faces.

Then he was running down the hall and out of the double doors of the school. He stepped up on a bench, caught a foot in the fence, and lifted himself over into the woods. Once his foot hit the ground, he shifted gears into a run.

Out in the drifts, the white burning my eyes. My body twisted as I ran through the knee-high snow. I scanned the dark above for the legionary's crest. And there, a riot exploding through the cold, across the path that Jeremiah had cleared. He lit low, filled with force, swept back across. No rest, no cover, weaving higher up toward his inversion, his natural law, his sandy wife. I'd never seen her before. Her tail and wings had been dipped in his color then dried to orange rust.

We were alone in the woods, running, Jeremiah's green jacket and hysterical laughter just out of reach. I had to tell them what I'd let happen, and I'd probably be fired. Maybe they already knew. I felt Carolina, Albrecht, and the principal watching us, receding, from behind the glass.

Jeremiah whooped and bounded. The school was out of sight. He followed after a spatter, a sound, a burst. I felt a violent, sudden, and pure joy slice my heart in half, a joy that said, Marry the siren, marry my life to emergency. I saw him fall in the snow and I heard him laughing.

The Taxidermist
Craig Eklund

THERE ONCE WAS A YOUNG MAN who, not one week past his twenty-second birthday, inherited a tremendous fortune and the control of a vast business empire, only to liquidate, before the market's closing bell the day of his father's death, every last asset and relinquish executive rights and responsibilities, all in order to pursue what he referred to only as his true calling, by which he meant, so it was to turn out, taxidermy. Years passed, however, before anyone came to know that, for even as he cashed out and handed over the reins, he said nothing more about the nature of his plans, and when the process was complete and all ties were definitively cut, he vanished without warning. Later, it was alleged that this disappearance was the first charge of his calling: to enter into the secret of leave-taking.

An extensive and thoroughgoing investigation was set in motion at the word that he'd gone missing—he was, after all, the scion of an old, powerful family. The only apparent trace was an empty boat dock in the Cayman Islands. After several months, the investigators had discovered no further leads and so, amid uncertainty and indecision, they pronounced him dead at sea. The word "suicide" was not used, but he had been, everyone confessed, a peculiar and withdrawn young man, nothing like his father, and who could account for the motives and actions of such an anomalous character? Four years later, he came back to life. The Associated Press reported that an island had been bought in his name with funds the official inquiry had been unable to account for. It was a frozen hunk of rock and lichens on the northern fringe of Canada's Northwest Passages. Needless to say, the news was received as a fantastic surprise and on its heels came headlines announcing the launch of a fleet of bulk freighters. Heaped with cranes and trucks, massive quantities of concrete and steel, and a wealth of cutting-edge synthetic materials, they forged up the frozen straits and closed in on this crest of earth breaking the sea's frosty surface. Construction was under way.

The enterprise was prodigious, an undertaking of regal ambition by any standard, but what the blueprint drew up was more bunker than pleasure dome. The greater part of the island was given over to the main building, an enormous hermetic structure with a concrete shell designed to endure the fiercest cold and the most extreme storm conditions (weather patterns having become, by this point in time, dangerously unpredictable). A desalination facility and a small hydro-electric plant were constructed on the island's eastern face. A dock was fashioned along the bay that inscribed the northern coast and the seafloor was drilled, blasted, and dredged to prevent glaciers from coming aground (the Northwest Passages being, at this point in time, known for a great deal of such traffic). The interior of the main building meanwhile was divided into a dozen showrooms, a large work-room, and a small wing of living quarters. The showrooms were immense and featured rows of different-sized risers illuminated by spotlights arranged in tracts across the ceiling. The workroom was too manifold in character to bespeak any coherent function. The living quarters were spartan. Finally, in a large back room of the do-mestic wing, a military-grade massively parallel supercomputer was installed—no one knew yet to what end, of course. In fact, at this point, no one knew what he was up to with any of this, for the strangest thing was that mid this commotion, which had all the makings of myth and legend, the young man himself was nowhere to be seen.

They said that he was insane. That he was a megalomaniac, a would-be dictator, a cult leader without a cult. A one-man conspiracy. One of history's great madmen taking shape. They attributed to him psychological disorders and sexual deviancies of every stripe. They accused him of crimes of every color. They said that the compound was fortified, that he was declaring war on the civilized world. They said that his plan was to let the place sink (sea levels having risen, around this point in time, beyond the mark of mere threat), that he intended to found a new Atlantis and bide the times below the cur-rent. They said that it was a giant nuclear fallout shelter, that he knew of some unknown catastrophe to come. They said it all, even that he was still dead. But in the end, the only thing they were right about was what he called it: the Linnaeum.

Family and friends had no contact with him. As it happened, they would never hear from him again. In light of his family's history, authorities of several sorts, not to mention many an influential pri-vate faction, were more than a little suspicious of his designs, but all their means came to no avail: He was nowhere to be found and his aims were just as concealed. What's more, there were in the works measures to secure this inaccessibility once and for all. Given the status of the surrounding waters as an international shipping passageway, plus the fact that the island was now a territorially independent entity with a net wealth that commanded no small respect, the possibility arose that the Linnaeum might be granted a technical form of de jure statehood with corresponding rights of sovereignty. His lawyers had begun pushing the case through international bureaucracies even as the foundations were being laid.

All of which is to say that he was in every way out of reach. The details and schematics of the project came trickling back with the construction workers, but nothing of its meaning and purpose, and only bare rumor about the author himself. Some believed that they'd espied him—a questionable presence on the outskirts of the work site, a figure for whom no one could account wandering about the half-finished halls—but none could be sure of it. The person in question certainly had none of the magnetism that (if it was him) had distinguished his father in his worldly heyday. Details were spare and vague and widely inconsistent, but what was relatively constant story to story was a sort of gradual awareness, as if he'd come to appearance without noise, without entrance, as if he'd always been diffused throughout it all but only now condensed and materialized (these are more or less their actual words). The world at large wanted to bleed him of a thousand outrageous confessions and what it got instead was a glance at a blurry snapshot of a shadow.

While these accounts teased the inflamed public, the construction entered its final stages. The pace was astonishing. With each passing week, walls were sealed off and systems powered on, and as each phase drew to a close, another band of workers shipped off. Day by day, the hallways emptied and hushed. It was only when the last crew had begun loading and battening down their equipment for departure that a ship charged with supplies arrived, bearing also the permanent staff. The Linnaeum was to be maintained by these dozen men and women: maintenance people and technicians of diverse specialties, a janitor, two housekeepers, a physician, and a chef. They came forged under every known climate, hammered out by every conceivable history. They were drawn by lavish salaries and undeterred by the clause in the contract that forbade any contact with the outside world for the entire term of employment. Naturally, they would all turn out to be cagey and reticent loners, but, whatever their motives, they were amenable to the conditions and fit for the task. Theirs are the first definitive eyewitness accounts. He stood on the pier as the ship berthed.

I was one among them that day, one who had willingly severed all connection to the world (for reasons I would no sooner divulge than any of them), one who had yoked himself to this strange and secret undertaking (for a considerable fee), and I saw him there, standing on the pier, blank and impassive, his gray suit vexed by the wind, and I was distinctly unimpressed. By all the noise that had run the daily round through every channel, journal, and website, by all the gravity and diligence and secrecy that had governed my hiring, I'd been led to believe in something more. Neither I nor any of my shipmates knew the purpose of this monumental endeavor, but there was an epic promise in it all that seemed to say that the spirit of our age had taken body out of the fog and haze and scattered passing hours and come to shape right here in this remote latitude. Unknown perhaps even to myself, I'd imagined I would now look it in the eye and call it to account. But the hope slipped through my fingers when I disembarked and finally came upon the figure on the shore.

With his hands held behind his back, he stood there before us, stock-still, unduly inanimate, rooted in the ground. Despite his poise, there was something fleeting and evasive about him, as if he wavered at the threshold of an unseen door. He appeared older than his years— that look of the youthfully ancient. His build was not small, his stature not short, but he seemed nevertheless dried and shrunken, a mere shaving of his old man. I wondered that all the grandeur of his robber-baron stock should be pruned to that of a mere bookkeeper. A minute or so passed before I was able to discern his voice amid the wind and waters and the din of construction cargo rumbling down the docks. We had been debriefed before departure and knew already what was required of us in our particular capacities, and so he held now to the task at hand, pronouncing not a word on the greater mission (a silence that he would maintain throughout our stay, with, to my knowledge, only two notable exceptions). He led us to our quarters, had us leave our suitcases in our rooms, and then put us to work unloading the boat. He was no more to be seen for the remainder of the day. And so we unpacked the cargo hold and stacked the huge pantries of our new home with crates of canned and dried goods, we piled the freezer with frozen meat and vegetables, we loaded the maintenance closets with tools and spare parts, we charged the infirmary with medicine and first-aid supplies. In short, we equipped the Linnaeum with all the provisions several lifetimes under these churning skies might call for. And as we stocked this ample storehouse, we could only wonder—silently, to ourselves—what was stashed there already in that secret cache we couldn't touch, what nameless future was held in waiting for us. The last boat, carrying the last construction crew, set off before our work was done.

It must be understood that the presence of these twelve men and women would hardly touch him: He was as good as alone with his art. For shortly it would come to light that he had, during his absence, answered his mysterious calling. Of course, no one knew where he had gone, where he had trained. Above all, no one knew why he had needed to disappear in the first place. And yet rumors do spread, even among the most circumspect souls. Over the years, I heard half a dozen accounts of his absence and training. They said he was a natural, entirely unschooled, that he'd worked a magnificent collection for an oil magnate in Abu Dhabi without ever trying his hand before. They said he'd trained with a renegade firm in the jungles of India, mounting specimens for throwback shikaris among the world elite. They said he'd passed the first two years as a poacher in Africa, living on the other side of the art, and then had disappeared again— yes, disappeared from his disappearance—to master the skills proper to his vocation. These stories ran their course and fell back into silence. But it was not without effect: The point in time came when we no longer referred to him by name but only and always as the Taxidermist.

He was a craftsman of a caliber never before seen. And also a purist of unique rigor, such that he devoted himself to a practice limited to the most final of mortal things. He was to be an artist of extinction, to put his hand only to the last instance of any given animal—the last blue-throated macaw, the last Mediterranean monk seal, the last (his ambitions were even so high) Siberian tiger anywhere in the world. It was a career with lucrative promise, to be sure, but time would reveal that he was to be the collector as well and his intention was to own—at ruinous cost, we can only imagine—every piece he was ever to touch. The Linnaeum was his workshop and gallery.

For a long time, this was all beyond the ken of the outside world and even within the Linnaeum dimly reckoned at best. On both sides, I kept his intentions as concealed as circumstances would allow. That is to say: I was the gatekeeper between the Taxidermist and the world. Shortly after the completion of construction, the supercomputer was booted up. It would be the only continuous link between the Linnaeum and the outside. It consisted of one hundred and twenty thousand processors arranged in thirty-six racks that subdivided the room into a sort of labyrinth, at the center of which was the interface.

The computer was designed for one purpose alone: to collect an un-thinkably large set of data from every corner of the information galaxy in order to determine the precise whereabouts of every animal of every species everywhere on the planet every second of the day. It was to be an all-knowing eye over the entire faunal world. The end-game was to pinpoint exactly when and exactly where the last of any given species—from the African elephant to the Old World sparrow—would fall. It was astonishingly effective. I know because I was the information technician at the Linnaeum. If I claim a unique insight into the Taxidermist's fate and ours, it is not without reason. I pre-sided over the frontier across which he and the world conducted their peculiar commerce.

My main duties were servicing the hardware and maintaining the server but at first my most urgent responsibility was to erase his tracks. No small part of his online activity contravened whole volumes' worth of international cyber laws. My task was exacting and I avow that I fulfilled it as well as could be expected. Of course, the opera-tion was enormous and unwieldy, and as it gathered speed, it made noise in a hundred different quarters at a time. It is, however, only in the nature of things that once his part (lawful or not) in the economic system was clarified, legal interest simply and definitively ceased. Even in the media, he was eventually downgraded from a sensational danger to an eccentric billionaire recluse, a crackpot of the familiar Howard Hughes stamp.

Needless to say, even to the information technician he was not going to willingly disclose this magnificent machine's purpose. He spoke to me no more than to any of the others—that is to say: almost never. He knew his way around advanced information systems and ran the program itself entirely on his own. My office was appended to the main computer room and my concern limited to technical support and maintenance. And so even for me, it came to full light only after the first hit. Those initial few weeks, the Taxidermist could be found sitting at the interface twenty out of any twenty-four hours, but I stepped inside only at points of scheduled service or when the hardware called for repair. I soon learned that knocking or other-wise announcing my presence was useless and simply entered and tended to whichever rack was in need. He would say nothing. I gen-erally couldn't tell for sure whether he even knew I was there. I would glance at him from time to time, around the corner of a cabinet, through the vacancies of removed blades. I would study him amid the steady gale of the cooling fans, from aboard the silent train of my own thoughts. He was inscrutable and I read there only my own empty conjectures. From my office, I was aware when he was online and able to observe the passage of incoming and outgoing information, but nothing of greater substance was within my reach. I could only follow an electrical trace that never lit upon any real sense and so I had no notion whatsoever what it all meant. It was from this distance then that I watched him home in on his first target and saw everything converge at a precise longitude and latitude of cyberspace—steadily, in tightening gyres, the Taxidermist, zeroing in. And when he struck, it was at last revealed. The first specimen. A California condor. The final California condor. *The* California condor.

It died in a zoo in Beijing (of all places) and touched ground at a private airport in Nunavut eighteen hours later, from where it struck off up the straits stashed away in the hold of a commercial fishing trawler. Thick clouds clenched over the sky as the vessel plied its way into the bay on the island's northern face. The boat docked and the crew rolled a small freezer down the gangway and onto the jetty. He had me meet them there. It was the middle of the night and all the others were asleep. I'm sure he suspected that I was more or less onto him already and therefore the logical accomplice, but perhaps he also had reasons for counting on my discretion. After all, I was under no illusions about the vetting I'd been put through before being hired. I led them up the path. He waited outside too, at a distance, beside the building, and did not intercept us as we passed up the walkway, but rather timed his approach so as to slip into our wake. It was as if the clouds had snuck in behind us through the open door. It occurred to me that this was the first outside glimpse into the Linnaeum since its completion and I knew how the crew saw it: enormous and empty, hollow as a bell. They hauled the freezer into the workroom. From the doorway, he spoke then, directing them to set it next to a large table. And then he thanked them. That was all. The door closed behind us and they set off into the choppy seas. The Taxidermist was left alone with his first piece.

The workroom, which, with its assortment of odd tools, exotic materials, and extraordinary equipment, had been the knottiest puzzle of all, was now revealed to be a state-of-the-art taxidermic factory. It was endowed to take on any imaginable specimen. This was in line with his singular practice, for at any moment he might find himself in need of any given utensil, chemical, or component, only to use it nevermore. That is: Extinction being a one-shot deal, he would not ever work the same animal twice and therefore every specimen would arrive with new demands. The variety was to be perfect, each individual figure unique. As a rule, taxidermy is a discipline that calls for steadfast patience and variegated skill. It's at once a craft, an art, and a science. Biology, chemistry, surgery, drafting, designing, modeling, molding, sculpting, welding, even whittling are all within its domain. I don't claim any expertise in these matters, but I had occasion to know firsthand the work of the world's greatest. I can say that the secret is in the pose. The word "taxidermy" (like the word "taxonomy") derives from the Greek "*taxis*," which we can translate only inadequately as "arrangement." More telling is how the term has been adopted by various fields. In architecture, *taxis* is the due proportion of ordonnance. In rhetoric, it is the systematic organization of language into a figure of speech. In biology, it is a life-form's response to a directional stimulus. It's a fecund word, and an elusive one, comprehending ideas of order, of sense, intention, and figuration, and even of the orientation of vital energies—the very shape, meaning, and purpose of life. And so it is in the art of taxidermy that the word fulfills the deepest demands of its etymology. In the *taxis* of the work—in, that is, the *pose*—order and meaning are brought to being. The pose is what transforms carrion into art. It's what brings the dead back to lifeless life.

Having defrosted the California condor and drained its blood, the Taxidermist selected a blade from his collection of a hundred-odd knives and skinned the bird. He then cleaned the pelt, salted it, and set it to dry on a frame. Done properly, these procedures are less straightforward than they sound. The mask requires particular delicacy in such a species and plumage is a tricky matter in and of itself. But these are questions of technique and it was only after the skin was cured that the art truly came into its own. It was only then that the Taxidermist conceived the pose—he read it, in fact, read it there in the hollowed-out pelt. What we have next comes at secondhand (I had little business in the workroom, after all), imparted by hushed voices over the dinner table: a series of still images, mental photographs taken by the maids, the janitor, snapshots of the Taxidermist under a surgical lamp, hunched over the condor's skin—the same image with every new memory, picture to picture a remarkable uniformity. For a week straight, each of the half dozen or so glimpses the day brought found him hunched and brooding over it. He must have examined every square centimeter a thousand times over. They caught him running his fingertips lightly across the surface or with his face drawn down until it grazed the plumes. He came at last to know the lay of every single quill. And he read it there—in the contours, in the fold of the feathers—he read the secret traces in the tissue, the life that was, the channels through which it once ran. He read the pose.

And then he brought it to life in clay and aluminum alloy. The workroom was furnished with a sculpting studio, a carpentry shop, a blacksmith's blast furnace, and a laboratory where he could cook up all brands of synthetic molds and casts. He called the elements to shape by these many names and dressed them in the skin that nature had shucked forever away. Again, I am no expert, but a masterpiece speaks for itself. It was as if the creature's every fiber had been restrung and set a-thrum again. It was sculpted out of the stuff of time, a span of evolution packed down into the very earth that had pared it to form over the millennia. Nothing less than death made quick. The upper body lunges forward. The wings curl off the shoulders, digging the gleaming remiges into the air. The neck plunges down at a sharp angle. It seems to want to stab its hooked beak into the ground, to gash and score the dirt and leave its ragged mark. The perfect image of itself. The condor's ankle was tagged and the Taxidermist wrote there in his own hand:

Species: *Gymnogyps californianus*
Place of Extinction: Beijing Zoo, Xicheng District, China
Time of Extinction: 5:28 a.m., December 13, 2--7.

He mounted it on a low riser in one of the largest showrooms, in the exact center of the huge, vacant space. The spotlight above was turned on and beamed down on it: a scavenger alone with its own carcass.

Of course it was only the first of innumerable pieces. The system strengthened with use and, in due course, a steady stream of specimens began to flow into the Linnaeum (for the times, to be sure, were to amply provide). His days and nights were given over more and more to the workroom—with each new arrival, new techniques, new tools, new chemicals, and new materials. Invariably, the animals died in zoos, drew their final breaths in foreign air. It turned out that he had dozens of cryogenic freezers just like the one the condor had been delivered in stashed away all across the globe. When the moment came, a freezer would be shipped in from the nearest depot to be packed with the corpse and then hustled out of cities and towns, through airports and down loading docks, across oceans and continents. Once arrived in the Linnaeum, the animals were grouped, showroom by showroom, in their rightful ecosystems, where each species assumed its position in line and stood in its place on its own respective square riser. The enormous, empty spaces filled with these empty presences. At any given moment, the Taxidermist had dozens of projects in development at once, all in different stages. I'd step outside to take in some fresh air and find myself watching a crane hoist off the deck of a freighter a truck-sized freezer containing the Asiatic buffalo. I'd glance into the workroom and see the island fox being sponged down in carbolic acid, the woodland caribou pickled in a tank, the Mona ground iguana tanned in a tub of alum. I gazed on once as he toiled several long hours pasting the Apache trout onto its manikin. I caught him in a moment of acute concentration adding the final touches of enamel paint to the Himalayan wolf's eyes. I observed the very curious spectacle of the meticulous installation, on a tall, thin riser in the Saline Wetlands Showroom, of the Salt Creek tiger beetle. Without ever setting foot off the island, I stood before creatures rarer and more outlandish than I'd ever dreamed. All of the earth's homelands, in time's wholesale clearing, emptied out here where every last creeping beast after its kind was transfigured into its own likeness.

Daily life inside this mute zoo settled into a surreal normality. Among the staff, an unvoiced accord maintained a certain distance between us all. We spoke together, of course. We played cards on Friday nights in the Alpine Ecosystem Showroom. We were cordial and familiar. Friendly even—but never friends, or so it was for most of us anyway. We kept to ourselves and did our jobs. And so time passed with a monkish uniformity. The selfsame day stretched into weeks, months, and then years. And all the time, at the edges of our willful enclosure, we were watched by the glassy eyes of yesteryear, and while we could hold them at bay, the Taxidermist lived squarely among them. I could hardly imagine such an existence: the gruesome dreariness, the stillness and silence that sucked at your vital reserves. It was an art of grisly magnificence and it could be borne for only so long, face-to-face.

Afterward, I surmised that this unrelieved strain was what brought it about (something I wouldn't understand until later would have me reconsider), but the first shake-up came as a complete shock. Early one July morning, a fleet of ships broke the iron horizon. He was nowhere to be found and we could only conclude we were finally being invaded, so, after some debate, a white flag was drawn up in front of the compound. It turned out that the ships were loaded with construction equipment. Straightaway they began knocking down walls on the southern face of the building.

He did not show himself until the third day. He called the entire staff before him. We gathered outside by the dock, in the same place where upon our arrival he'd first addressed us all as a group—which was the only time, until now, he had ever addressed us all as a group. A thin veil of cirrus clouds was cast over the sky and the sun seemed impossibly far away. He stood there once more, stock-still, hands behind his back. We had aged, all of us, but it was only then that I realized how completely the Taxidermist had shed his youth, how fully he had assumed the biding ancientness that had so long hung about him. He began to speak. He told us that a new wing was being added to the Linnaeum in order to reflect what he referred to as the new world. He explained that climatic conditions across all of the planet's ecosystems had come to fluctuate so drastically that all distinctions had been rendered untenable. Nowhere did there remain the environmental stability necessary to characterize and differentiate regions. And as chaos metastasized and installed its homogeneity of absolute instability, the global climate and the population dependent on it came now to constitute a single enormous new ecosystem. He called it the Warmed World. He anticipated skepticism and rejoined that the island was set within an anomalous pocket of relatively constant cold, an atmospheric concentration of low temperature created by the very heat that was tightening around it like a vise. He was totally calm. It would have been far less disquieting had he been raving and foaming at the mouth. He said that the earth had been reduced to one one-hundredth of its former species. He said that those that remained, the last survivors, would all end up here, in this immense new hall. Absolute zero, he said, was within sight. All in all, it was more than he'd said these many years combined and the first time he had ever uttered a word touching his true concerns. His voice grew hoarse as he spoke and finally slipped into a rasp so soft I doubt any of us heard his closing words.

Due to technical difficulties in adapting the addition to the preexisting structure, construction proceeded with less speed and efficiency than it had so many years ago, but by and by the new showroom was completed. It featured a huge glass dome fabricated with durable nanofiber. The dome loomed over the space, stretching all the way down the southern wall, opening upon leagues of gray waters, the blank sky, and the blanker horizon. From above, the Warmed World Showroom must have looked like a giant snow globe or some exotic crystal seed. He was different after that. It was nothing any of us could point to, of course, but he was different and our lives too had changed. Every incoming specimen was now installed in the new hall and the other showrooms were neglected altogether. Forgoing sleep, he took to passing among the ranks of the last survivors all through the darkening hours. I discovered him there more than once, pacing slowly from piece to piece, lost in unknowable thoughts, staring into eyes that stared back from a moment beyond time. The moon never seemed so cold as it did through that glassy sky at night.

The dismissals that began shortly thereafter were taken by the staff as a blessing. The majority of us, in fact, were already appraising our options toward a quiet way out when, without warning, he started discharging us, one or two at a time, by means of a note taped to bedroom doors and with severance pay substantial enough to convince those who remained to bide our time rather than quit. In a matter of months, the island's living population was reduced to seven.

By now, I had more than an inkling of what was unsettling him, but even I could not foresee what came next. It was over a year after the completion of the new wing. I was in the computer room replacing a dead processor when he came in. I sensed right away that something was amiss, but couldn't place it. I did not think he saw me there and I was long past the point of trying to address him, and so I gazed on in silence as he went straight to the interface, sat down, and stared up at the screen. On the surface, everything was as usual and yet underneath it all I felt something astir. I realized what only when the siren went off: A faint scent of gasoline had trailed him in and not come to my full awareness until the fire alarm sounded. Confusion, suspicion, panic, and haste—it was all primed to crash down on me, but for several moments, I was enveloped by a perfect calm. The siren wailed and a recorded voice informed us over the loudspeaker that a fire had broken out in the northeastern quadrant. I watched him. I carefully set the processor back in its rack and slowly made my way toward the door and I watched him the whole time. It was all too clear: He wasn't going to budge. And then, just as I reached the threshold, he spoke.

"And I too await the hour when I will meet my maker."

All I could see was the back of his chair and the top of his head— a dark crest against the background of the glowing monitor. I waited there for a full minute, but he did not speak again. I ran off down the hallway then, overcome at last by the noise and adrenaline.

The fire struck a gas line and the blast rocked the whole building and blew to pieces a large section of the outer wall. The Riparian Zone Showroom was in rubble by the time I careened around the corner and hit the heat and chaos headfirst. We went at it with hoses and fire extinguishers, we fought side by side, in solidarity, with staunch resolve, but it was an utter inferno and our efforts choked and sputtered in the smoke that drove us back, step by step. My colleagues' faces seemed strange to me under the searing light, these faces I'd known through the still and icy decades, contorted now, straining, desperate and febrile, glistening in sweat. It scratched at the surface of things in me long buried, longer dead. I was nearly overborne by the urge to let the fire extinguisher clatter to the ground, call on them all to follow suit, and watch the flames consume the place. I came to my senses. By the time the blaze was fully doused, the Savanna Showroom too was nothing but cinders and charred wreckage. We were weary and feverish and covered in soot. More than anything, we were stunned by the sudden violence that had crashed over our island refuge on the far side of time's tide. And the crisis was not over. A considerable portion of the Linnaeum's shell was demolished. It was late February and the wind penetrated deep into the building. It took us thirty-six hours to throw together a makeshift wall and it was no permanent fix. Without a professional crew and new materials, the damage could not be repaired, and over the coming days it became clear that the Taxidermist did not intend to take any action. The best we could do was shore up the barrier with what resources remained from the construction. The result was not reassuring. It held off the unruly brunt of the weather, but no one knew how long that would last and there was no telling with what stealth the more subtle chill might infiltrate.

I never let anyone know what I knew, but they were suspicious of him. They all noticed, of course, that he was the only one not fighting the fire. It would eventually come to light that the sprinkler system had been deactivated. There were few explanations for how the blaze might have ignited and fewer still for its rapid spread in a building constructed largely of fire-resistant materials. His detachment throughout the disaster and the recovery was disconcerting, to say the least. What it all added up to, none of them could be sure, but grave misgiving could have thrived on less.

Six months after the fire, I found myself part of the next (and penultimate) deportation off the island. There were three of us. We boarded an outgoing yacht that had brought in the brown rat. The Taxidermist was nowhere in sight. We weighed anchor and the waves kicked up a few miles out and I watched the island fall over the horizon—slipping away to its silent destiny, as I to ours. The final three—the chef, a mechanic, and a housekeeper—were kept on for another four and a half years. They were by no means equal to the task of maintaining the entire facility and, one by one, utilities broke down and subsystems hit upon glitches, some to be patched up, some never to work again. The Linnaeum steadily deteriorated. And meanwhile they—the chef, the mechanic, and the housekeeper—passed each other at great distances in the hallways and showrooms, like ships at crossing prospects, until they finally came abreast one morning on the jetty, luggage in hand, all three bound for the same voyage back home.

It must seem out of order that I was not a member of this long-retained party, that I was sent off not early but untimely enough to belie my significance and uniqueness in the scheme of things, and in this, perhaps, is the key to it all. Above and beyond any other distinction I might claim, I was essential to the supercomputer's performance, which was itself essential to the Taxidermist's mission, and sometime before the construction of the Warmed World Showroom, I began to suspect that something was awry here in the central nervous system of the enterprise. Now on my end, let it be said, everything was in working order. The hardware was as sound as ever. But there was something strange afoot in the distribution of the computer's online activity. From the beginning, information had passed largely through the same channels: to and from zoos and preservations, smugglers and underground market dealers, transportation and communication firms, governmental and law-enforcement agencies. The margins of these thoroughfares saw some exchange, but it was always minimal. An uptick in peripheral activity was the first sign that the case had altered. For a long while, I attributed it to mere fleeting anomalies in the extinction pattern. It escalated, however, and I realized that whatever was going on, it couldn't be accounted for so easily. This was something else altogether and I had no idea what. Despite the influx of specimens, the Taxidermist also began around this time to spend more of his day before the computer. Naturally, as the aberrations multiplied, my gaze began to gravitate toward his monitor while I ran my rounds through the racks, and it was just a matter of time before I found myself going out of my way to get whatever glimpse I could, and so it is likely that he caught on, likely that he knew that I saw him sitting there, before the screen, hour after hour, staring at an unceasing stream of meaningless combinations of letters and numbers and typographic symbols.

I don't claim to know what this means. But I do know that it was in the midst of my first suspicions that reconstruction began and somewhere about when they kicked into high gear that he set the Riparian Zone and Savanna Showrooms on fire and spoke to me those lone enigmatic words. I do know that it was shortly thereafter that I was released.

However you have it, the Taxidermist was now the Linnaeum's only living inhabitant. The deliveries persisted for some time. And so he continued to wait outside at a distance and steal in behind the new arrivals, always silent, always composed. The building's disrepair appeared ever greater before the eyes of the deliverymen, even as the cold, which had long slipped through the chinks and fissures of our deficient barrier, chased them back away. Besides these brief visits, the only other line to the outside world was the computer and the phenomenon that I had observed could not have resolved itself, would instead certainly accelerate and finally disrupt all communication, even as the machine, left unattended by my hands, would without a doubt slowly break down. Concurrently, the deliveries too would taper off, the supply line would discontinue. It would be just a matter of time before the Taxidermist was cut off entirely from what was called the living world.

It is now a question of how he would interpret this.

And again I must assert my unique privilege. For he told me himself.

He would come to two conclusions. First, that the supply line had discontinued because the supply had died away, that no more specimens arrived because the last of the last survivors was gone. That is: Every animal species was now extinct. Second, that the computer returned endless reels of dumb signs void of mind and intent and no more ships docked at the island pier, that he neither saw nor communicated with anyone anymore because the last of the human species too was gone. That is: the last but one.

What remained to be done stood before him with authority. He had no choice. All known procedures were out of the question, of course, but that did not relieve him of the charge. The broad principles were plain enough. The challenge was to hone a technique on the whetstone of pure theory. And the technique had to be flawless—there was no test subject. Once more, the Taxidermist faced the absolutely unrepeatable.

For him, it had till now only ever been a question of the skin, never the innards, ever about the preservation of the dead, never the curing of the living, and so his research took him from Egyptian mummification to modern embalming, from experimental chemistry to mystic thanatology. All traditional knowledge mastered, every facet of the problem still demanded groundbreaking insights and methods. He dwelled on it for many quiet months. The program he at last developed involved successive injections of synthetic and natural embalming solutions—highly diluted at first, but as the body grew habituated, ever more concentrated. Alongside this, a gradual weaning off liquids was called for, plus the infusion of Epsom salts and mineral compounds into a restricted diet. The cold that, in the neglect of the heating equipment, was slowly pervading the Linnaeum now revealed itself to be a boon and was factored into his calculations. Everything was coordinated so as not to shock the system but to ease it into demission—to have shutdown coincide with the final touch of preservative.

Once the plan was devised and the chemicals were concocted, his workday was reduced to a rate of dosages per hour. Nothing else remained but to let time bleed away as he wandered the Warmed World, day in, day out, the last of living beings, withdrawing ever deeper into his flesh, settling slowly into the stasis that had so long surrounded him, slumping toward the zero degree with every dose: the soundest, coldest mineral slumber. He forwent food entirely those several endmost weeks. And as the moment approached, he made the concluding arrangements. He prepared the final several dozen syringes ahead of schedule. Time and energy were increasingly precious. Seated at a table in the back of the showroom, he wrote the tag:

> Species: *Homo sapiens*
> Place of Extinction: The Linnaeum
> Time of Extinction:

He did not stir from that table for days, but sat in a quietude disturbed only by the hourly injection. From above, up in the steeled skies over the island, all would have seemed stilled already—the speck of life that had floated so long under the glass globe, so languidly, come at last to rest.

And yet you would have seen him from up high as he stood at the appointed hour and looked toward the riser where the final syringe awaited him.

And you can imagine him then:

Once and only once more he passes through the ranks of the last survivors, to the front of the Warmed World, the crown of the kingdom—passes the mummichog, the giant tube worm, the Northland tusked weta, the carrion crow, the black-backed jackal, the beatic dwarf olive. He plows forward over the frigid ground with ever-flagging speed, recedes into the stillness underfoot at every step. He inches toward the head of the pack and is soon outstripped by time's slow creep, vies in speed with their enlivened shadows, and is taken up by that silent herd marching west to east, driving back the dawn. Finally, he arrives. And he lifts his leg then, slow as night, levers himself onto the riser and into place, grinding, muscle by muscle, to a stop. He takes the last syringe off the platform. He draws it aloft. He coaxes it into his left cephalic vein and depresses the plunger and the serum drips a drop at a time into his coagulated bloodstream. He draws the needle out, cell by cell. He drops the syringe and the thin glass shatters the silence. And he cringes over at the waist then into a gesture that takes shape over days. The accumulated solution oozes through the congealed slough that clogs his veins, fixing his every atom into place—the art he'd only ever known from without brought within, coiling him into expression: the final mudra of himself and his kind. And he urges his right arm down, tick by tick, across his legs, edging his hand forward, eroding his way through space, toward the tag wrapped around his left ankle, toward the stop that every second seems to push two seconds away, until he reaches the penultimate moment, the pause before the definitive stab, the breath before the last gasp.—And you will imagine him there for a small eternity: Waiting. Pen in hand. Waiting. Pen poised. Waiting for the time when it will have been. Waiting to write the moment of his own death.

NOTES ON CONTRIBUTORS

EMILY ANDERSON's fiction and poetry have appeared in numerous publications, including *McSweeney's*, *Caketrain*, and the *Kenyon Review*.

RUSSELL BANKS is the author of many novels, most recently *Lost Memory of Skin*, and six short-story collections, including the forthcoming *A Permanent Member of the Family* (both Ecco), which contains the titular story that appears here. "A Permanent Member of the Family" is © 2013 Russell Banks.

MARTINE BELLEN's most recent collection of poetry is *Wabac Machine* (Furniture Press Books). Her other books include *GHOSTS!* (Spuyten Duyvil Press) and *The Vulnerability of Order* (Copper Canyon Press).

REBECCA BRIDGE is a poet, essayist, and screenwriter who lives in Seattle. Her work has previously been published in *Boston Review*, *Columbia Poetry Review*, *Sixth Finch*, *notnostrums*, and elsewhere. Her collection of writing essays and exercises, *Clear Out the Static from the Attic*, is forthcoming from Write Bloody Publishing.

Novelist, cut-up artist, and Beat postmodernist WILLIAM S. BURROUGHS (1914–1997) is the author of such canonical works as *Junky* and *Naked Lunch* (both Grove Press). The recipient of the Ordre des Arts et des Lettres, he published nearly thirty books in his lifetime, as well as collaborating with artists such as Laurie Anderson, Jim Morrison, Gus Van Sant, Nick Cave, and Tom Waits.

EDWARD CAREY is a writer and illustrator. His novels *Observatory Mansions* (Crown) and *Alva and Irva* (Houghton Mifflin Harcourt) have been published in fourteen countries. Hot Key published *Heap House*, the first volume of his young-adult Iremonger trilogy, in September.

H. G. CARRILLO is the author of the novel *Loosing My Espanish* (Anchor Books). His short stories have appeared in *Conjunctions*, *Kenyon Review*, *Iowa Review*, *Glimmer Train*, *Ninth Letter*, *Slice*, and elsewhere. He teaches at George Washington University.

GILLIAN CONOLEY's seventh book, *Peace*, will be published by Omnidawn in the spring of 2014. City Lights will publish her translations of three books by Henri Michaux, *Thousand Times Broken*, in the fall of 2014.

SUSAN DAITCH is the author of three novels, *L.C.* (Dalkey Archive Press), *The Colorist* (Virago), and *Paper Conspiracies* (City Lights), as well as a collection of short fiction, *Storytown* (Dalkey). "Fall Out," a novella, was published this year by Madras Press in support of Women for Afghan Women.

MONICA DATTA's work appeared earlier this year in *Web Conjunctions*. She is currently writing an opera libretto and a novel, from which this piece is excerpted. This is her first appearance in print.

"The Taxidermist" is CRAIG EKLUND's first published story.

TEMPLE GRANDIN is a designer of livestock-handling facilities for the United States and many countries around the world, as well as a noted author and speaker on the subject of autism. Named one of the one hundred most influential people by *Time Magazine* in 2010, she is the author of numerous books including *New York Times* bestsellers *Animals in Translation: Using the Mysteries of Autism to Decode Animal Behavior* (Scribner) and *Animals Make Us Human: Creating the Best Life for Animals* (Houghton Mifflin Harcourt). The HBO movie about her life story, *Temple Grandin*, won seven Emmy awards and a Golden Globe.

BENJAMIN HALE is the author of the novel *The Evolution of Bruno Littlemore* (Twelve) and the recipient of the Bard Fiction Prize and a Michener-Copernicus award. His fiction and nonfiction have appeared in *Conjunctions*, *Harper's*, *The New York Times*, *The Washington Post*, and elsewhere. He teaches at Bard College.

KEVIN HOLDEN is the author of two chapbooks, *Identity* (Cannibal Books) and *Alpine* (White Queen Press). He lives in Connecticut.

NORA KHAN is a researcher and teacher interested in games, digital humanities, and the nexus between creativity and cognitive studies. Her short fiction has been published by *Hunger Mountain* and *American Literary Review*, and she writes regularly for *Kill Screen*.

Cover artist SIR EDWIN HENRY LANDSEER (1802–1873) was an English artist celebrated during his lifetime for his paintings of animals, particularly those of dogs. Popular among both the middle class and the aristocracy (Queen Victoria commissioned work from him), he modeled the lions that grace the base of Nelson's Column, and the Landseer Newfoundland dog is his namesake.

MICHAEL PARRISH LEE's stories have appeared in *Scrivener Creative Review* and *Web Conjunctions* and his essays have appeared in *Novel: A Forum on Fiction* and *Studies in the Novel*. He teaches at Leeds Metropolitan University.

PAUL LISICKY's books include *The Burning House* (Etruscan Press), *Unbuilt Projects* (Four Way Books), *The Narrow Door* (forthcoming from Graywolf Press), and others. He teaches in the MFA program at Rutgers-Camden.

ADAM McOMBER is the author of *The White Forest* (Touchstone) and *This New & Poisonous Air* (BOA Editions). He is the associate editor of the journal *Hotel Amerika* at Columbia College Chicago, where he also teaches creative writing and literature.

SANDRA MEEK is the author of four books of poems, most recently *Road Scatter* (Persea Books) and *Biogeography* (Tupelo Press), winner of the Dorset Prize. She is the co-founding editor of Ninebark Press, poetry editor of the *Phi Kappa Phi Forum*, and director of the Georgia Poetry Circuit. She teaches at Berry College.

GWYNETH MERNER is a graduate of the MFA program at Washington University in St. Louis. This is her first appearance in print.

The notable Belgian-born French writer and artist HENRI MICHAUX (1899–1984) was known for his forays into human perception. In addition to books such as *Voyage en Grande Garbagne* (Gallimard), *Au pays de la magie* (Athlone), and *Ici, Poddema* (Mermod), he produced visual work in India ink, watercolors, and oils. The excerpt from *Watchtowers on Targets* published here was conceived in collaboration with the abstract expressionist Roberto Matta and will appear in Gillian Conoley's translation of *Thousand Times Broken: Three Books by Henri Michaux*, #61 in the City Lights Pocket Poets Series (Fall 2014).

SARAH MINOR is an MFA candidate in creative nonfiction at the University of Arizona. Her work can be found online at *Word Riot*.

RICK MOODY is the author of five novels, three collections of stories, a memoir, and, most recently, the collection of essays *On Celestial Music* (Back Bay). He writes about music regularly online at the *Rumpus*, and writes songs for the Wingdale Community Singers.

KYOKO MORI has published three nonfiction books: *Yarn* (GemmaMedia Books), *Polite Lies*, and *The Dream of Water* (both Holt), and four novels: *Barn Cat* (GemmaMedia Books), *Stone Field True Arrow* (Metropolitan), *One Bird*, and *Shizuko's Daughter* (both Holt). She lives in Washington, DC, with her two cats and teaches at George Mason University and Lesley University.

BRADFORD MORROW is the editor of *Conjunctions* and the recipient of the PEN/ Nora Magid Award for excellence in literary editing. He is the author of six novels and his most recent books include *The Diviner's Tale* (Houghton Mifflin Harcourt) and the fiction collection *The Uninnocent* (Pegasus Books). He is currently at work on *A Bestiary*, a collaboration with virtuoso guitarist Alex Skolnick. A Bard Center fellow and professor of literature at Bard College, he lives in New York City.

JAMES MORROW is the author of nine novels, including *The Last Witchfinder, The Philosopher's Apprentice* (both William Morrow), and the Godhead Trilogy (Harcourt). He has received the World Fantasy Award, the Nebula Award, the Grand Prix de l'Imaginaire, and the Prix Utopia. His recent novella, *Shambling towards Hiroshima* (Tachyon), won the Theodore Sturgeon Memorial Award.

ANDREW MOSSIN teaches in the intellectual heritage program at Temple University in Philadelphia. His writing has appeared in *New Ohio Review, Hambone, Talisman, Jacket, Callaloo*, and other publications.

JOYCE CAROL OATES is the author, most recently, of *Black Dahlia & White Rose*, which received the 2013 Bram Stoker Award from the World Horror Association, and the novel *The Accursed* (both Ecco). Her new collection, *Evil Eye* (Mysterious Press), contains a novella, "The Flatbed," originally published in *Conjunctions:58, Riveted: The Obsession Issue* (Spring 2012).

DALE PETERSON is the author, co-author, or editor of seventeen books, the most recent of which is *Giraffe Reflections* (University of California Press).

JANIS E. RODGERS is a poet and anthropologist currently based in Southern California. More information on the Fongoli Chimpanzee Project and Faleme Chimpanzee Conservation Project addressed in her essay can be found at savannachimp. blogspot.com and facebook.com/falemechimpanzeeconservation, respectively.

DAN ROSENBERG's first book, *The Crushing Organ* (Dream Horse Press), won the 2011 American Poetry Journal Book Prize. He co-edits *Transom*.

BENNETT SIMS is the author of the novel *A Questionable Shape* (Two Dollar Radio). His fiction has appeared in *A Public Space, Electric Literature, Orion, Subtropics, Tin House,* and *Zoetrope: All-Story.* He lives in Iowa City.

TERESE SVOBODA's most recent novel is *Bohemian Girl* (University of Nebraska Press), named one of the ten best Westerns of the year by *Booklist.*

COLE SWENSEN is the author of fourteen books of poetry and a collection of critical essays. She is the recipient of the 2004 PEN USA Award in Translation and the editor of La Presse, a nano-press dedicated to contemporary French writing.

LYNNE TILLMAN's most recent collection of stories is *Someday This Will Be Funny;* her second essay collection, *What Would Lynne Tillman Do?,* is forthcoming in January (both Red Lemonade Press).

SALLIE TISDALE's most recent book is *Women of the Way* (Harper San Francisco).

FREDERIC TUTEN's books include *Tintin in the New World* (William Morrow), *The Adventures of Mao on the Long March* (Citadel Press), and *Self Portraits: Fictions* (Norton).

DR. VINT VIRGA is a veterinary behaviorist and the author of *The Soul of All Living Creatures* (Crown/Random House). Renowned for his expertise on human-animal relationships, he works as a consultant to zoos and wild-animal parks on animal behavior and well-being and has appeared as a featured guest on *ABC World News, PBS Nature,* and *National Geographic Explorer.*

WIL WEITZEL is currently at work on a novel set in Pakistan's Hindu Kush range. His fiction and poetry have appeared or are forthcoming in *Southwest Review, New Orleans Review, White Whale Review, Chautauqua,* and elsewhere. He teaches at Harvard University.

Eduardo Jiménez Mayo
& Chris N. Brown, eds.
Three Messages and a Warning:
Contemporary Mexican
Short Stories of the Fantastic
"A landmark collection."
—*World Literature Today*

Angélica Gorodischer
Trafalgar
(trans. by Amalia Gladheart)
"Fascinating stories."—*Reforma*

The Unreal and the Real:
Selected Stories of Ursula K. Le Guin
"A masterclass in contemporary fiction."
—*New Zealand Herald,* Best of 2012

Alan DeNiro
Tyrannia and Other Renditions
Eleven stories exploring the personal and political.

Claude Royet-Journoud: *Four Elemental Bodies*

[translated from the French by Keith Waldrop]

Royet-Journoud's Tetralogy assembles his central volumes *Reversal, The Notion of Obstacle, Objects Contain the Infinite,* and *Natures Indivisible.*
He is one of the most important contemporary French poets whose one-line manifesto: "Shall we escape analogy" signaled a revolutionary turn away from Surrealism and its lush imagery. He explores loss as if it were the threshold we have to cross to fully enter language.

Poetry, 368 pages, offset, smyth-sewn, original paperback $20

Ray Ragosta: *A Motive for Disappearance*

Against a background of traumatic events we hear the voice of the outsider or exile.
"Ray Ragosta, like the serpent swallowing its tail, does not describe the event, but things close in, as in a dark room or desert. His poems convey the emotional intensity of the gap between articulation and experience; between the possibility of expression and the effort toward that expression."—Gale Nelson

Poetry, 88 pages, offset, smyth-sewn, original paperback $14

P. Inman: *per se*

Inman fractures the conventions of language in order to build everything up again from a more elemental level. In *per se*, the composers Luigi Nono, Hans Lachenmann, and Morton Feldman provide musical structure for his jazz-inflected words in motion. The book lives in the tension between the free, multi-directional movement of words and the highly orgazined macro-structures.

Poetry, 88 pages, offset, smyth-sewn, original paperback $14

Elfriede Czurda: *Almost 1 Book/ Almost 1 Life*

[translated from the German by Rosmarie Waldrop]
Runner-up for PEN Award for Poetry in Translation and shortlisted for Best Translated Book
This volume contains almost all of Elfriede Czurda's first book and all of her second, *Fast 1 Leben.*
Coming out of the experimental *Wiener Gruppe,* Czurda is not averse to thumbing her nose at the experimental imperative. In *Almost 1 Life,* the ruling avant-garde has licensed "monomania" as official language and punishes misuse by expelling the offender: into reality. Which is exactly where Czurda positions herself.

Poetry, 96 pages, offset, smyth-sewn, original paperback $14

Orders: www.spdbooks.org, www.burningdeck.com

NOON

A LITERARY ANNUAL

1324 LEXINGTON AVENUE   PMB 298   NEW YORK NY 10128

EDITION PRICE $12 DOMESTIC $17 FOREIGN

Best American Short **Stories**

Best **American** Poetry

Best American Essays

Best American **Science**

&**Nature** **Writing**

the **Pushcart**

Prize anthology

Since 2006 *Ecotone* is the only publication in the country to have had its work reprinted in all of these anthologies. Find out why Salman Rushdie names us one of a handful of literary magazines on which "the health of the American short story depends."

REIMAGINING PLACE

ecotone

ecotonejournal.com

All animals have **feelings.**

Choose compassion.

Find out how you can make the world a more loving place for animals. Visit **PETA.org.**

PETA

Be the voice
for those who have no voice

Join us
worldwildlife.org

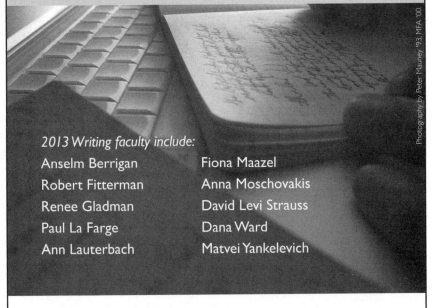

superstition [review]

an online literary magazine

[art, fiction, interviews, nonfiction, poetry]

recently featuring...

Aimee Bender
David Kirby
Susan Steinberg
Lee Martin
Kamilah Aisha Moon
Adam Johnson
Alix Ohlin
Ira Sukrungruang

"I would recommend Superstition Review to anyone who wants good, honest writing."

The Review Review

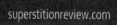